A FIRE BURNING

A PETER BLACK THRILLER

DAVID ARCHER

VINCE VOGEL

RIGHTHOUSE

PRAISE FOR THE PETER BLACK SERIES

ISBN-13: 978-1-63696-411-9

ISBN-10: 1-63696-411-7

Cover design by: Damonza

Printed in the United States of America

www.righthouse.com

www.instagram.com/righthousebooks

www.facebook.com/righthousebooks

twitter.com/righthousebooks

PETER BLACK THRILLERS
Burden of the Assassin (Book 1)
The Man Without A Face (Book 2)
Unpunished Deeds (Book 3)
Hunter Killer (Book 4)
Silent Shadows (Book 5)
The Last Run (Book 6)
Dark Corners (Book 7)
Ghost Operative (Book 8)
A Fire Burning (Book 9)
Dawnlight (Book 10)

PROLOGUE

6 SEPTEMBER 1976

DENG XIAOPING'S MIND WAS A WHIRLWIND OF thoughts as he walked through the hushed corridors of Zhongnanhai. This place, so synonymous with the revolution, the CCP, and much that had happened in his life up to this point, brought back the memories of those turbulent years—the arguments, the exile, and the pain of his son's death. Yet, amidst the chaos and the accusations of being a counter revolutionary, he had always remained steadfast in his vision for China. Now, summoned urgently to Mao Zedong's deathbed, the weight of the nation's future pressed down upon him like a millstone.

He reached Mao's bedroom, its dim light and heavy scent of medicinal herbs creating an almost surreal atmosphere. Mao lay frail and ghostly pale, his once robust frame now reduced to a skeletal shadow. Shallow breaths barely lifted his chest.

Deng approached the bedside, the gravity of the moment palpable. "Chairman Mao, it is Deng. I am here," he said softly.

Mao's eyes fluttered open. "Deng... you've come," he whispered. "Sit by my side."

Deng sat down, leaning in to catch Mao's faint words. "Deng,

I have... little time left. The doctors say my heart cannot... endure much longer. I will slip... into a coma any time now."

"I understand, Chairman. You must conserve your strength."

"No, Deng. There are things... I must say. My... my cultural and social reforms... they have not rid the people... of their need for western consumerism," Mao said, his voice strained with effort.

Deng listened intently as he continued. "You... you were right, Deng. When we argued... all those years ago. Right when you said... that it was better to join the devil... and beat him from within. And I was wrong about... what happened to your son, Deng Pufong. I was wrong for sending you to the factory and wrong for not seeing... your vision more clearly... at the time," Mao confessed. A rare moment of vulnerability shone in his eyes.

Deng's voice carried a hint of sadness when he said, "Chairman, that was a long time ago. We must look forward."

Mao breathed heavily, the effort taxing his frail body. "Now I see it, Deng. Your vision... it is the only way. Economic reforms... must happen. We must... marry ourselves to them."

Deng began nodding. "I will make sure our people prosper, Chairman," he said firmly. "We will adapt, but our ultimate goal will remain."

"Then you have my blessing... go after the puritans. My wife... the Gang of Four. They will never understand and must be dealt with," Mao said, each word a struggle.

Deng's expression was one of steely determination. "Whatever our differences, Chairman Mao, you will always be the father of China and its true visionary."

Mao nodded weakly. "Then go... make that vision happen."

Deng stood, looking down at Mao with a mixture of respect and resolve. Mao closed his eyes, exhausted but at peace with his decision. Deng then exited the room, the future of China now resting heavily on his shoulders.

ONE

FORTY-EIGHT YEARS LATER

THE PHONE CALL HAD COME OUT OF THE BLUE, PETER answering it with surprise in his voice. "Kara? It's been a while. What's up?"

On the other end, Kara Tate's voice was tense, almost urgent. It had immediately put him on edge. "Peter, I need to see you. Right away."

"Right away? What's going on?"

She'd hesitated, the weight of her words heavy even over the line. "I can't explain over the phone. It's... too sensitive and way too..."

Kara's voice broke off into a series of violent coughs. Peter's concern deepened. "Kara, are you okay?"

More coughing followed, sounding raw and painful. When she finally managed to speak again, her voice was weaker. "I'm... I'm fine. Just a bit under the weather. But this can't wait, Peter. Can we meet?"

"Sure. When and where?"

Without missing a beat, she replied, "This afternoon, at our old spot—the café on East 5th. Say, four?"

He'd paused, memories flooding back from the countless times they'd breakfasted at the old café, then he'd agreed. "All right. I'll be there."

Six hours later, Peter sits in the café, waiting. The clock on the wall says four-twenty-two. She's twenty-two minutes late.

As he stirs his now lukewarm coffee, memories of his time with Kara flood back, triggered by the familiar surroundings of Enzo's Café. Their relationship had been as intense and unpredictable as the lives they led. They had met just over a year ago while Peter, a CIA operative, had been chasing a jihadi collective known as the Wolf Pack. Unbeknownst to him, investigative journalist Kara Tate was also pursuing a lead to the same group. Their paths had collided in a whirlwind of danger, violence, and intrigue.

He remembers the adrenaline-fueled partnership that laid the groundwork for something deeper. In the midst of the tumult, they had found a strange connection. When the dust settled on their adventure, they started dating. Early on, they began living together, and in the brief moments he wasn't in the field or she wasn't working on an article, they would spend every second with each other. Those moments were filled with intense passion, exploring each other physically in a way that made the rest of the world disappear.

However, the very intensity that brought them together also made their relationship feel transient and unreal. They would go months without seeing each other, only to reunite with a fervor that was as exhausting as it was exhilarating. The relationship became fraught with complications. When they were together, it was a sex-fueled escape, a brief respite from their demanding lives. But the emotional side of the relationship never had a chance to grow. They never evolved beyond being sexual partners.

After a year of this tumultuous existence, it became clear that their relationship, while passionate, was unsustainable. Their lives were too demanding, their work too consuming. The inevitable parting loomed over them, casting a shadow on their fleeting moments of joy. But despite the chaos, despite the brevity, Peter had come to care deeply for Kara. Their love, though brief and fiery, left a lasting impression on him, the impact of their time together lingering on.

"Excuse me, sir. Would you like anything else?" The waiter's voice pulls Peter from his reverie.

He looks up, momentarily disoriented. "Another coffee, please," he says, offering a tight smile.

As the waiter walks away, Peter glances at the clock again. Four twenty-four. He sighs, the memories flooding back. His mind drifts to a moment they shared in this very place. It had been a rare sunny autumn afternoon, and the café was bustling with life. The two of them had managed to carve out some time from their hectic schedules to meet for lunch.

They sat by the window, the sunlight streaming in and casting a warm glow on their faces. Kara was animated, her eyes sparkling as she recounted a recent adventure for an article she was working on about a former entrepreneur who, when his company went under, robbed his staff's pension fund and disappeared. Peter listened intently, a smile playing on his lips as he watched her.

"And then, just as I was about to give up, the guy shows up on one of the balconies, and it's him. You should have seen the look on his face when I showed up with a camera!" Kara laughed, her voice full of life.

"I can imagine. So is he in custody?" Peter chuckled.

"Oh, yeah. The second I got my shots and my statement..."

"Which was?"

She rolled her eyes. "He told me to shove my camera where the sun doesn't shine and that he had nothing to say."

Peter laughed.

"Anyway," Kara continued, "I'd already alerted the cops. Interpol was waiting around the corner. They caught him as he and his mistress were packing their stuff. He's being extradited from Thailand tomorrow."

"Another corrupt SOB gets his comeuppance at the hands of Kara Tate," Peter said with a sly smile.

They shared a plate of sandwiches and a pot of tea, their conversation flowing easily despite the weight of their respective worlds. For a brief moment, the mayhem of their lives seemed distant, and they were just two people enjoying a quiet lunch together. As they finished their meal, Kara reached across the table and took Peter's hand, her touch warm and reassuring.

He had felt a sense of peace he rarely experienced in life. It was a memory he held on to, a reminder of the brief but precious moments they shared amidst the storm.

The sound of the café's door opening pulls Peter back to the present. He glances up, hopeful, as the memory fades and reality sets in.

It's someone else entering the café. Not Kara.

Peter's heart sinks, but he remains patient. He knows Kara wouldn't have contacted him if it weren't important. He sips his fresh coffee, eyes flicking to the door every few seconds, waiting.

TWO

It's now six o'clock. Unable to reach Kara on the phone, Peter drives to her apartment. His mind is a firestorm of anxiety and fear. As he turns onto her street, his heart sinks at the sight of flashing blue lights. The street is awash with the disorderly illumination of police cars.

Officers are everywhere, their uniforms stark against the backdrop of emergency lights. The air buzzes with the murmur of radio chatter. Neighbors stand huddled on the sidewalk, their faces masks of concern and curiosity. The usually quiet street now feels like a scene from a nightmare.

Peter parks his car hastily, barely taking the time to shut off the engine. He steps out, the cacophony of the scene crashing over him. He pushes through the throng of onlookers, his eyes fixed on the entrance to Kara's building. The flashing lights create a disorienting strobe effect, heightening the sense of urgency.

An officer steps into his path, raising a hand. "Sir, you can't go any farther. This is a restricted area."

Peter's voice is tight with worry. "I'm looking for Kara Tate. She lives here. Is she all right?"

The officer's expression shifts slightly, a flicker of sympathy in his eyes. "I can't give you any information right now. Please step back."

The sense of impending doom gnaws at Peter. Each passing second is an eternity. As he shows his CIA ID, the officer's eyes widen slightly before he nods and radios ahead to warn his colleagues. Peter steps past, his heart pounding as he ascends the stairs to the seventh floor.

Each step feels heavier, the sense of dread intensifying. He passes concerned neighbors, some speaking to police officers taking statements. One neighbor's voice rises above the rest.

"I heard the scream and just knew something was wrong. That's why I called you," the woman tells a nearby officer, her face pale and drawn.

Peter's heart tightens with each step. The higher he goes, the heavier he gets.

Reaching the fourth floor, he sees an officer standing guard outside Kara's apartment door. As he shows his ID once more, Peter struggles to maintain his composure.

"It's an active crime scene," the officer says, handing him a pair of shoe protectors and gloves, "so you'll need to put these on."

"Of course," Peter responds, taking them and numbly putting them on. His movements are automatic, his thoughts circling each other.

He steps inside, the familiar scent of Kara's apartment now mixed with the metallic tang of blood. The sight before him makes his stomach churn. Inside the door lies a dead woman, a bullet hole in her forehead, blood pooling on the floor. She's wearing her coat, and beside her, a bag lies open, its spilled contents strewn across the carpet—dusters, bleach, spray bottles.

Peter recognizes her immediately as Rosa, Kara's cleaner. She must have just made it through the door, probably called Kara's name. Then she saw a strange person or people. Saw the gun. It is such a horrific scene—someone so innocent murdered for being in the wrong place at the wrong time. It leaves Peter struggling to breathe.

His mind is filled with questions. Where is Kara? What happened here? He steels himself for the answers.

As he stands in the hallway, glancing at the ransacked furniture, he becomes overwhelmed by memories of happier times. Countless times he had entered this once warm place, sharing laughter and whispers with Kara as they'd tumbled inside and made their way to the bedroom. The image of her warm smile and the sound of her voice fill his mind—the absolute opposite to the present horror.

He comes to, staring at the open doorway of the living room. That's where all the action appears to be taking place.

Camera flashes illuminate the room. CSI in coveralls and face masks move around methodically. Peter steps to the doorway, his heart pounding. Inside, all the curtains are closed, casting the room in shadow. The room triggers a memory of quiet evenings spent together, cuddling on the sofa, watching old movies, and talking about their dreams. He can almost hear her laughter, the warmth of her presence.

But that all goes cold by what he sees.

Kara is sitting in a chair in the middle of the room, the rest of the furniture pushed to the sides. He can tell already that she's dead. Her blond hair is matted with blood, her wrists duct-taped to the arms of the chair, her fingers poking out at broken angles. Like the rest of the apartment, the room has been ransacked: drawers are out, the cushions off the couch, the fabric cut open by someone looking to see if something is hidden inside.

The sight is almost too much to bear. Peter's breath catches in his throat, his vision blurring.

"Kara..." he whispers.

The name hangs in the air, a lament for what's been lost. He takes a step closer, the world narrowing to the shattered remnants of his life laid bare in this room. The pain of her loss sears through him, but he knows he must hold it together. He needs to find out who did this and why.

Peter moves into the room, weaving between the CSIs, and comes before Kara. The sight is horrific. Kara Tate has been brutally beaten. Her bloated, bloodied, mutilated face is unrecognizable from the woman he was—no, is—in love with. Someone must've really wanted something from her; and by the looks of things, she wasn't willing to give it up.

Peter struggles to maintain professional detachment, overwhelmed by horror and grief. Rage burns in his eyes as he takes in the brutality of Kara's death.

"I will find them. I promise," he whispers.

Just as these faint words leave his lips, a man steps up beside him. "Detective Mendez," he introduces himself. Mendez is wrinkled along the forehead, but with an otherwise calm demeanor, signs of a seasoned detective. His eyes are sharp and questioning.

"My colleague downstairs informs me that you're CIA," Mendez says.

"I am," Peter replies blankly, still staring at Kara's mangled face.

"Was she working with you?"

"No. She wasn't. Our relationship was... personal."

"So nothing to do with national security?"

"Not to my knowledge."

"How well did you know her?"

"We were close. Once."

While they speak, Peter quickly assesses the situation. These weren't professional torturers—they haven't been trained by some state apparatus. No psychologist has taught them these barroom techniques. They've used no method other than brute force. The people who did this tried to beat it out of her. A more subtle torturer wouldn't have needed to make such a mess.

"How'd it go down?" Peter asks Mendez.

"They broke into the place using a pick set. Oh, and that was after they'd disabled all the building's CCTV, so there's no footage of them. They hit the street's cameras, too. Bastards," he hisses at the end.

Peter doesn't think he's cursing them out for taking out the cameras. No, the detective is cursing them out for what they've done to these poor women.

They are bastards. Monsters. Dead men.

"What does the evidence tell you?" Peter asks.

"That they snuck inside. Kept the noise down low enough for the victim not to hear their approach. They surprised her in the bedroom while she was putting on her makeup."

She was getting ready to meet me, Peter thinks.

"They dragged her into here," Mendez goes on, "attached her to the chair, and, well, as you can see, they went to town on her. My people think they must've been working her for at least twenty minutes when the cleaner showed up."

Peter glances out the door at the body of Rosa.

"The cleaner let herself in," Mendez continues, "stumbles upon the scene, and gets shot. But not before she lets out a big ol'scream that the woman living below hears and calls the cops."

"I take it they were gone by the time you got here."

"Yes, they were. No sign. They used gloves, and the neighbors never saw anything. Meaning they were smart enough not to be spotted leaving."

Peter realizes that they're professional in one degree: apart from the cleaner showing up—an unforeseen anomaly—the operation was pretty smooth. So not trained torturers (or at least in the traditional sense), but experienced enough to plan and undertake an operation. *Special Forces?*

"As you can see," Detective Mendez says, "she clearly didn't want to tell them what they wanted to hear."

"They were after something," Peter states.

"Yeah. That's what we think."

"Do you know what it was or if they found it?"

"Not really. The place is a mess. They were scared off before they could finish. Shot the first victim, then the second."

The bullet has entered her right cheek. 22. with a suppressor, because the hole is neat. They've shot her in the face.

Peter looks around the room. The chaos of the apartment reflects the chaos in his mind, a fire burning. He knows that finding out what Kara knew and why she was killed is the key to everything. The determination in his eyes hardens, the fire raging deep within them. What he does next won't just be about revenge. It will be about finding the truth. All of it.

Peter leaves the living room and explores the rest of the apartment. The kitchen is the same: ransacked drawers, broken dishes, and overturned chairs. The disorder is overwhelming. He remembers mornings here, Kara making coffee, the aroma filling the air as they shared stolen moments of peace before the world demanded their attention. He sees her in his mind, vibrant and alive, nothing like the current sad scene of destruction.

"Where did you hide it, Kara?" he mutters to himself.

He moves to the bedroom, a place of intimacy and trust. The bed is unmade, evidence of a hurried struggle. Personal items are strewn across the floor. He is hit with the memory of waking up next to Kara, her soft smile greeting him in the morning light. The images, the sounds, the smells fill his mind, bringing with them a fresh wave of pain that swallows him.

Then, a specific memory surfaces.

One morning, he had woken up to find Kara doing something secretive in her closet. She had been kneeling at the doorway, half her body buried within it. He had asked what she was doing as she placed a loose ventilation grill back into the wall at the back of the closet. She had turned to him, rolling her eyes with a playful grin. "Great. Now you know my stash spot," she had said.

In the present, Peter's hands tremble as he approaches the closet. Using a quarter, he pries open the ventilation grill on the back wall inside, his heart pounding with hope and fear. Inside, he finds three MiniDV cassette tapes. One of the cases has nothing written on the label. On another is written *Grand Junction*, and on the other is *Petrov Interview*. He realizes this is what the killers were after.

Carefully, he pockets the evidence, keeping an ear out for the possibility of one of the police coming his way. "This is it. This is what they wanted," he whispers to himself as he slips the tapes into the inside of his canvas field jacket.

He then replaces the grill and steps back from the closet, taking a moment to steel himself. The grief and rage swirl inside him, but he knows he has to keep moving. There are answers to find and justice to serve. With a final glance at the closet, he turns and leaves the room, the cassettes safely hidden and a new resolve burning in his heart.

Peter returns to the living room, the police still processing the scene, unaware of the vital evidence he holds in his jacket. He surveys the room, his face a mask of calm determination.

"Will there be security here tonight?" he asks the detective.

Detective Mendez sighs, shaking his head. "I don't think they'll be back, and we can't extend the budget. The department's resources are stretched thin as it is. Once we clear the scene, it'll be unguarded until morning."

Peter's mind races, but he masks his thoughts, keeping his expression neutral.

"Good," he says, nodding.

As Mendez looks at him curiously, Peter keeps his gaze steady, giving nothing away. But inside, his resolve hardens.

He leaves the apartment, the weight of his mission clear in his mind. Tonight, the hunt begins.

THREE

IT WAS ONLY TWO HOURS AGO WHEN THEY REMOVED the bodies and left. It is now nighttime. Having returned to the apartment, Peter now waits in the shadows of Kara's bedroom. A window lies open, the breeze blowing the curtains. He sits holding her sweatshirt, the Nike one she used to jog in, pressing it to his face and breathing in her scent, a bittersweet mix of memories and pain. Mostly pain.

He recalls lying in bed with her, the soft glow of the bedside lamp casting warm light over them. Wrapped in each other's arms, they often chatted away the late hours, just the two of them.

"You know, I could get used to this," Kara said, smiling softly.

Peter brushed a strand of hair from her face. "What, lying in bed all day?"

She laughed softly. "No, silly. Just being with you like this. It feels... right."

"It does. I wish we could freeze time and stay like this forever," he replied, gazing into her eyes.

"Me too. It's like the world just fades away when I'm with you." Kara sighed contentedly.

Peter kissed her forehead. "You make everything better, Kara. Even the tough days."

"You do the same for me, Peter. I don't know what I'd do without you," she said, nestling closer.

They lay there in silence for a moment, just holding each other, feeling the warmth and comfort of their connection.

"I love you, Kara," Peter whispered.

"I love you too, Peter. Always," she whispered back.

Peter shudders as he breathes in the sweatshirt. He hasn't had many women in his life. Kara was one. A piece of her is embedded in him forever.

A faint sound breaks the stillness—the slight, almost imperceptible scratching coming from the front door as someone cautiously uses a pick-set to get through the lock.

Peter's grip tightens on his pistol as he watches the shadow of a figure move stealthily into the apartment, heading straight for Kara's bedroom—straight for him. The intruder's movements are precise, practiced. Peter's heart steadies, but he remains calm, every muscle coiled and ready.

As the intruder steps into the bedroom, Peter moves swiftly. He steps out from behind the door, moves toward the man, and pistol-whips him across the back of the head. The blow sends him crashing to the floor. In a flash, Peter is on top of him, pressing the barrel of his SIG Sauer to the back of the guy's head, disarming him of the pistol he keeps in an underarm holster and slipping it into the back of his own jeans.

The man is silent, his body tense beneath Peter's weight. Peter quickly searches him, finding no ID, but a tattoo catches his eye— a tattoo on the back of the guy's neck. It's an iron gauntlet curled into a fist with spikes along the knuckles.

Bringing his mouth to the guy's ear as the intruder lies prostrate, Peter whispers, "Did you really have to pull her teeth out and break her fingers?"

The guy remains silent, his breath ragged.

"You came for this," Peter holds one of the small video cassette tapes in front of the guy's face. "I couldn't find anything to play it on. What's on them, and why did you kill my friend to get them?"

"Fuck you," the guy murmurs in a voice filled with defiance.

Peter's grip tightens on the pistol, his anger barely contained as he shoves the barrel into the back of the guy's neck. "You think this is a game? You think you can walk in here and take what you want after what you did?"

The intruder says nothing, his silence infuriating.

Peter presses the barrel harder into the man's skull. "Who sent you?"

Silence is the guy's only response. Peter knows he won't get answers easily, but he also knows he can't let this guy go. Not without understanding what he's dealing with.

Peter leans in closer, his voice a deadly whisper. "You have no idea what you've started. And I promise you, I'll find out who you are and who you're working for. Then I'm going to dismantle your entire operation. You're going to wish you never came here."

It is then that Peter hears something beyond the guy's breathing. A whispering is coming from his ear. That's when Peter spots the comms unit and snatches it from the guy's ear, placing it in his own.

"Hey, Davey," a voice murmurs. "You got it yet?"

Peter takes the earpiece out and speaks into it. "Where are you?" he asks before listening intently.

"Who is this?" the voice demands.

Peter hears the dull bass of the guy's voice coming from outside the apartment. "Where are you?" Peter repeats.

"Davey?!" the guy shouts.

That's when Davey pulls his face away from Peter's hand and cries out, "Ronny! He's got the—"

Peter smashes him in the back of the head, knocking him out. Listening, he hears the other guy's almost silent approach. Both men are professionals. They move with the skill of hunters. But Peter has been a hunter his whole life. He's not about to be another man's quarry. He's already two steps ahead.

Peter moves to the open window, stepping silently out onto the ledge of the seventh-floor apartment. He shimmies along the outer ledge of the building, the nighttime traffic honking below him, the crisp air blowing him around. At little farther on, he stops beside the living room window, listening.

Ronny has just crept into the apartment and is searching the small one-bedroom unit. The guy's flashlight beam crosses the living room, and Peter tucks himself in as it shines through the window.

Ronny leaves the living room to inspect the rest of the apartment. Peter slips the window open quietly, having left all the latches off in case of this exact scenario.

As Ronny reaches the bedroom, finding the unconscious Davey, Peter slips into the living room, creeping into the hallway just as Ronny reaches the open window in the bedroom. The killer cautiously sticks his head out; it is the only place he can think that the attacker would be. But the attacker, Peter, is fast approaching from behind.

Ronny spots his reflection in the glass, though, and whips around.

Peter and Ronny face off, their eyes locked in a deadly stare.

"Was it you who broke her fingers?" Peter asks.

Ronny merely glares at him. The tension in the room is so thick you could chew it, the tight space of the apartment adding to the claustrophobic intensity that buzzes in the air.

"I hope you know how to fight," Peter says.

"Yes, I do," Ronny breathes as he drops his shoulder in a feint, then lunges at Peter with a powerfully flicked jab to the face. Peter sidesteps, grabbing a lamp from the nearby table and smashing it into Ronny's head. The thing shatters. Ronny staggers but quickly recovers, his eyes blazing with rage.

Peter drops the broken lamp and assumes a Muay Thai stance. Ronny comes at him, Peter using his elbows and knees to keep his opponent at bay. Ronny counters with a Krav Maga move, aiming a quick jab to Peter's throat. Peter deflects it with his forearm and follows up with a swift knee strike to Ronny's ribs, the impact reverberating through the small room.

Ronny grabs a heavy ceramic vase, swinging it at Peter's head. Peter ducks just in time, and the vase smashes against the wall, pieces flying everywhere. Then he counters with a low leg sweep, a classic Jiu-Jitsu move, taking Ronny's legs out from under him. Ronny crashes to the floor but quickly rolls away as Peter attempts to stomp on his throat, grabbing a kitchen chair and using it as a shield.

Peter presses the attack, throwing a series of rapid punches, Bruce Lee's Wing Chun techniques on full display. He strikes the chair repeatedly, each blow weakening Ronny's defense, Peter whacking a leg off with one jab, another with a hook. Ronny kicks out, catching Peter in the shin and causing him to stumble.

The fight now in the kitchen, Ronny uses the brief respite to grab a frying pan from the kitchen counter and swings it at Peter. Peter blocks with his forearm, the impact jarring but not enough to stop him. He manages to catch Ronny's wrist and twists, forcing him to drop the pan before slamming his elbow into Ronny's face, using a powerful Muay Thai elbow strike.

Ronny reels back, blood streaming from his nose. He grabs a curtain rod, plucking it from above a window, and swings it like a staff, aiming for Peter's head. Peter ducks and comes around the back of Ronny, then uses an Aikido wrist lock to disarm him, the rod clattering to the floor.

Ronny is desperate now. He lunges at Peter with a knife he pulls from his boot, slashing wildly. Peter steps inside the attack, using a Judo hip throw to send Ronny crashing into the wall. The knife skitters across the floor, out of reach.

Peter pins Ronny against the wall, his grip like iron, pulling his SIG Sauer with his free hand. "Who sent you to kill her?" he demands.

Ronny just grins, his teeth bloodied.

"Who?!" Peter shouts, driving the barrel of his pistol into Ronny's cheek. He cocks it. The guy continues to stare at him, defiant. Peter fires a bullet right beside his ear, the edge of the blast catching him, grazing the side of his face.

"Who?" Peter asks again, his voice low and dangerous.

The guy says nothing, so Peter shoves the gun right into his chin.

"Who?" he snarls.

That's when they're interrupted. Someone bursts into the apartment. Peter whirls around with Ronny, using him as a human shield, his gun aimed at the two men entering the apartment. But they don't look like these guys. They're chubby, out of shape, and wearing the distinctive blue uniform of NYPD.

"NYPD!" one of them shouts at Peter. "Put your gun down and let him go!"

Peter has no other choice but to surrender. He lowers his gun, releasing Ronny, who collapses to the floor. The cops move in, guns trained on Peter, their expressions wary and confused.

Peter steps back, hands raised.

"I'm CIA," he tells them. "You'll find my ID in my pocket."

"I don't give a damn who you are," the cop says as he comes around Peter, takes his gun, and begins placing him in handcuffs.

Peter's mind races, calculating his next move. He knows he'll have to find another way to get the answers he needs. For now, he'll play along, biding his time until he can strike again.

FOUR

THE INTERROGATION ROOM IS STARK AND COLD. A single light overhead casts harsh shadows up the whitewashed brick walls. Peter sits handcuffed to a metal table, his expression calm but alert. The scent of metal and body odor hangs in the stuffy air, and there's a sense of being in a tomb as the room is buried deep within the precinct.

As he waits, Peter's mind drifts to the two men who attacked him. He wonders where they are now. Are they sitting in another interrogation room on the other side of the wall? He hadn't finished talking to them. He hopes he gets the chance to reacquaint himself with them. The information they hold could be crucial, and Peter is determined to extract it, one way or another.

Detective Mendez enters, carrying a file and a cup of coffee. He looks upset.

Peter is the first to speak. "You said there wasn't going to be any security on her apartment," he says, eyeing the detective as Mendez sits down opposite.

Detective Mendez studies him back for a moment before speaking. "I lied," he replies flatly. "Now tell me, Peter Black, CIA officer, what the hell were you doing back at my crime scene, seriously assaulting suspects?"

"They were back to finish what they started," Peter replies evenly.

"So you told my officers. You said they were looking for those video cassettes you had on you."

"Yes. They're crucial to figuring this thing out. Where are they now?"

"Being booked into evidence."

"Have you watched them?"

"Not yet. I've got a guy trying to source a camcorder that'll run them."

"You need to keep a close eye on those tapes."

"Look, Agent Black..."

"Colonel, not agent," Peter interrupts. "We have military ranks. I'm a colonel. We don't call ourselves agents in the CIA."

Mendez frowns. "Well, Colonel, I have two badly beaten men sitting in cells who won't tell me why they were meeting you in the dark of my crime scene."

"I wasn't there to meet them."

"No. You were there to ambush them," Mendez retorts dryly. "Well, I'd like to know why."

"That's what I was trying to find out when your officers showed up and stopped me."

Detective Mendez becomes visibly frustrated. "Why didn't you tell me about planning an ambush?" he asks. "The NYPD could have helped out. Why take matters into your own hands?"

"I'm trained to handle these situations. The people who killed her wouldn't hesitate to kill again. I needed to act fast. Unfortunately, your officers showed up before I was able to extract my information."

"What were you planning to do to them?"

Coldly, Peter replies, "Anything I needed to."

Mendez shudders.

Switching roles, Peter asks, "Have you identified them yet?"

"No. Their prints aren't on any records, and neither of them has been forthcoming with a name."

"Then their records have been removed," Peter says firmly. "Because they are definitely ex-forces. The one with the gauntlet tattooed on the back of his neck has a scar on his upper arm. It looks like a tattoo's been removed by surgery. I bet it was a military tattoo. Their movements, their gear—it all screamed highly trained professionals."

"That's what we figure, too," Mendez says. "What exactly was the victim..."

"Kara Tate," Peter snaps. "Her name wasn't 'the victim.' It was Kara Tate."

"Okay. Then can you tell me what Kara Tate was working on? What kind of information could be worth killing her for?"

"Like I told you, she was going to tell me everything at the meeting."

"And the CIA? Are you sure this has nothing to do with your agency?"

"I was telling the truth earlier, this has nothing to do with official operations. Nevertheless, I do believe whatever was on those tapes I found at the apartment is important to my agency."

"It's also important to my murder investigation."

Peter just stares at him. "Look. Shouldn't you already have some idea of what she was into?" he says. "I mean, Kara's laptop and computer weren't at the apartment. I'm guessing you took them."

"Then you'd be guessing wrong. During our search, we didn't even find a phone. We're under the impression that your friends took it all."

"Not my friends," Peter seethes. "Now, I've already wasted enough time. I take it you've called my superiors."

"I have. He's on his way. Guy named Deacon. But you forget. This is NYPD's jurisdiction. You're in a lot of trouble here, Peter. Assault with a deadly weapon, obstruction. So give me something to work with."

Peter gives him an earnest look. "I'm sorry. I wish I knew more."

Mendez leans back, his frustration evident. "You must know more about these guys. Who they might be working for?"

Peter considers his words carefully. "Look, the one guy with the tattoo on the neck—an iron gauntlet curled into a fist with spikes along the knuckles—that's not something you see every day. It could be linked to a private military contractor or some rogue faction."

Mendez nods, jotting down notes, then asks, "Why didn't Ms. Tate go through official channels if she had such important information? Why come to you?"

"She trusted me," Peter replies. "And she probably thought she could handle it without putting it in the hands of the authorities who might compromise her source or the information."

Mendez sighs again, rubbing his temples. "This is a mess, Black. I need to know what we're dealing with here. If there's a larger threat, we need to be prepared."

"I understand," Peter says. "But I can't give you more than what I have right now. Those film cassettes might hold the answers we both need. Have you thought about the titles yet?"

The detective takes a deep breath, his eyes hardening. "Petrov could be anyone, but I'm hoping once I speak with those she worked with, I'll find out. As for the other, Grand Junction, it's the same: it could be a place or a business, anything. I mean, there's a pizza parlor not far from here named Grand Junction. I'm hoping once I speak with Ms. Tate's editor, it'll become clear who it is."

Good luck, Peter thinks. *Kara was notorious for protecting her sources and not telling her editor who they were.*

"We will go through those films with a fine-tooth comb," Mendez goes on. "In the meantime, you're not going anywhere. Your boss will be here soon, and we'll see what he has to say."

Peter nods, knowing he has to bide his time. Once Deacon is here, he'll get him to take over the investigation. He hopes that those tapes will be theirs before Detective Mendez's people get him something to play them on.

Detective Mendez then stands up, grabbing the file and his coffee, and leaves the room.

Peter realizes that the real battle is only just beginning. He needs to be ready for whatever comes next.

FIVE

PETER SITS IN A DIMLY LIT CELL, THOUGHTS OF KARA and the conspiracy swirling in his mind. The distant hum of activity in the precinct fades as he contemplates his next move. The starkness of his surroundings contrasts sharply with the storm of memories and speculations brewing within him like black clouds.

There is a rumble of thunder coming, a lightning bolt heading straight for the people behind Kara's murder.

He pushes away the rage and reflects on the situation, contemplating the three MiniDV tapes. He hopes that Mark Deacon turns up soon so that they can take them from the NYPD and examine them themselves. He's sure this is CIA territory, that it reaches far beyond New York City. The titles—*Petrov Interview, Grand Junction*, and the possibilities of what could be on the unlabeled tape—revolve in his mind like a carousel of half clues.

Petrov interview, he muses. *So Petrov must be a person. Otherwise, why interview him, right? But Grand Junction? The detective was right. It could be anything.* The uncertainty gnaws at him, each possibility more troubling than the last.

Then his mind coughs up two names: *Davey and Ronny. David and Ronald. David and Ronald who?* The names circle in his thoughts, elusive and frustrating. During the interrogation, he had not shared the detail of the names with Mendez, only giving him what the detective already had: the titles of the tapes, the tattoos on the men. But their names are Peter's. Let NYPD figure out their own case. He has his to follow.

Peter shifts uncomfortably, the chains of his handcuffs rattling slightly. He needs to stay focused, to get to the bottom of this. The information those tapes contain could be the key to unraveling the conspiracy that has cost Kara her life.

Oh, Kara.

The thought of her brings a fresh wave of pain. Her laugh, her smile, the way she made him feel like he could take on the world —all of it is now a haunting memory. He knows he has to keep moving forward, for her and for the truth.

A FLOOR BELOW, in separate interrogation rooms, the two men are being grilled. All they do is sit there in smug silence as Mendez questions one and his partner questions the other.

Mendez leans forward, his voice steady but firm. "Who sent you?"

The man whom Peter knows as Davey remains silent, a slight smirk playing at the corner of his lips. Mendez's frustration grows as he continues to press for answers.

"Why did you kill her? What's on those tapes that was worth taking her life?"

Davey finally mumbles something, his voice low and almost inaudible. Mendez doesn't catch it at first and has to lean in closer. "What did you say?"

Davey looks directly at Mendez, his eyes cold and unflinching. "What does any of it matter when you're all going to be dead very soon?"

JUST AS AN EERIE feeling creeps up the back of Detective Mendez, two people creep toward the precinct roof from the adjacent building. Resembling spirits, they are manifestations of Davey's threat, dressed all in black, wearing gas masks, body armor, and carrying assault rifles. They also have canisters of gas slung over their shoulders. The night is dark and quiet, perfect cover for their operation.

Crouched at the edge of one rooftop where it joins that of the precinct, one of them, a woman, touches her ear.

"Team One in place," she says. "Over."

"You have eyes on the HVAC?" a man's gruff voice on the other end asks. "Over."

"Copy that, Team Leader. I have eyes on the HVAC. Over."

The eyes behind her mask are fixed on a fenced-off structure in the corner of the police precinct roof. The HVAC system—heating, ventilation, and air conditioning—looks like a series of large, metallic boxes and ducts, humming softly as they manage the airflow and temperature inside the building. The central unit is a sizable, box-like structure with vents, grills, and fans, connected by a network of pipes and ductwork. Its presence is unassuming yet crucial, a lifeline of air for the entire precinct.

"Then stand by for Phase One," Team Leader confirms. "Over."

"Copy that. Over and out."

———

AT THE SAME TIME, another two operatives, Team Two, work their way through a sewer below the precinct. The air is thick with the stench of waste and damp, the narrow tunnels amplifying every sound. They too are clad in tactical gear and gas masks, their footsteps reverberating softly as they move.

Team Leader checks a digital map, the screen glowing faintly in the darkness. "This is it," he says as they reach a solid wall, patting it with his gloved hand. The concrete is cold and slick with moisture.

The two men begin unpacking explosives, the metallic clinks of their equipment echoing through the sewer. As they work, one of them asks the other, Team Leader, "Are you sure this is all going to work? I mean, this plan is a little on the fly."

"The plan's rushed, I accept that," Team Leader replies, carefully setting the charges. "But Leadership has provided us with all the support we need. It is vital that we get those tapes."

"Fucking Davey and Ronny. How'd they screw this up so bad?"

With this question hanging in the air, the two men complete their task. Team Leader adjusts the fuse, ensuring that it's secure and ready. Then he speaks into his comms. "Command, you getting me? Over."

———

PARKED A BLOCK FROM THE PRECINCT, a fifth operative wearing a headset sits in the back of a van in front of multiple monitors. This is Command. On the screens is the live CCTV feed from inside the precinct. He watches the footage from the interrogation rooms, observing Mendez and his partner questioning Davey and Ronny.

Upon hearing Team Leader, Command replies, "Loud and clear. Over."

"Are you set for Phase One? Over."

"Oh yes. You ready? Over."

"We are. Over."

"Then it's happening in three... two... one."

Command presses a key on his keyboard, and all the footage inside the precinct goes into a loop, showing recordings from ten minutes ago, the transition seamless and undetectable to anyone watching in real time. Checking the cameras on the roof, he sees that they too show previous footage.

"Phase One is complete," he says into his comms. "Over."

———

ON THE ROOF, Team One gets the go-ahead.

"Initiate Phase Two," Team Leader's rough voice gurgles in their ears. "Over."

"Copy that," the male of the two says. "Initiating Phase Two. Over and out."

They leave their spot and move silently across the precinct roof. With the CCTV in a loop, the cameras won't pick up their approach. The night air is cool and still, the only sound the faint hum of the city below.

Reaching the fenced-off HVAC ventilation system, they work quickly, using bolt cutters to snip through the metal links. The sharp snick of the cutters is almost drowned out by the hum of the HVAC unit.

They access the system and release the gas canisters into the ducts, twisting their taps as they begin to hiss. The woman watches intently as the gas begins to waft into the system, a thin, almost invisible plume that disperses rapidly.

"Phase Two is complete," she says into her comms, eyes fixed on the gas swirling into the intake.

"Good," Team Leader says. "Then we'll see you on the other side. Over and out."

Inside the precinct, the gas begins dispersing throughout the building quickly. It snakes through the ducts and vents, spreading like a silent, invisible fog. Officers begin to choke and cough, their eyes watering as the gas fills their lungs. Panic surges through the ranks as they realize something is terribly wrong.

"Gas! We're being... gassed!" one officer manages to shout between coughs, his voice raspy and desperate.

Chaos ensues. Officers stumble and grasp at their throats, some collapsing to the floor, others trying to make their way to the exits. The sounds of choking and coughing resound through the halls, blending with the frantic shouts and the clatter of fallen equipment.

In the interrogation room, Mendez and his partner exchange horrified glances as the gas begins to seep in, making them cough. Mendez reaches for his radio, but only static greets him. He leaves the room, trying to get the attention of anyone outside, but the thick, acrid gas makes it hard to breathe, let alone shout. Shoving his shirt over his mouth, there is only one thing to do. He begins running toward the armory where he knows there are gas masks. And heavy guns.

Inside the cell block, prisoners begin to panic, slamming their fists on the cell doors, crying out for an assistance that will not be coming. In his cell, Peter spots the stale air shift subtly, carrying with it an unfamiliar, sweet odor. Experience tells him immediately that it is knockout gas seeping in through the ventilation. He springs into action, grabbing his shirt and pressing it over his nose and mouth, dampening it with water from the bottle Mendez had left him with. The fabric feels cool against his skin, offering a fragile barrier against the encroaching gas.

———

INSIDE THE VAN, the fifth operative, Command, watches the monitors intently as all the telephone calls from inside the precinct are intercepted and diverted to him via an electronic stingray device. Some of the screens flicker with the looping footage, creating a false yet eerie sense of calm inside the chaotic building. His headset crackles to life with a call from a panicked lieutenant calling in from inside the building.

"Emergency Dispatch," Command says.

"Dispatch... this is the... 18th Precinct," the lieutenant coughs. "We got gas coming into the building through the ventilation."

"We are aware of the situation 18th," Command replies, his

tone calm and reassuring, pretending to be an emergency worker. "Assistance is on its way. Just hold on."

He disconnects the call, his face betraying no emotion as he continues to monitor the situation.

The voice of Team Leader crackles in his ear: "Phase Three ready. Over."

Command glances at the monitors, ensuring that everything is still running smoothly. "You hearing that, Team One?" he says into his comms.

"Loud and clear. We're ready on our end. Over," comes the response from the roof.

"Phase Three is a go, Team Two," Command says. "Over."

———

POSITIONED a safe distance away from the explosives, Team Leader steadies his nerves and speaks into his comms. "Phase Three initiate. Over."

With a press of a button, they detonate the explosives.

Inside the precinct, the sense of dread is thickened by the sudden rumble that shakes the building. The ground trembles, and from the basement, dust and smoke billow up, mingling with the gas and making it impossible to see.

The explosion takes out most of the wall in the basement shower unit. The force of the blast sends debris flying into the changing rooms and gym, the sound of crumbling concrete and twisting metal filling the air. The water main is hit, water spraying out everywhere, slowly flooding the wreckage. Several police officers, who are already coughing and spluttering from the gas, are caught in the explosion. The blast's impact crushes them under the rubble, their cries of agony quickly silenced by the overwhelming chaos.

Upstairs, the rumble is felt throughout the building. Detective Mendez, already struggling to breathe, is thrown off balance as the floor beneath him shakes. He exchanges frantic glances with his fellow officers, realizing the situation is much worse than they imagined.

Peter, in his cell, feels the vibration of the blast. He knows what is coming. The gas is making it hard to think, but he forces himself to stay focused. Trapped inside this room, there is nothing he can do.

In the van, Command watches the monitors, satisfied with the progress. "Phase Three complete," he says into his comms. "Proceed to infiltration. Over."

The operatives in the sewer move quickly through the newly created breach, their path clear. They navigate the dark, smoke-filled gym, making their way to the building's north stairwell. The plan is unfolding perfectly, and they are now within reach of their objective. The confusion inside the precinct works to their advantage, and they press on with unwavering determination.

———

On the roof, Team One smashes their way through the bulkhead doors using sledgehammers and enters the top of the precinct's south stairwell. The sound of the doors giving way resonates through the building, mixing with the distant rumble of the explosion and the muffled cries of the gas-choked officers.

They move swiftly, senses heightened as they descend the stairs. Halfway down, they surprise a police officer who has managed to cover his mouth and hasn't been knocked out by the gas. His eyes widen in shock the second he spots the intruders, tactical gear and gas masks making them look otherworldly. Instinctively, he raises his pistol, his finger poised on the trigger.

But Team One is quicker to the draw. In a fluid motion, the male operative raises his assault rifle and fires. The sharp crack of the gunshot reverberates through the stairwell, and the officer crumples to the ground, his weapon clattering uselessly beside him.

Team One doesn't break stride, stepping over the fallen officer and continuing their descent, their mission clear, no time to waste, the sounds of mayhem growing louder as they approach the lower levels, the mixture of gas, dust, and smoke making the atmosphere increasingly oppressive. They are a well-oiled machine, driven by the urgency of their mission and the knowledge that failure is not an option.

———

COMING UP FROM BELOW, Team Two reaches the third floor and enter the interrogation suite.

"Their signals are coming from just ahead of your position," Command's voice says through their comms. "You shouldn't be—"

"Drop your weapons!" voices shout.

Some officers who have managed to avoid being knocked out by the gas have spotted them. The second Team Two throws themselves into cover, the officers open fire. Bullets ricochet off the walls, narrowly missing the operatives as they dive for shelter behind a corner of a wall.

Without missing a beat, Team Leader pulls the pin from a frag grenade, leaves the cover of the wall, and sends the grenade sailing through the air. It lands at the feet of the two cops, who barely have time to react. Their eyes widen in horror as they scramble to get away.

The grenade explodes with a deafening roar, sending shrapnel and debris flying in all directions. The shockwave shakes the entire floor, adding to the uproar. The two officers are thrown to the ground, quickly getting to their feet and running.

The operatives seize the moment. They open fire on them, the staccato bursts of their assault rifles echoing through the confined space. The fleeing men are caught in the hail of bullets, their bodies jerking violently before collapsing to the floor.

All hell has broken loose.

IN THE MEANTIME, Team One moves swiftly down the stairwell, heading toward the evidence lockup on the fifth floor.

Command's steady voice comes over the comms. "Team One, status update. Over."

"Team One here," the female says. "Moving to the fifth floor. Encountered minimal resistance so far. Over."

"Copy that," Command replies. "Team Two, status update. Over."

"Team Two here," Team Leader's gruff voice says. In the background there is the sound of gunfire. "We've come across heavy resistance at the interrogation suite. However, we are still proceeding to location. Over."

"Copy that," Command says. "Team One, ETA to evidence lockup. Over."

"One minute out," the female relies. "Over."

———

INSIDE HIS CELL, Peter breathes through his vest, his shirt blocking up the ventilation grill on the wall. Trained to withstand this type of sedative, he forces himself to recite the multiplication tables aloud, his voice a hoarse whisper, each number a lifeline, pulling him back from the brink of unconsciousness—"twenty-one, twenty-eight, thirty-five, forty-two, forty-nine..." It keeps him alert as he listens intently to the commotion outside. The walls shake with distant explosions, gunfire, shouts, and screams pulsating through the hallways. The lights flicker sporadically, casting eerie shadows in the small cell.

The sound of the door unlocking catches his attention. Two men in gas masks suddenly burst in. For a split-second he's not sure what is about to happen, but then he recognizes their clothing; it is a uniformed officer followed by Detective Mendez. Both men are breathless and urgent.

The officer comes around Peter and begins unlocking his handcuffs. Lifting his gas mask slightly, Detective Mendez speaks. "As you can see, we're under attack," he says. "And if you're as good with a gun as I think you are, then you can help us."

When Peter's hands are free, Mendez hands him a handgun. Peter takes it, feeling the familiar weight in his hand.

"You'll need this, too," Mendez says, handing Peter a gas mask.

Nodding grimly, Peter puts the mask on and then checks the handgun over. It is a Beretta M9 with a twelve-round mag. He feels a sense of purpose settle over him, the chaos around him sharpening his focus.

"We need to secure those tapes," Peter says, his voice muffled by the mask. "Where are they?"

"Evidence Room on the fifth floor," Mendez replies.

"Lead the way."

———

Team One reaches the Evidence Room, a trail of unconscious bodies lining the gray carpet tiles. The gas reached this area quickest and with the most potency. The room is filled with the sight of officers slumped over desks and sprawled on the floor, their bodies limp and unresponsive.

Among the disorder, the eerie silence is punctuated only by their footsteps. The female operative gestures to a computer terminal with a curt nod.

The male operative moves swiftly to the computer. He connects a small device to the terminal, bypassing the security protocols with ease.

"You know what?" the male says, glancing around.

"What?"

"It would be much quicker and easier if we just burned it down."

"We have to be sure," the woman replies. "Now try and find out where they are."

———

Team Two reaches the interrogation rooms, looking like ghosts as they glide through the thick haze of gas that permeates the air. Trails of smoke flow from the barrels of their assault rifles, and not all the bodies in their wake were incapacitated by the gas. Many of them have been permanently incapacitated by bullets.

Using their lock-picking tools, the two operatives quickly work on the doors. The click of the locks being disengaged preludes the doors creaking open, and the operatives step inside, their eyes scanning for their companions.

In the dim light, Davey and Ronny are huddled low to the ground, their bodies pressed against the cold concrete. They have their sweatshirts pulled over their mouths, desperately trying to filter out the noxious gas. Their eyes are wide but alert, and the two men are readied for this opportunity to escape.

As the operatives approach, Davey raises his head slightly, recognizing the familiar tactical gear. "About time," he mutters, his voice muffled by the fabric.

Ronny, crouched beside him, nods in agreement. "We thought you'd never get here."

"You should be thankful we came at all," Team Leader retorts brusquely.

The operatives waste no time. One of them produces a pair of bolt cutters and quickly severs the handcuffs restraining Davey and Ronny.

"Here," Team Leader says, handing them comms earpieces and gas masks. Davey and Ronny quickly place the comms into their ears, then don the masks, the fresh air a welcome relief from the choking gas.

As they secure the masks, the operatives pass them Heckler &

Koch HK416 assault rifles. Davey checks the magazine, his eyes narrowing with determination. "Let's get out of here."

Ronny nods, his grip on the assault rifle tight. "What's the plan?"

"We regroup and extract," one of the operatives replies. "Now get ready. We need to get you out of this mess."

―――――

ON THE FIFTH FLOOR, the tension is palpable. "Got it," the male operative in Team One says triumphantly.

"Where?" the woman demands.

"It's in Section B, Shelf Four, Bin Twelve."

"Where is that?" she asks as she uses a key she removed from one of the unconscious officers to open the cage door of the Evidence Room.

The male operative checks a map of the layout on the wall beside the terminal. "It's the third aisle on the right," he calls out to her. "The shelves are probably numbered. Look for item number 89644, tagged with case number 23-9785."

The female searches along the shelves, her eyes scanning the numbers quickly until she finds Bin Twelve. "Got it!" she declares, finding the tapes and shoving them into a bag. "Is this really all it's about?" she asks herself, sealing the bag and shoving it over her shoulder. "Three stupid cassette tapes."

―――――

PETER, Detective Mendez, and several other officers reach the fifth floor, their faces set with grim determination.

Peter turns to the group, his eyes sharp. "Two of you wait here," he commands. "The other two, you need to go up to the sixth, cut across to the other stairwell and wait there. We need to cut them off on both sides."

The officers nod, understanding the urgency of the situation.

They split into two groups, one staying behind while the other heads for the stairwell.

Mendez steps forward. "What are you going to do?"

"Flush them out."

"You can't go in there alone. It's madness."

Peter meets his gaze, a steely resolve in his eyes. "I'm always better working alone," he replies in a steady voice.

Mendez hesitates, clearly torn, but finally nods. "Be careful," he says.

Peter gives a brief nod, then turns and disappears through the doors leading to the offices of the Evidence Room, disappearing into the depths of the building, his mind focused on the mission ahead.

———

WITH THE TAPES SECURE, Team One heads for the north stairwell. Everything is going smoothly. Until now.

Before they get the chance to hit the stairwell, gunshots ring out, accurate and deadly, seemingly from nowhere, sending them diving for cover behind desks.

The male operative sits breathing heavily, his chest heaving. He's been hit, his body armor having stopped several bullets. Despite the protection, he struggles to catch his breath, suspecting a fractured sternum from the heavy impact.

"You okay?" the woman whispers into her comms.

"Pretty... much," he gasps.

"Can you fight?"

"Uh huh."

"Then we fight!" She bursts from cover, but there is no one to be seen at the doorway where the gunshots came from. Her instincts kick in, and she swings around. He's there, in the opposite doorway. Before she can get a shot off, he's fired the Beretta. A bullet grazes her leg as she dives back behind the desks.

She can hear him running, leaping over desks, getting into

cover. The man stands up sharply and sprays the air with his machine gun.

"No!" the woman shouts. "He's—"

More gunshots from the opposite side of the room. One hits the male in the arm.

"Fuck!" he cries out as he goes down.

The woman crawls on all fours, then stops and listens. She can't hear anything above her companion's heavy breathing and groaning, but she is sure whoever is attacking them is moving as quietly as they can, using the environment to shield themselves, waiting for the two of them to move. She also acknowledges that his shots have been almost perfect thus far.

Peeking, she scans her environment. The room feels haunted, every shadow a potential threat, every creak of the building a harbinger of doom. The oppressive atmosphere is thickening quickly, and she can sense their hunter—a ghostly presence stalking them with unerring precision.

"Team Two," she whispers into her comms. "We are under attack. Someone is hunting us. We need your assistance. Over."

"This is Team Two. Copy that. We're on our way. Over."

The woman remains motionless, her breath shallow, straining to hear any sign of movement. The silence is deafening, broken only by the ragged breaths of her injured companion. She grips her weapon tightly, her knuckles white, knowing their hunter is out there, closing in—a stooped tiger roaming the long grass.

Daring, she pokes herself out of her cover, remaining down low on all fours. In the hazy air, she catches a glimpse of a shadow moving silently across the room. Her heart pounds in her chest, and she steadies her breathing, focusing on the task at hand. The hunter moves like a phantom, only his shadow showing for the briefest of seconds on one of there walls, blending into the surroundings, his presence felt more than seen.

Peter moves toward her with the grace of a predator, his movements silent, his eyes scanning for any sign of his prey. He knows the operatives are skilled, but this isn't his first rodeo. He inches closer, using the desks and overturned furniture as cover.

The woman senses him before she sees him, a cold shiver running down her spine. She spins around, her weapon raised, but he is already in motion. Peter fires, forcing her to dive farther into cover.

She screams out as another bullet catches her in the thigh, tucking herself into the pillar she's dived behind as tightly as she can, the shock coursing through her body, making her shake, while the warm blood flows down her numb leg.

The male operative, still struggling to breathe, manages to lift his weapon and spray the area with gunfire. The bullets ricochet off the walls and furniture, filling the air with the frenzied sound.

But Peter is gone, already hidden behind his next piece of cover, his mind calculating his next move.

"Team Two, we need you now!" the woman hisses into her comms.

"We're close," comes the reply. "Hold on."

Gazing at her partner on the other side of an aisle, she says, "We need to move."

The two of them nod at each other, steeling themselves for what comes next. At exactly the same time, they burst from cover, guns blazing, but are quickly pinned back by several well-placed shots. The man takes another hit, grunting in pain as the impact drives him back, the bullet punching another dent into the body armor, sending shockwaves through his ribs. The woman narrowly avoids a similar fate, a bullet whizzing past her head.

With her partner struggling for breath and pinned behind a column, she tries to crawl away, desperate to escape, her movements frantic. But she crawls straight into a shadow that emerges from behind a desk, her enemy having tracked her movements like a wolf stalking an injured deer.

Peter grabs her from behind, an arm wrapping around her neck, the hand of his other arm plucking her assault rifle from her, his knee striking the back of her injured leg, forcing her down. She struggles briefly, but his grip is unyielding.

He leans in, bringing his lips close to her ear, about to say something when gunfire erupts outside the door. Ronny and Davey have reached Mendez and the officer guarding the southern stairwell. The officer is armed with a Benelli combat shotgun, the blasts resounding through the building, followed by heavy machine gun fire.

On the opposite side, emerging from the northern stairwell, is Team Two. They instantly open fire on Peter, sending him diving away from the woman, who scrambles to safety.

Peter rolls behind a desk, the bullets tearing through the air above him.

In the stairwell, Ronny and Davey look to press their advantage, advancing with military precision. Mendez and the officer fight back fiercely, the confined space amplifying every gunshot, every shout.

"Hold the line!" Mendez shouts, his voice barely audible over the cacophony.

Peter sits up against a desk. Pinned down, he assesses the situation. He knows he's outnumbered and outgunned—the Beretta only has a single bullet left. As gunfire reverberates through the fifth floor, he peeks through a small gap in the desks that lets him see his enemies.

Team One has joined Team Two in the northern stairwell. That's where the tapes are. It's also where the biggest danger is. Even though two of them are injured, the four of them have enough firepower to take on an army. Peter has just the one bullet.

At the opposite end of the room, he sees Mendez and the officer struggling to hold their ground, the shotgun blasts from the Benelli punctuating the air with each thunderous shot as they try to defend themselves from Ronny and Davey. The two men are relentless, their assault rifles barking fire as they press forward.

The Benelli runs dry, and all the officer can do is fold his body into an alcove. It isn't long before Mendez is out of ammo, the detective pressing his body into a corner by the door as bullets hit the wall close to his head, sending plaster shards into the air.

Back at the northern stairwell, Teams One and Two are readying to leave, Team Two positioned to defend their position, while in the background, Team One checks their wounds.

"How you doing back there?" Team Leader asks as his eyes scan the office space for Peter.

"Just a flesh wound," the female operative answers.

"How about you?" Team Leader asks the male.

"My arm's numb," he answers, holding his injured right arm, a grimace on his face. "I think the bullet's still in there."

"Can you move?"

"Hell yeah."

Team Leader touches his ear. "Ronny? Davey?" he calls into his comms. "We're leaving."

In the stairwell, Ronny ignores the command. He's too busy moving toward the stricken officer, who is trapped in the alcove. Ronny, his assault rifle aimed on the edge of the alcove, moves slowly, taking one step at a time.

"Ronny, leave him," Davey hisses at him, one eye on the door to the fourth floor, where they can cross the precinct to meet the others. "We gotta go."

But Ronny isn't listening; there is a blood lust in his eyes. It has something to do with his utter hatred for all forms of authority.

"You're gonna need to run to me," Mendez calls across to the officer.

But when the officer goes to leave his place, gunfire sends him back again, Ronny roaring with laughter.

Peter's gaze flicks between one stairwell and the other. In the southern stairwell, the officer and Mendez are more than likely going to die if he doesn't help them. But on the other hand, the tapes—the only evidence they have—are there in the northern stairwell.

As Mendez cries out, "Move, man! Move!" Peter spots an

opportunity. A fire extinguisher hangs on the wall nearby, its bright red color standing out against the murky air. Using the desks as cover, he reaches it, plucking the extinguisher from the wall. Pulling the pin, he aims it at the northern stairwell. With a swift squeeze of the handle, a thick cloud of white powder erupts from the nozzle, filling the air and obscuring the vision of the operatives standing there.

The sudden burst of powder creates a temporary shield, allowing Peter to move without being targeted by gunfire. He sprints toward the southern stairwell. As he reaches the doorway, he sees Ronny advancing on the officer trapped in the alcove. Without hesitation, Peter aims the extinguisher at Ronny's face and unleashes another blast of powder. The white cloud engulfs Ronny, causing him to stumble, blinded by the sudden onslaught.

Peter seizes the moment, charging at Ronny with the extinguisher held high. He swings it downwards with all his might, the heavy metal cylinder connecting with Ronny's head with a sickening crunch. Ronny staggers, dropping his rifle, and Peter strikes again, ensuring he won't get up.

Seeing his comrade disappear in a white cloud, Davey can't wait any longer. He's forced to flee, leaving Ronny to his fate.

"Wait here," Peter tells Mendez and the officer before leaving them. He returns to the fifth-floor offices armed with nothing but the single bullet chambered in the Beretta. The operatives have already moved from the stairwell. Peter can just make out the patter of their boots as they descend in a panic.

That's when he spots Davey below. Peter fires his last bullet but misses by mere centimeters, the bullet whipping past Davey's ear. He moves to follow but is stopped when a muzzle flash explodes from lower down in the stairwell, sending him diving as bullets ping off the metal railings.

Then there's silence. Nothing except the sound of his own pounding heart. When he thinks it's safe, Peter peels away from his cover.

DAVEY REACHES the others in the basement, his breath coming in harsh gasps.

"Where's Ronny?" Team Leader asks.

"Gone" is Davey's curt response.

"What do you mean?"

"I mean gone. Now we need to go."

The urgency in Davey's voice leaves no room for argument. Team Leader nods, turning his attention to the others. The female operative, her thigh grazed by Peter's bullet, winces as she shifts her weight. The male operative from Team One cradles his arm, a bullet lodged painfully within it.

"Let's move," Team Leader commands.

Supporting their injured comrades, the five operatives make their way across the damaged gym. The floor is littered with broken equipment and debris from the breach explosion. They reach the showers, where the gaping hole in the wall leads into the sewers.

Climbing through, they move as quickly as their injuries allow, the sounds of their footsteps bouncing off the damp, grimy walls.

"Keep moving," Team Leader urges. "We can't afford to slow down."

The operatives push themselves, adrenaline fueling their steps despite the pain.

———

PETER FOLLOWS CAREFULLY down the stairs. Reaching the basement, he traces the operatives through the gym, his eyes locked on the blood trail left by the injured. The gym is a mangled mess, but the trail is unmistakable. It leads him to the changing rooms, where he spots a service weapon hanging on a peg by its holster. He takes the Beretta out, checks it over, and cocks it.

Following the blood to the showers, he finds the breach in the wall. The air is thick with dust, making visibility practically zero as he steps over the unconscious littering the floor. He enters the sewer, the darkness pressing in around him—but he can hear the faint movements of the operatives up ahead.

Peter moves cautiously, his senses on high alert. The sound of rushing water and the echo of the distant footsteps guide him. But his caution isn't enough. As he comes around a bend in the sewer, muzzle flash ignites in the darkness ahead. He instinctively dives for cover, the bullets ricocheting off the walls around him.

Heart pounding, he waits for a break in the gunfire, then the sound of the operative moving off to join the rest of his group. When it comes, he moves swiftly, keeping low as he follows the trail. By the time he catches up with them, he sees the open manhole above, faint light streaming down. Peter climbs up, his muscles tense with anticipation.

Emerging from the sewer, he catches a glimpse of rear lights disappearing into the night. A van is pulling out of the construction site the manhole opens into, but it's too far to make out the license plate number. Frustration wells up inside him as Peter watches the van vanish.

"Maybe some other day," he whispers into the night.

SIX

THE 18TH PRECINCT IS A DISASTER ZONE. WITHIN THE building, emergency services personnel in gas masks move with a bleak efficiency, their muffled voices blending with the cacophony of sirens and shouts.

Peter, bruised and exhausted, moves through the wreckage with a determined focus. His muscles ache, but he pushes through the pain, helping to evacuate the building. He loads the unconscious onto stretchers. Others, he lifts onto his shoulders, carrying them out of the building and handing them off to paramedics. His mind is a raging sea of thoughts, but he forces himself to stay in the moment, to keep moving.

The street outside is a symphony of emergency vehicles—ambulances, fire trucks, and police cars lining every inch of asphalt. The blue and red lights create an eerie glow against the thickening dusk. Paramedics and firefighters in gas masks work tirelessly. The fire department has set up large industrial fans and ventilation systems to suck the gas out of the building, the equipment humming loudly as it works.

The press, held back by the police cordon, shout questions and snap photos, their voices a distant background noise to the immediate crisis.

Among this bedlam, Mark Deacon and Kirsty Lange arrive at the scene, both equipped with gas masks for the occasion. Deacon, a composed and authoritative figure, strides through the chaos with an air of command. His tall frame and sharp features are a stark contrast to the tumult around him. Beside him, Kirsty Lange, a thirty-three-year-old operations officer, stands out with her dyed gray hair and hipster look.

They show their badges to the police officers manning the barricade and are promptly let through. As they approach the precinct, they spot Detective Mendez directing operations near the entrance. Deacon and Kirsty walk up to him, their IDs held out for inspection.

"Ah, CIA," Mendez says. "You here to take my case?"

"Probably," Deacon replies.

"Good. Because I'd like to retire in one piece, and tonight almost cost me my life. So you're welcome to it."

"Nevertheless," Deacon says, "before I do, I'd like to know where my operative is."

Mendez's expression softens. "Your operative saved my life," he says in a solemn tone. "Probably saved a lot more of my people tonight by chasing those bastards outta here. Clipped one of them, too."

"Yes, I heard," Deacon says, his gaze scanning the area. "Did the man survive?"

"No. Your guy, Peter, hit him so hard he broke his neck."

"And where is Peter?"

"There."

Mendez points to a row of ambulances where Peter is helping load a stretchered body into the back of one. His face is streaked with sweat and grime, his movements deliberate but weary. Deacon nods to Mendez, a silent acknowledgment of his gratitude, before he and Kirsty begin making their way toward Peter.

"Peter," Deacon calls out as they near.

Peter looks up, his eyes widening slightly in recognition. He straightens, his exhaustion momentarily forgotten. "Mark. Kirsty."

"You look like hell," Kirsty says with a half-smile.

"You should see the other guy," Peter replies, managing a tired grin.

Deacon's eyes scan Peter, noting the bruises and the exhaustion etched into his features. "You okay?"

Peter manages a tired smile. "Been better. But I'm still standing."

Kirsty looks around at the mayhem. "So you gonna tells us what exactly happened here?"

Peter's face grows grim. "A well-coordinated attack. They knew exactly what they were doing."

Deacon's expression hardens. "We need to understand their strategy. Can you walk us through it?"

Peter nods, wiping sweat from his brow. "Yeah, I can. But we'll need to go inside."

The three put their gas masks on, Peter pulling his down from atop his head. He then leads Deacon and Kirsty into the building, navigating through the debris and the bustling emergency personnel. The remnants of the attack are everywhere: shattered glass, overturned furniture, and the occasional body covered with a sheet, waiting to be taken away.

"They hit us hard and fast," Peter explains as they move through the wreckage. "First, they looped the CCTV feed, then released gas through the HVAC system to incapacitate as many officers as possible."

Kirsty listens intently, her mind piecing together the information. "How did they get in?"

"Two teams," Peter continues. "Team One accessed the roof and deployed the gas. Team Two came up through the sewers and breached the basement. They coordinated their movements perfectly."

As they head to the stairwell, they pass by a group of paramedics tending to wounded officers. Deacon's face remains impassive, but his eyes are sharp, absorbing every detail of Peter's account.

"They breached the interrogation rooms and freed two of their own," Peter says. "Davey and Ronny. I killed Ronny, hit him a little too hard with a fire extinguisher, but Davey got away."

Deacon asks, "And the tapes?"

Peter's jaw tightens. "That's what they were after. Managed to get them in the end."

Kirsty nods thoughtfully. "Okay, let's see where they breached the building."

Descending the stairs, they hit the basement and what's left of the gym and the shower blocks.

"Watch your step," Peter advises as they reach the showers, where a gaping hole in the wall reveals the attackers' point of entry and escape. CSI teams are already there, meticulously combing through the debris for evidence. The air is thick with the smell of wet concrete and sewer grime.

As they step through the hole into the sewer, the walls begin vibrating as subway cars rumble by, just a few feet away on the other side of the slimy brickwork.

"They came through here," Peter says, his voice resonating in the confined space. "Used the sewers to get close without being detected."

Deacon inspects the walls and the remnants of the breach, his expression thoughtful. "Any leads on where they went after this?"

Peter nods. "From here, they made it through the sewer about six hundred feet and climbed out. That's where they got in some type of van."

"Did you see it?" Kirsty asks.

"Only its rear lights," Peter replies, his voice oozing with disappointment. "All I can say is it looked like a van."

They continue through the sewer, the stench intensifying as they go deeper. Their footsteps echo off the damp, grimy walls.

Eventually, they reach an open manhole that leads to the derelict land of a construction site. CSI are all over the manhole and the site, already making casts of the tire tracks.

"The city's on lockdown," Deacon points out, "but I'm sure they're at a safe house inside New York where they'll lay low until things cool down. Then they'll move away."

SEVEN

SOMEWHERE IN QUEENS, WITHIN THE SHADOWED confines of an apartment safe house, five of the attackers, including Davey, gather to catch their breaths after the manic escape from the precinct. Their sixth member is in a bedroom, on an encrypted line speaking to Leadership, his muffled voice reverberating gently through the wall. The atmosphere is tense, a volatile mix of relief and anxiety.

The apartment is sparsely furnished, with a few chairs and a small table serving as the main gathering point. The low wattage bulb casts long shadows, amplifying the sense of unease among the group. They sit around the table, visibly shaken, their breaths heavy and labored.

Davey leans back in his chair, running a shaking hand through his disheveled hair, a testament to the fierce encounter they have barely survived. The distant wail of sirens serves as a constant reminder of how close they came to being caught.

In the background, a police scanner mumbles away, its monotone voice a steady undercurrent of tension. "...all eastern exits from Manhattan have been blockaded... heightened security measures in place... I need both ends of the Lincoln Tunnel blocked..." Simons, a lean man with a sharp jawline, intense green eyes, and a long ponytail, sits by the police scanner, listening carefully, his face illuminated by its dim light. This is who liaised with them from the van, the man they called Command over their comms.

The only female among them, grimacing with pain, is sewing her own thigh wound. Her hands gently tremble as she threads the needle through the torn flesh, but her face remains set in determination. The pain is intense, but she bites her lip and pushes through it. Her name is Rebecca, or Raven to her friends.

It was her mother who gave her the nickname Raven because of her long jet black hair—like the wings of a raven. Apart from the hair, she's tall, wiry, athletic, more than a match for any man that can swing a fist. She's also very pretty, something she tries hard to hide but pulls off with limited success.

Across the room, another attacker, a tall, well-built man with sharp eyes, is removing a bullet from another man's arm. He has deepset eyes, a shaved head, and a thick, gray beard braided at the end. His name is Marcus. He works quickly and efficiently, using pliers to extract the bullet, while the wounded man clenches his jaw, stifling his groans of pain.

The big guy wincing and grimacing is Travis, or Mad Dog as he's known among the group. And no, his mother didn't give him the nickname. It came from his time as a Special Forces operative working the most secret missions in places the USA wasn't supposed to be.

The room is filled with the sounds of suppressed grunts, the soft clinking of metal on metal, and the distant hum of the police scanner. It is Raven who breaks the silence among the group, her voice trembling with a mix of grief and frustration. "I can't believe we lost Ronny."

Davey, with his close-cropped gray hair and heavy stubble, tries to console her, though his own voice is heavy with fatigue. "I know, babe. But we're lucky to have gotten out of there at all."

He places a hand on her shoulder, giving her a tender squeeze. She gives him a sad but appreciative look, touching the hand.

Mad Dog, cringing as the bullet is finally pulled free, speaks up. "Who the hell was that guy? He wasn't no cop."

Davey's face hardens. "I think it was the guy from the apartment. The one who ambushed us."

"Whoever he was, he was like a goddamn phantom," Mad Dog remarks.

"And one hell of a fighter, too," Davey adds. "You saw what he did to Ronny's face. I ain't never seen a man beat Ronny in a fight. Never. He was a SEAL team champion. Best fighter I ever seen."

Marcus leans forward, holding the bloody bullet. "Did you get a look at him?"

Davey shakes his head. "No. Only Ronny did. The first I knew he was in the apartment was when he was shoving me down on the ground and putting a gun to my head. All I got was his voice—this low growl. Then when Ronny came running in, he smashed me with his pistol, knocking me out."

Mad Dog turns to Raven. "How about you, Raven? He got pretty close to you. You see his face through that gas mask?"

Raven shivers, the memory clearly unsettling her. "It was just like what Davey said. The guy got the drop on me before I even saw him coming. He was behind me the whole time. If it wasn't for Davey and Ronny showing up, I'd be dead."

Sitting by the scanner, listening keenly, Simons speaks up. "Well, whoever he is, we're away from him now."

The group nods, but the tension remains. The thought of the mysterious attacker gnaws at them, a shadowy figure whose presence they can't shake.

Marcus looks thoughtful. "You think the journalist told the Feds what she found out?"

Raven shakes her head. "If she did, we'd know by now. But that guy... he's not just any fed."

The room falls silent again, each member lost in their thoughts. As they wonder how much Kara Tate had uncovered and whether her investigation reached the federal authorities, the door to the bedroom opens, and their leader walks in, his presence commanding immediate attention.

His name is Joseph, but the group calls him by his last name, Frost. Frost is a man in his late forties with a lean, athletic build that speaks to years of rigorous training and discipline. His sharp, angular features are marked by a few small scars, hints of a past filled with conflict. His eyes are a piercing blue, intense and calculating, always scanning his surroundings with a hawk-like vigilance. He has short, salt-and-pepper hair, neatly trimmed, and a closely cropped beard that adds to his rugged appearance.

"Leadership is ready to meet," he announces.

Raven looks up from where she's tending to her injuries. "All of us?"

Frost shakes his head. "No. Just me... and Davey."

As he sits beside Raven, Davey frowns, his eyes narrowing in confusion. "What?"

Frost's expression remains stoic. "They claim that you're compromised. The police have images of you. Of your face. You and Ronny. They need you to hide."

Davey's frustration is obvious. "Hide? Where?"

Frost steps farther into the room, his voice steady and authoritative. "They have a secure location. Somewhere they'll keep you safe."

Davey's anger flares. "Safe from what? We got out, didn't we?"

Frost's gaze is unyielding. "They think the guy who attacked us might be CIA. He might be on to you specifically, David. It's for your own protection that you should disappear."

"So what? I just go off with them?" Davey's voice is a mix of disbelief and resentment.

"That's what they say. Me and you are gonna meet them tomorrow once we're disguised. That's when I'm supposed to give them the cassettes."

Raven, still sewing her wound, speaks up, her voice laced with concern. "What about the rest of us?"

Frost looks at her, his expression unreadable. "You stay here and lay low. Follow the protocols. I'll be back once we've met with Leadership and sorted everything out."

Davey's jaw tightens, but he nods reluctantly. The reality of his situation is undeniable. Frost's words, though unwelcome, are necessary.

Frost's eyes sweep the room, ensuring that his orders are understood. "Get some rest," he tells them. "We've still got a lot of work ahead of us."

With that, he turns and heads back to the bedroom, leaving the group to absorb the gravity of their situation.

EIGHT

AT THE CITY MORGUE, PETER, DEACON AND KIRSTY stand around the dead body of the attacker known as Ronny. The body lies on a cold metal table as Kirsty scans the face with her phone, waiting as a progress bar begins filling up, the image being processed through the system. The morgue is cold and sterile, with harsh fluorescent lights casting a clinical glow over the stainless steel tables and white-tiled walls.

Deacon speaks first. "This is the one you fought in Kara Tate's apartment, right?"

Peter nods. "Yes."

Kirsty studies the bruised face. "Hence the broken nose, cut eye and bruises."

Peter points to the chest. "You see the tattoo of the gauntlet over his heart?"

They look closely at the numerous tattoos covering Ronny's body, finally spotting the gauntlet among the curly hairs of his chest.

"I see it," Deacon says.

"The other guy had one on the back of his neck," Peter informs him. "Exactly the same."

"Could be group regalia," Kirsty suggests.

"That's what I thought," Peter adds.

Deacon takes a photo of the tattoo with his phone.

"I'll put it through the system," he says.

Just then, Kirsty's progress bar completes, and she checks the screen.

"Nothing on his face," she reports.

Deacon's frustration is palpable. "That's impossible. He must have a passport or a driving license. How can his face not have turned up on anything?"

Peter adds, "His prints aren't in the system either. That detective couldn't find them. I told him in the interview that someone must've gone through the system and wiped them."

Deacon checks his phone again. "Nothing on the regalia, either."

"They were definitely American. A mix of Midwest and Southern accents," Peter says. "They must've been trained to fight like that in the US military. Which means they must be known somewhere."

"And yet we can't find them," Deacon says.

Kirsty nods. "It can be only one thing. Someone must've pulled them from the system. A very sophisticated hacker or some other group. Turned them into ghosts."

A moment of silence follows as they all digest this unsettling information. Deacon then asks the question that has been weighing on all their minds. "Where's Kara?"

Peter swallows hard. "In one of the other cabinets. They're gonna move both bodies to the hospital where the pathologist will examine them."

Deacon reaches out and touches Peter's shoulder, offering silent support. "I am sorry, Peter."

Peter stares hard at the dead face of Ronny. "The best way to honor her is to find out what she was into. Get to the bottom of it. Then," he adds in a low growl, "we can tear it apart."

NINE

THE TIME IS ALMOST THREE A.M. WHEN PETER SHOWS up at his son Michael's place. It's a small apartment in Greenwich Village, where Michael lives with his girlfriend, Mayu. Peter awakens them by knocking on the door. Michael, groggy and concerned, opens it to find his father standing there, looking worn out and grief-stricken.

"Dad?" Michael rubs his eyes, trying to shake off the remnants of sleep. "What's going on?"

Peter's voice is heavy with exhaustion. "I'm sorry for the late hour, Mikey. Can I come in?"

Michael steps aside, nodding. "Of course."

Peter enters the small hallway, the warm light from a tall lamp casting a soft glow on the walls. He hears the gentle padding of feet and looks up to see Mayu emerging from their bedroom, her dressing gown wrapped tightly around her.

"Peter?" Mayu's voice is filled with concern as she approaches. "Is everything okay?"

Peter manages a weary smile. "I'm sorry for waking you both. I need to tell you something in person."

They move into the kitchen, where Mayu begins making coffee, the scent mingling with the residual warmth of the apartment. Peter sits down at the kitchen table, his voice heavy with grief. "Again, I'm real sorry to have woken you both, but I needed to tell you this in person before I have to leave New York. It's Kara... Kara is..." He almost can't say the word. "...dead."

Michael, shocked, sits down heavily. "What? How? What happened?"

Mayu's eyes fill with tears. "Oh God."

Peter takes a deep breath, trying to find the right words. The memories of Kara flood back, making it hard to speak—first her smile, then her broken mouth. "She was... she was murdered. Tortured for information first, it seems. Police found her last night at her apartment."

Michael's voice shakes. "But we only saw her a week ago when we had lunch together at Enzo's."

"Did she mention anything about her work?" Peter asks.

"She seemed a bit distant," Michael replies, "but she didn't talk much about work. Just said it was stressful and taking her all over the country."

All over the country? Peter ponders.

"Did she say where?" he asks.

"Not exactly."

Mayu, her voice trembling, adds, "She told us she was going out west to follow a lead. She seemed really nervous about it. We never saw her after that, and though I messaged her once or twice, I saw that the messages weren't being read. When I called, it went straight to voicemail."

Peter's expression is grave as he listens. "Yeah. That adds up. The police couldn't find her phone, and when she called me, it was from a payphone."

Mayu nods, wiping away a tear. "Even though she never said anything, I could tell something was weighing on her. I just wish I had pressed her more."

The room falls silent, each of them lost in their thoughts. The enormity of Kara's death and the mystery surrounding her final days weigh heavily on them. The coffee is served in the same heavy silence, the three then nursing their mugs, their blank eyes staring out.

It is Peter who finally breaks the silence. "After the police left," he says, practically to himself, his voice heavy with exhaustion, "I waited at the apartment. Two guys showed up."

Both Michael and Mayu widen their eyes.

"What'd you do to them?" Michael asks, looking very serious.

"I captured them but was interrupted by the cops. We were all taken back to the 18th Precinct. The two guys and me."

"The 18th Precinct?" Mayu says, frowning. "Why does that ring a bell?"

"That's when all hell broke loose," Peter continues. "Their buddies attacked the precinct."

Michael's eyes widen in shock. "We saw it on the news."

"That's where I remember it," Mayu adds. "The terrorist attack. You were there?"

"Yeah, I was there," Peter replies. "They were after some tapes Kara had hidden."

Mayu narrows her eyes. "Tapes?"

"They were those old tapes you used to put in camcorders."

"What was on them?"

"No one knows. There was nothing at Kara's I could play them on, and the cops never got a chance to see them."

Mayu's eyes go blank as she thinks about it. "They must have contained footage of whatever she was into."

"And whatever it was," Peter adds, "must've been something really, really important—worth risking their lives to get back. Worth taking on a whole police precinct filled with cops."

"The news said they used some type of gas," Michael says.

"Yeah. They gassed the building, blew a hole in the basement, and stormed the place. We managed to fight them off, but not before they got what they came for."

Mayu's voice trembles as she asks, "Why would someone do this? What was Kara working on that was so dangerous?"

Peter shakes his head, frustration on his face. "I don't know yet. But I'm going to find out."

Once more, the room falls silent, each of them returning to their thoughts. Though Kara and Peter's relationship had lasted barely six months, her presence in the lives of Michael and Mayu had been much more significant. It had become a point of contention for Kara that in those six months she had spent much more time with his son than with Peter, having befriended both Michael and Mayu early on. When Peter and Kara finally split, Kara had come to the couple, fearing that it would mean the end of them as well, and together they had decided that just because her relationship with Peter was over, it didn't mean their friendship had to end. The news of her death, therefore, has hit Michael and Mayu almost as hard as it hit Peter.

Almost.

Peter finally speaks, his voice soft and tired. "I know it's late, but can I stay here tonight? I don't think I can handle a hotel right now."

Michael's expression softens. "Of course, Dad. We'll make up the couch for you."

Mayu, her eyes filled with empathy, adds, "You can stay as long as you need."

Peter nods, feeling the warmth of his family's reassurance. "Thank you."

TEN

MORNING LIGHT FILTERS THROUGH THE THIN
curtains of the safe house, casting a soft glow on the worn furniture. Davey stands by the door, his disguise already in place as he looks at Raven. She is checking the bandages around her thigh. Their eyes meet, and the world outside seems to fade away for a moment.

"You take care of yourself," Davey says.

Raven steps closer. "You too."

Davey nods, wrapping his arms around her in a tight embrace. "I'll miss you."

She leans up, pressing a soft kiss to his lips.

The group doesn't exactly allow relationships—not in the traditional sense. Frost permits what he calls 'coupling,' but marriage and children are strictly forbidden. The objective, the mission, is paramount. There's no time for anything except their ultimate goal. Nevertheless, over the past year, since Davey had arrived at the group like so many of the lost, Raven has grown close to him. When Frost proposed last night's rescue and retrieval mission, she had been one of the only ones to agree immediately. Even Mad Dog had hesitated, only relenting when he saw that a woman was showing more balls than he was. The reason she'd been so eager hadn't been the tapes; it had been Davey.

They hold each other for a moment longer before Frost clears his throat from the doorway. "We need to go."

Davey pulls back, giving Raven a final, lingering look. "Stay safe."

"You too," she says, watching as he and Frost leave.

The duo exits the apartment block into downtown Queens, blending in with the morning crowd of workers heading to their jobs. The streets are filled with people in business attire, their expressions focused and hurried. Frost and Davey walk with purpose, their disguises ensuring that they don't stand out.

Reaching a parking garage a block from the building, they get into a nondescript car. As Frost adjusts his seat, they overhear two neighbors talking.

"I take it you saw the terrorist attack that happened last night," one neighbor asks.

"Yeah, it's all over the news. Scary times we're living in," the other replies.

Frost and Davey exchange a glance but say nothing, driving off into the flow of morning traffic. The radio is tuned to a news station, the broadcaster's voice filling the car with updates.

"...last night's attack has left the city in shock. Authorities have not released the names of the deceased or who the attackers were. There is also further speculation that it may be linked to the death of investigative journalist Kara Tate. Tate was found..."

Davey switches it off. "That's enough of that."

Frost nods, his expression grave. "You did what you had to do, Davey," he says.

Davey shudders. "Yeah," he says, his voice trembling slightly, "but you weren't the one who had to torture her, were you?"

Frost says nothing, just keeps his eyes on the road as they drive north through Queens. The rest of the journey is uneventful, the city's morning bustle surrounding them. Eventually, they arrive in the suburb of Bayside, pulling up outside a nondescript house in a quiet neighborhood.

They get out and approach the house, knocking on the door. It is opened by a man who gestures for them to enter but says nothing. Inside, the hallway is dimly lit, with old, patterned wallpaper lining the walls. It looks like no one has lived here in years.

The man who let them in, a tall figure with a stern expression, places a finger on his lips to instruct them to remain silent. He produces a thermal imaging device, a sleek, high-tech gadget designed to detect hidden electronics and bugs.

The morning light oozing through the thin curtains barely reaches into the hallway. Davey and Frost stand still as the man switches on the device. He first scans Davey, moving the device methodically from head to toe. The thermal imager displays a clear image, showing only the expected heat signatures. Satisfied, the man nods and moves on to Frost, repeating the process.

He gets the same response: nothing. The man finishes the scan and motions for them to follow him farther into the house.

They are led into a living room where another man sits behind a table, a video camera set up in front of him. The room is sparsely furnished, with only a few pieces of furniture and the smell of stale coffee lingering in the air. The man who let them in stands behind them both—a silent reminder of the scrutiny they are under.

Frost hands over the tapes, carefully placing them on the table. The man at the table picks each one up, inspecting them closely before setting them aside.

"You haven't made any copies, have you?" he asks, his tone flat.

Frost shakes his head. "What would we make copies on?"

The man merely nods and turns his attention back to the tapes.

"What's on them, anyway?" Frost asks.

The man who led them in steps forward, about to speak, to tell them not to ask questions, but the seated man raises a hand to silence him. "You might as well know," he says. "The woman you killed was investigating several of our groups and members. She had unmasked figures in our organization and was going to publish an article revealing their names and pictures. We couldn't allow that to happen. Our plans, which you are well aware of, Frost, are at a delicate stage. Exposure now would be catastrophic. What you and your men did last night will win us the war one day."

"Good," Davey interjects, his voice tight. "Because we lost a brother last night to get those tapes."

"We've all lost people," the man replies bluntly. "And we shall lose many more before this is done. Now, David O'Brian, I need you to go into the back room with my companion here so he can prepare you for your voyage to your new safe house."

Davey looks at Frost, his eyes filled with worry.

"It's okay, Davey," the leader says.

They embrace in a warm farewell. Then Davey goes off with the man who answered the door, leaving Frost alone with the other.

"You make sure to look after him," Frost tells the seated man. "He's a loyal soldier. Remember that."

"Don't worry. We have other jobs for him. He'll still get to be a soldier. Just not here. Not at the moment."

Frost watches Davey disappear down the dim hallway, before turning back to the man at the table, his voice low.

"Just make sure he doesn't lose himself along the way."

The man nods, his eyes hard. "None of us come out of this the same, Frost. You know that."

ELEVEN

Peter is with Kara. They're at her apartment on the day she broke up with him. She has her back to him, staring out the window at the gray autumn day outside. The dream is vivid, filled with the melancholic ambiance of that fateful day. Rain pelts against the windowpane, creating a rhythmic backdrop to their tense conversation.

"Kara, please." Peter's voice breaks the silence.

Her voice trembles, her back still turned to him. "I just can't go on like this."

Peter can hear the sorrow in her voice and sees her playing with her necklace, unable to face him.

"I'll quit. I'll leave the agency," he says, taking a step forward.

Kara shakes her head, still not turning around. "No. The CIA practically made you. The horror they put you through up there in Alaska with those two women was awful. Yet still, you stay loyal to them."

"I mean it. I'll quit," Peter insists, taking another step.

"And what will you do, Peter?" she sighs, still not turning. "You said yourself that you were lost without the CIA."

Peter thinks about it and begins to realize he's in a dream. The room around him darkens, the atmosphere growing ominous. His frown deepens as the once familiar apartment warps into something darker and more sinister.

"Wait..." Peter murmurs, confusion setting in.

He steps forward, takes Kara by the shoulder, and turns her around, only to be confronted by her battered, beaten, dead face. Her lifeless eyes stare back at him, and the shock jolts him awake.

Peter bursts up from the couch, breathing heavily, covered in sweat. His heart pounds in his chest, the remnants of the nightmare lingering in his mind. The sight of her mutilated face slowly fades. As his breathing settles and his heart rate returns to normal, he becomes aware of another sound: his phone rattling on the coffee table.

He reaches for it, his hand still trembling. The caller ID displays Mark Deacon's name. Peter takes a deep breath and answers, his voice steady despite the lingering effects of the dream.

"Are you still at your son's?" Deacon asks.

"Yeah," Peter replies, rubbing his eyes.

"Then come down and meet me outside. Something's happened."

"What?" Peter asks, his senses sharpening.

"Not over the phone," Deacon says, and the line goes dead.

Five minutes later—roughly the time it took him to brush his teeth, put his shoes on and leave the apartment—Peter is sitting in the passenger seat of Deacon's car.

"On my instructions," Deacon begins, "the pathologist started Kara's autopsy early, at around four a.m. Upon examining the body, he immediately noted unusual physical conditions— skin burns, discoloration that didn't correspond to the apparent cause of death."

Peter, now fully alert, focuses on every word. "Go on."

"During the autopsy, he observed unexpected internal burns and organ damage. He sent tissue samples to the lab, making sure they went straight to the top. Three hours ago, the lab got back to us. The samples revealed unusual cell damage."

Peter's mind races. "Radiation?"

Deacon nods. "Yes. I called a radiologist in. She suggested radiation based on the cellular damage. A toxicologist was brought in to test for poisons and chemicals—standard tests returned negative. It wasn't poison. Then we used a Geiger counter." He pauses before adding ominously, "It went crazy."

Peter's jaw tightens.

"They confirmed the body was contaminated," Deacon continues. "The forensic team returned to the crime scene to test for radiation contamination. The vent at the back of the closet showed up, as well as the box the tapes had been kept in at the precinct. Those tapes were contaminated too," Deacon explains.

Peter frowns. "But there's no sign of the origin of the contamination?"

"No. No sign of the contaminant. Wherever she was exposed was somewhere else," Deacon says, glancing at Peter.

"What about the guy I killed?" Peter asks.

"No. He wasn't contaminated," Deacon answers.

Peter muses loudly, "So what in the hell do a bunch of ex-military guys who've had their identities erased from all government systems have to do with radiation?"

Deacon nods. "That's what we need to figure out."

That's when something clicks inside Peter.

"Grand Junction," he says suddenly.

"What?" Deacon asks, confused.

"I googled Petrov and Grand Junction last night. Petrov could be anything, but Grand Junction showed up as Grand Junction Nuclear Waste Management Plant," Peter explains. "And not just that. It's in Colorado, and last night, my son told me that the last time he saw Kara, she was saying that she was going out west."

Deacon's eyes widen. "Could be. But first we need to see her editor. I've arranged a meeting."

Deacon hands Peter a Geiger counter. "Oh, and before we get there, I need you to check yourself. The ME said Kara was only a low-level contaminant, but you still could be affected."

Peter checks himself with the Geiger counter, but nothing happens. The device remains silent, its screen showing no readings.

Deacon looks relieved. "That's good. Now let's go find out what she was into."

TWELVE

PETER AND DEACON ARRIVE AT THE EDITOR'S OFFICE. The atmosphere inside the office is tense, the editor having only learned of Kara's death a few hours ago. Ms. Julia Harmon, a seasoned journalist with a sharp eye and a calm demeanor, sits behind a large wooden desk, glancing off to the side, staring out the window at the high-rises, lost in thought. The office is cluttered with stacks of papers, old issues of the magazine framed and hanging on the walls, as well as various awards and accolades.

She stands as they enter. "Peter, it's been a while. And you must be Mr. Deacon. Please, have a seat," she says, gesturing to the chairs in front of her desk.

Deacon nods. "Thank you for meeting with us on such short notice, Ms. Harmon."

Peter and Deacon take their seats, and soon they are talking about Kara. Ms. Harmon's voice is steady, but there's a hint of sadness in her eyes.

"Of course, I was devastated to hear about Kara," she says. "She was one of our best. The world has lost one its shining lights this morning."

Peter leans forward. "Kara mentioned she was working on

something big. Something that went further than she had anticipated. Can you tell us anything about it?"

Ms. Harmon sighs, her gaze distant. "Kara was always chasing leads, but this one... she was different. She seemed more paranoid, more cautious. She promised it would be huge, but she didn't share the details with me. She said it was too dangerous—that I could be in danger just knowing what she'd discovered."

Deacon chimes in, his tone probing. "Did she mention any specific names? Like Petrov or Grand Junction?"

Ms. Harmon shakes her head. "No, those names don't ring a bell. She kept her cards close to her chest. All I know is that she was working on it for months and that it involved some high-level corruption. That's all she'd tell me."

Peter continues, "We found video cassette tapes in her apartment, the type used in old analogue video cameras. Do you know why she would have been using one instead of, say, her phone?"

Ms. Harmon nods. "Yes, she borrowed the camera from me. Said she needed it for evidence that she couldn't risk being traced digitally. She was very particular about it, said it was crucial for her investigation."

Deacon's brow furrows. "So she was paranoid that she was being tracked, then?"

Ms. Harmon hesitates, then says, "Yes, she was. Kara got rid of all her electronic equipment recently. She was calling me from pay phones, faxing things across. She'd become very paranoid."

Peter's eyes narrow in thought. "At the apartment, I didn't see any signs of electronic equipment either. The police didn't find anything. Are you saying she'd gotten rid of her computer and phone herself?"

Ms. Harmon nods. "Yes. Which was unusual for her. She was always so tech-savvy, but this time she was avoiding anything digital. She said it was safer that way."

That pretty much ends the meeting. Ms. Harmon stands, offering her hand. Deacon rises and shakes it firmly, followed by

Peter. Then they leave the office, feeling the weight of the unknown.

"What do you think?" Deacon asks Peter as they reach the car.

"She was definitely on to something big. We need to find out more about Grand Junction. And Petrov, if we can. Someone has to know something."

Deacon nods, starting the car. "Let's get to work. We're not stopping until we find out what Kara was digging into."

As they drive away, the sense of urgency grows. They have more questions than answers, but their resolve is unshakable. Together, they will uncover the truth, no matter how deep they have to dig.

THIRTEEN

OVER THE NEXT FOUR DAYS, A SPECIALIZED CIA TEAM conducts a thorough review of all available information and evidence related to Kara's contamination. They meticulously analyze her movements, interactions, and any potential sources of radiation she could have encountered. There are black spots in her timeline, days where there's no trace of where she was—and the more they look into her movements over the last month, the more black spots they find.

In this day and age, we take it for granted that everywhere we go, we have our phones. These little devices are always collecting and sending data—essentially tracking our movements. Remove them, and we remove an investigator's best tool for knowing where someone was and when.

This was why Kara got rid of everything digital in her life. She didn't want to be tracked. So after a thorough look into her recent life, the team has been unable to locate where she came into contact with the radiation. All they have is Grand Junction.

Data analysts sift through historical and current data about the Grand Junction site, scrutinizing recent activity, satellite imagery, and intelligence reports. Yet nothing out of the ordinary emerges. The Grand Junction site, built on an old mine that was once one of the country's deepest coal mines until its closure in the 1940s, seems unremarkable. The facility's primary function is waste management, mostly dealing with chemical waste from industrial plants with little nuclear activity these days.

Despite this, CIA Director Sandy McLean is currently coordinating with the Department of Energy (DOE), which oversees the Grand Junction site, seeking more information about the current status of the site, as well as access.

But this is where they hit a snag.

In a CIA operations room, Peter and Deacon sit at a conference table, a large screen displaying maps and data about Grand Junction.

Peter leans forward, studying a satellite image. "Everything seems above board. No incidents, no unusual activity. Just routine waste management."

"But Kara found something," Deacon says.

"Maybe it wasn't Grand Junction," Peter says, doubt in his voice. "Maybe it was some other place she got contaminated, and Grand Junction is something else entirely, a coincidence and we're jumping to conclusions."

"I don't believe in coincidence," Deacon mutters as his eyes trace the lines of a report.

With this hanging in the air between them, the door opens, and Director Sandy McLean enters the room, a grave look on her face. "We have a problem," she announces.

Peter and Deacon look up, their expressions turning serious. Sandy takes a seat, folding her hands on the table.

"The DOE won't budge," she says. "There's not enough evidence to allow us to send in an investigative team to Grand Junction. A name on a now missing tape and the fact that Kara Tate was contaminated are not enough. The plant can't afford to have its operations compromised by shutting down for a week for us to investigate."

Peter clenches his fists. "So what are they willing to do?"

Sandy sighs. "They're willing to allow us to speak with the

plant's administrator, Thomas Jacks. That's it. A single interview at the plant, in Jacks' office. A Q&A, no more."

Deacon frowns. "An interview? That's all? We need access to the site, to their records. There's no way we'll get anything substantial from a single conversation."

"I know," Sandy replies. "But that's all we have right now. So you'll have to make the most of it."

FOURTEEN

THOMAS JACKS' CAREER TRAJECTORY IS TYPICAL FOR A man in his position. Jacks, a graduate of MIT with a degree in chemical engineering, climbed the ranks through various roles in waste management and environmental safety. He eventually became the administrator of the Grand Junction site, overseeing the plant's operations with a reputation for efficiency and adherence to regulations. There's nothing remarkable about his record, just a solid, steady career.

Peter and Deacon arrive at Grand Junction on a cold October morning, and are greeted by the head of security, a morose looking man with an abrupt manner. After being outfitted with hard hats and hi-vis vests, they are led through the plant to the office of Thomas Jacks.

They find Jacks standing by his desk. He is a tall, slender man with a completely bald head, thick black eyebrows, and pale skin. He greets them with a nod.

"Mr. Deacon, Mr. Black, welcome to Grand Junction," Jacks says. "Please, have a seat."

Peter and Deacon sit down, their expressions serious. Jacks takes his seat behind the desk, folding his hands in front of him.

"Thank you, John," Jacks says, turning to his head of security. "I'll take it from here."

The security man nods, not even acknowledging Peter and Deacon as he exits the office, closing the door behind him.

"We appreciate you seeing us, Mr. Jacks," Deacon begins.

"Of course," Jacks replies. "How can I help?"

Peter leans forward. "Have you had any break-ins or incidents at the plant recently?"

Jacks shakes his head. "No, we haven't had any unauthorized entries. Not in the last few years at least, and that was only a few tree huggers messing around. Security here is very tight. We monitor all access points 24/7."

"What about the mines beneath the plant?" Deacon asks. "Are they still accessible?"

Jacks raises an eyebrow. "The mines have been closed off for years. They were sealed after the plant was built. No one goes down there anymore."

"Have you heard the name Kara Tate?" Peter asks.

Jacks' expression darkens slightly. "Yes, there was something on the news. Is that the investigative journalist who was recently murdered in New York?"

"That's correct. Do you know anything about her investigation?"

Jacks shakes his head. "No, I don't. I only know what's been reported in the news. She usually wrote about high-level corruption, I believe. But that's all I've heard."

"What about any unusual activities or individuals around the plant in the last few months?" Deacon probes further.

Jacks considers the question for a moment. "Nothing comes to mind. We have a very strict protocol here. Any unusual activity would be reported immediately."

"Do you have any recent hires or anyone who has left the company unexpectedly?" Peter asks.

Jacks shakes his head again. "No, our staff turnover is quite low. Most of our employees have been with us for years."

Peter and Deacon exchange a glance. They have exhausted their immediate questions.

"Would it be possible to review the last month's worth of CCTV footage?" Deacon asks.

Jacks gestures to a stack of DVDs on his desk. "I anticipated that request. Here are the recordings. Consider it a goodwill gesture."

"Then that's all," Deacon says, standing up.

They take the DVDs.

"We appreciate your time, Mr. Jacks," Peter says.

Jacks stands as well. "If you have any other questions or need further assistance, please don't hesitate to contact me."

They shake hands, and Peter and Deacon leave the office, feeling the weight of their empty-handed investigation. As they walk back through the plant, the hum of machinery seems louder, like it's boring into their heads.

Once outside, Peter glances at Deacon. "Well that was a waste of a trip."

Deacon nods. "At least we have the CCTV footage. Maybe there's something there."

Peter turns back toward the building. "I get a feeling he wouldn't have given us them if there was."

FIFTEEN

THE FUNERAL TAKES PLACE A WEEK LATER. THE SKY IS overcast as Peter, Michael, and Mayu arrive at the cemetery. The past week has been a blur of grief and frustration. Peter and Deacon, along with the specialized CIA team, have meticulously analyzed the CCTV footage from the Grand Junction site. They watched and rewatched the entire month's worth of footage, scrutinizing every frame for any sign of Kara.

Alas, there were no break-ins, no anomalies, and no sign of Kara anywhere near the plant, externally or internally. They went so far as to get Kirsty Lange to go over the code of the footage, and all that did was confirm that none of it had been altered. Kara Tate had not been anywhere near the Grand Junction site.

The air at the cemetery is heavy with sorrow and the scent of rain that has yet to fall. The crowd gathered is larger than Peter expected, a testament to Kara's impact on those around her. Friends, contacts, fellow journalists, and those simply touched by her journalism are in attendance, their faces somber and reflective.

Kara's editor, Ms. Julia Harmon, stands near the front, her expression a mixture of grief and stoic resilience. Nearby, Kara's parents are supported by friends and family, their faces etched with anguish. The coffin is a gray, ugly thing. It is made of lead to contain the radiation contamination, and it rests on a stand covered with flowers to hide its ugliness.

Peter stands beside Michael and Mayu, his gaze fixed on the sealed coffin beneath the mounds of colorful flowers. Michael's arm is wrapped around Mayu, who clings to him, her tears silent but steady. The pain of losing Kara is manifest in each and every one there, but Peter's own grief is mixed with a burning resolve.

As the service proceeds, several of Kara's fellow journalists speak, sharing memories and praising her relentless pursuit of truth. The crowd listens, their heads bowed, as each speaker's words echo the loss felt by all.

After the eulogies, the pallbearers step forward to lower Kara's coffin into the ground. The sight of the lead coffin disappearing into the earth is almost too much for Peter. He clenches his fists, his nails digging into his palms as he fights to maintain his composure.

Nearby, a group of Kara's colleagues circulate a petition. They are animated, their voices hushed but intense as they gather signatures and plan their next steps. Some talk of organizing protests, determined to demand answers about Kara's death.

One of the journalists, a young woman with fiery red hair, approaches Peter. "We're gathering signatures to demand an independent investigation into Kara's death. Would you—"

Peter cuts her off, his voice flat. "No."

The woman looks taken aback. "But we need answers. We need to—"

"Petitions and protests won't get you the answers you're looking for," Peter tells her. "Trust me on that."

The woman opens her mouth to argue but sees the steel in Peter's eyes and backs off, nodding reluctantly. She returns to her group, leaving Peter standing there, the weight of his conviction heavy on his shoulders.

As the service concludes, people begin to disperse, offering condolences to Kara's parents and each other. As the last pockets make their way towards the exit, Kara's mother leaves her husband's side and approaches Peter, who has stayed behind at the graveside. The mother's eyes are filled with a mixture of sorrow and something else: anger.

"Peter, I just wanted to say thank you for coming," she says softly. "I know you and Kara didn't last long as a couple, but she always spoke so highly of you. She used to say you were the most honorable person she ever met."

Peter can only nod, unable to find the words. Kara's mother takes his hands, her grip firm despite her trembling. "You were there when the police found her, weren't you?" she asks, her voice barely above a whisper.

Peter nods.

"Do you know who did this to my daughter?"

"No," he replies. "But I sure as hell aim to find out."

She swallows her tears, a determined look replacing her sorrow. "There was something else that Kara used to say about you. She said that as well as being the most honorable person she ever met, you were also the toughest son-of-a-bitch she ever met."

Peter says nothing.

"Is there some truth in that?" she asks.

Peter nods.

"Then you find them, Peter. You find them and you make them pay for destroying my beautiful little girl."

With that, she lets go of his hands and leaves, her resolve adding fuel to Peter's own.

SIXTEEN

One month later, the investigation into Kara has gone cold, and other business has come up. Peter finds himself in Israel, being escorted through the Sde Teiman detention center by a stern-faced Mossad colonel. The hot desert sun beats down on them as they walk, the air filled with the sound of distant drills and the bursts of gunfire from the gun range. Inside the facility, the atmosphere shifts to one of tense silence, punctuated by the occasional shout from a guard or cry from a prisoner.

Behind mesh walls, men in gray sweatpants and sweatshirts sit with their arms raised above their heads, black hoods covering their faces. Armed IDF soldiers stand watch, their expressions impassive as they monitor the detainees. The scene is a bleak reminder of the harsh realities of conflict.

The Mossad colonel, a tall man with a sharp jawline and piercing blue eyes, speaks in a clipped tone as he briefs Peter. "Ibrahim al-Farouk. One of the bigger fish we've pulled out of Gaza. A top-tier operative in his organization."

Peter listens intently, his eyes scanning the rows of prisoners as they walk. "What can you tell me about him?"

The colonel continues, "Al-Farouk was directly involved in the

October 7 massacre. He personally led the attack on the Be'eri kibbutz."

Peter's expression hardens. "What else?"

The colonel pauses before responding, his voice tinged with disgust. "There is film of him beheading people at kibbutz Be'eri. We also have two witnesses who claim to have seen him rape at least three hostages."

Peter's jaw tightens as he processes the information. "How did you capture him?"

"During fighting in one of the tunnels," the colonel replies. "He was cornered and put up quite a fight, but we managed to subdue him. He's been here ever since." The colonel then adds, "Now he's claiming to have vital information about an imminent attack on US soil."

Peter glances at the colonel. "Do you think he's credible?"

The colonel's expression darkens. "A rat will do anything to save itself once it is cornered. When they took him in the tunnels, he killed two men before they wounded him and dragged him out of there. He was lucky to survive that. Now he wishes to see how far he can stretch that luck."

Peter is eventually led to a dark, oppressive room with a single lightbulb dangling from the ceiling, casting a harsh, flickering glow. The air is thick with apprehension and the stench of human sweat. Ibrahim al-Farouk, bruised and bloodied, sits with his hands zip-tied. His eyes are wild as he looks at Peter, searching for any hint of mercy. Peter sits across from him, a notebook open on the table, the pen poised to record any useful information.

Ibrahim al-Farouk's voice is strained, barely more than a whisper. "You are really from the US?" he asks like he can't believe it.

"Yes," Peter replies. "Now tell me what you have."

"I know the identities of a cell in the US planning an attack. You'll need me to stop it."

Peter, scribbling in his notebook without looking up, responds calmly. "I'm listening. Start with the names."

Ibrahim glances nervously, the fear evident in his eyes.

"There's Farid Hassan, Ammar Ali, and Yusuf Kareem. They're operating out of New York, planning something big."

Peter's pen moves steadily. "Farid Hassan, you say?"

"Yes, yes," Ibrahim replies eagerly. "He's the mastermind. You need to get me to the US, into protective custody. I can help you find them, help you stop them."

"And Ammar Ali, what's his role?" Peter asks, still not looking up.

Ibrahim leans forward as much as his restraints allow, desperation in his voice. "Ammar handles the logistics. He's crucial to their operations."

Peter's voice remains steady. "And Yusuf Kareem?"

Ibrahim's eyes dart around the room. "Yusuf is the financier. Without him, the cell falls apart. You need me to get to them."

Peter finally looks up, his expression unreadable. "Interesting names."

Hope flickers in Ibrahim's eyes. "So you'll take me to the US? Put me in custody there? I can give you more details, like where they are and what identities they are living under, but I need assurances."

Peter leans back in his chair, considering. "Assurances?"

"Yes, protection. Safety. You know what they'll do to me here. I can help you. I can give you everything you need," Ibrahim pleads, nodding vigorously.

Peter pauses, then leans forward, his eyes narrowing. "You seem pretty eager to get to the US."

"I have valuable information! I'm your best chance to stop the attack," Ibrahim says desperately, his voice rising.

Peter sighs, closing his notebook with a deliberate motion. "You know, the funny thing is, those names you just gave me?"

Ibrahim's tension is palpable. "Yes?"

Peter's voice is cool and controlled. "Farid Hassan is dead. Ammar Ali is serving life in a federal prison. And Yusuf Kareem has been in custody for months."

Panic creeps into Ibrahim's voice. "No, no, that's not possible. You need me!"

Peter stands up, pushing his chair back with a loud scrape. "It was a nice try, Ibrahim, but you're not getting out of this one."

"Please, you have to believe me. I can give you real names, real information. Just take me to the US!" Ibrahim pleads.

Peter leans close, his voice low and cold. "You made your decision when you decided to behead innocent people."

"No, please..." Ibrahim's eyes widen, his voice trembling with fear.

"This is the end of the line for you," Peter says firmly, turning to leave.

He exits the room, slamming the door behind him. The sound reverberates through the oppressive space, a final punctuation to Ibrahim al-Farouk's fate.

Outside the cell, Peter finds the Mossad colonel waiting, his posture tense but expectant. Peter's expression is grim as he approaches.

"He's trying to get out of his fate," Peter says. "But fate has other ideas."

The colonel nods. "He thinks he can bargain his way to safety. Typical. Did he give you anything useful?"

"Just a bunch of lies. Names of people who are either dead or already in custody. He's desperate," Peter replies.

"Desperation makes men dangerous," the colonel says. "But it sounds like you handled it well."

Peter nods. "Thanks for the support, Colonel. Now I need to get moving."

"Good luck, Mr. Black. If you need anything from us, you know where to find me," the colonel says, extending a hand.

Peter shakes it firmly. "I appreciate that."

As Peter walks back to his vehicle, his phone rings. He glances at the caller ID and sees Deacon's name.

"Mark, what's the update?" Peter asks, answering the call.

"We've got a breakthrough, Peter. Remember Ronny?" Deacon's voice crackles through the line.

"Of course I do. What about him?" Peter replies, intrigued.

"Kirsty had the idea of using his blood to trace his DNA. We then ran it through some ancestry sites. Turns out, we got a hit," Deacon says, his tone excited.

"A hit? How solid?" Peter asks, his interest piqued.

"Pretty solid. We found someone who's a 98 percent match to be his sister," Deacon explains.

"That's something. Who is she?"

"Her name's Sarah Anderson. We dug into her family tree and found she has an estranged brother," Deacon reveals.

"And the brother?" Peter prompts.

"Ronald Anderson."

"Ronny," Peter murmurs to himself.

"Ex-Navy SEAL," Deacon goes on. "After his discharge, he joined a militia. One that's listed as a domestic terrorist group. The group is relatively small and under the radar, which makes their recent actions in New York all the more puzzling."

"What's their name?"

"The Iron Brotherhood. Their symbol is..."

"... an iron gauntlet," Peter finishes as he gets into his car and immediately puts the A/C on full blast.

"Yeah. Just like the tattoos," Deacon says. "They should have come up when I sent off the photo, but they didn't. The group is known—I've found several paper files on them in archives. Not just that, but I found paper copies of Ronald Anderson's military file, but nothing about him on the system."

"It's like we said, they've hacked the system," Peter interjects as the sweat cools on his face. "Wiped them from it."

"Kirsty and the other analysts have spotted other anomalies in official records. Someone's forensically wiped the group and all members. We think that there could be other groups and individuals that aren't there on the digital system."

"What's the next step?" Peter asks.

"Well, the Iron Brotherhood are our only lead, except for the dead end of Grand Junction and whoever Petrov is, so that's where we go. We're looking at ways to infiltrate the group, and I've decided you're going to be our man on the inside. You up for that?"

"What do you think?"

"I thought so. We'll brief you on the details as soon as you're back. Be ready, Peter. This one's going to be tough," Deacon warns.

"Always am. See you soon, Mark."

"Safe travels," Deacon says before hanging up.

Peter starts the car, a new resolve burning in his heart. He knows the next phase of his mission, and he's ready for it. But glancing at the passenger seat, he flinches. For a split second he thought he saw someone sitting there. It looked like Kara. Like she was sitting there right beside him.

Shaking it off, he puts the car in gear and pulls out of there, prepared to dive deeper into the shadows to find the truth and deliver justice.

SEVENTEEN

It takes a few days to finalize Peter's cover story. Right now, he sits in a conference room at CIA headquarters, being briefed by Mark Deacon and Kirsty Lange.

"All right, Peter," Deacon starts, handing Peter a thick dossier. "Your cover name is Jack Reilly. Former Marine Corps sergeant."

Peter flips through the dossier, nodding as he takes in the details. "Jack Reilly. Got it. What's my story?"

Deacon leans forward. "You served sixteen years in the Marines, multiple tours in Afghanistan and Iraq. Honorably discharged four years ago after sustaining injuries in a roadside IED explosion during the last days of Afghanistan. I thought that burn scar on your left hip will come in handy. As well as that, you've got several commendations for bravery and leadership."

Peter absorbs the information, his expression thoughtful. "And after the military?"

Deacon continues, "You struggled to adapt to civilian life. Took a series of low-paying jobs, none of which gave you the structure or purpose you had in the military. You grew increasingly frustrated, feeling abandoned by the government and society."

Peter nods, understanding the mindset. "Sounds about right. What pushed me over the edge?"

"Political radicalization," Deacon explains. "You became disillusioned with the direction of the country. Started joining online forums and local militia groups, where you found a sense of belonging. Your views became more extreme, focusing on anti-government and nationalist ideologies."

Peter listens intently, piecing together his new identity. "And my recent activities?"

Deacon outlines the next steps. "You became a prominent member of a local militia group. Participated in armed protests and rallies. Connected with other former military personnel who shared your views. You attended clandestine meetings, discussed strategies, and shared intelligence. However, you got bored. Didn't think they were serious enough. That's what attracts you to the Iron Brotherhood."

Kirsty Lange interjects, "Your military training makes you valuable. Tactical knowledge, marksmanship, and leadership abilities. You're there to prove your loyalty and commitment to their cause. Show them you're in for the long haul."

Peter's face hardens. "And my objective?"

Deacon's tone is serious. "Gain their trust, uncover their plans and connections. Gather intel on their operations, leadership, and any links to the broader conspiracy. Those men who attacked the precinct were using military equipment, from the bombs they used to blow a hole in the wall to the guns they were holding. Someone bigger than the Iron Brotherhood supplied those weapons and ordnance. Find out who they are."

Peter closes the dossier and looks up, his eyes burning with resolve. "Jack Reilly, disillusioned Marine, ready to infiltrate and bring these guys down from the inside."

Deacon nods approvingly. "Exactly. Be prepared to make tough decisions. This is deep cover, Peter. They can't suspect a thing."

Peter's voice is firm. "I've got it."

There's a brief moment of silence before Kirsty Lange steps forward. "All right, Peter," she begins, "let's talk about how you're going to get in with the Iron Brotherhood."

Peter leans in. "I'm all ears."

"Your access will come via an intermediary," Kirsty explains. "His name is Ray Collins. He's a former Army buddy of Ronald Anderson's. After leaving the military, he fell into the militia scene and eventually started working with the Iron Brotherhood. He's not high up in their ranks, but he's trusted enough to make introductions."

"How do we know he'll vouch for me?" Peter asks, his brow furrowed.

"We've been keeping tabs on Collins for a while," Kirsty replies. "He's been involved in several smaller militia activities, nothing that's put him on the most-wanted list but enough to get our attention. We've intercepted some of his communications and know he's looking for more muscle for the Brotherhood."

Peter nods, understanding the plan. "How do I make contact with Collins?"

Deacon steps in, handing Peter a burner phone. "We've arranged for you to meet him at a secluded bar in Omaha, Nebraska. It's a known hangout for militia members, so your presence there won't raise any suspicions. Collins will be there expecting you."

Peter takes the phone, his mind already working through the details. "And what's my approach?"

"Be direct but cautious," Deacon advises. "Collins will want to know why you're interested in the Brotherhood. Stick to your story—disillusionment, a desire for change, and a willingness to take action. Mention your military background and drop a few names from your supposed past interactions in militia circles. We've provided you with all the details you need."

"What if he asks for proof?"

Kirsty reassures him, "We've got you covered. Your backstory includes a few notable incidents and operations. We've created false records and even some digital footprints. If he checks, everything will hold up. Just stay confident."

Peter leans back, taking it all in. "What's the next step after meeting Collins?"

Deacon continues, "If Collins buys your story, he'll introduce you to some of the lower-ranking members of the Iron Brotherhood. From there, you'll need to prove yourself through a series of minor operations. Once you've gained their trust, you'll be introduced to the core group."

Peter's expression hardens with resolve. "And who's that?"

"Take a look at the screen," Deacon says as he clicks the remote for the flatscreen on the wall.

The first image appears: a man in his late forties with a lean, athletic build. His sharp, angular facial features are marked by a few small scars. His piercing blue eyes stare out from beneath short salt-and-pepper hair, neatly trimmed, with a closely cropped beard. "This is Joseph Frost. He's the leader of the Iron Brotherhood. His background is a mix of special forces military and extreme nationalist ideologies. He's charismatic, but ruthless."

Deacon clicks the remote, and a new image appears: a big, wide-jawed man with a menacing look. "That's Travis 'Mad Dog' Morgan. Ex-Green Beret. While in the military, he was known for taking on the hardest missions. We suspect that anything big that the Brotherhood is planning, he'll be at the center of."

Deacon clicks on the next face. "Next, we have Daniel Carter, their explosives expert." The image of a wiry man with intense eyes appears on the screen. "He's a former Army EOD, got discharged under questionable circumstances. We suspect he's responsible for a string of bombings targeting government buildings."

Peter scribbles notes. "Carter. Got it. Who else?"

Deacon clicks again, and an image of a tall, well-built man

with sharp, deep-set eyes, a shaved head, and a thick, gray beard plaited at its end appears. "Then there's Marcus Kane. Ex-con, muscle for the Brotherhood. He's been in and out of prison his whole life. Known for his strength and ruthlessness, he's suspected in several assaults and armed robberies before he began running with the Brotherhood. Now he does Frost's bidding and is said to be his second in command."

"Markus Kane," Peter mutters as he writes.

"Yeah, you won't miss him. Big guy, lots of tattoos," Deacon says, moving to the next image. "Then there's a newer addition to their ranks, a tech genius named Jason Simons." The screen shows a lean man with a sharp jawline, intense green eyes, and a long ponytail. "He's the one who handles their cyber operations. We believe he's the link to the recent cyber attacks, though we haven't pinned anything concrete on him yet."

Peter frowns. "Tech guy. Could be trouble if he sniffs me out online."

"Exactly. Be careful with him," Deacon warns. "Finally, there's Rebecca 'Raven' Hart." The image of a striking woman with long jet black hair appears. "She's high up, possibly second only to Frost and Kane. Former intelligence analyst, extremely smart and dangerous. She's suspected of orchestrating several high-profile kidnappings and assassinations."

Peter raises an eyebrow. "A former analyst? How'd she end up with this group?"

"Disillusionment, same as the others. She's highly respected within the Brotherhood, and her loyalty to Frost is unwavering. Don't underestimate her," Deacon advises.

Peter takes a deep breath. "That's quite the lineup. Anything else I should know?"

Deacon nods. "Just remember, these aren't your average extremists. They're well-trained, well-armed, and highly motivated. Each of them brings a unique set of skills to the table, and they're all fiercely loyal to Frost."

Peter's expression is confident. "Understood. I'll keep my eyes open and tread carefully."

"Good," Deacon says. "Your first priority is to gain their trust. Once you're in, gather as much intel as you can on their operations and their plans. We need to dismantle this group from the inside out."

EIGHTEEN

Two days later, Peter, now living as Jack Reilly, finds himself in a secluded bar on the outskirts of Omaha. It's late evening, and the bar is bathed in soft light, with small groups of people huddled in corners, talking in low voices. A jukebox plays a country song in the background, adding to the rustic, clandestine feel of the place. Peter scans the room and spots Ray Collins sitting at a table near the back.

Ray is a rugged man in his late thirties, with a shaved head and a weathered face that speaks of hard years. He nurses a beer, occasionally glancing around the room, his eyes sharp and alert.

Peter takes a deep breath, steeling himself for the encounter, and makes his way through the bar. He navigates past worn tables and faded chairs, finally reaching Ray' table.

"Ray Collins?" Peter asks.

Ray looks up, his gaze scrutinizing. "You must be Jack Reilly."

Peter nods. "That's right. Mind if I join you?"

Ray gestures to the empty chair. "Have a seat."

Peter sits down, maintaining eye contact. Then Ray leans forward, lowering his voice. "So you're looking to join the Brotherhood?" he asks.

"I'm looking for a place where I can make a difference. Heard you're the guy who can make introductions."

Ray nods slowly, assessing Peter. "We'll see. Got to make sure you're not just talk."

Ray signals the bartender for another round of drinks, then leans back in his chair, his expression one of cautious curiosity. "So what's your story? How'd you end up here?"

Peter takes a sip of his drink, feeling the warmth of the liquor settle in his chest. "Served sixteen years in the Marines. Got discharged after an IED took out my convoy, killing two of my buddies, maiming another three. I survived with just cuts, bruises, and a mean scar on my hip. Thought I'd just about had all the luck I was due. Time to leave. After that, I tried to adjust to civilian life, but it didn't stick. Got tired of watching this country go to hell. Figured it was time to do something about it."

Ray nods thoughtfully. "You'd be surprised how many times I hear that. What makes you different?"

Peter leans in, his voice steady. "I'm not just another armchair warrior. I've got the skills and the drive. I'm ready to take action, whatever it takes."

Ray studies him for a moment, then nods, seemingly satisfied. "All right. We've got a job lined up. Consider it your initiation."

Peter's pulse quickens. "What's the job?"

"I'll show you."

Ray leads Peter to a back room of the bar, where a small group is gathered around a pool table. The surface is covered with maps and the air is thick with cigarette smoke. Whispers fly among the men as they glance at Peter with suspicion.

"This is Jack Reilly," Ray announces, his voice cutting through the murmurs. "He's looking to join us."

Peter recognizes two of the men around the pool table from the photos he's been poring over for the past four days. One is Marcus Kane, his thick gray beard plaited at the end. Another is Daniel Carter, the Brotherhood's explosives expert, his intense eyes following Peter as he and Ray join the group.

Marcus Kane steps forward, his gaze fixed on Peter.

"Another recruit, huh?" Marcus says gruffly. "Hope you're not just talk."

Peter meets his gaze, his expression calm and unyielding. "You'll see soon enough."

Ray turns to the group. "Jack's gonna join us for tonight's job."

Peter moves closer to the pool table, where a detailed map of a building is spread out. At the top, in bold letters, is written *City Hall*.

"City Hall?" Peter remarks, raising an eyebrow.

"Oh yes, City Hall," Marcus affirms, a malicious grin spreading across his face. "See, while the mayor and his cronies are spending this evening at a charity gala to celebrate some self-congratulatory bullshit while their city sinks further into the swamp, we're gonna light a fire the whole city's gonna see."

NINETEEN

Nighttime in Omaha. The group is en route to City Hall. The van they've all piled into rumbles through the desolate streets, bouncing slightly over the potholes. Peter, now fully immersed in his role as Jack Reilly, sits in the back, scanning the devastation outside from the back windows. The streets are filled with drug addicts—zombified, ragged people shuffling along aimlessly or simply holed up in a doorway in makeshift tents.

The dim streetlights cast eerie shadows on the boarded-up buildings. The once-thriving neighborhood is now a picture of despair and decay. There is a sense of hopelessness that hangs in the air, the remnants of a community let down and left to the drug dealers—ravaged by addiction and neglect.

Marcus Kane, sitting in the passenger seat, breaks the heavy silence with a voice filled with disdain. "You want to know why we're hitting Omaha City Hall, Jack?"

Peter, maintaining a calm demeanor, responds, "I think I can work it out."

Marcus gestures to the streets, his eyes reflecting the anger and frustration he feels. "Look at this place. These streets used to be full of businesses, full of hope. Now they're filled with zombies. Omaha has one of the worst drug epidemics in America. Our great nation is under the scourge of narcotic addiction, but our politicians and police officers merely look the other way."

Peter watches the scene, taking in the heartbreaking sights. "It's sad."

Marcus intensifies, his voice growing more passionate. "It's more than sad, it's a damn tragedy. Our country is sick, Jack. People are leeching off of each other, every human interaction reduced to nothing more than a transaction. No one cares about long-term goals or greater purposes anymore—everyone's just chasing short-term pleasure, addicted to their own selfish desires."

Peter, thoughtful and playing his part, says, "Society's lost its way."

Marcus nods. "Exactly. The Founding Fathers would be ashamed to see what's become of their great nation. They built this country on principles of hard work, community, and faith. They had the pioneer spirit—a willingness to suffer and strive for a better future. But look at us now. We've corrupted those values, lost our way, and forsaken our God."

The vehicle turns a corner. Less than five minutes later, the city couldn't look any more different. The potholed roads have given way to wide boulevards, the boarded-up buildings replaced by tall, neat stone structures. Everything is clean, well-maintained, and bustling with activity.

As they drive past the columned front of a luxurious hotel, Marcus gestures to the brightly lit venue where a gala charity event is taking place. The contradiction between the opulence and the despair they just saw is striking. The hotel is beautifully decorated with well-dressed attendees mingling outside, the gala in full swing.

Marcus Kane, his voice filled with contempt, gestures toward the hotel. "Look at that. Just a block away from all that misery, the mayor and his cronies are having a ball—quite literally. A charity event, they call it—but in reality, it's a fundraiser for his next campaign."

Peter nods. "Quite the contrast."

Marcus Kane's passion flares as he continues. "These so-called leaders live in their bubbles, throwing lavish parties and pretending to care while the rest of the city rots. They're disconnected from the real struggles, the real suffering. They make promises, hold these events, but it's all a show. Nothing changes."

They turn a corner, the hotel's bright lights fading into the background.

"So what's the plan?" Peter asks.

Marcus's fervor is palpable. "We need to remind the people of their power. We need to show them that we can reclaim our nation from those who've betrayed it. The Founding Fathers wouldn't sit idly by while their country fell apart—they'd take action. And so will we."

Peter nods in agreement. "It's time for a change."

Marcus's determination is unwavering. "Damn right. We're going to ignite a revolution, one act at a time. And that's why we're going to burn down City Hall. To send a message that we, the people, will no longer stand by and watch our country rot from the inside out."

They reach Omaha City Hall. The building looms ahead, dimly lit by footlights. Security cameras poke out at the corners and a few security guards in gray uniforms patrol the perimeter.

The van pulls into a narrow alley adjacent to the building. The rumble of the engine ceases, replaced by the faint hum of the city's nightlife in the distance—including the sound of the mayor's gala. The four men sit in silence for a moment, each lost in his own thoughts, steeling themselves for what comes next.

Marcus Kane is the first to move. He slides the door open and steps out, his boots crunching on the gravel. Peter follows, with Ray and Daniel Carter close behind. The alley is dark, the tall buildings on either side blocking out the streetlights.

"Stay close and keep quiet," Marcus whispers, leading the way. He moves with a purpose, smooth and practiced like a cat. Peter thinks he recognizes him from the attack on the 18th Precinct, but he can't be sure.

The group follows, their footsteps barely making a sound against the pavement. City Hall looms ahead, a symbol of the power and corruption they have come to confront. The building is pristine, imposing, and guarded.

As they approach, Marcus gestures for them to stop. He scans the area, noting the positions of the security cameras and the guards patrolling the perimeter. Earlier, in the backroom of the bar, Marcus had gone over the intel gathered from their recent surveillance of the building. He made sure to verse Peter and the others in the routes and habits of the security guards.

Marcus motions to Ray, who nods and steps forward, producing a small device from his backpack.

"Jam the cameras," Marcus orders.

Ray works quickly, setting up the jammer and activating it. A faint buzz indicates that the cameras are now useless, their feeds disrupted.

Peter notes the sophistication of the device, understanding that only the best militaries in the world has access to such technology.

Marcus then turns to them. "Ray, Danny, set the fires at the back," he instructs in a low voice. "Jack and I will head to the roof."

The group splits up, Marcus and Peter heading to the fire escape on the side of the building while Ray and Carter move toward the back alley.

With the cameras down and the guards out of the way, Peter and Marcus reach the fire escape without hassle. There, they use snips to cut their way through the mesh cage that surrounds the stairs. In less than a minute, they are in.

The metal structure creaks under their weight, but they move quickly and quietly, their years of experience showing in their fluid, controlled motions. As they ascend, the city's sounds become more distant, replaced by the occasional clink of their shoes on the iron steps.

Reaching the rooftop, Marcus pauses to take in the view. The gala's lights flicker brightly in the distance. He points to a cluster of ventilation ducts. "We'll start the fire there. The vents will help it spread fast."

Peter nods. They move to the ducts, working efficiently. Both men remove their backpacks and pull the canisters of gasoline from them. They then begin to douse the area, making sure that the gas runs down the ventilation into the building. Each carries ten liters, enough to get things going.

Once the canisters are empty, Marcus turns to Peter. "You light it," he says. "Call it your initiation."

Marcus had stated earlier that the alarms would go off immediately and the six guards stationed in the building would easily evacuate. Still, Peter feels uneasy about the act, even if it is essential he remain in deep cover.

Hesitating less than a few seconds, Peter strikes a match, the small flame flickering in the night air before he touches it to the trail of gasoline. The fire catches immediately, spreading quickly.

Marcus watches the flames for a moment before turning to Peter. "Once it burns through the roof and drops into the building, the whole place will go up. They'll be too busy trying to put out the fire Ray and Carter are setting at the back to notice this one."

Peter nods. The flames grow, licking up the sides of the ducts and beginning to consume the rooftop. Marcus gives a satisfied nod. "Let's move."

They make their way back to the fire escape, descending swiftly. The glow of the fire above them intensifies, casting eerie shadows on the alley below. As they reach the ground, they hear the faint shouts of the security guards coming from the back of the building. Ray and Carter have succeeded in setting the trash cans ablaze, creating the decoy fire.

The group reconvenes at the base of the fire escape. "Time to go," Marcus tells them.

But before they can move, a cry pierces the night. Peter whirls around and spots a security guard trapped on one of the upper floors, his silhouette visible against the backdrop of the growing flames.

Peter doesn't hesitate. "I'm going back."

Daniel Carter grabs his arm. "What the hell are you doing? You're gonna get us caught!"

Peter responds, "That guy's just a minimum-wage blue-collar worker. He doesn't deserve to die doing no more than trying to make a buck."

Carter's anger flares. "He's protecting criminals!"

Peter's voice is firm. "He's just trying to earn a living. If the Brotherhood isn't about protecting guys like that, then I'm in the wrong group."

Without waiting for a response, Peter pulls his arm away and sprints back to the fire escape, where he begins to climb. The metal structure sways under his weight, the heat from the fire intensifying the higher he gets. Reaching a window on the trapped guard's floor, he smashes it with his elbow, the glass shattering around him as he hauls himself inside.

The smoke is thick, choking, but Peter pushes forward, listening for the guard's cries. He moves quickly through the offices, the flames already starting to consume the furniture and walls.

"Help! Help!" The guard's voice is faint but clear enough to guide Peter through the maze of cubicles and burning debris.

He spots the man at the far end of the floor. He's stopped shouting and is now coughing wildly. He must've been in the room when the fire came down from the ventilation. A thick wall of flames cuts him off from the stairwell.

Thinking quickly, Peter rips down a set of thick drapes from one of the windows. He soaks them in the water pouring down from the sprinklers. Wrapping himself in the drenched fabric, he charges through the flames, feeling the heat sear his skin even through the wet barrier.

Reaching the guard, who is now unconscious, he hoists the man over his shoulder, covering them both with the damp drapes.

With the flames closing in, Peter retraces his steps, moving as quickly as he dares through the inferno. He makes it back to the window, the fire escape just outside.

Peter carefully lowers the unconscious guard out the window and onto the fire escape, then climbs out himself, the flames licking at his heels. He descends quickly, the guard slung back over his shoulder, and reaches the ground just as the fire roars even higher, consuming the floor they had just vacated.

A short distance away from the blazing building, Peter lays the guard down gently on the ground. The night air is thick with the acrid smell of smoke and the distant wail of sirens. He kneels beside the unconscious man, placing two fingers on his neck to check for a pulse. The guard's skin is clammy, but the pulse is steady, albeit weak.

Peter leans closer, pressing an ear to the guard's chest to listen to his breathing. A moment later, the guard begins to cough violently, his chest heaving as he expels the smoke from his lungs. His eyes flutter open, dazed and confused, but alive.

Assured the guy has survived, Peter leaves him, moving swiftly to the alley.

The van is idling when he reaches it. Carter, Ray, and Marcus are waiting inside, their faces a mix of anger and grudging respect as Peter gets into the back.

"You're insane," Carter mutters as Ray puts the van in gear and rolls them out of there.

Marcus raises a hand. "Back off, Carter. Reilly's right. We're here to protect the people, not harm them." He turns to Peter. "You've got guts, Reilly. And honor. I like that."

They disappear into the night, the flames of City Hall rising behind them.

TWENTY

THE NEXT DAY, PETER IS ON HIS WAY TO A SECURE location where the core members of the Iron Brotherhood are gathered. He sits in the back seat of an SUV being driven by Daniel Carter. Peering out the window, he takes in the desolate scenery. They pass through a small, dilapidated town, its streets lined with boarded-up shops and abandoned houses. The few remaining residents move listlessly, their faces dripping with defeat and despair. *This is what happens when systems fail*, Peter can't help thinking.

Marcus Kane sits in the front passenger seat, turning occasionally to glance back at Peter. "This place used to be alive, you know," Marcus begins, his voice heavy with a mix of anger and nostalgia. "Factories churning out goods, warehouses full of supplies. Families had jobs, kids went to decent schools. There was a sense of community."

Peter nods, understanding the bitterness in Marcus's tone. "What happened?" he asks, already knowing part of the answer but wanting to hear Marcus's perspective.

Marcus sighs, looking out at the crumbling remains of what was once a thriving industrial hub. "Outsourcing," he says with a sneer. "Everything we used to make and store here is now made and stored in China. Cheaper labor, they said. More efficient, they said. But they didn't think about the lives they were destroying here. I mean, what's the point in cheaper goods if no one's got any wages to pay for them?"

The SUV continues down the narrow, winding road, passing rusted-out cars and overgrown lots where weeds choke what used to be manicured lawns. "Factories closed down one by one," Marcus continues. "People lost their jobs, their homes, their dignity. This town, this whole area, just fell to pieces."

Peter watches a group of ragged children playing in a yard filled with junk, laughing and yipping as the decay surrounds them. "So the Iron Brotherhood moved in?" he asks.

Marcus nods. "We saw an opportunity. This place might be a ghost town, but it's perfect cover for us. Secluded, forgotten by the outside world. The authorities don't come here anymore, and the people... they've given up hope. But we haven't."

They drive on, the road narrowing as it winds through dense forest. The trees form a thick canopy overhead, blocking out the already weak light of the overcast sky. The sense of isolation deepens, and Peter feels the weight of the place pressing in on him.

After what feels like an eternity, the trees open up to reveal a sprawling, abandoned industrial complex. The main building, a massive, decrepit warehouse, looms ahead, its windows shuttered over and its walls covered in graffiti. Despite its rundown appearance, however, there is a sense of purpose about the place.

They drive through the rusted gate, passing armed guards who nod curtly as they enter. The guards are a stark reminder that while this place may look abandoned, it is anything but. The Iron Brotherhood has made it their stronghold.

The SUV comes to a stop in front of the main building. Marcus turns to Peter with a grim smile. "Welcome to the Iron Brotherhood's sanctuary," he says. "The only place around here that's still inhabited."

Peter steps out of the vehicle, his eyes scanning the area. Members of the Brotherhood move purposefully around the compound. The air is thick with the scent of gun oil and the faint tang of explosives. Peter knows that this place, though destitute and forgotten by the world, is a hive of activity and planning.

As they walk to the entrance, Marcus continues, "This place might look like hell, but it's our hell. And we're going to use it to strike back at the people who have left us for dead."

Peter is led into the heart of the building, to an office at the back. Inside is a large table at the center occupied by various people. The walls are adorned with maps, tactical diagrams, and various weapons. The group of men and women gathered around the table exude a mixture of suspicion and authority. Peter recognizes them. They are Travis "Mad Dog" Morgan, Jason Simons, and Rebecca "Raven" Hart. They scrutinize Peter as he steps into the room.

Ray leads the way, introducing Peter to the group. "This is Jack Reilly. He more than proved himself last night in Omaha."

Mad Dog, a broad-shouldered man with a wild grin, leans forward. "We'll see about that. You up for more than just petty vandalism, Reilly?"

Peter meets his gaze, unwavering. "I'm here to do whatever it takes."

Rebecca "Raven" Hart, a striking woman with long, jet-black hair and piercing eyes, speaks coolly. "Loyalty is earned, not given. We'll be watching you closely."

Peter nods. "Understood."

Jason Simons, a wiry man with a suspicious look, interjects. "And if you turn out to be something other than what you claim?"

Peter's confidence doesn't waver. "Then you deal with me accordingly. But I'm here to stay."

At that moment, Joseph Frost steps into the room. His commanding presence immediately silences the group. Frost is a tall, lean man with sharp, angular facial features marked by a few small scars. His piercing blue eyes and short salt-and-pepper hair give him an air of authority.

"Welcome to the Brotherhood, Reilly," Frost says in a voice dripping in calm authority. "We'll see where your loyalties lie soon enough."

Peter looks around the room, feeling the weight of their gazes. "I won't let you down."

Frost smiles slightly, a hint of menace in his expression. "For your sake, I hope not. Let's get to work."

After that, Marcus Kane takes Peter on a tour of the place. The group's hideout was once a major meatpacking and processing facility, which thrived until the 1980s before falling on hard times and closing down. The building was later stripped of its equipment and repurposed as a warehouse, which also eventually closed in 2010. Its significant advantage for the Brotherhood lies in its massive array of underground refrigerator units. The Brotherhood has stripped these units, transforming the chambers into spaces filled with weapons, supplies, and makeshift sleeping quarters.

The hideout, despite its outward decrepitude, is a hive of organized chaos. Men and women move with purpose, each deeply involved in their tasks, whether it's cleaning weapons, setting up surveillance equipment, or plotting their next move on large, detailed maps.

Peter is impressed with the sheer scale of the operation. He wonders how these people managed to secure the finances for such an extensive setup. During the briefing, Deacon had mentioned that the Iron Brotherhood was formed in 2017. How, then, had they grown to this size in less than nine years?

As Marcus Kane guides him around the weapons caches, Peter spots guns not available on the domestic market. There's an FN SCAR-H (Mk 17), a battle rifle used by special forces. They also pass several Barrett M107A1 sniper rifles lined up, boxes of .50 BMG ammunition stacked beside them. The M107A1 is used to engage light-armored vehicles, fortified positions, and long-range targets. What in the hell is the Iron Brotherhood doing with them? Next, they pass crates of Rheinmetall MG3s, a German general-purpose machine gun chambered in 7.62x51mm NATO. Belt-fed, it is renowned for its high rate of fire and effectiveness in both infantry and vehicle-mounted roles.

Someone is supplying them with military hardware flashes through Peter's mind. *But who?*

He turns to Marcus as they walk. "This is quite the setup. How did you manage to pull all this together?"

Marcus smirks, a hint of pride in his expression. "We've got connections. People who believe in our cause and are willing to support us. You'd be surprised how many folks out there feel the same way we do about the state of this country."

———

PETER BEGINS his first week with the Iron Brotherhood, eager to observe and integrate himself into their day-to-day operations, aware that every move he makes is being scrutinized.

On his first morning, he joins the group for physical training. The sun is barely peeking over the horizon when they start, the chill in the air not enough to deter them as they make off from the hideout into the surrounding woodland, a long line of joggers. The drills are grueling—running, an obstacle course they've built out there in the middle of the field, and hand-to-hand combat exercises. Peter, with his CIA training, keeps up easily, earning nods of approval from Marcus Kane and wary glances from Travis "Mad Dog" Morgan.

"Not bad, Reilly," Marcus says, slapping Peter on the back after they finish a round of shooting drills. "Looks like you've still got it from your days in the Marines."

Peter nods, keeping his expression neutral. "Just trying to stay sharp."

Mad Dog, standing nearby, watches with narrowed eyes. "Let's see if you can keep it up," he mutters, barely loud enough for Peter to hear.

In the afternoon, Peter helps with the maintenance of their

arsenal. The task is meticulous—cleaning and organizing weapons, checking ammunition, and ensuring everything is in working order. He works silently, his movements efficient and practiced. Daniel Carter, working at a nearby table, occasionally glances over but remains distant.

"Need any help?" Peter asks, approaching him, having finished his own work.

Carter shakes his head without looking up. "I've got it," he replies curtly.

Peter nods, noting Carter's aloofness. He understands the man's caution; trust is not easily earned in this environment.

———

ON HIS SECOND DAY, the group heads out to a gun show to sell and trade arms.

They leave the hideout early in the morning in several vehicles. The drive is tense but filled with anticipation. Marcus Kane sits next to Peter in the lead SUV, explaining the nuances of arms trading and the importance of discretion.

"Listen, Reilly," Marcus says, his voice low and serious. "These gun shows are a goldmine for us, but they can also be a trap if we're not careful. Your job today is to oversee the transactions and make sure everything goes smoothly. Got it?"

Peter nods. "Got it. I won't let you down."

The gun show is bustling with activity when they arrive. Vendors showcase their wares, and potential buyers inspect firearms with keen interest. The air is filled with the stench of gun oil and the sound of haggling.

As he helps with sales, displaying his extensive knowledge of weaponry, something that impresses the others, Peter observes Rebecca "Raven" Hart.

She moves through the crowd with ease, coordinating with other militia groups present at the show. Her demeanor is friendly but calculating, gathering intelligence with every conversation.

Her long jet-black hair and striking features make her stand out, but it's her sharp mind that truly sets her apart.

Peter can't help feeling drawn to her.

"Jack," she calls, beckoning Peter over. "Meet Carl. He's with the Midwest Patriots. They might be interested in some of our hardware."

Peter shakes hands with Carl, exchanging pleasantries and discussing potential deals. Raven watches closely, evaluating Peter's ability to navigate these social interactions. He doesn't let himself down, even if he feels like he's being more than assessed; he's being sussed out.

———

ON PETER'S THIRD DAY, the Iron Brotherhood attends a meeting with other militia groups. A convoy of vehicles leaves the rundown warehouse and heads north through West Virginia. The drive takes them through the desolate remnants of the old rust belt, passing by economic ruins and ghost towns that once thrived but now stand as haunting reminders of better days. Or *fairer days*, as Joseph Frost puts it.

Seeing all these factories and warehouses in ruins, Peter begins to feel that the workers of America—once its lifeblood—have been abandoned. Left to fall into dilapidated ruins in exchange for a better profit margin.

They drive deep into the countryside until they reach a secluded cabin high up in the Appalachian foothills.

Upon arrival, the leaders of the Iron Brotherhood, Patriot's Frontline, Sovereign Sentinels, and Liberty Defenders gather around a large table in the dimly lit cabin. Peter stands at the back with several others, the wooden structure bursting at its seams.

Joseph Frost stands at the head of the table, commanding attention. "The government is tightening its grip, so we have to unite."

Liam Hayes, leader of Patriot's Frontline, agrees. "We've operated independently for too long. It's time to pool resources."

Raven offers weapons in exchange for cooperation. Evelyn Stone, leader of Sovereign Sentinels, counters with explosives.

Travis "Mad Dog" Morgan seeks logistical support for an operation in Baltimore. Derek James offers untraceable vehicles in exchange for rally assistance.

It is when there is mention of *Leadership* that Peter's ears prick up. "For this next phase," Frost says, "Leadership has given us encrypted devices to communicate with them." He nods at Mad Dog, who picks up his backpack and begins doling out small portable devices.

"These devices," Frost goes on, "allow our communications to be completely hidden. They run off of end-to-end encryption, employing ephemeral encryption keys that are generated exclusively for each session and discarded immediately after use. This makes it practically impossible for any intercepted communications to be decrypted later."

Each group leader takes the device, staring down at it. Peter gazes at them, too. They are highly sophisticated, and he wonders just who in the hell has invented these for this ragtag band of broken brothers and sisters.

As the meeting concludes, Frost's voice carries their resolve. "Our unity is our strength. Divided, we fall. United, we rise. Let's make this work."

———

DAYS FOUR, five, and six are pretty mundane. They involve more training, more gun cleaning, more drills. It isn't until day seven that something interesting happens.

Joseph Frost takes Peter aside for a private conversation. The two step away from the group, finding a quiet corner of the hideout.

"Reilly, you've proven yourself this week," Frost begins, his piercing blue eyes studying Peter intently. "You've got the skills and the nerve we need."

Peter nods, meeting Frost's gaze. "Thank you, sir. Just doing my part."

Frost smirks, nodding slightly. "We have a mission coming up. Something big. We need to pick up a shipment from the port in Baltimore. It's been smuggled in, and we expect things could get very heated with the Feds."

Peter listens intently, his mind racing with possibilities. "What's the shipment?" he asks.

"Something that's gonna help us," Frost replies, his smirk widening. "I need people with ice in their veins to oversee it. Think you're up for it?"

Peter's confidence doesn't waver. "Absolutely."

Frost nods, seemingly satisfied. "Good. Get some rest. We leave later tonight."

TWENTY-ONE

THE NIGHT AIR IS THICK AND HUMID AS PETER, MARCUS Kane, Jason Simons, and Daniel Carter approach the entrance to the Baltimore docklands in an indistinct sedan—the untraceable vehicle supplied by Derek James of the Liberty Defenders. The drive has taken them six hours, and it's now almost midnight.

The faint orange glow of the streetlights casts long shadows on the cracked asphalt, and the distant sounds of ships creaking and waves lapping against the piers add a muted soundtrack to their approach.

Peter grips the steering wheel, his eyes scanning the road ahead as they near the gatehouse. The docks are quiet at this hour, save for the occasional rumble of a boxcar or the clatter of machinery in the distance. As they pull up to the gate, the large, imposing figure of a security guard steps out of the small booth, a flashlight in one hand and a clipboard in the other.

"Stay calm, follow my lead," Carter murmurs from the passenger seat, his voice low and steady.

In the back, Marcus Kane and Jason Simons sit in silence, their presence adding to the weight of the moment. Peter nods, easing the car to a stop. The guard shines his flashlight into the vehicle, first at Peter, then at Carter, before moving the beam to the backseat where Marcus and Simons are seated before approaching the driver's side window.

"Evening, fellas. Papers, please," the guard says, his tone gruff but routine.

Peter reaches into the glove compartment, pulling out a manilla folder containing the fake IDs and paperwork they've prepared. He hands them over, his face a mask of calm. The guard flips through the documents, his eyes flicking between the photos and the men in the car. The moment stretches, tension humming beneath the surface.

"You're here to pick up a vehicle, right?" the guard asks, glancing up.

"That's right," Carter replies smoothly from the passenger seat. "We won't be long."

The guard nods, seemingly satisfied, and hands back the paperwork. "All right, you're clear. Gate 12 is where you'll want to go. Stay on the marked lanes, and don't wander. It's quiet tonight, but the foreman doesn't like any funny business."

Peter nods in acknowledgment, taking the papers back. "Will do. Appreciate it."

The guard steps back, waving them through. Peter shifts the car into drive and slowly rolls forward, his pulse steady as they pass the barrier. The docks spread out before them, a labyrinth of containers stacked high, their metal sides gleaming dully under the sparse lighting.

As they navigate the narrow lanes between towering crates and dormant cranes, Peter keeps his eyes on the road, but his mind is racing. The cover has held so far, but the real challenge is yet to come. In the back, Marcus Kane and Jason Simons remain silent, their gazes fixed ahead, the weight of the mission settling between them as they approach Gate 12.

The time for second thoughts is long past. Now it's all about execution.

They enter Gate 12, the area eerily quiet with only a few dock-workers moving around. The docks are lit by floodlights, but the aisles between the containers are pitch black, the tall stacks blocking out the light.

Peter, scanning the area, spots their target. "There it is. Container 47B," he whispers.

He parks the sedan, and all four men get out. They approach the container quickly and quietly, their footsteps barely making a sound on the cracked asphalt. Marcus Kane steps forward, pulling out a small flashlight to illuminate the lock on the container. He carefully enters a numerical code into the digital keypad attached to the lock. After a tense moment, the lock beeps and clicks open.

Peter moves forward and swings open the heavy doors, revealing a black van. The key is balanced on top of a rear wheel. Unlocking it, the team swiftly opens the back doors and begin checking the contents. Peter spots immediately that the van is packed with explosives.

Jason Simons, after a thorough inspection, confirms, "Everything's here. Now let's get going before anyone notices."

Peter and Marcus Kane head to the front of the van. Peter slides into the driver's seat, the leather creaking under his weight, while Marcus takes the passenger seat, already pulling out his phone to contact Frost. Behind them, Carter and Simons move swiftly back to the sedan, the urgency of their task reflected in their brisk movements.

As Peter turns the key in the ignition, the van's engine rumbles to life, a low growl that echoes in the stillness of the docks. He adjusts the rearview mirror, catching a glimpse of the sedan's headlights flickering on as Carter and Simons follow suit. The two vehicles then begin to roll out of the maze of containers and back toward the main gate.

Marcus dials Frost's number and the line connects after a couple of rings. "It's done," Marcus says, his voice low but firm. "We're on our way out now. Should be clear in about ten minutes."

There's a brief pause on the other end before Frost replies,

"Good. Keep it smooth, and don't take any chances. I'll be waiting for the signal once you're clear."

Marcus nods, though Frost can't see it, and hangs up. He turns to Peter, who's maneuvering the van through the narrow lanes, the container stacks looming on either side like the steep walls of a canyon. "All we need is to get past the gate and we're home free."

Peter grunts in acknowledgment, his focus on the road ahead. The exit looms closer, the gatehouse a small, solitary structure against the backdrop of the sprawling docklands. The sedan keeps pace behind them, headlights casting long shadows across the asphalt.

Just as they near the gate, Peter's heart stops dead. In the rearview mirror, flashing red and blue lights appear like unwanted specters. The distinctive whirl of a siren breaks the silence, and Peter curses under his breath.

Marcus Kane, panicking, shouts, "Shit, the Feds are here!"

Peter, calm and collected, replies, "Stay calm. I've got a plan." He then speaks into the radio. "Carter, follow my lead."

Peter drives the black van through the docks, keeping out of sight. He takes a series of sharp turns, using the shipping containers as cover. The van weaves through the narrow paths, the engine revving softly, his eyes sharp as he scans for an escape route.

Daniel Carter, anxious, exclaims over the radio, "We're gonna get caught! There's no way out!"

Peter reassures him, "Trust me. I've got this."

He maneuvers the van skillfully, staying hidden in the labyrinth of containers, evading the flashing lights and the growing noise of the sirens.

"We're running out of time!" Marcus snaps, his voice betraying the anxiety that's creeping all over him.

Peter doesn't reply, his eyes focused as he steers around another tight corner, the van almost striking the edge of a rusted container. The sedan behind them mirrors every move, Carter and Simons maintaining their pace despite the rising fear that gnaws at their nerves.

The whir of a helicopter grows louder, its searchlight cutting through the darkness, sweeping the area with an unrelenting eye. Peter knows they only have a minute before the Feds close in on their position.

"We need to take the next left," Peter orders, his voice steady.

Marcus glances at him, confusion flashing across his face. "That'll take us farther into the docks."

"Exactly," Peter says, a small, grim smile tugging at the corners of his mouth. "We're not getting out the way we came in. We need to disappear."

He takes the left, the van slipping deeper into the docklands, the container stacks growing taller, the lanes narrower. They're heading toward the most derelict part of the docks, where abandoned industrial buildings loom like forgotten giants.

Carter's voice crackles over the radio, a mix of frustration and fear. "Reilly, what the hell are you doing?"

Peter glances at Marcus, who's gripping the dashboard like a lifeline, and then presses the button on the comms. "Trust me, Carter. I know exactly what I'm doing."

He floors the accelerator, the van speeding through the desolate landscape, the hum of the helicopter like a ghost that refuses to be shaken.

They weave through the deserted alleys of the industrial zone, the once-thriving factories now nothing more than hollowed-out shells. Peter slows the van as they approach a series of interconnected buildings, their windows broken, their walls scarred by time and neglect. It's here, among these relics of a bygone era, that Peter knows they can find temporary refuge.

"There!" Peter says, pointing to a nondescript lockup door, half-hidden by the overgrown weeds and debris that have overtaken the area. He pulls the van to a sudden stop, tires screeching on the cracked pavement. Carter is right behind them, slamming on the brakes, the sedan skidding to a halt mere inches from the van's bumper.

Peter jumps out, his heart pounding but his mind clear. He sprints to the lockup door as the helicopter's spotlight sweeps dangerously close. The sound of sirens is growing nearer, an omnipresent threat that's closing in from all sides.

"What the hell are you doing?" Carter shouts from the driver's window of the sedan.

Peter ignores him as he searches a pile of bricks. In the van, Marcus Kane thinks he knows what's happening.

"Hurry, Peter!" he urges, his eyes darting nervously between the sky and the door.

Ignoring the pressure, Peter finds the key among the bricks and shoves it into the lock. The mechanism clicks, and he throws the door up with a grunt, revealing the shadowy interior of the lockup—a hidden sanctuary within this warren of dereliction.

"Inside, now!" Peter commands.

Marcus is the first to respond. Leaping across the cab into the driver's seat, he taxis the van into the lockup. Peter motions frantically for Carter and Simons to follow, and they waste no time guiding the sedan inside the small garage space. As there is a third vehicle inside, the vehicles barely fit, their bumpers almost touching the walls on all sides as they squeeze in.

Peter slams the lockup door down just as the helicopter's beam sweeps over the area, narrowly missing them. They are plunged into darkness, the only sounds being their heavy breathing and the distant wail of the sirens as they speed past.

The men's hearts pound against their ribcages. Peter leans against the cold, metal door, listening intently to the world outside. The sirens begin to fade, and the helicopter's whir grows distant, the searchlight moving away from their hiding spot.

After what feels like an eternity, the noise recedes completely, leaving behind an eerie silence.

Marcus exhales sharply, his relief evident. "Jesus, that was close."

Carter, still sitting in the sedan, slumps back in his seat, wiping the sweat from his brow. "I think I'm gonna need fresh pants."

Jason Simons, who has been silent through the entire ordeal, turns to Peter and finally speaks, his voice hoarse. "What now?"

Peter looks around at them, the men who have just narrowly escaped a federal dragnet. "Now we get to work," he says, his voice calm but authoritative.

Peter opens the back doors of the black van, revealing the crates of explosives inside.

"We need to transfer all of this to the other van," Peter says, pointing to a tarp-covered vehicle at the back of the lockup. He pulls off the cover, revealing a nondescript white van, similar in size to the one they just drove in but slightly older and worn—and not black.

As they start unloading the explosives, Peter begins to explain. "I've got an old Marine buddy here in Baltimore, Jim 'Rusty' Blake. We served together in Iraq. When Frost informed me about Baltimore, I thought there was a chance we might be walking into a setup. Too many things were lining up too smoothly, so I reached out to Rusty. He's the one who got us access to this lockup, left the key for me, and arranged for this second van."

Marcus grunts as he hefts a heavy crate from the first van, his face strained with the effort. "Smart move, Reilly. Never hurts to have a backup."

Peter nods, lifting another crate with ease. "You've always got to have a plan B. If you don't, you're asking to get caught. Especially in this line of work."

Carter, who has been suspicious of Peter's judgment throughout their time together, pauses for a moment, his hands still gripping the crate he's carrying. He looks at Peter with a newfound respect, realizing that this man is not just a driver or a soldier but someone who thinks several steps ahead. Even he can't help but admire that.

"So this Rusty," Carter begins, setting down the crate in the new van. "He's reliable?"

Peter chuckles as he places another crate next to Carter's. "As reliable as they come. He's got his own reasons for staying off the grid, and he knows how to keep his mouth shut. He didn't ask too many questions, just set things up the way I asked."

They finish stacking the last of the crates in the new van and wipe the sweat from their brows. Peter then slams the rear doors of the van shut and locks them, his mind already shifting to the next phase of the plan.

"We'll leave the other vehicles here," he says. "If the Feds trace us to the docks, they'll waste time searching the abandoned van and the area around it. We'll be long gone by the time they realize we've swapped vehicles."

Marcus Kane leans against the side of the van, folding his arms across his wide chest. "Not bad, Reilly. Not bad at all."

Peter allows himself a small smile, knowing that earning Marcus' respect is no small feat. But there's no time to dwell on it. "Let's get moving," he says. "We'll take the back roads out of the city, avoid the main routes."

TWENTY-TWO

PETER STANDS INSIDE A RUSTING PAYPHONE AT THE corner of a lot. Not far from him is a diner, a relic of a better time, its once-bright neon sign now flickering weakly against the blue-gray sky. Inside, through the smudged windows, he can see Marcus, Carter, and Jason Simons hunched over plates of greasy eggs and bacon, their faces showing the weariness of men who've been on the run for too long.

The metal is cold to the touch, and the phone cord feels stiff and brittle as he lifts the receiver. He drops a couple of quarters into the slot, then dials a number from memory.

The line clicks once, then twice, before a familiar voice answers. "That you, Reilly?"

"Yes, it is," Peter says, glancing back at the diner to make sure no one's paying him any attention. "It worked."

Deacon's voice is calm, measured. "You're sure?"

Peter leans against the metal frame of the payphone. "Yeah, I'm sure. They trust me more than ever. Daniel Carter even gave me a compliment—didn't think he had it in him."

There's a faint chuckle on the other end of the line. "That's good to hear. The FBI did their part then?"

Peter nods, even though Deacon can't see him. "Yeah, they

showed up right on time, just like we planned. We had to dodge them through the docks, but they made sure I got to the lockup before they backed off. The guys think I pulled off some kind of miracle."

"Perfect," Deacon replies, a hint of satisfaction in his tone. "This'll give you the credibility you need to keep moving up in the group. We're getting closer, Peter. Just stick to the plan, and we'll get what we need."

Peter's gaze drifts to the horizon, where the highway stretches out into the distance, empty and forlorn. "Understood. But this thing with the FBI... we can't keep pulling stunts like that. They're already jumpy, and it's only gonna get worse the deeper I go."

Deacon's voice softens, taking on a more reassuring tone. "We won't push it too far. Just keep doing what you're doing. You've got them where we want them. Stay sharp, and remember why you're there."

Peter tightens his grip on the phone. "Yeah, I know."

It's then that he spots someone on the far side of the lot—a shadowy figure, like a ghostly apparition. For a fleeting second, he sees Kara standing there, staring at him. But a passing truck blocks his view, and when it's gone, so is she.

Deacon's voice shakes him. "Take care of yourself, Peter. You're in deep, but you're doing good work."

Peter swallows the lump in his throat. "Thanks, Mark. I'll be in touch."

He hangs up the phone, the clatter of the receiver echoing in the quiet lot. For a moment, he just stands there, breathing in the crisp morning air, trying to shake the lingering feeling of being watched by a ghost. Then he straightens up and heads back to the diner.

The bell above the door jingles as he steps inside. The warm, greasy air wraps around him, very different from the coolness outside. He slides into the booth next to Marcus, who's halfway through a stack of pancakes.

Marcus glances up from his plate, a rare smile crossing his face. "How's your mom?"

Peter forces a smile, playing the part. "She's good. Just worried about me, you know how it is."

The lie slips out easily, just another part of the job. But as he looks around the table, at the men who now trust him more than ever, he can't help but feel the weight of the truth pressing down harder with every step he takes closer to the edge.

TWENTY-THREE

TWO DAYS LATER, JOSEPH FROST APPROACHES PETER AS the latter sits on his bunk, cleaning and checking over a series of pistols. Peter observes that he's a little pale and that there's a slight tremor in Frost's hand.

"Reilly, we've finalized our next target," Frost states.

Peter is all attention, placing the Glock 17 he's holding to one side.

"We're hitting the New York Stock Exchange," Frost says.

Peter, taken aback, responds, "The NYSE? That's... audacious."

Frost nods, Peter noticing a sheen of sweat on his forehead. "It's the heart of American capitalism—the nest in which the vipers trade and sell off our futures. Disrupting it will send shock-waves through the entire financial system."

Peter understands the rationale immediately. "The economic impact alone will be devastating."

"Exactly," Frost continues, though his voice sounds slightly strained. "The chaos will weaken their financial control and show our power. Now usually I wouldn't involve a greenhorn in such a delicate operation, but you've more than impressed everyone, and I can't think of a better guy to be on the team. Are you in?"

Peter meets Frost's gaze, resolute. "Absolutely. Let's do it."

Frost leads Peter into the operations room. There, the other members of the team who will be performing the attack are waiting: Raven Hart, Marcus Kane, Mad Dog Morgan, Jason Simons, and Daniel Carter. Each of them gives Peter a curt nod as he enters the room with Frost.

They then begin meticulously preparing and planning the attack, set to happen in one week, gathering around a table covered with maps and blueprints of the NYSE building.

Joseph Frost addresses the team. "This is it. The biggest operation we've ever attempted. We're going to strike at the heart of the financial world."

Raven nods, her expression steely. "We'll be hitting them when they least expect it. The security will be tight, but once we've surveyed the site, we'll have a plan to bypass it."

As the preparations continue late into the night, Frost occasionally rubs his temples and leans on the table for support, but the others are too focused on the plan to notice.

By the end of the meeting, each member of the team knows their role and responsibilities. But as they disperse, a pale looking Frost suddenly wavers.

"Joseph?" Peter asks, concerned.

Frost waves him off but staggers slightly. "Just a bit lightheaded. I'll be fine."

Before he can protest further, Raven rushes to his side. "You forgot your insulin again, didn't you?"

Frost nods weakly, sinking into a chair. "I got caught up... didn't realize..."

Raven sends Jason off to retrieve the insulin. Peter watches from the sidelines, a new understanding dawning on him. Joseph Frost, the formidable leader, is a type 1 diabetic.

———

THE DRIVE to New York is long and tense. The group is silent for most of the journey, each member lost in their own thoughts.

As they enter Brooklyn, the familiar sounds and sights of the Big Apple greet them. The hum of traffic, the distant honking of horns, and the buzz of city life fill the van. They navigate through the crowded streets, eventually making their way to Brighton Beach. The safe house is hidden in a nondescript building, blending seamlessly with the surrounding apartment blocks and small businesses.

The van pulls into an alleyway, the headlights cutting through the darkness as they approach the rear entrance of the building. When they park, Frost steps out first, scanning the area before gesturing for the others to follow.

The safe house is a cramped apartment, its windows covered with thick, dark curtains to block out any prying eyes. The décor is sparse—just the essentials. A couple of worn couches, a table littered with scratches, and a kitchenette that looks like it hasn't been used in years. The air is stale, carrying the faint scent of must and old cigarettes.

As they begin to unpack their gear, the tension in the room starts to ease slightly. The group starts talking in low voices, their conversations punctuated by the rustling of bags and the clinking of weapons being set down.

"Feels like only yesterday since we were last here," Marcus Kane remarks, setting a duffel bag on the floor. "Never thought we'd be back so soon."

"Yeah, last time was a real mess," Mad Dog adds, his voice gruff as he instinctively rubs his arm. "Can't believe we pulled that off."

Raven glances up from her pack. "Wasn't much of a choice. We had to get it done. And we did."

Peter, pretending to focus on his gear, listens intently, piecing together the fragments of their conversation. His heart skips a beat as he realizes they're talking about the last time they were in New York—when Kara was killed and the precinct was attacked.

"Yeah," Jason Simons chimes in. "The only difference this time is no Davey or Ronny."

There's a heavy silence that settles over them as each contemplates their absences. It's Frost who breaks it.

"They should've never got caught going back to the apartment," he says.

"They should never have got caught by the cleaner," Mad Dog adds. "That's where it all went wrong. It forced Davey to shoot the journalist there and then."

Peter's blood runs cold. *Davey. Davey was the one that shot her.* The name burns into his mind like a brand. He now knows exactly who killed Kara. Who pulled the trigger.

But before he can dwell on it, he hears himself asking, almost reflexively, "What happened to him? Davey, I mean."

The room falls silent for a moment, the question hanging in the air like an axe. Frost steps forward, his presence commanding attention. His icy blue eyes fix on Peter, and the room seems to grow colder.

"That's enough," Frost says. "What happened to Davey is none of your concern, Reilly. We've got bigger things to focus on right now."

Peter nods, falling silent as the conversation abruptly shifts. The others take the cue and drop the subject, but Peter's mind is already racing, the pieces of the puzzle beginning to come together. He knows now who killed Kara, but he also knows he has to play it smart. He can't afford to tip his hand, not yet. Not until he knows more.

———

THE NEXT DAY, they begin their initial reconnaissance of the NYSE. The building stands majestic and imposing, a hub of activity as tourists and workers bustle about, unaware of the dangerous plot unfolding right before them—like sheep unaware of the circling wolves. The Brotherhood members merge with the crowds, pretending to be tourists and blue-collar workers.

Peter and Marcus Kane are dressed in reflective vests and blue work jackets bearing the Con Edison logo, each holding a hard hat under their arm. The uniforms allow them to blend in seamlessly as average workers, appearing as two utility employees checking infrastructure layouts while they walk around the building with a map in hand.

Marcus Kane, pointing to the map, says, "We'll start by getting a lay of the land. We need to know every entrance, exit, and guard post."

Peter nods. "Agreed. Let's split up and meet back here in two hours with our observations."

Peter heads to the main entrance, meticulously noting the security checkpoints and the frequency of guard patrols. His eyes catch every detail, from the metal detectors to the guard rotations. He memorizes it all.

Raven, dressed as a tourist, her hair bleached blond, has joined a tour group Wall Street Walks, and is being taken around the interior of the building by a tour guide. She moves through the interior, her focus on the trading floor and key financial offices. She observes the flow of people, the security protocols in place, and the timing of employee movements. Her sharp eyes catch the nuances of the building's daily operations.

Simons, dressed in the brown uniform of a UPS driver, has been tasked with the technological aspects. He discreetly identifies surveillance cameras and potential blind spots, taking note of the security systems, assessing where they might exploit weaknesses or disable the cameras without triggering alarms.

Marcus Kane, outside, examines the exterior of the building. He looks for discreet places to plant explosives without drawing attention. His experienced eye spots structural weaknesses and potential cover spots, creating a mental checklist of his findings.

After several hours, they reconvene at a nearby café, huddling around a table and sharing their findings in hushed tones.

Raven whispers, "The trading floor is heavily patrolled. We'll need to time our movements perfectly if we're going to plant explosives inside."

Marcus Kane adds, "The exterior has some good spots, but we'll need to be quick and discreet."

ON THE SECOND DAY, they gather in the apartment, standing over maps and blueprints of the NYSE. The dank air of the safe house is lit by low wattage bulbs, the curtains all drawn, Brighton Beach no more than a mere hum outside. The maps are marked with notes and observations.

Raven points to one. "We'll plant the explosives here, here, and here. These spots give us the best chance to maximize damage."

Simons nods. "I've identified a few blind spots in the camera coverage. We can use those to our advantage."

It is then that their explosives expert, Daniel Carter, explains his side of the plan.

"We'll place the charges here and here," Carter says, pointing to the blueprint, before taking a detonator and holding it up to the group. "We'll use these detonators—simple, but effective. It'll take some time to wire everything, but it should get the job done."

Peter interjects, "You're using standard detonators?"

"Yeah, what of it?" Carter replies with a hint of irritation.

"Standard detonators are fine, but they're slow to wire and prone to failure if the wiring isn't perfect. I've got a better idea."

Peter picks up a different type of detonator from the table.

Marcus Kane looks curious. "What do you suggest, Reilly?"

Peter holds up the dual-trigger detonator, brought just in case. "These are dual-trigger detonators. They're quicker to set up and have a higher success rate. Plus, they allow for a manual override if needed. We can wire these in half the time and ensure they go off without a hitch."

Carter looks defensive. "I've been doing this for years. My setup works."

Peter remains calm. "No doubt, but time is critical. The Feds are getting smarter and faster. We need every advantage we can get. This setup will save us precious minutes and reduce the risk of a misfire."

Marcus and Frost exchange a glance, considering Peter's suggestion. The tension in the room slowly rises as everyone waits for their decision.

"He's got a point," Frost finally says. "Time is of the essence, and we can't afford any mistakes."

Marcus turns to Peter. "Show us how it's done, Reilly."

Peter steps forward, taking over the setup. He quickly and efficiently wires the dual-trigger detonators, explaining each step as he goes. "These wires connect here, and the manual override goes here. This way, if something goes wrong, we can still detonate the charges remotely."

Jason Simons, watching from a distance, remains skeptical. "And you're sure this is foolproof?"

"As foolproof as it gets," Peter replies confidently. "I've used this setup in the field more times than I can count. It's reliable and quick."

The group watches as Peter completes the setup in record time. Marcus and Frost look impressed, while Carter's irritation is evident as his top lip curls.

"Well done, Reilly," Frost says, patting Peter on the back. "You've just saved us a lot of time."

Carter grudgingly acknowledges Peter's contribution. "Yeah, good job."

Peter nods. "Just doing my part."

TWENTY-FOUR

THE DAY BEFORE THE ATTACK, THE NEW YORK SAFE house buzzes with an anxious energy as Peter approaches Joseph Frost.

"Frost, I think I should do one last sweep of the stock exchange. Make sure there aren't any last-minute changes in security," Peter says confidently. "I mean, I've spent the last two days recording their routines. It'd be bad if there was some sudden change."

Frost agrees. "Good idea, Reilly. But don't take too long. We need everyone sharp for tomorrow."

"I'll be quick."

With Frost's approval, Peter leaves the safe house, the cool air of New York hitting his face as he steps onto the sidewalk. He takes a circuitous route, weaving through crowded streets, blending in with the throngs of people. His eyes dart around, scanning for any sign of being followed. Satisfied that he's in the clear, he heads into a nearby Seven-Eleven.

Inside, the fluorescent lights hum overhead as Peter makes his way to the electronics section. He selects a pay-as-you-go cell phone, cheap and relatively untraceable. He moves to the counter, handing over a few crumpled bills and watching the cashier with a detached calm. As he pockets the phone and receipt, he glances over his shoulder, ensuring that no one from the group is treading on his heels. His movements are deliberate, cautious.

Back outside, Peter blends into the city's rhythm, slipping into the anonymity of the crowd. He makes his way toward the Riegelmann Boardwalk, the vast Atlantic spreading out beyond the beach. The chatter of tourists, the distant sound of a street performer, and the squawking of gulls provide a familiar background noise as he walks, the phone hidden in his jacket pocket.

Getting about a mile away from the safe house, Peter pauses, scanning his surroundings to ensure he still isn't being followed. Satisfied, he pulls out the phone, removes the SIM card from its packaging, and inserts it. His fingers hover over the keypad for a moment before dialing a number from memory.

As the phone rings, Peter continues walking, blending back into the flow of people. When the line clicks open, a familiar voice speaks on the other end.

"Is this secure?" the voice asks.

"As secure as it gets," Peter responds in a low voice. "I've got intel. We're hitting the New York Stock Exchange tomorrow."

"How and when?" Deacon asks.

"We're planting explosives at key points inside and outside the building. They'll detonate during the opening of tomorrow's trading."

"Then we need to move fast."

"I've already got a plan," Peter says. "I convinced the team to use dual-trigger detonators instead of standard. That way, the signal can be blocked. You've got something that can do that, right?"

"I'll shut down every mobile phone tower in NYC if I have to."

"Good. I've written down the bomb locations and the contact number for the trigger. Do you have someone near Brighton Beach?"

"I can have someone there in less than five minutes."

"Perfect. I'm going to stash a notepad with everything on it underneath the trash can opposite the entrance to Nathan's Hotdogs on the Riegelmann Boardwalk."

"I'll get a guy out there ASAP."

As Peter walks, he glances around, always conscious of the possibility of being watched. "Deacon," he continues, "you also need to let us plant the bombs, then set on us as we leave. But you have to let us get out of the area."

"What do you mean?"

"You need to foil the attack but let us escape."

"My buddy in the FBI won't be thrilled about that," Deacon grumbles.

"If we escape, it'll fracture the group. There's no way we'll return to the Brotherhood's hideout in West Virginia. My notes include the hideout's location. Raid it, and you'll scatter us. It'll make it easier for me to split the group and reach the guys supplying them with all this gear—Leadership."

Deacon is silent for a moment, considering. "Okay. Sounds good. I'll get the signal blocked and create a plan to chase you out of there. What's your escape route?"

"We're using the sewers."

"Same as when they hit the precinct," Deacon notes.

"Yeah, but this time we've got a boat waiting at the Hudson River."

"Got it. I'll have a team of bomb disposal experts at the NYSE, undercover as maintenance staff. My FBI contact will have his people in chase mode. Just make sure none of your Brotherhood pals get too heroic and start shooting the place up."

"I'll do my best to get them out of the area as quickly as possible," Peter replies. "And another thing. I found out who pulled the trigger on Kara."

"Who?"

"David Smith. Davey."

"Where's he now?"

"I don't know. Frost got cagey when I asked."

"Alright. I'll run his name through the system, see what I can dig up."

Peter reaches the trash can opposite Nathan's Hotdogs. The boardwalk is quiet this early in the morning, so no one notices as he tips it over and slides the notepad, wrapped in plastic, underneath.

"One more thing," he says into the phone, scanning his surroundings. "Joseph Frost is a type 1 diabetic. I'm pretty sure he gets his insulin from a black market peddler to avoid any medical records."

Deacon muses on the other end. "Interesting. I'll see if I can trace his source."

"Do that," Peter replies. "The notepad is in place. It's got all the bomb locations, the timing for the hit, and when we're set to leave. Don't let your guys in the FBI jump the gun. Let us get clear."

"I will. And Peter?"

"Yeah?"

"Stay safe."

"Always do," Peter says, ending the call.

TWENTY-FIVE

THE MORNING AIR IS CRISP AS THE TEAM GATHERS IN the shadows of Manhattan's towering skyline, the sun just beginning to creep over the horizon. Peter takes a deep breath, steadying himself for the mission ahead. Today is the day.

Frost and Raven are the first to move. Dressed in the plain uniforms of cleaning staff, they approach the New York Stock Exchange with practiced confidence, making their way up the steps and past the stone columns. Their fake IDs pass scrutiny with ease as they are waved through the security checkpoint. Bags checked, nothing suspicious found. They exchange a glance, a silent confirmation that the operation is underway.

Once inside, they make their way to the cleaning cupboards, retrieving their trolleys. A fellow cleaner, oblivious to their true intentions, remarks with a chuckle, "You guys are new, huh?"

Frost gives a nonchalant nod. "Yeah, just filling in."

"Darn agency's always sending new folks," the cleaner adds with a roll of the eyes.

With that, they push their trolleys down the gleaming corridors, making their way to some empty offices on the second floor. The building is still waking up, only a few early risers present. Shutting themselves in a large corner office, they draw the blinds of the internal windows and make their way to the outer windows. Frost and Raven open them wide onto the almost deserted road of New Street that runs along the back of the building.

Outside, Mad Dog Morgan, Peter, and Daniel Carter wait below, bags of explosives in hand. Peter and Mad Dog throw their bags first. Both sail cleanly through the open windows, caught deftly by Frost and Raven. But when Carter tosses his, it clips the edge of the window frame and tumbles back down. Everyone's hearts freezes, the sweat pricking their skin as Carter lunges to catch it before it hits the ground.

"Jesus Christ, Danny," Mad Dog snarls, snatching the bag from him. "Give it here."

With a grunt, Mad Dog throws the last bag himself, sending it perfectly through the window. Frost and Raven catch it smoothly, and the three men below exhale in relief.

While Frost and Raven close the windows and retreat into the building, Mad Dog, Carter, and Peter split up to begin placing the bombs along the outer edges of the building. Each moves with purpose, their actions a choreographed dance of precision and efficiency. As they work, Jason Simons sits in a maintenance van parked nearby, eyes glued to a laptop. He monitors mobile chatter, watches the building's internal cameras, and listens to a police scanner. His voice crackles over their earpieces, a steadying presence in the midst of their operation.

"Keep moving," Simons advises. "No unusual activity on the scanners or cameras... yet."

Inside, Frost and Raven maneuver their way into the trading room. The vast space is still quiet, the first few traders trickling in. While Frost pretends to mop the floor, keeping his eyes out for anyone watching, Raven expertly deposits one bomb under a desk and another in a trash can. More traders arrive, the energy slowly building for the day's activity. Their task complete, they move on, leaving the trading room behind.

They make their way to the third floor via a service elevator, then move along to an empty office next to the server room, the location for the last bomb. This one is critical—it will destroy the NYSE's computer system, sending the financial world into chaos. Raven crouches low, securing the bomb in place while Frost keeps watch.

Outside, Peter, Mad Dog, and Carter finish planting the last of the bombs along the building's perimeter. They signal to Simons, who replies swiftly.

"Bombs are in place. Waiting for your exit before we detonate," Simons informs them.

Frost and Raven slip out of the building through a back exit, meeting up with Peter, Mad Dog, and Carter in the narrow side street of Exchange Place, within the shadows of the scaffolding which covers the southern edge of the building.

Raven is the first to speak. "Well, that went—"

She's cut off by the sudden screech of tires echoing down the street. Four black vans skid to a halt on the corner of Exchange Place and Broad Street. As they stare at them, armed SWAT teams pour out the back doors.

"FBI!" someone shouts, and the alley erupts into pandemonium.

Peter's instincts kick in as the first shots ring out. The team scatters, half of them ducking behind a dumpster, while the others take cover in doorways. Bullets ricochet off the brick walls and the metal scaffolding, the air filling with the rat-a-tat-tat of automatic gunfire.

Peter opens a large duffel bag and pulls out their weapons—M4A1 carbines. He tosses one to each of them, the rifles caught and immediately cocked.

"Bounding overwatch!" Frost barks, his voice cutting through the chaos. "Mad Dog, Carter—lay down fire! Peter, Raven, with me!"

Mad Dog and Carter immediately emerge from their cover and drop to one knee, their rifles barking out rapid, controlled bursts. The sound of gunfire echoes off the brick walls, forcing the SWAT officers to duck behind their vehicles and whatever cover they can find.

Peter, Raven, and Frost sprint down the narrow street, keeping low as bullets ricochet off the ground and walls around them. They reach the end of the alley and dive behind a large dumpster, barely managing to avoid a hail of return fire.

"Now us!" Frost signals.

Raven nods, raising her weapon as Peter and Frost do the same. Together, they unleash a barrage of suppressive fire, their rounds pinging off the SWAT vehicles and forcing the officers to take cover again.

"Move!" Frost yells back at Mad Dog and Carter.

Mad Dog and Carter rise from their positions, sprinting toward the shelter where Peter and the others are hunkered down. The SWAT team struggles to return fire, pinned by the relentless suppression.

As Mad Dog and Carter dive into cover beside them, Frost doesn't waste a second. "Next position! Go, go!"

This time, Peter leads the charge, his legs pumping as he darts across the street to a doorway recessed in the wall. Raven and Frost are right behind him, taking cover just as bullets tear through the air where they'd been moments before.

Mad Dog and Carter once again lay down fire, their shots precise and steady, keeping the SWAT team pinned. The exchange is intense, the air thick with the crack of gunfire and the sharp smell of cordite.

Peter reloads quickly, his hands moving on autopilot before leaning out to provide cover for Mad Dog and Carter. "Go!" he shouts over the din.

Mad Dog and Carter push off from the wall and sprint toward the doorway, narrowly avoiding a burst of gunfire. They crash into the cover, breathing hard but uninjured.

"We're almost there!" Frost shouts. "Final push!"

The team makes one last coordinated move, Peter and Raven

covering Mad Dog, Carter, and Frost as they race toward the van where Simons waits with the back doors wide open.

"Get in, get in!" he yells as they pile into the van, Peter and Raven last, the doors slammed shut behind them.

The SWAT team braces, expecting the van to make a desperate break for it, so they quickly shoot out the rear tires to prevent any escape. But when the van remains eerily still, the engine dead, their tension deepens. Something isn't right.

The team leader signals for a slow, cautious advance. They move in, weapons trained on the vehicle, surrounding it. The van sits ominously, its darkened windows giving nothing away.

"Ellis," the leader speaks into his comms, "use explosives to open it up."

With the rest of the team providing cover, Ellis approaches the van, carefully affixing a small amount of plastic explosive to the rear doors. The charge is set quickly, his movements efficient from countless repetitions in training.

"Clear!" Ellis shouts, retreating to a safe distance. The team hunkers down, eyes fixed on the van as he triggers the detonator.

The explosion is sharp, a controlled blast that rips through the rear doors with a flash of light and a cloud of smoke. The sound echoes down the alley, debris clattering to the ground as the force dissipates. The SWAT team waits a heartbeat, letting the smoke begin to clear before moving in.

Weapons at the ready, they close in on the van, expecting a confrontation. But as the smoke thins, revealing the interior, they find nothing. The van is empty, its rear compartment devoid of any signs of the fugitives.

"Inside, inside!" the leader orders, his frustration mounting. They peer inside the van, scanning every corner.

One of the SWAT members taps his comms. "Van is empty. Repeat, the van is empty."

Another officer, crouching low, notices something unusual. "Sir, down here."

The leader leans in, his eyes narrowing as he spots the source of their escape—a large, round hole in the floor of the van, revealing an open manhole beneath. The van had been strategically parked over it, the perfect cover for a clean getaway.

"They're in the sewer," one of the officers reports, his voice tinged with disbelief. He pauses, awaiting further orders. "Do we follow?"

The response comes back. "Negative. Repeat: do not follow."

The team stands down, frustration and disbelief settling in. The SWAT leader steps back, taking in the scene—the blown-open van, the empty interior, and the clever escape route.

Peter and the others race through the sewers, the stench and darkness engulfing them. Frost leads the way, his mind racing. How had the FBI known?

In a voice dripping with vexation, he orders, "Detonate the bombs."

Simons dials the number on his burner phone. They all expect to feel the ground shake, but nothing happens.

"I said detonate them," Frost says angrily.

"I am," Simons says. "Something's blocking the signal."

"I knew we should've used standard detonators," Carter mutters, casting a suspicious glance at Peter.

With the situation rapidly deteriorating, Peter glances back the way they came. "Forget the bombs! We're being chased. We need to move, now!"

Frost snaps out of his grim thoughts, his eyes locking on to Peter's. The urgency is clear. "He's right. Let's go! We'll regroup later."

The team snaps into action, pushing the failure from their minds. There's no time to dwell on it—they're not out of the woods yet. As they sprint through the labyrinth of tunnels, the darkness swallowing them, the only thought driving them forward is survival.

They eventually emerge at the banks of the Hudson River, where Marcus Kane waits in a powerboat at the end of a jetty. A little relief washes over them as they climb aboard.

"What the hell happened?" Marcus demands as they all settle into the boat.

"They knew we were coming," Frost growls, the fury clear in his voice. He looks back toward the city, anger and betrayal seething within him. "Now get us out of here."

Marcus guns the engine and the boat roars to life, speeding away from Manhattan's looming skyline. Behind them, the city remains eerily silent, unaware of the catastrophe that has just been averted—or of the dark plans still simmering beneath the surface.

TWENTY-SIX

AFTER THEIR NARROW ESCAPE, THE GROUP GOT themselves quickly out of New York. Moving under the radar, they began their journey across the country, using a network of safe houses and contacts to avoid detection.

As they made their way south, traveling by night and sticking to backroads, they received some devastating news: their hideout had been raided. Most of the Iron Brotherhood was now scattered or captured, with many members currently behind bars. Their weapons caches had also been seized, leaving the remnants of the group vulnerable and disarmed.

With their network crumbling and their base now compromised, the team realizes they can no longer rely on their old contacts and resources. They're forced to abandon their plan to regroup back at base, instead disappearing further into the shadows toward Colorado. They move cautiously, knowing that they're now fugitives with a weakened support system.

The last remnants of the Iron Brotherhood finds itself wounded and in hiding on a secluded ranch in Colorado. Nestled deep in the woods and surrounded by the Rockies, the ranch is peaceful and serene, something that doesn't fit with the burning anxiety that grips the group. They now live in constant fear of discovery, always ready to move at a moment's notice.

Inside the ranch, they spend their time watching the news, tracking every development, and planning their next move. The weight of their recent escape lingers, a constant reminder of how close they came to being caught.

Raven, her nerves frayed, says, "We can't stay here forever."

Joseph Frost, ever the steady leader, responds calmly, "We're safe for now. We just need to stay vigilant. We'll move when we have a solid plan."

The group falls silent, the tension almost unbearable, like someone is slowly removing all the oxygen from the room. The peaceful setting outside only heightens the contrast with the turmoil within. Every creak of the floorboards, every rustle of the pine and spruce trees that surround them, puts the group on edge as they await their next move.

Peter watches them carefully, noting the growing paranoia. He knows that their fear of discovery could lead to rash decisions, and his thoughts are already turning to the future, planning how he can stay ahead of the Brotherhood while keeping his true mission intact. The serene ranch may be a temporary haven, but the danger is far from over.

On their second day at the ranch, more bad news comes their way as the group huddles around a small TV in the ranch house, the flickering screen casting a dim light over their tense faces. The news anchor's voice fills the room.

The anchor reports, "The FBI has named Daniel Carter and Jason Simons as suspects in the recent plot to blow up the New York Stock Exchange. Authorities are urging anyone with information on these men to come forward."

Marcus Kane's face hardens with anger. "How did they get your names?"

No one says anything. As for their leader, Joseph Frost glances around the room, meeting each of their eyes before nodding toward a small bedroom down the hall. "I need to make contact with Leadership," he mutters, grabbing the encrypted device from the arm of his chair.

Without waiting for a response, Frost heads into the bedroom, closing the door behind him. The silence in the cabin grows heavier in his absence. Peter, Raven, Mad Dog, Carter, and Simons exchange uneasy glances, the weight of their circumstances pressing down on them.

Minutes tick by, feeling like hours. The murmur of Frost's voice occasionally filters through the door, but none of them can make out what he's saying.

Finally, the door creaks open and Frost steps out. His face is grim, the lines of worry etched deeply into his features. The usual calm determination in his eyes has been replaced with something darker, more uncertain.

Addressing the group, Frost says, "They want Danny and Jason to go into hiding."

"Just like with Davey," Raven points out.

Frost turns to her, an apologetic look on his face. "Yes, just like Davey. And just like Davey, they've been compromised. It makes sense for them to go into hiding."

Raven, visibly upset, speaks up. "But we've heard nothing from Davey since you dropped him off. Nothing."

Frost, trying to soothe her, replies, "Because it's too dangerous for him to contact us. Not when the Feds know his face."

Raven's voice trembles with desperation. "But what's to stop him sending a message so we know he's not dead?"

The word "dead" hangs in the air, creating a somber mood that settles heavily over the group. The silence that follows is thick with unspoken fears, each member grappling with the realization of how isolated and vulnerable they've become.

From the edges, Peter watches them carefully, noting the rising paranoia and the cracks forming in their unity. The release of their names and photos was Peter's idea, included in the notes he left for Deacon. Now he watches as the plan takes hold, the seeds of discontent sowing themselves into the fabric of the group.

THE NEXT MORNING, they gather at the edge of the ranch to say farewell to Daniel Carter and Jason Simons. The atmosphere is heavy with emotion as the pair prepare to leave. Peter watches the scene unfold, taking in the camaraderie and the genuine family vibe among the group.

Joseph Frost hugs Daniel Carter tightly. "Stay safe out there," he says, his voice a little thickened by emotion.

Peter can't help thinking about the file he read on Carter. He'd served multiple tours in the Middle East, only to return home and struggle with PTSD, feeling abandoned by the very government he fought for. The disillusionment is clear in his weary eyes as he prepares to leave.

Once Frost lets Carter go, the latter hugs it out with Marcus, Raven, and Mad Dog. All except Peter, who he gives a curt nod to.

Jason Simons is next, Frost wrapping his arms around him. "Don't worry," Frost tells him. "Leadership will look after you. Just get to the meet, and they'll take care of it."

It's Marcus' turn next. "It'll all be all right," he whispers to him.

Raven and Mad Dog take their turns, and once again, Peter merely receives a nod.

Simons gives a final nod to the group. A graduate of MIT, his tech business was crushed by larger corporations with government ties just after the 2008 crash, and he lost everything. He believes the government favors big business over small entrepreneurs, a belief that pushed him to join the Brotherhood in his quest for justice.

As they depart, the group watches them go, their hearts heavy but resolute. Peter absorbs the moment, understanding more deeply the powerful mix of personal grievances and shared purpose that binds these people together. It's a reminder that, despite their dangerous path, they see themselves as a family, united by their anger and loss.

TWENTY-SEVEN

A WEEK LATER, THE GROUP HAS ADAPTED TO THEIR NEW reality. The ranch isn't linked to the electrical grid, and the running water comes from a well. They have a diesel generator but thus far have kept its use down to a minimum—running it only when they need to use the water pump or in the evenings when they gather around the old television set to catch up on the news.

Too dangerous to run into town for groceries, they live off the land, hunting deer, fishing, and snaring rabbits for food. Peter, who discovered a bow and arrows in the cabin, impresses the group with his hunting skills. The bow's silence is a crucial advantage—no gunshots to echo through the mountains, alerting anyone to their presence.

The cabin is basic, with limited amenities. A wood stove provides heat and serves as their cooking source. The lack of modern conveniences is a constant reminder of how precarious their situation has become, each day a struggle to remain hidden and survive.

They take turns keeping watch, eyes constantly scanning the skies for signs of the authorities. The sound of helicopters overhead has become a continual nuisance, their eyes searching the sky until the chopper fades from view, hoping that its presence is just an innocent coincidence.

Often, Raven accompanies Peter into the forest, her own skill with the bow second only to his. It is during these hunting trips that the pair grow closer. Tracking deer through the dense forest, they are able to gain a brief escape from the pressures of their hidden life, a chance to connect in a way that feels almost normal.

One morning, as they creep over a ridge, they spot a stag grazing by a stream, its coat shimmering in a wedge of golden sunlight that breaks through the canopy above.

The stag is majestic, a rare and beautiful sight in the otherwise harsh environment they've grown accustomed to. The moment feels almost magical, a fleeting interlude of peace in the midst of their tumultuous lives. Peter, his breath steady, slowly draws the bow, eyes locked on the target.

"Easy does it," he whispers as he lines up his shot.

But before he can release the arrow, Raven gently touches his arm. "Wait," she says softly. "Let's just watch him."

Surprised, Peter lowers his bow, and they both lie down side by side on the ridge, watching the stag in silence. The world around them seems to pause, the only sounds the quiet gurgle of the stream and the occasional rustle of leaves as the wind moves through the trees. The stag moves gracefully, oblivious to the two humans observing it, its movements a picture of calm in a world filled with chaos.

"I haven't seen anything so beautiful in a long time," Raven whispers, her voice barely audible over the soft murmur of the stream.

Peter's gaze is fixed on the stag. "Me neither. It's... something special."

Raven turns her head slightly to look at Peter, studying him for a moment before speaking. "It's moments like this that make everything else seem... distant. Like maybe there's still something good left out there."

Peter meets her gaze, the sincerity in her eyes reflecting the same thoughts he's been having. "Yeah," he murmurs. "Sometimes it's easy to forget that."

They continue to watch the stag in silence. In this peaceful interlude, surrounded by the beauty of the natural world, the harshness of their reality fades away, replaced by a quiet understanding and a connection that seems ethereal.

As the stag eventually wanders off into the forest, Peter and Raven remain lying side by side, the moment lingering between them.

Turning onto their backs, they lie on the ground, staring up at the clouds that drift lazily across the sky. Raven breaks the comfortable silence, her voice thoughtful.

"Do you have anyone, Reilly?" she asks, her tone soft, almost hesitant.

Peter glances at her, a moment of uncertainty passing through him. "You mean romantically?"

"Yeah."

Peter sighs, his gaze returning to the sky. "I did."

Raven's curiosity is piqued. "What happened to her?"

Peter pauses, the memory heavy in his mind. "She died."

Raven's voice is filled with sympathy. "How?"

Peter goes to speak, but the words catch in his throat. Before he can answer, Raven quickly interjects, realizing she may have crossed a line. "No. I'm sorry. I shouldn't have asked."

Peter shakes his head slightly, his voice soft but steady. "No, it's okay. She was murdered."

Raven gasps. "Oh God. Did they catch the guy?"

Peter's mind flashes back to a moment he's tried hard to bury —the feel of David Smith's collar in his grip, the fury that burns through him. "Yeah," he says, his voice tight with barely controlled anger. "But he got away."

Raven looks at him with a mix of understanding and sadness. "Is that why you joined? Because your woman was killed and the police let you down."

Peter nods. "Something like that."

There's a moment of shared silence before Peter, curious, asks, "How about you? Were you and David... you know, together?"

Raven thinks for a moment, her expression thoughtful. "Not like a husband and wife. A marriage could never survive this shit. No. But we were close, and we shared a bed. So I guess you could say we were a couple."

Peter watches her, sensing there's more beneath her words. "You miss him?"

Raven is honest, her voice tinged with a mix of emotions. "A little, maybe. But not as much as I thought I would."

Peter's next question is gentle, almost as if he's afraid of the answer. "Where do you think he is?"

Raven's eyes soften, her voice filled with a hope she's not sure she believes in. "Safe. I hope."

They lie in silence for a while longer, the connection between them deepening with each shared word. The clouds drift by above, indifferent to the pain and loss they've each endured. In this quiet moment, surrounded by the peace of the forest, they find a fragile solace in each other's company, a brief respite from the harsh world that awaits them back at the ranch.

TWENTY-EIGHT

PETER AND RAVEN RETURN TO THE CABIN WITH FOUR squirrels they managed to kill. It's far from the venison they had hoped for, but it's something. However, as they approach the cabin, they sense something is wrong. There is a tension in the air that wasn't there earlier, and as they get closer, they hear a commotion inside.

Entering the cabin, they find it in disarray. Mad Dog Morgan and Marcus Kane are standing over Joseph Frost, who is slumped in a chair in the kitchen, pale and sweating profusely. The usually unflappable leader looks weak and vulnerable, a stark contrast to his normal commanding presence.

Peter steps forward, his concern evident. "What's going on?"

Mad Dog answers, "It's Frost. His diabetes is out of control. The insulin injections we got in Illinois must be faulty or no good, because they're not working."

Raven's worry spikes. "What do you mean, not working?"

Marcus, his expression stern, explains, "We got it off our usual guy, but none of it is working. I think we've been scammed. I'm not sure if he'll make it."

Peter realizes that Deacon has worked fast. It took them six days of zig-zagging from New York to reach Illinois, and in that time, Deacon had managed to get to their insulin contact and provide him with the fakes.

He looks at Frost, who's struggling to keep his eyes open, his skin clammy and pale. Without proper medical care, Frost's condition could turn fatal, and the group's already fragile stability could shatter completely.

Peter plans on being the hero.

Raven moves closer to Frost, her face a mix of angst and single-mindedness. "There has to be something we can do," she says. "We can't just let him die."

Marcus Kane, looking defeated, adds, "He could slip into a coma any moment."

"We need to go into town," Mad Dog says. "I spotted a pharmacy when we drove in. But we can't do it during the day."

"But we can't wait until nightfall," Raven urges. "Look at him. He could die any moment."

Peter steps forward. "I'll hike down into town. Get him what he needs from the pharmacy. Steal it if I have to."

Raven doesn't hesitate. "I'll go with you."

Marcus says, "Okay. But be careful. Stealth is the key."

Peter and Raven quickly gather what they need—dark clothing, sturdy boots, a small bag for the insulin. With a final glance back at the cabin, where Frost lies barely conscious, they set off.

After a grueling hike through the rugged terrain, they finally reach the outskirts of the small mountain town of Ouray. The town is quiet, with only a few people milling about, but as they approach the pharmacy, they see that it's filled with customers. Peter scans the area, searching for a way to get what they need without drawing too much attention.

Across from the pharmacy, a department store has set up a large New Year's Eve fireworks stand outside its doors, the bright colors of the display catching Peter's eye. As well as that, whoever is supposed to be manning the counter is absent.

Peter points to the stand, a plan forming in his mind. "Look, the department store has a fireworks stand. We can use that to create a distraction."

Raven follows his gaze and quickly nods. "Let's do it."

They move quickly, crossing the street and approaching the stand. The area around it is deserted, and the boxes of fireworks are stacked high, ready to be sold for the upcoming holidays. Peter grabs a handful of the fireworks, setting them up in a cluster, while Raven takes out a lighter.

She hands it to Peter, her eyes scanning the street to ensure they're not being watched. "Here, light it all up."

Peter takes the lighter and ignites the fuses. The fireworks sizzle to life, the crackling sound growing louder as they prepare to launch. He then tosses them in a box filled with more fireworks.

Peter and Raven quickly move back, taking cover behind a parked panel van.

Seconds later, the fireworks explode into the sky, bright colors bursting overhead with loud bangs and whistles, turning the store front into a mess of explosions and color. The sudden commotion grabs the attention of everyone in the area, including the customers and staff inside the pharmacy. People rush outside to see what's happening, their curiosity piqued by the unexpected display.

With the street now filled with onlookers, Peter and Raven slip into the pharmacy unnoticed, the distraction working perfectly. Inside, Peter quickly locates the pharmacy refrigerator, tugs open the door, and scans the shelves for the insulin they need. Raven watches from the doorway, her heart pounding as the noise from the fireworks fills the air. She gazes at the crowd, which is still distracted by the display, the staff from the store trying their best to put it out. "Hurry, Jack," she urges, her voice just above a whisper.

As Peter finishes collecting the insulin, his eyes catch sight of a small display of pay-as-you-go cellphones near the counter. Without a second thought, and making sure Raven is still focused on the street, he quickly snatches one and slips it into his pocket, keeping the action as discreet as possible.

"Got it," he says, rejoining Raven at the door. "Let's go."

They exit the pharmacy as quietly as they entered, the bag of insulin safely tucked out of sight. As they move steadily away, the sound of fireworks continues to reverberate in the distance, the chaos masking their escape. Heading back toward the safety of the forest, they carry with them the hope of saving Frost.

———

Just over an hour later, they arrive back at the cabin, hearts pounding and lungs burning from the grueling hike. However, the urgency that had driven them forward fades into a chilling stillness as they step inside. A gloomy quiet hangs over the living room.

Peter rushes to Frost's side, but one look at his pale, lifeless face tells him everything he needs to know. Frost's body lies slumped in the chair, his breathing stopped, the signs of life gone. The bag of insulin in Peter's hand feels heavy, useless now. Mad Dog and Marcus stand with their backs to them, staring out of the window at the mountains. When they turn, their faces are filled with shock and sorrow.

Raven's voice trembles as she speaks. "We're too late."

Peter slowly places the bag of insulin on the table, his heart sinking with the realization. They were so close—just minutes away from saving Frost's life—but those minutes had been the difference between life and death. The journey, the risk, the hope they had clung to—it had all been in vain. Peter doesn't get to be the hero. Not today.

Marcus Kane, his voice thick with emotion, breaks the silence. "He's gone," he says. The finality of the words hang in the cold air of the room.

Mad Dog stands by, his fists clenched, anger and grief warring in his eyes. "We should have gotten better insulin. That fuck sold us poison."

Raven goes over to him, placing a hand on Mad Dog's arm, her voice soft but filled with sorrow. "We couldn't have known."

Mad Dog nods, but the weight of failure and the death of their leader presses down on him. Joseph Frost, the man who led them through so much, is gone, and with him, a part of the group's strength and resolve.

In the quiet of the cabin, they all realize that the road ahead has just become much darker.

TWENTY-NINE

THE GROUP MOVES IN SOLEMN SILENCE THROUGH THE
dense woods, grief-stricken and somber-faced. The early morning
light seeps weakly through the trees, casting long, jagged shadows
across the forest floor. Frost's cloth-wrapped body lies on a
makeshift stretcher, carried upon the shoulders of Marcus Kane,
Mad Dog, Peter, and Raven. The air is cold, the chill matching the
sorrow that grips them all.

After what feels like an eternity, they reach a small clearing
where they have prepared a pyre of logs and sticks. It's a secluded
spot, far enough from the ranch to ensure they won't be discovered but close enough to serve as a final resting place for the man
who led them through so much.

With careful, reverent movements, they place Frost's body on
the pyre. The silence is deafening, only broken by the rustle of
leaves and the occasional birdcall. Each of them takes a moment
to gather their thoughts, knowing this is their last chance to say
goodbye.

Marcus Kane steps forward first, his face hard but his voice
soft. "Joe Frost was more than just a leader. He was a brother. A
man who never backed down, never gave up. He taught me what
it means to fight for something bigger than myself." His voice

cracks slightly, but he presses on. "We wouldn't be here without him, and we owe it to him to keep going. No matter how hard it gets."

Mad Dog nods, stepping up beside Marcus. "Frost was a tough bastard," he says, his voice rough with emotion. "He could get under your skin, but he did it because he cared. Because he wanted us to be strong. We're gonna miss him, but we'll make sure his fight doesn't end here."

Raven approaches next, her eyes glistening with unshed tears. She looks down at Frost's body, then back at the group. "Joe believed in us," she says softly. "Even when we didn't believe in ourselves. He saw something in each of us worth fighting for. I won't forget that. And I won't forget him."

Peter stands slightly apart from the others, his thoughts racing as he listens to their words. He only knew Frost for a short while, but in that time, he had come to understand the strength and resolve that bound this group together.

The group stands in silence for a moment longer, then Marcus speaks again, his voice firm. "We're going to carry on. For Frost and for ourselves. We don't need a leader to keep fighting. We have each other, and that's enough."

Lighting the torch he holds, he steps forward, the flames flickering in the crisp morning air. He lowers it to the pyre, setting the dry wood ablaze. The fire catches quickly, the flames consuming the logs and sticks, and soon, Frost's body is engulfed in the bright, crackling heat.

As the flames rise, Raven moves closer to Peter, seeking comfort in his presence. She wraps her arms around him, leaning into his side, and he puts an arm around her in return. They stand together, watching the fire, the warmth of the flames making the cold emptiness left by Frost's death even worse.

THIRTY

NEXT MORNING, PETER SETS OUT INTO THE FOREST alone, his bow slung over his shoulder. Fall is slowly turning to winter, the frost-laden leaves crunching underfoot, the early morning mist still clinging to the underbrush. Raven is back at the cabin, occupied with other chores, giving Peter the solitude he needs.

He makes his way deeper into the woods, his footsteps soft on the hard ground. Only the birds make any sound. After a while, he reaches a familiar landmark—a stack of rocks beside a large, gnarled tree. Peter stops, glancing around to ensure he's alone, then kneels by the rocks.

Carefully, he begins to unearth the hidden item within. He moves the rocks aside until he reveals the phone he took from the pharmacy, wrapped securely in plastic. He had hidden it here the other day while out with Raven.

With the phone in hand, Peter stands and takes a few steps away from the tree, finding a spot with a clear signal. His heart beats a little faster as he unwraps the plastic and dials Mark Deacon's number, the familiar digits coming easily to him. He waits, each ring thrumming gently like a heartbeat in the quiet of the forest.

Finally, the line clicks, and Deacon's voice comes through, steady and businesslike. "Reilly, what's your status?"

Peter keeps his voice low, glancing around as he speaks. "Joseph Frost is dead."

There's a pause, then Deacon's tone shifts, intrigued. "How?"

"You really have to ask?" Peter puts to him. "*We* killed him when you replaced his insulin with sugar water."

"I sense that upsets you."

"It does. I could have gotten to Leadership with Frost still alive."

"You feel bad for him dying?"

"I do."

Deacon's response is devoid of emotion. "Joseph Frost was responsible for dozens of deaths. He was planning on making that thousands. If we have to kill our way to the top, then so be it. These people are the enemy, Peter."

Peter's voice tightens, his anger barely controlled. "No. They're not. They're just misguided blue-collar guys. Guys who used to be proud of this country before it took everything they had from them."

Deacon's tone turns icy. "You're starting to sound like one of them. Don't be going all Stockholm on me. Don't forget what they did to Kara."

The name echoes through Peter's skull for a moment. A prickling sensation crawls up his spine, and he instinctively snaps his gaze toward the forest. There, shrouded in the mist between the trees, Kara stands, her eyes fixed on him, a bullet hole marring her cheek.

Deacon's voice crackles through the phone, bringing him back. "Look, I'm sorry about Frost, but these things happen in a conflict. And believe me, that's what we're in. Now, tell me, are you any closer to getting that encrypted communication device they use to talk to Leadership?"

Peter exhales, frustration creeping into his voice. "It's difficult. Like Frost, Marcus keeps it close."

Deacon's voice takes on a calculating edge. "You have to get it."

"But how?"

"Things get lost when people have to move. Maybe the next time you all move out, the same could happen to the device."

"I'll try."

"You do that. Because if you can get that thing to me and Kirsty, then we can break into it, maybe find a way to uncovering who exactly Leadership are—find out who's pulling everyone's strings. Now what about any links with Grand Junction?"

"Negative on that. There's been—"

Suddenly, the sharp sound of a twig breaking nearby explodes in Peter's head, cutting through his speech like a gunshot. His heart skips a beat, adrenaline flooding his system. Without hesitation, he ends the call abruptly, stuffing the phone into his pocket.

The forest around him is eerily silent, the usual background noise of rustling leaves and distant birdsong absent. Peter's senses are on high alert, every nerve in his body tingling with primal instinct. He stands still for a moment, listening, eyes scanning the thick, frost-ridden trees for any sign of movement.

The forest, once a place of solitude and refuge, now feels menacing, every sound amplified in his heightened state of awareness, the mist now cloaking a thousand enemies. Peter moves quickly but quietly, making his way back to the cabin. He constantly looks over his shoulder, half-expecting to see someone emerge from the trees.

"Probably just be an animal..." he mutters to himself, though the words do little to ease his nerves. "Either that or someone's on to me."

THIRTY-ONE

LATER IN THE EVENING, YOU CAN PRACTICALLY CHEW the tension in the cabin as the Iron Brotherhood gathers around Marcus Kane. Everyone is on edge, waiting for Marcus to reveal their next mission. Peter stands slightly apart, his eyes subtly fixed on the encrypted communication device in Marcus's hands, trying to figure how he'll get it to Deacon. But even as he tries to focus, his mind keeps drifting back to the woods—the sound of that twig snapping. Who was it? Was it just an animal, or has one of them seen him on the phone? The uncertainty gnaws at him, feeding his growing paranoia.

Marcus Kane finally speaks, his voice serious. "Leadership has been in touch. We've got our next mission. It's an extraction."

Raven asks, "Who's the target?"

Marcus's expression darkens as he replies, "A former Russian oligarch living in hiding in the United States. He's a billionaire, living in a mansion in Beverly Hills, surrounded by his own private security force."

Mad Dog asks, "What's the target's name?"

Marcus's voice is steady as he replies, "Yuri Petrov."

Boom! It's as if a bomb explodes in Peter's head. *Petrov.* The name on the tape. The connection he's been searching for, suddenly laid out in front of him. The implications are staggering—Petrov is more than just a target; he's the key to everything. But what if Marcus or Raven were on to him? The thought crashes through his head, erasing any sense of achievement. Did they follow him back to the cabin? Will he even get as far as Petrov before they turn on him?

Marcus's voice breaks through Peter's spiraling thoughts. "Leadership claims that he's only going to be in LA for another three days. After that, he'll be moving. So we need to pack up and move out right now."

———

In less than an hour, the group leaves the cabin, moving swiftly and silently into the woods. They hike for two hours, the forest around them growing darker as they push forward. Their destination is a tarp-covered SUV hidden deep in the trees, a vehicle they had stashed for just such an occasion.

When they reach it, they quickly uncover the SUV and load their gear inside. The engine roars to life, and Marcus Kane takes the wheel. After twenty minutes of bumping along an uneven dirt track, they hit a winding mountain road. Instead of the main ones, they stick to back roads, avoiding major highways to stay off the radar. The landscape shifts around them. As they drive from the rugged, pine-covered mountains of Colorado, the scenery gradually transforms into the arid, sun-baked deserts of the Southwest before eventually giving way to the golden rolling hills and vibrant coastal valleys of California some seventeen hours later.

Approaching Los Angeles, the landscape becomes increasingly urban, and soon they are driving into a suburb on the edge of the eastern part of the city. The neighborhood they enter feels like a forgotten relic of a better time. Rows of foreclosed homes line the cracked streets, their windows dark and lifeless. Most of the houses stand empty; some have never been occupied, their front doors boarded up or hanging ajar, signs of neglect and abandonment.

The lawns, once meticulously manicured, are now wild with overgrown weeds, creeping up the walls and spilling onto the sidewalks. Rusted mailboxes lean precariously, their flags permanently down, as if surrendering to the decay around them.

They park the SUV and quickly move into one of the ghost houses. The inside is sparse but functional, a temporary shelter in the midst of enemy territory. The group begins unpacking their gear, their minds already on the mission ahead.

But as Marcus Kane reaches into his bag, his hand comes up empty. His eyes widen, and panic flashes across his face. "Where the hell is it?" he mutters under his breath.

He tears through his bag, throwing gear aside in a frantic search. His voice rises, sharp with fear. "Where the hell is the device?"

The others freeze, the tension spiking as they realize the gravity of the situation. Marcus's eyes dart around the room, landing on each of them in turn. "Check your bags! Now!"

Raven and Peter immediately start rummaging through their gear, the urgency of the situation clear in their movements. Mad Dog scowls but does as he's told, ripping open his duffel and tossing its contents onto the floor.

Marcus's panic escalates as each of them comes up empty-handed. "It's not here! It has to be here!"

Mad Dog straightens up, his face a mask of irritation. "Maybe you left it in the SUV."

Marcus points to the door, his voice cracking with anxiety. "Go check! Now!"

Mad Dog grumbles but heads out to the SUV, moving quickly despite his frustration. Marcus resumes his frantic search, muttering to himself, his hands shaking as he tears through his gear.

Raven glances at Peter. "It's got to be somewhere, right?"

Peter, his mind racing with the implications, tries to remain calm. "Maybe it slipped out during the hike."

Marcus turns on him angry-faced. "Don't say that."

Mad Dog returns, his expression foreboding. "Nothing in the SUV. It's not there."

Marcus stops dead in his tracks, the realization hitting him like a punch to the gut. "No... No, no, no! This can't be happening!"

He looks around at the group, his face pale with fear. "Leadership will kill us if they find out we lost it!"

THIRTY-TWO

OVER THE NEXT FEW DAYS, THE GROUP SETS UP A meticulous surveillance operation on the mansion in Beverly Hills where their target, Yuri Petrov, is hiding. The mansion is a fortress of opulence, perched high in the hills, surrounded by high walls and state-of-the-art security systems. The group uses the natural elevation of the surrounding hills to their advantage, setting up positions that give them a clear view of the property without risking detection.

The operation runs like clockwork, with each member taking turns on shift, binoculars and long-range cameras in hand. From their hidden vantage points, they watch the mansion like hawks, noting every detail, every movement. Petrov lives like a king, constantly surrounded by a bevy of beautiful women and a small army of bodyguards, all heavily armed and alert.

Marcus Kane watches through the binoculars, his tone serious. "The place is full of little nooks and crannies. Small rooms and tight passageways. A firefight will be tricky. We'll need to hit them hard and fast."

Peter, thoughtful as he studies the scene through his own set of binoculars, nods in agreement. "We'll need to time this perfectly. One mistake and we're done."

Even as he speaks, however, Peter's mind is elsewhere, gnawed by a constant, creeping paranoia. The snapped twig back in Colorado still plays on his mind. The sound had been too close, too deliberate. Did someone see him with the phone? Is it possible that someone in the group is on to him? The thought nags at him, an itch he can't scratch, and he finds himself constantly looking over his shoulder, especially at Marcus Kane, whose own paranoia has been growing since the loss of the encrypted communication device.

During this time, the stress of the mission begins to push Peter and Raven closer together. The long hours spent on surveillance duty, the tension of being on constant alert, and the high stakes of their mission all contribute to the bond that forms between them. They find solace in each other's company, a brief respite from the pressure building all around them.

As the sun dips below the horizon, casting long shadows across the sprawling estate, Peter and Raven lie prone in the bushes on a ridge overlooking Petrov's mansion. The foliage offers just enough cover to keep them concealed, while still providing a clear view of the opulent fortress below. Peter peers through his binoculars, adjusting the focus as he scans the property.

"He's got a couple more guards posted at the back entrance now," Peter mutters, making a quick note in the small notepad he's carrying. "Seems like they're tightening security even more as night falls."

Raven shifts slightly beside him, her own binoculars trained on the mansion. "It's almost like they know we're watching."

"Maybe," Peter replies. "It's probably more that he's just paranoid."

"He should be," Raven adds.

They lapse into silence, the only sounds around them the distant hum of the sleepless city. Peter finds comfort in these moments, the quiet before the inevitable storm. He glances at Raven, her face partially illuminated by the soft glow of the setting sun.

"Can I ask you something?" she says suddenly, breaking the silence. Her voice is soft, almost hesitant.

"Fire away," Peter says.

"What do you want to do when all of this is over? Assuming we get out of here alive."

Peter considers the question, the future feeling like a distant, unattainable thing. "I've thought about it," he lies, lowering his binoculars for a moment. He's playing the part of Jack Reilly. "Sometimes I think I'd like to disappear somewhere quiet, away from all of this. Maybe live by the sea. But... I'm not sure I'll ever get that chance."

Raven smiles faintly, though there's a hint of sadness in her brown eyes. "I used to dream about something like that too. A little cabin in the mountains, where no one could find me. A place to start over."

Raven shifts her position slightly, her gaze still fixed on the mansion.

"Do you ever fear dying?" she asks, her voice quieter now, as if the question itself is a fragile thing.

Peter's grip tightens on the binoculars. "I do," he says, his voice low. "But I'd rather die doing something I believe in than live with regrets. What about you?"

Raven is silent for a moment, as if weighing her own thoughts. "I think about it sometimes," she admits. "But what scares me more is the idea of dying for nothing—of all this being for nothing."

Peter nods, understanding the sentiment.

Raven suddenly shifts the conversation, her voice soft but with an edge of vulnerability. "David, my ex... he has this fear of drowning. His father was a commercial fisherman and drowned at sea when David was a kid. It messed him up. He'd have these nightmares, waking up in a cold sweat, convinced that he'd meet the same fate."

Peter listens, making a mental note for if he ever happens to get to David Smith, the man who murdered Kara. "That must have been hard on him."

"It was," she says. "He could never shake it, no matter how hard he tried. It was like this shadow that followed him everywhere."

Peter studies her face, the shadows of dusk softening her features. He shifts his position slightly, turning to face her more fully, his eyes searching hers. "Raven," he begins, his voice low, almost a whisper, "we've both lost a lot... but maybe, just maybe, we don't have to lose everything."

She meets his gaze, her expression softening. For a moment, neither of them moves, the weight of what's unspoken hanging in the air. Then, almost as if drawn by an invisible force, Peter leans in, closing the small distance between them. His hand brushes against hers, and she turns fully toward him, her eyes locking on to his. The world around them fades, the mansion, the mission, the danger—all of it slips away as Peter cups the side of her face gently. He hesitates for just a second, searching her eyes for any sign of doubt. But there is none. Raven leans in, her breath mingling with his as they close the final gap.

Their lips meet, and for a brief, perfect moment, the chaos of their lives is silenced. The kiss is tender, yet filled with the unspoken fears and hopes they both carry.

When they finally pull back, their foreheads rest against each other, both of them breathing a little heavier, but calmer somehow. Peter looks into her big brown eyes, the warmth of the moment still lingering between them.

"Whatever happens," he says softly, "we'll get through this together."

Raven nods, a small, genuine smile tugging at her lips. "Together," she echoes, her voice steady despite everything.

———

THE GREYHOUND STATION is a short walk away from the lot of foreclosed houses they're hiding in. The closer Peter gets, the faster his pulse races. He's supposed to be getting food from the local store, but he has a more urgent mission to accomplish first.

Once inside the station, Peter moves quickly but carefully, scanning his surroundings to ensure no one is watching him too closely. He finds a row of storage lockers tucked away in a corner. He slips the encrypted device into one of them, feeling a surge of relief as he locks it up. But there's no time to dwell on it—he heads straight to the mailing kiosk inside the station, where he prepares an envelope and mails the locker key to the local CIA station—to Mark Deacon.

The act of sealing the envelope feels like closing a chapter, but Peter knows it's only the beginning. With the deed done, he allows himself a brief moment to breathe, feeling some of the crushing weight lift from his shoulders.

But he knows better than to let his guard down. He's still in the lion's den, and the mission is still looming.

THIRTY-THREE

Mark Deacon steps out of his car, crosses the street, and walks into the air-conditioned Greyhound bus terminal. The atmosphere is gritty, the late-night travelers weary as they wait for their buses in a space that feels almost frozen in time.

Deacon walks briskly to the row of storage lockers near the back of the station. His steps resonate softly in the quiet terminal, the hum of fluorescent lights overhead adding to the surreal stillness. Deacon finds the locker number he's after, his heartbeat steady as he pulls the key from his pocket.

The key slides into the lock with a soft click, and the door swings open. Inside, just as Peter had promised, is the encrypted device, nestled in a black plastic bag. Deacon retrieves it quickly, his hands steady, before closing the locker door with a quiet thud. He spares a glance around the terminal, ensuring that no one is paying attention to him, then turns and walks back the way he came, his pace unhurried but deliberate.

As he exits the terminal, the cool December night air hits him. He heads back to his car, parked a short distance away under a flickering streetlamp.

Deacon opens the driver's door and slides into the seat. Beside him, Kirsty Lange sits in the passenger seat, her sharp eyes immediately focusing on the device as he hands it to her.

"You think you can break into it?" Deacon asks as he starts the car.

Kirsty gazes down at the device, her fingers already moving to examine it with a practiced touch. "I can try," she replies.

Deacon goes to start the car when his phone buzzes in his pocket. He glances at Kirsty, who is already engrossed in examining the encrypted device, then pulls it out. The caller ID shows Director Sandy McLean, and his jaw tightens for a moment before he answers.

"Director McLean," Deacon says, forcing a casual tone.

"Deacon." McLean's voice is crisp, all business. "What's the status of the operation? Any updates?"

Deacon's mind races, quickly crafting a response. "Everything's proceeding as planned, ma'am. We're making progress, but it's slow going. You know how these things are."

There's a pause on the other end, a silence that feels weighted. "And Peter Black? Where is he in all this?"

"Peter's still on compassionate leave, ma'am," Deacon replies smoothly. "I still thinks he's not over Kara Tate's death. He needs more time to recover. It's been rough on him."

"I see," McLean responds, her tone slightly skeptical. "Hasn't he had enough time by now? We need every capable hand on deck, Deacon. Especially with the situation escalating."

"I'll bring him back in," Deacon promises. "Maybe put him on a desk somewhere. Keep him busy but out of harm's way."

"Good," McLean says, her voice softening just a fraction. "The last thing I want is him seeking revenge. We can't afford any loose cannons, especially not now."

Deacon murmurs his agreement, and the call ends with the usual formalities. As he puts his phone away, he notices Kirsty watching him, a frown creasing her brow.

"Why doesn't Director McLean know that Peter's already undercover?" Kirsty asks, her voice low but insistent.

Deacon shifts in his seat, his eyes fixed on the road ahead. "She wouldn't approve it," he says after a moment. "Using a man like Peter on home soil... it's too risky in her eyes. And with 'Leadership' and everything else lurking around, I'd rather keep my cards close to my chest."

"Even with McLean?" Kirsty presses, her skepticism clear.

"It's not just McLean," Deacon replies, his voice taking on a more guarded edge. "It's all those politicians she reports to. I don't know who to trust anymore. And neither should you."

THIRTY-FOUR

PETER, RAVEN, MAD DOG, AND MARCUS KANE ARE clad head to toe in black tactical gear, the night air cool against the fabric of their body armor. Each of them carries a Beretta M9 holstered at their sides, an M4A1 carbine slung across their chests, and smoke grenades strapped to their vests. Their faces are hidden behind black balaclavas, and night vision goggles rest on their helmets, the ocular lenses currently flipped up as they move silently through the shadows toward the perimeter of Petrov's place.

The mansion looms ahead, its luxury now a target rather than a symbol of wealth. The group moves into position, ready to execute the plan that's been days in the making. Tonight, they will extract Yuri Petrov.

Peter and Raven break off from the group, moving swiftly but quietly toward the building's power junction. The junction is concealed behind a utility shed at the edge of the grounds. Unlike the rest of the property, it isn't covered by cameras.

Mad Dog and Marcus wait in the shadows, their breath held, while Peter and Raven prepare to plunge the mansion into power-less darkness.

Peter crouches down beside the junction box, his body tense

as he waits for the cover of a passing car. When the vehicle finally approaches, its speakers blaring loud music through open windows, he seizes the moment. The noise of the car masks the sound of metal on metal as Peter wedges a crowbar into the seam of the box's locked doors and pries them open with a quick wrench.

With the doors hanging ajar, Peter swiftly removes a compact set of tools from his pouch. He selects a wire cutter and a small, flathead screwdriver. Every second counts. As he works, Raven stands nearby, her M4A1 held steady, eyes sweeping the perimeter.

The mansion looms behind them, its opulent interior visible through the floor-to-ceiling windows that stretch along much of this side. Inside, figures move about, unaware of the shadows outside working under the cover of darkness.

Peter quickly identifies the power line of the mansion's security systems. With a swift motion, he cuts through the wire, the sound barely more than a faint snip in the quiet night. All the little blinking red lights on the cameras go out—the eyes are blind. He then uses the screwdriver to sever the backup line, ensuring there will be no emergency power kicking in. Finally, he cuts the main power, plunging the mansion into darkness. The exterior footlights flicker and die, and inside, the glow from the windows snuffs out, leaving the grand structure as nothing more than a dark silhouette against the sparkling star-lights of Beverley Hills.

Peter straightens. "Power's down."

Raven nods. "Everyone, get into position. Over," she murmurs into her comms.

At her command, the group synchronizes their movements, snapping down the ocular lenses of their night vision goggles. The world around them shifts into shades of green, every detail illuminated in the artificial light of their NVGs.

"Phase two commence. Over," Marcus Kane whispers.

In perfect harmony with one another, the four of them begin launching a barrage of smoke bombs and flash grenades through the large glass windows of the mansion. The grenades crash through the elegant panes, shattering the night with the sound of breaking glass.

Petrov's luxury mansion is transformed into a war zone. Thick clouds of acrid smoke billow through the rooms, swirling around the ornate furniture and priceless art. The flash grenades detonate, filling the mansion with bursts of blinding light that bounce off the walls, disorienting anyone caught in their glare. The chaos is immediate and overwhelming. The once-calm and controlled environment has turned into a maelstrom of noise, light, and confusion.

Marcus Kane's voice cuts through the disarray, barking orders over the comms. "Go, go, go!"

Mad Dog's face lights up with a manic grin, adrenaline pumping through his veins. "Time to have some fun," he growls.

Two security guards, coughing and spluttering from the thick smoke, stumble out into the garden. Mad Dog doesn't hesitate. He squeezes the trigger twice of his carbine, the gun kicking back against his shoulder as the shots ring out in the night. One, two— the guards drop to the ground, their bodies collapsing into the grass before they even realize what hit them.

Inside the mansion, the remaining security team regroups, their training kicking in. They rush to a cabinet at the end of a corridor, rip it open, and begin pulling out gas masks. Each man grabs one and hurriedly fits it over his face, the rubbery material muffling their shouts as they pass masks to one another.

Their charge, Yuri Petrov, stands at the center, his eyes wide with fear. One of the guards thrusts a mask into his hands, and Petrov wastes no time in putting it on. The rubber hides the terror on his face, but his eyes dart around wildly behind the glass.

The security team braces themselves as they form a protective circle around Petrov. They are trained for this, and they will fight to protect their charge. The air is thick with smoke and tension as they prepare for the inevitable confrontation. The battle has begun.

The four attackers split up as they move toward the mansion. Peter creeps along the outer wall, heading toward a side entrance. Mad Dog slips through a window at the rear, his boots crunching on the broken glass. Marcus Kane enters through a service door on a lower floor, his eyes studying every corner, every shadow. Raven remains outside, her gaze sharp and unwavering as she watches for any sign of Petrov trying to slip past them.

Petrov and his men are at the back of the mansion. Closing in on their position, Peter slows, catching a glimpse of the bodyguards through the narrow crack of a partially open door. They are stationed at the end of a corridor, clustered around a doorway. Peter's instincts tell him that Petrov is just beyond it.

Mad Dog and Marcus converge on his location. Without a word, Peter signals them with hand movements. Mad Dog and Marcus nod, moving into flanking positions. Then, with everyone in place, Peter pushes the door open a little wider, takes a flash-bang from his vest, pulls the pin, and lobs it down the hallway. It clatters against the hardwood floor, skidding to a stop at the edge of the men.

The grenade explodes with a deafening burst of light and sound. The corridor is instantly filled with blinding white light, the flash flooding the bodyguards' vision.

Inside the room, Petrov sits on a bed, shaking uncontrollably, his gasps reverberating in the tight confines of the mask.

The guards barely have time to react. The moment the flash-bang goes off, the team moves in. Peter sweeps in low, his carbine steady as he fires off controlled bursts, dropping the first guard before he can raise his weapon. Mad Dog is on the second guard in an instant, his trigger finger a blur as he takes him down with precise shots. Before the last guy can react, Marcus takes him out, a single round to the chest sending the man to the floor.

With the bodyguards neutralized, the mansion falls eerily silent except for the sound of Petrov's labored breathing. Peter steps into the bedroom, his weapon trained on the oligarch, who is now hyperventilating on the bed, his eyes wide with terror behind the mask.

"Don't move," Peter commands.

He doesn't need to say it. Petrov is already frozen. Peter steps closer with the smooth, efficient movements of a seasoned predator. He reaches into his pocket and pulls out a set of zip-ties. "Stand up," he orders, and Petrov shakily complies, his knees nearly buckling under him.

Peter spins him around, securing his wrists behind his back with the zip-ties.

The initial assault has gone smoothly; the guards are down, and Petrov is in their custody. But just as Peter finishes securing the ties, the sound of screeching tires cuts through the air outside. Mad Dog, stationed by a window, quickly glances out, and his expression darkens. Two vans have skidded to a halt outside the mansion, and armed men are pouring out.

Mad Dog's grin fades. "More are coming!" he shouts. "Get ready!"

Outside, Raven's heart quickens as she spots the armed men running across the yard, each of them wearing night vision goggles. She takes a deep breath, her rifle steady as she picks her targets. The first guard falls with a single shot to the chest, crumpling to the ground before he even knows what hit him. The second follows a split second later, Raven's aim deadly precise.

But as she adjusts her position, the remaining guards, having spotted her muzzle flash, open fire, forcing her to dive behind a low stone wall at the edge of a swimming pool. Bullets tear into the wall, sending chips of stone flying. She grits her teeth, pressing herself flat against the ground as the sound of gunfire explodes in her ears.

Inside the mansion, there's no time to waste. Peter tightens his grip on Petrov, forcing the oligarch to move quickly as Mad Dog and Marcus provide cover.

"We need to get out of here now!" Peter hisses, guiding Petrov toward the rear exit.

They move swiftly, but they can hear the guards entering the building behind them, their boots pounding against the polished flooring as they storm inside. The tension winds itself around them like barbed wire, tightening by the second.

As they reach the back of the mansion, Peter glances over his shoulder. The guards are right there, their shouts resonating through the hallways.

"There!" one of them shouts, pointing at them.

"Mad Dog, cover our rear!" Marcus orders.

Mad Dog whips around to face the corridor. "Come on!" he cries as he charges forward, his M4A1 barking out rounds, eyes lit up with adrenaline.

Behind him, Peter, Marcus, and Petrov reach the base of a staircase, its polished marble steps disappearing upward to the mansion's upper level. Peter knows they have to move fast—the reinforcements are closing in, and the only viable escape route is through the upper floor and out the back.

"Upstairs, now!" Peter orders, giving Petrov a rough shove toward the staircase.

Behind them, Mad Dog holds his ground, his M4A1 roaring as he lays down suppressive fire. The men at the end of the corridor hesitate, caught off guard by the ferocity of Mad Dog's onslaught. But as Mad Dog prepares to move back up the stairs with the others, a door to his right creaks open.

Before he can swing his gun around, a guard emerges from the room, weapon already drawn. The man had flanked him, slipping around the building's edge and climbing through a broken window to outmaneuver Mad Dog. A gunshot cracks through the corridor, sharp and sudden. Mad Dog stumbles, a crimson stain blossoming across his side as the bullet tears through a gap in his body armor. The pain is immediate and searing, but he grits his teeth, refusing to go down without a fight.

With a surge of adrenaline, Mad Dog manages to lift the carbine and squeezes the trigger. His shots are true, striking the guard square in the chin, the bullets ripping through his face. The man drops instantly.

From the top of the stairs, Marcus hears the shots and whirls around, eyes wide with shock. "Mad Dog!" he cries, starting back down to help.

Peter grabs him by the arm. "We can't!" he tells him sharply. "We have to keep moving!"

Marcus hesitates, torn between loyalty and survival but knowing the mission is more important. He nods, his face hardening as he turns back to continue up the stairs.

Mad Dog drops to one knee, his breathing painful as his lungs fill up with blood. He can see the remaining guards charging toward him. There's no way out, and he knows it. But if he's going down, he's taking as many of them with him as he can.

With a grim smile, Mad Dog reaches into his vest and pulls out a flag grenade. His vision blurs as he pulls the pin, the metal ring falling to the floor with a faint clatter. The guards freeze, their eyes widening in horror as they realize what's about to happen.

One of them manages to shout, "Grena—!" before the explosion tears through the corridor, a deafening roar that shakes the walls and sends debris flying in every direction. The blast consumes everything in its path, the shockwave rattling the entire mansion.

From the top of the stairs, Peter and Marcus feel the tremor beneath their feet. But there's no time to grieve. Peter tightens his grip on Petrov and pulls him forward, driving them toward the rear exit. Mad Dog's sacrifice has bought them precious time, but they know it won't be long before more guards or backup arrives. They need to get out, and fast.

Emerging from the broken windows at the rear of the mansion, the cool night air hits them like a jolt. But before they can even take a breath, they're ambushed.

Three guards burst from the shadows, weapons raised.

Marcus instinctively dives for cover over a low wall at the edge of the property, disappearing down the hill on the other side as bullets chase him. Peter, caught in the open with Petrov, doesn't have that luxury. Thinking quickly, he yanks the oligarch in front of him, using him as a human shield. He presses the barrel of his Beretta M9 to Petrov's temple, the cold metal digging into the man's skin.

"Back off!" Peter snarls. The guards hesitate, their guns trained on him, but the sight of their employer's terrified face gives them pause.

Peter can feel Petrov trembling under his grip, the man's fear being worn like a suit. The guards shift uneasily, unsure of their next move.

Suddenly, a sharp crack splits the night. One of the guards staggers, a spray of blood erupting from his chest as he drops dead to the ground. Raven emerges from the darkness, her rifle smoking.

The surprise is enough to break the remaining guards' focus. As they whirl around, trying to locate the new threat, Peter seizes the moment. He fires off two quick shots, the bullets finding their marks with deadly accuracy. The men fall to the ground, their weapons clattering uselessly on the patio beside them.

Peter doesn't lower his gun, his eyes scanning the area for any more threats as Raven approaches quickly.

"Where's Mad Dog and Marcus?" she asks.

"Mad Dog's dead," Peter replies. "Marcus just dived down that hill."

They rush to the edge of the hill, peering into the darkness below. The slope is steep, and in the faint moonlight, they can barely make anything out. There's no sign of Marcus. But before they can even think about finding him, the distant wail of sirens reaches their ears, growing louder by the second.

"We have to move," Peter says, his voice urgent.

Without another word, they sprint to the getaway vehicle

parked a short distance away, Peter dragging Petrov. When they reach the car, Peter slams the butt of his pistol into the back of the oligarch's head, knocking him out cold. He then shoves the unconscious man into the trunk, slamming it shut with a finality that reverberates in the night.

Raven jumps into the passenger seat as Peter slides behind the wheel. He starts the ignition, the engine roaring to life. The sirens are closer now, their piercing cries cutting through the night.

"What about Marcus?" Raven asks as she glances back toward the hill.

"We can't wait," Peter replies. His tone leaves no room for argument as he shifts the stick into gear, the car roaring to life as he floors the accelerator, the tuned-up engine responding with a guttural growl. The tires scream against the pavement as they tear out of the driveway, the mansion shrinking rapidly in the rearview mirror. The sirens are still distant, but Peter knows it won't be long before the police close in. Gazing down the hillside, he sees blue flashing lights.

He navigates the winding roads of Beverly Hills with precision, the car hugging each turn as they speed through the meandering hillside. The narrow streets twist and coil like a serpent, but Peter handles them with ease, his eyes sharp, his hands steady on the wheel. The world outside blurs into a dark canvas of shadows and streaks of light as they fly past gated estates and high walls.

Raven glances nervously out the passenger window, her eyes darting to every approaching headlight, every driveway that might conceal another threat. As they crest a hill, the city sprawls out beneath them, a glittering sea of lights stretching to the horizon. But Peter has no time to appreciate the view. He needs to put distance between them and their pursuers—fast.

"Hold on," Peter mutters, his voice tight with focus.

He downshifts and slams on the gas, the car surging forward. The road ahead curves sharply to the left, a hairpin turn that would send most drivers careening off the edge. But Peter isn't most drivers. He eases into the curve, letting the momentum carry them through the turn, the tires gripping the asphalt with just enough force to keep them on the road.

As they straighten out, the blue and red flash of police lights suddenly appears in the distance, reflected off the walls of the canyon ahead. A roadblock, just as he expected.

Peter grits his teeth. "We're going off-road," he decides.

Raven nods, her knuckles white as she grips the edge of the seat. A narrow dirt trail veering off the main road, barely visible in the dark. Without hesitation, Peter yanks the wheel hard to the right, the car skidding as it leaves the road and plows onto the rough trail.

The car bucks and jolts as they race down the uneven path, the headlights cutting through the dense underbrush. Dust and gravel spray up behind them, the rear tires struggling for traction on the loose surface. The police lights vanish from view, obscured by the thick trees and steep terrain.

Peter pushes the car harder, threading it through the narrow gaps between trees, the suspension groaning under the strain. They're deep in the wilderness now, the city far behind them. The only sounds are the roar of the engine and the rhythmic thud of the wheels on the rough trail.

Finally, they crest a ridge, and the trail begins to descend, opening up into a wider dirt road. Peter guns the engine one last time, and the car shoots down the hill, emerging onto a deserted highway that cuts through the wilderness. The smooth asphalt is a welcome relief after the rough trail, and Peter lets out a breath he didn't realize he was holding.

"We're clear," he says, the tension in his voice finally easing. He glances over at Raven, who is still scanning the road behind them.

She nods, her shoulders relaxing. "We did it."

"We need to get as far away from LA as possible," Peter says. "No stopping until we reach the safe house."

Raven agrees, and Peter shifts the car into a higher gear, the engine purring as they accelerate down the empty highway. The lights of LA fade into the distance, swallowed by the vast darkness of the wilderness. The road stretches out ahead, a long, winding path to safety.

THIRTY-FIVE

THEY DROVE A WHOLE DAY TO REACH THE NEXT SAFE house, a lonely cabin in the foothills of Wallowa County, Oregon. Once again, they were being guarded by a mountain range, the jagged gray peaks standing like dutiful sentinels.

The safe house is quiet, the only light coming from a flickering TV screen in the corner of the room, snowflakes tapping gently against the windowpanes. They hit snowfall the second they'd crossed into Oregon, the flakes getting thicker the farther north they traveled.

Peter and Raven sit side by side on a worn couch, eyes fixed on the news report playing out in front of them. The footage on the screen shows aerial shots of the mansion in Beverly Hills, now a smoldering ruin after the explosion of violence the night before. Reporters speak in hushed tones, baffled by the carnage, but none of the dead have been identified. There's no mention of Marcus, no confirmation that he was among the fallen—or that he was captured.

Peter sighs heavily, rubbing a hand over his tired, bedraggled face. "No word is good. I guess," he mutters. "It means he could be out there somewhere."

"But without Marcus," Raven says, "we've lost contact with

Leadership. We don't know what to do with Petrov." She glances at Peter. "It means we're on our own out here."

A muffled sound comes from the back bedroom. It's Petrov, bound to a radiator by his wrists, his legs secured tightly and tape covering his mouth. Peter's eyes flick to the open door, waiting until the noise subsides before turning back to Raven.

When his gaze reaches her, a single tear slips down her cheek, and she abruptly turns to face him.

"Reilly," she whispers, her voice barely holding back the tide of emotion threatening to overwhelm her. "Can you hold me, please?"

Peter's heart clenches at the vulnerability in her voice. He leans toward her, gently pulling her into his arms. "Come here," he murmurs softly.

Raven collapses against him, burying her face in his chest as the tears begin to flow. She shakes with the force of her sobs, the adrenaline of the past twenty-four hours giving way to raw, unchecked emotion—Mad Dog's death, Marcus's disappearance, all of it flooding her overstretched mind.

Peter holds her tightly, his hand running soothingly up and down her back. As he starts to pull away, she clings to him, not ready to let go.

"Stay," she whispers. "Please."

They stay like that for another five minutes, and when they do part, Peter reaches over to a nearby shelf and retrieves a bottle of bourbon and two glasses, setting them on the small table in front of the couch. The light from the fireplace flickers across the room as he pours the whiskey, the liquid sloshing gently in the glasses.

He hands one to Raven, then settles beside her, their bodies close. The warmth of the fire and the whiskey does little to chase away the chill that lingers in their bones, but it's a start.

"I can't stop seeing Mad Dog's face," she whispers. "Every time I close my eyes, he's there."

They cling to each other. Raven's fingers thread through Peter's hair as she presses closer, seeking solace in his embrace.

"Stay with me," she whispers against his lips, her voice a plea. "Don't leave."

"I'm not going anywhere," Peter breathes before kissing her.

Their hands move with a sense of desperation, clothes falling away as they shift to a bed in the far corner of the room, Peter kicking the door to the bedroom closed with his heel as they pass it, shutting Petrov out. The need to feel, to forget the pain if only for a moment, drives them forward. Falling onto the bed, the world outside the cabin ceases to exist as they find comfort in each other's touch, their movements raw and intense, driven by a need to escape the darkness closing in on them.

THIRTY-SIX

PETER LIES AWAKE IN THE DIM LIGHT OF THE EARLY morning, his mind occupied with thoughts of the days to come. Raven is fast asleep, nestled into him, her breathing slow and steady as she rests against his chest. The warmth of her body is comforting, but Peter can't shake the unease that gnaws at the edges of his thoughts.

As he stares up at the ceiling, he hears a faint sound coming from the other room. It's subtle at first, but then he recognizes it —the sound of Yuri Petrov stirring.

Carefully untangling himself from Raven, Peter moves slowly so as not to wake her. She stirs slightly but doesn't open her eyes, her exhaustion keeping her deep in sleep.

Slipping out of bed, his movements are silent as he makes his way to the other room. The cabin is quiet, the only sound the gentle whine of the floorboards under his feet. He steps into the small room where Petrov is being kept, his eyes immediately locking on to the Russian, who is struggling against the restraints that bind him to the radiator. The moment Petrov sees Peter, he stops, his eyes widening in fear.

Peter raises a finger to his lips, signaling for silence. "Stay quiet," he whispers.

He pulls a small flick knife from his pocket and approaches Petrov, the blade glinting in the early morning light that filters through the curtains. Petrov freezes, his breath hitching as Peter kneels beside him and carefully cuts the zip tie securing him to the radiator. Then he moves to the restraints on Petrov's ankles, slicing through them with the same precision. The Russian watches him closely, his eyes flicking between Peter's face and the knife in his hand.

With Petrov's legs freed but his wrists still bound and the tape still covering his mouth, Peter helps him to his feet. Placing a thick coat around the oligarch's shoulders, he then guides him outside. The morning air is frigid, the chill biting through their clothes. Snow falls gently from the sky, blanketing the ground and trees in a soft, white cover. Their breaths show in the cold air, puffing out in clouds as they walk toward a wooden bench at the edge of the property, the snow crunching beneath their shoes.

Peter guides Petrov to the bench, sitting him down and taking a seat beside him. Reaching out, he gently peels the tape from his mouth. For a moment, they sit in silence, the snowflakes settling quietly on their shoulders.

Peter's voice breaks the stillness. "You were Kara Tate's source, weren't you?"

Petrov sighs, his breath visible in the cold air, the sound heavy with resignation. "Yes," he admits quietly, his gaze fixed on the snow-covered tree line. "I was."

"Then I'm going to need you to tell me exactly what you told her."

The early morning light casts long shadows across their faces, adding weight to Petrov's words as he begins to speak.

"How much do you know about Kara Tate and the evidence she gathered?" Petrov begins.

"There were three video cassettes," Peter replies.

Petrov chuckles softly to himself. "Yes, she had become deeply paranoid of modern technology. Too easy to hack into. Did you watch what was on those tapes?"

Peter shakes his head. "I wasn't allowed. Leadership made us hand them over." It's a lie, but he must play the part.

Petrov's lips curl into a wry smile. "Leadership, huh? Well, one of those tapes is an interview with me. Another is her copy of video evidence of secret meetings between various communists from 1976 to 1986. The third I'm not aware of."

Peter's confusion deepens. "Communists?"

"Yes," Petrov says, leaning forward slightly. "Communists outlining a new Cold War strategy. A strategy that involves using America's own system against itself. A strategy that is well underway." He lets these words hang a while in the cold air before continuing. "You see, despite what people think, the Cold War never ended. It merely entered a phase of Shadow War."

Peter listens intently as the snow continues to fall, blanketing the forest in a serene yet deceptive quiet.

"In the late '70s and '80s, China opened its economy under Deng Xiaoping," Petrov explains. "These reforms seemed to align with Western economic principles but were actually part of a larger strategy to infiltrate and destabilize capitalist economies."

Peter leans in. "How did the Soviets fit into this?"

Petrov nods, pleased that Peter is following along. "They too had their part to play. A young, ambitious Mikhail Gorbachev saw the need for drastic change and was eventually ushered into power. His subsequent policies of Glasnost and Perestroika appeared to reform the USSR, but they were really designed to present a friendly face while subtly undermining Western confidence and stability. Boris Yeltsin was his biggest ally in this, pushing for reforms that seemed pro-Western but were aimed at exploiting economic vulnerabilities."

The snow thickens around them as Petrov continues to unravel the conspiracy, his voice steady and sure. "This strategy didn't die with the collapse of the Soviet Union. It evolved, integrating with global networks, infiltrating corporations, governments, and media. The aim has always been to weaken the West from within, using its own freedoms and systems against it."

Peter's mind races as he processes Petrov's words.

"And now," Petrov says, his voice dropping to a conspiratorial whisper, "those pulling your strings are using this strategy to further their own agenda. Leadership isn't who you think they are. They're not fighting for freedom—they're part of this plan, playing their role in destabilizing the world. The economic ruin you see everywhere in today's USA, the reason you people join your little gangs. It's all the doing of your Leadership."

Peter feels a cold chill run down his spine as Petrov's revelations settle in.

The Russian's voice is steady as he continues to speak. "The Fall of the Berlin Wall in 1989 was a pivotal moment," he says, his tone reflective. "But it wasn't the straightforward victory for the West that everyone thought it was. It was a strategic move. The influx of Western goods and lifestyle into the former Eastern Bloc led to increased materialism, which, in turn, sowed the seeds of economic instability not just in Germany, but across Europe and beyond."

Peter nods slowly, the pieces of the puzzle beginning to fall into place. "And the economic booms and crises in the '90s?" he prompts, eager to understand the full scope of the manipulations.

Petrov's eyes narrow as he continues, his voice taking on a darker edge. "The tech boom, the Asian financial crisis—all of these events were exacerbated by hidden manipulations. The rise of China in the 2000s, for example, wasn't just a natural progression. It was a calculated move that led to massive trade imbalances and economic dependency on China by the West. Every move was part of a larger strategy to destabilize the global economy."

"And what was your role in all this?" Peter asks.

"I was one of those in charge of the mass Russian privatization scheme of the early '90s," Petrov says, his voice tinged with a mix of pride and regret. "To the world, it seemed like a way to introduce capitalism to the former Soviet Union. But in reality, it was a means to consolidate power and wealth in the hands of a few while creating economic chaos. What should have been a pathway to prosperity became a mechanism for the oligarchs to seize control, leading to widespread corruption and instability."

"So you were a key player in both the Soviet and post-Soviet strategies," Peter remarks.

Petrov nods, his gaze meeting Peter's, the intensity in his eyes clear. "Yes," he admits without a trace of hesitation. "The goal was always to destabilize the West, even through apparent reform. By the time the world will come to realize what has happened, the foundations of Western dominance will already be beginning to crack. Every crisis, every economic downturn, is another step toward weakening the global order.

"And the Shadow War continues, more dangerous than ever, hidden from view. The West let its guard down, believing that the ideological battle was over. But it never ended—it just went underground, becoming more insidious, more deeply embedded in the very systems the West prides itself on."

He shifts slightly on the bench, his mind seemingly traveling back through the decades as he recalls the strategic moves that have kept this covert war alive. "Take North Korea, for example. Under Kim Il-sung, the country remained isolated, shunning the reforms that swept through other communist states. But this wasn't just out of stubbornness. It was a calculated move, agreed upon in secret discussions. North Korea's role was to act as a constant thorn in the side of the West, ensuring perpetual distraction and division."

Peter's brow furrows as he processes this new information. "So Kim Il-sung maintained North Korea's isolation deliberately to keep the US and its allies preoccupied?"

Petrov nods gravely. "Yes. While the West was busy dealing with the threat posed by North Korea's provocations, it diverted attention from the larger, more subtle moves being made by other players in the Shadow War. Each crisis, each conflict, was part of a broader strategy designed to weaken the West from within."

"So all these global conflicts," Peter puts to him, "—North

Korea, the Middle East, all the economic crises of the past forty years—they're all interconnected?"

"Yes," Petrov says. "Each event is a thread in a much larger web. The goal has always been to destabilize the West, to make it second-guess its own values, its own systems. The more the West becomes mired in conflicts, both external and internal, the weaker it becomes. And the more it weakens, the more those who orchestrate these events can tighten their grip on global power."

For a moment, the two men do nothing but stare ahead, the gravity of their conversation hanging heavily in the air. The early morning snow begins to ease, but the shadows of the past remain, casting a long and ominous specter over the present.

Peter finally breaks the silence. "So who exactly are Leadership, then?" he asks.

Petrov meets Peter's gaze, his expression grave. "Leadership are your handlers," he explains. "They come from the CCP—the Chinese Communist Party—and from what's left of the so-called Russian Federation. They're the ones pulling the strings, running the Iron Brotherhood and various other domestic groups within the US. Groups like yours are being used to coordinate the start of a civil war. The goal is simple: send America into disarray, weaken it from within, and pave the way for a communist takeover. They intend to unfurl the hammer and sickle over the White House."

Peter feels his blood run cold at the enormity of what Petrov is describing. The Iron Brotherhood, the cause they think they're fighting for, was nothing more than a pawn in a game of global domination by the enemies of their country. "And why did you turn on them?" he asks, trying to make sense of Petrov's motivations.

Petrov's expression hardens, his eyes burning with conviction. "The world they envision is one of complete control," he says passionately. "No innovation, no freedom. A totalitarian hellhole where a man cannot express himself, cannot live freely. I couldn't let that happen. I had to act, to expose them for what they are."

The weight of Petrov's words settles over Peter like a heavy shroud. He's about to ask about Grand Junction, but before he can, the sound of a car approaching cuts through the quiet morning air. His instincts kick in, and he quickly grabs Petrov's arm, pulling him back inside the cabin. Peter is just closing the door behind them when the car's headlights pierce the falling snow.

With Petrov secured once more to the radiator, Peter peeks through a crack in the curtains. The car comes into view, pulling up to the cabin. For a moment, Peter readies himself for a fight, the Beretta gripped in his hand—are they being found out? Is this the end? But then the car door opens, and out steps Marcus Kane, looking exhausted but alive.

Raven, who had been stirring in her sleep, wakes up and joins Peter at the window. Her eyes widen in incredulity and relief. "It's Marcus!" she exclaims, rushing outside.

Peter watches from the doorway as she runs to Marcus, the two embracing tightly.

"I'm so glad you're okay," Raven says, her voice thick with emotion as she clings to Marcus.

"I made it," Marcus replies gruffly. "Barely."

Peter steps out onto the porch, watching the scene with a mixture of emotions. The group is reunited, a small glimmer of hope shining through the dark cloud that hangs over them. But even as they embrace, sharing in the relief of survival, Peter can't shake the weight of Petrov's revelations.

THIRTY-SEVEN

THE MIDDAY AIR IS CRISP AND FRESH AS THE SUN RISES high over the Wallowa Mountains, casting a warm glow over the cabin.

Peter and Raven are preparing to leave for the local store to gather supplies. They stand by the doorway, adjusting their gear and making sure they have everything they need for the trip. Marcus Kane leans casually against the doorframe, watching them with a knowing grin. Despite the seriousness of their situation, there's a glint of something like amusement in his eyes.

"You two make a good team," Marcus says, his voice carrying a note of approval. "Keep looking out for each other."

Raven, caught off guard, feels a flush of warmth creep up her cheeks. She glances at Peter, a shy smile tugging at the corners of her lips. "Thanks. I guess."

Peter returns the smile. "We appreciate your blessing, Marcus."

For a moment, the tension between the three eases, replaced by a sense of camaraderie. But the brief respite doesn't last long. Marcus's expression shifts to something more serious as he reaches into his pocket and pulls out a small piece of tech. Peter's eyes narrow as he recognizes the familiar shape of an encrypted communication device.

"You got another one," Peter says, more a statement than a question.

Marcus nods. "Yeah. Leadership wasn't happy about the last one going missing, but they left me this in a deposit box. They made it clear that we don't have any more room for mistakes."

Raven's gaze flicks to the device, her brow furrowing with concern. "And you've made contact?"

"Yes," Marcus replies. "Leadership's keeping a close eye on us now. They want to know every move we make."

Peter takes a deep breath, his thoughts immediately turning to Yuri Petrov and the implications of what he learned that morning. "What are we planning to do with Petrov?" he asks.

Marcus's expression hardens. "Leadership wants us to bring him to them," he says. "We'll get the location at some point today. Then we'll make the handover."

The small town is quiet, another tiny mountain community forgotten by everyone except the handful of tourists that visit each year. As Raven heads inside the local store to gather supplies, Peter slips away, finding a secluded spot behind the building. The alley is empty, the walls of the store shielding him from prying eyes. He pulls out the pay-as-you-go phone, its cheap plastic surface cold against his palm, and quickly dials Deacon's number.

The phone rings once, twice, before Deacon picks up, his voice brisk and businesslike. "Reilly, what's the update?"

Peter glances around, ensuring no one is nearby to overhear. "I've got news," he says in a low, urgent voice. "Leadership is a secret communist alliance."

There's a moment of silence on the other end of the line, followed by Deacon's incredulous response. "What?"

"Petrov spilled everything," Peter continues. "The video cassettes Kara had contained footage of secret meetings between the communists from 1976 to 1986, as well as an interview with Petrov himself."

Deacon's dubiousness is obvious, even through the phone. "This is way out there. Are you sure he was telling the truth?"

"He said the Cold War never ended," Peter explains. "It just became a Shadow War. The Soviets and the Chinese have been manipulating global events to destabilize the West. Petrov claims the Iron Brotherhood and other groups are being used to start a civil war. How far are you into decrypting that device I got for you?"

"Kirsty's getting there," Deacon replies. "But I'll tell her to hurry up. Something big is coming, isn't it?"

"Yes," Peter confirms. "And we need to be ready."

"Where's Petrov now?" Deacon asks.

"Marcus Kane is going to take him somewhere," Peter answers. "However, I've placed a tracker on Petrov. One of the ones you gave me."

"Good thinking," Deacon says. "That'll help us keep tabs on him. What about Grand Junction?"

"I didn't get the chance to ask. Marcus showed up as we were speaking, and I had to get him back inside."

"Then maybe I can answer a little of that. Looking into the mines underneath Grand Junction, we found something. It didn't really bother us at the time, but now you mention the Chinese and the Russians, it's making more sense."

Peter's heart pounds in his chest. "What?"

"The abandoned mines underneath Grand Junction are owned by a conglomerate of companies," Deacon explains. "Namely, companies based in Moscow and Beijing."

Peter's stomach churns as the pieces begin to fall into place. "Then that must be what Kara meant—whatever caused her to be contaminated with radiation must be down there. Mark, you need to get into those mines."

Deacon's response is swift and determined. "Leave it to me."

Peter goes to end the call, but Deacon's voice stops him. "One more thing. I need you to make sure the group watches the six o'clock news this evening. There'll be something important on it."

Peter frowns. "What?"

"What you told me about David Smith and the others going into hiding got me thinking. I've gone to some effort to plant a story. One that might just begin to pull at the cracks in your group. Just make sure they see it."

"Will do. Speak soon."

Peter hangs up the phone and turns around, already bracing himself to head to the store. But when he does, he stops dead in his tracks. Raven stands there, just a few feet away, her expression a blend of curiosity and something darker—suspicion. The usual background noise of the small town—the distant hum of cars, the chatter of a passerby—fades, leaving only the thick, tense silence between them.

"I was wondering who it was you've been calling," Raven says.

Peter's mind races. His thoughts collide, piecing together what this means, and his stomach drops as he realizes that Raven has been watching him for longer than he'd thought. "It was you who spotted me in the woods that day, wasn't it?" he says.

Raven nods, her eyes never leaving his face. "Yes. I saw you using the phone. So are you going to tell me who it is you've been secretly calling?"

A cold knot of dread forms in Peter's gut. He knows he has to think fast, say something that will satisfy her curiosity without revealing the dangerous truth.

"Look, I'll admit it," he says. "I've been breaking the Brotherhood's no-contact policy, but it's not what you think."

Raven's brow furrows. "What do you mean?"

Peter pauses, letting the silence stretch just long enough to make the lie more convincing. He needs her to believe this. "I have a son," he says finally. "He worries about me. I've been calling him to put him at ease. My own father was never there when I was growing up. It was horrible not knowing where he was. I can't do the same to my own child."

Raven's suspicion seems to melt away, replaced by sympathy. Her expression softens, and she reaches out to touch his hand. "Oh, Reilly, I had no idea. That must be so hard for you."

Peter nods, doing his best to keep his face composed, to play the role of the concerned father. "It is," he says, forcing a sigh, "but I had to keep him from worrying. I'm sorry I didn't tell you earlier."

Raven's lips curve into a gentle smile. "I understand now."

She leans in then, her lips meeting his in a tender kiss that is warm and reassuring, a signal that she believes him, that she trusts him. And with it, Peter can't help feeling a sense of shame and guilt for lying to her like this.

THIRTY-EIGHT

IN A SECLUDED CORNER OF A COMPUTER LAB DEEP within CIA Headquarters, Kirsty Lange hunches over her workstation, her eyes fixed on the three screens before her. Her fingers fly across the keyboard, her expression one of intense concentration. She has been working on decoding the encrypted device for three days, and now, she feels she's close to breaking through. The screen flickers, lines of code streaming past, and then suddenly, it all clicks into place. The encryption shatters, and the data within the device begins to unfurl before her eyes.

Without wasting another second, she picks up her phone, dials a number, and when it answers, she practically cries, "Mark, get over here!"

Mark Deacon takes less than a minute to reach her workstation from his own office. He immediately leans over her shoulder, his eyes scanning the screen. "Okay," he says. "What've we got?"

Kirsty clicks through the data, her voice steady as she explains. "There are at least ten other encrypted devices, all across the US. These devices are connected to various groups, all of them following orders from what we assume is 'Leadership.' But here's the thing—the messages self-delete after they're read, so I'm unable to recover any previous communications."

Mark frowns. "So we can't see what they've been planning, only that these devices are active and in use."

"Exactly," Kirsty confirms. "But there's more. The devices are all connected to five master devices—Leadership's devices. These master devices are the source of the commands, and they're spread out across the country, issuing orders to the others."

Kirsty clicks on a map, which displays the various locations of these master devices. The screen zooms in, and five red dots appear, blinking ominously on a map of the United States.

Mark's breath catches in his throat as he notices something alarming. "Those dots... are they moving?"

Kirsty nods, her eyes widening. "Yes, they're mobile. But look at this." She taps a few keys, bringing up the recent locations of the master devices. "They've been visiting the same location repeatedly. Look at the pattern—they keep returning to the same place."

Mark leans in closer, his eyes narrowing as he studies the map. The red dots converge on a specific point, the same place they have all visited multiple times. His heart sinks as he recognizes the location. "That's close to the Grand Junction site," he murmurs. "The mines beneath it."

Kirsty nods again. "The data shows that all five master devices have been in or near those mines. Whatever's going on down there, it's critical to their operations."

Mark straightens up, the urgency of the situation hitting him full force. "We absolutely need to get down there," he says. "We need to find out what's in those mines and why Leadership keeps returning."

Kirsty hesitates for a moment, then adds, "But what about clearance? We can't just waltz into a restricted area without it."

Deacon groans softly, then speaks up. "Director McLean's been a little frosty about the whole thing. She wants us to wrap it up, set the FBI on the last members of the Brotherhood, and leave off Leadership. She thinks that once we have Marcus Kane, we'll be able to figure who's financing the whole thing. She's not anxious for us to dig any deeper—or looking into the Cold War aspect. She practically laughed me out of her office when I mentioned it."

Kirsty frowns. "So what do we do?"

Deacon lets out a resigned sigh. "We'll have to go on our own. No clearance, no backup—just us."

She gives him a tight smile. "Then let's hope we can bring back something that can be used to stop this."

THIRTY-NINE

INSIDE THE CABIN, THE FLICKERING LIGHT FROM THE TV casts long shadows on the rough wooden walls. The group sits in tense silence, their eyes glued to the screen as the news anchor's voice drones on, the words like lead weights falling on their heads, heavy with implication.

"...the human remains found earlier today in a storage container at the Port of Baltimore have been identified as those of David Smith," the anchor reports, the name sending a chill through the room. "Authorities believe he was involved in the death of journalist Kara Tate. Tate was found..."

The screen cuts to a photo of David Smith.

Raven stares at the screen, her face pale and drawn, the shock written in every line. "They told us he was to go into hiding..." Her voice trails off as she turns to Marcus Kane, eyes wide with fear and disbelief. "How many others have gone into hiding over the years to avoid exposure? Danny, Simons... Did we send them to their deaths, Marcus?"

Marcus Kane sits frozen. "I... I need to speak with Leadership," he mutters, his voice hollow.

Peter watches from his seat, his expression carefully neutral, but inside, he knows exactly what's happening. Deacon set this up

—the story is the plant he mentioned, one designed to sow doubt and fear.

Next to him, Raven's shock gives way to horror. She stares at the television, her voice a whisper. "They killed them."

Marcus bristles, his voice rising in defense. "We don't know that. It could be something else."

But Raven isn't having it. She turns on him, anger and pain mingling in her voice. "What else, Marcus? What else could it be?"

Without waiting for an answer, she bolts from the cabin, the door slamming shut behind her. Peter hesitates for only a moment, but then quickly grabs a thick coat from the hook by the door and rushes after her, the cold night air biting at his skin as he steps outside. Behind him, he can hear Marcus frantically dialing on the encrypted device.

Peter chases after Raven, his boots crunching on the snow-covered ground. Snowflakes fall steadily, his breath visible in the frigid air as he tracks her through the freshly fallen snow. He finds her in a clearing, her shoulders shaking with sobs as she leans against a tree.

He approaches slowly, then gently wraps the coat around her shoulders before pulling her close. Raven collapses into his embrace, her tears soaking through his shirt as she cries into his chest. The forest is silent around them, the only sounds her muffled sobs and the distant rustle of wind through the snow-laden branches.

"It's okay," Peter whispers softly. "I'm here."

Raven clings to him, her voice breaking as she speaks. "I thought we were fighting for something real. Now I don't know what to believe. Have I wasted my life for a cause that's just... bullshit?"

Peter tightens his hold on her. "It's not bullshit," he murmurs. "We believed in it for a reason. But maybe we need to rethink who we're following."

She pulls back slightly, looking up at him with tear-filled eyes. "I had doubts before, but now... now they're tenfold."

Peter strokes her long black hair, his touch gentle. "You're not alone in this. I'm beginning to doubt exactly who Leadership is, but we'll figure it out together."

Raven nods, but the uncertainty still lingers in her eyes. As they stand there in the clearing, surrounded by the darkness of the forest and the falling snow, Peter knows that the seeds of doubt have been planted deep. The final remnants of the Iron Brotherhood is fracturing, and soon, the truth they've been running from will come crashing down around them.

A minute later, they turn and head back toward the cabin. As they step inside, they can hear Marcus Kane's muffled voice from the bedroom. He's on the encrypted phone, speaking with Leadership. His tone is hushed but urgent, the seriousness of the conversation clear.

Peter pauses, listening to the low murmur of Marcus's voice. "What do you think they'll say about it?" he asks, glancing at Raven.

Raven opens her mouth to respond, but before she can get the words out, the bedroom door swings open, and Marcus steps out, his face pale, his eyes wide.

"Leadership wants to meet with me personally," Marcus announces, his voice tight. "They have something to show me."

Raven cuts her eyes at him. "How do you know you won't end up in a storage container?" she asks, her tone biting.

Marcus meets her gaze directly, his expression hardening. "Leadership claims it's not David," he says, his voice firm, almost defiant.

Raven doesn't back down. "Then how did the Feds identify him?" she presses.

Marcus shakes his head, the confusion evident on his face. "They don't know. But they want to show me something." He pauses, taking a deep breath. "You two are to go on from here to

Nashville for the Patriot Front march happening in three days. I'll be there to meet you."

Raven's anger flares. "And what?" she demands, her voice rising. "What then?"

Marcus steps closer, his own voice taking on a pleading edge. "Leadership states that by then I will have all the answers for our future. Just trust me, Raven. If you can't trust in Leadership, then trust in the guy who's been your friend for the past five years. Trust a brother, okay?"

Raven looks at him, the tension between them stretching thin, like heated wire. After a long moment, she nods, though her reluctance is clear. "Okay. But you better meet us there with the right answers."

Peter steps forward. "Are you taking Petrov?"

Marcus nods. "Yeah."

"Then I want to go with you. His people could be looking for him. You might need help if you're ambushed."

Marcus shakes his head firmly. "Leadership only wants me to take him. They said it has to be just me."

Peter doesn't back down. "You'll need backup. Two of us would be safer."

But Marcus stands his ground. "Leadership's orders are clear. It's just me. You need to go to Nashville and get ready for the march. I'll meet you there with the answers."

Raven crosses her arms, frustration etched on her face. "Marcus, this doesn't feel right."

Marcus Kane looks at both of them, his eyes filled with a desperate need for them to understand. "Trust me. Trust that I'll get the answers we need. It's the only way."

The room falls silent, his words hanging in the air like the snowflakes rattling the window panes. For now, all they can do is trust that Leadership will give Marcus the answers they need, even if every instinct tells them otherwise.

FORTY

THE EARLY MORNING LIGHT DRIFTS INTO THE CABIN, casting a pale glow across the worn wooden floor. Outside, the world is blanketed in snow, the soft white flakes still floating down from the gray sky. The air inside is filled with the sounds of hushed conversations and the rustling of gear as everyone prepares to move. Peter crouches by Yuri Petrov, who is still secured to the radiator, his eyes darting nervously between Peter and the others outside the room.

Peter's hands are steady as he unfastens the ties holding Petrov in place. Petrov's voice is low, edged with anxiety. "What are your friends going to do with me?" he asks, his eyes searching Peter's face for some hint of reassurance.

"Hand you over to Leadership," Peter replies calmly.

Petrov scoffs, the sound bitter. "Leadership? You mean the puppeteers pulling your strings."

Peter meets his gaze, his voice soft but firm. "Something like that."

Petrov's demeanor shifts, his fear bleeding into desperation. "And you're just going to let them? After everything I told you?" His voice rises slightly, pleading.

Peter pauses, his eyes locked on to Petrov's. "Just keep your mouth shut and you might live," he says, his tone low and measured, almost a whisper.

He helps Petrov to his feet, the man's legs shaky but steady enough. Moving quickly, Peter places a strip of tape across Petrov's mouth, silencing any further questions or protests. He then leads him into the next room, joining the others. The cabin feels even smaller now, everyone burdened with the knowledge of what's to come and the uncertainty of how it will all play out.

As they gather outside the cabin, the cool morning air is heavy with tension. Snow continues to fall steadily, blanketing the ground and muffling their movements as Peter leads Yuri Petrov, bound and gagged, toward the car.

Marcus stands by it, his eyes hard as he looks at the Russian. "Get him into the trunk," he orders.

Peter obeys, guiding Petrov into the trunk with care. Once the Russian is tucked inside, Marcus approaches with a syringe, the liquid inside catching the morning light as he administers a sedative. Petrov's eyes flutter as the drug takes hold, his low-level struggles weakening to nothing. Peter then lifts the unconscious man's legs, holding them steady as Marcus winds duct tape around them, ensuring that even if Petrov regains consciousness, he won't be able to kick or make any noise.

"That should keep him quiet," Marcus says as he straightens up, his gaze lingering on the trunk before he slams it shut.

With the task done, the three of them step back. It's time to part ways.

Raven steps forward, her voice serious and filled with concern. "Be careful, Marcus. We'll see you in Nashville."

Marcus nods, his expression stoic but with an edge of something deeper—perhaps worry, or perhaps resolve. "You too. Stay safe." He then turns to Peter, his eyes narrowing slightly. "And you," he adds, his voice carrying a note of trust but also a warning, "look after her."

After that, they watch Marcus climb into the car, the engine roaring to life. The vehicle lurches forward, the tires crunching over the snow as Marcus drives away, the car soon disappearing down the narrow, snow-covered dirt road that snakes through the forest.

For a moment, Peter and Raven stand in silence, the sound of the car fading into the distance. The world feels still, as if holding its breath in anticipation of what will happen now.

FORTY-ONE

Marcus Kane's car moves steadily through the north Oregon countryside, the narrow winding road almost deserted of traffic.

Almost.

Mark Deacon maneuvers his sedan about 200 yards back, carefully keeping a bend in the road between them at all times. His eyes constantly flick to the screen of his phone, tracking the red dot that marks Petrov's location—courtesy of the tracker Peter discreetly placed on him.

Deacon's team, consisting of Aria Shah and Kirsty Lange, is spread across three different vehicles, all carefully positioned to maintain their surveillance without drawing attention. They've been trained for this—tailing a target without ever making their presence known. The relay-like formation they're using allows them to stay hidden, with each of them taking turns in the lead, ensuring that Marcus never sees the same car in his rearview mirror for too long.

As the landscape shifts subtly, leaving behind the mountains of Oregon, then gradually transforming from the rolling hills of northern Idaho to denser forests as they head toward Montana, the team drive in staggered intervals, sometimes switching lanes or letting other cars pass between them and Marcus Kane's vehicle.

Deacon lifts the radio to his lips. "We'll switch cars at the next rest stop. Kirsty, you'll take the lead."

"Copy that," Kirsty replies. "Preparing to take point."

Deacon approaches the planned rest stop, a small, nondescript area off the highway, where another vehicle waits for him. As he pulls into the dirt lot, Kirsty is already pulling out in an SUV. The switch is quick, seamless—just another step in their carefully coordinated operation. Deacon then changes cars, and before you know it, he's back on the road in a pickup truck.

The convoy continues east, the landscape around them growing more rugged as they move closer to the Montana border. The early morning has given way to the pale light of mid-morning, the sun casting a bright but cool glow over the snow-covered treetops.

After an exhausting eleven and a half hours on the road, Deacon, Aria, and Kirsty finally converge outside Billings, Montana. The city sprawls out before them, a mix of rugged industrial buildings and modern developments. The Yellowstone River winds its way through the outskirts, and the distant Rims, steep sandstone cliffs, rise up against the horizon. Billings has the feel of a city caught between the old and the new, its roots in oil, agriculture, and the railroad still evident, even as it pushes forward into an uncertain future.

Each of them arrives in a separate vehicle, maintaining a low profile as they approach a failed business park on the edge of the city. The park was once touted as a future hub of local commerce, expected to create 10,000 jobs, but the reality has fallen far short. Now it's a ghostly, half-abandoned complex with fewer than 1,000 employees, most of the buildings empty and the surrounding area eerily quiet.

Deacon, Aria, and Kirsty park their cars in the shadows of the deserted buildings, the only movement around them the occasional drift of a plastic bag. They keep a close watch on the business park, its sleek, modern architecture now a hollow reminder of unfulfilled promises. The high fences topped with razor wire and the security cameras that still scan the area are remnants of what was supposed to be a bustling center of innovation.

Deacon spots Marcus Kane's car pulling into the complex, the vehicle disappearing behind the high fences as it's let inside by a pair of heavily armed guards.

"Damn, he's going inside," Deacon whispers into the radio. "We can't follow him in there."

Aria, parked a few hundred yards away, echoes his concern. "What now?"

Kirsty, parked a little farther back, replies, "I could try to hack into their security feeds, but it'll take time."

"Do it," Deacon orders, his eyes never leaving the entrance to the business park.

Inside her vehicle, Kirsty's fingers fly over the keyboard of a laptop as she begins her work, tapping into the business park's network. The minutes tick by, each one feeling longer than the last, but within less than five, she's in.

"Got it," Kirsty announces triumphantly. She pulls up the security feeds, the screen flickering to life with images from inside the complex. "We've got eyes."

Deacon and Aria huddle around their own screens, synchronized with Kirsty's, watching as Marcus Kane hands his car over to two security personnel—Yuri Petrov still in the trunk. The men get into the front, then begin driving it away toward one of the warehouse buildings at the back of the complex.

"Where's Petrov going?" Aria asks.

"Wherever it is, there's no security feed," Kirsty notes as the car disappears from the camera's view. "Or at least not one I can get into."

Aria asks, "What do we do about it?"

"There's nothing we can do," Deacon replies. "For now, we focus on where Marcus Kane is going."

They watch as Marcus Kane is led inside a five-story Lego

brick. Switching to the internal cameras, Kirsty acting as director, they observe a security guard guide Marcus to a conference room on the second floor, where two men await him, one standing, the other sitting behind a desk.

Kirsty leans closer to her laptop, adjusting the volume. "We've got sound," she says.

The conversation inside the conference room becomes clear as the volume increases. Marcus Kane's voice is the first they hear.

"What is this place?" he asks, frowning as he glances around. "I thought we were meeting somewhere... different."

The standing man, his demeanor calm and collected, offers a faint smile. "This isn't just any place, Marcus. It is our base. In order to fund the Brotherhood and other groups like it, we need a way of moving our money inside the country without alerting the authorities."

The other man, leaning forward in his seat, speaks with measured calm. "These operations require capital, infrastructure, and the ability to move funds without raising suspicion. That's where businesses like this come in. It's the perfect cover, and it allows us to keep the Brotherhood and other organizations fully operational."

Marcus's skepticism doesn't fade. He nods slowly but remains uneasy. "I get that. But this..." He gestures vaguely around the room. "This doesn't feel like what I signed up for. We're supposed to be fighting for our country, not playing corporate games."

The standing man smirks, his tone dismissive. "And we are fighting. But to win, you have to use every tool at your disposal. This business park, these companies—they're just tools. They launder the money and the influence we need to support our cause. Without them, the Brotherhood would be nothing more than a ragtag group, easily crushed."

Marcus Kane then shifts the conversation, the edginess in his voice deepening. "Speaking of the Brotherhood... what about David Smith? I need to know what happened to him. Was he the one found in that container in Baltimore?"

The two men exchange a quick glance, and the sitting man sighs, his expression serious. "Marcus, the man inside that container... wasn't David. We believe that the report is nothing but a ruse."

"A ruse?"

"Yes."

"Then if it's a ruse, where are David and the others?" Marcus demands.

"David and the others are—"

But before the sitting man can finish, his phone buzzes on the table, the plastic rattling against the polished mahogany. Answering it, his expression grows tense as he listens to the voice on the other end.

"What do you mean?" he demands, his tone sharp. "...How long ago?" He glances upward, staring straight into the camera, then turns to the standing man. His next words chill Deacon and the team to the bone. "We've been hacked."

The feed cuts out abruptly, the screens in each vehicle going black. Around the perimeter of the business park, there is a sudden increase in activity. Security guards move with purpose, shouting into their radios, jumping into SUVs. The vehicles begin leaving the gatehouse, heading in their direction.

"Time to move," Deacon orders over the radio. The three engines hum to life as the team pulls out from their hidden spots, quickly heading off into the flow of traffic.

Aria's voice crackles over the radio, tense. "What about Petrov?"

Deacon's jaw tightens. "There's nothing we can do. Not now."

They speed away from the business park, the threat of pursuit looming behind them, Deacon's mind racing with the knowledge that the stakes have just been raised even higher.

FORTY-TWO

Peter and Raven arrive in Nashville as the sun sets, casting a dusky orange glow over the city. The streets are alive with agitation, a city on the brink of something dangerous. The atmosphere is charged with energy, the kind that crackles in the air before a storm. The sidewalks are packed with people from all walks of life, but the majority are grim-faced and purposeful, their expressions hardened by the ideologies they carry.

As they navigate the crowded streets on foot, Peter scans the faces around him, noting the variety of groups converging in the city. White supremacists with shaved heads and tattoos, some wearing T-shirts emblazoned with hate symbols, move in tight-knit packs. Their presence is imposing, many of them clad in body armor, AR-15s slung over their shoulders.

In stark contrast, Antifa members and other leftist movements have also made their presence known. Dressed in black, many with their faces covered by masks or bandanas, they chant anti-hate slogans as they march on the opposite side of the street.

The police are out in force, creating a barrier between the groups. Clad in riot gear, they stand in knots, their faces obscured by helmets and visors, batons at the ready. The blue and red lights of their vehicles flash intermittently, reflecting off the storefronts and casting eerie patterns across the asphalt. They are a presence but not a deterrent—more like the watchful eyes of a referee in a game that could turn deadly at any moment.

Peter keeps Raven close as they move through the throngs of people, her hand in his. The noise is overwhelming—chants from the Antifa crowd, angry shouts from the supremacists, the steady hum of police radios, and the occasional bark of a command. Overhead, helicopters circle, their rotors chopping through the air, adding to the dizzying cacophony.

"This place is about to blow," Peter says. He glances around, every instinct on high alert. "We need to keep our heads on a swivel."

Raven nods, her eyes scanning the crowd with the same vigilance. "Let's get to the bar. We need to touch base with the others."

They push through the hordes of people, the din of voices growing louder as they near the heart of the city. The bar they're heading to is tucked away on a side street, its neon sign flickering in the night. The entrance is discreet, a small door beneath a faded awning, but the sound of voices and music spills out into the street. It's a place where the various factions converge, a neutral ground of sorts where the Iron Brotherhood and others gather before the storm hits.

As they enter, they are struck by a wall of sound. The bar is a riot of noise and movement, packed with Iron Brotherhood members, those who escaped arrest at the hideout celebrating and swapping war stories. The air is thick with the smell of beer, sweat, and the underlying tension that seems to follow them wherever they go. It's a place of camaraderie, but also a simmering aggression, the kind that could explode at any moment. The walls are adorned with flags and symbols, all representing the Brotherhood's twisted vision of patriotism.

Raven guides Peter through the crowd, weaving between clusters of men and women clad in leather jackets and combat boots. Their faces light up as they spot Raven, their expressions a mix of respect and rough affection. Peter can feel the weight of their gazes on him, sizing him up, but Raven's presence by his side seems to grant him a measure of acceptance.

They reach a well-known spot at the back of the bar where several members from different chapters of the Iron Brotherhood are gathered. The atmosphere is slightly more subdued here, but the energy is still palpable. Conversations are punctuated by bursts of laughter, the clinking of glasses, and the occasional thud of a fist on the table.

Peter's original contact, Ray Collins, is there; a stocky man with a grizzled beard and a broad grin. He spots them and stands, raising his voice above the din. "Raven! Reilly!" Turning back to his companions, he announces loudly, "Everyone, this is Jack Reilly. He's the guy I told you about. The one that saved that security guard out in Omaha."

A cheer goes up, and one of the members, a tall man with a scar running down his cheek, steps forward, grinning as he extends his hand. "Welcome, Jack! Heard good things about you."

Peter takes the offered hand, shaking it firmly. "Good to meet y'all," he replies.

Ray claps Peter on the back, then wraps an arm around Raven's shoulders. "How are you, Becky? You good? I saw the news. How you holdin' up?"

Raven leans into Ray slightly, her weariness showing. "I'm good, Ray. Just a little exhausted is all. Glad to see you got out of West Virginia safely."

"I was lucky," Ray says. "Me and a couple of the others were out collecting supplies when the raid happened. Look," he then adds in an undertone, "about Davey. Leadership must've had a reason."

Raven gives a tired smile. "You sound like Marcus."

Ray's expression shifts slightly, a flicker of unease crossing his face as he glances around. "And where is our new leader?"

Raven's smile fades. "He had to meet with Leadership," she says quietly.

Ray's face goes a shade paler, his eyes narrowing as if trying to mask his worry. "Yeah," he murmurs. "And what, he's gonna meet us here?"

"Yeah," Raven replies, her tone lacking conviction. "I'm sure he'll make it. He was dropping something off to them."

As Ray is pulled into another conversation, Raven finds Peter among the crowd. Her earlier energy seems to have drained away, replaced by a heavy exhaustion that weighs down her shoulders and stoops her back. Her eyes, normally sharp and alert, are now half-lidded, the day's events clearly taking their toll.

"Jack," she says softly, her voice almost lost in the noise of the bar. "I need to find a place to sleep. Can you come with me?"

Peter's concern is immediate. "Of course," he replies. "Let's go get some rest."

He wraps an arm around her waist, guiding her through the crowd and out of the bar. Outside, it has begun steadily raining, the chill in the December air forcing both to pull the collars of their coats up. The noise of the bar gradually fades behind them as they walk through streets still buzzing with the coiling tension of the city.

A few blocks away, the crowds thinning to just a few knots of people lingering in the streets, they find a quiet, out-of-the-way motel. It's not much, but it's enough—a place where they can shut out the world for a while.

The room is simple, with a bed, a small dresser, and a television mounted on the wall—nothing fancy, but it offers the privacy and respite they desperately need. Raven walks over to the bed and sits down on its edge, her shoulders slumping as the heaviness of the day catches up with her.

She runs a hand through her hair, her expression conflicted and weary. "This is all too much, Jack," she sighs. "I've never felt so confused."

Peter joins her on the bed. "What do you mean?" he asks.

Raven looks down at her hands, fidgeting with her fingers as if searching for the right words. "One of the biggest reasons is because of you," she admits. "I feel something for you... and it's making everything so complicated."

Peter feels a sharp pang of guilt in his chest. He knows what he's doing—playing a role, keeping secrets, betraying the trust Raven has placed in him. But as much as he cares for her, the memory of Kara's death is a constant reminder of why he's here, why he can't afford to let his emotions cloud his judgment. He's on a mission, and no matter how much it hurts, he can't allow himself to lose focus.

He takes her hands in his, his gaze steady. "I care about you too, Raven," he says softly, his voice tinged with the guilt he can't quite shake. "But we need to stay strong. There's so much at stake, and we can't afford to let our guard down now."

Raven looks up, meeting his eyes. There's a vulnerability there, a raw openness that makes Peter's heart ache. But he holds firm, knowing that this moment of honesty is as much as he can give her.

"Get some rest," he murmurs, releasing her hands and standing up. "We'll figure this out. But for now, you need to sleep."

Raven nods, her expression still conflicted, but there's a sense of relief in her eyes as well. She undresses, then moves farther onto the bed, pulling the covers over herself. Peter watches as she settles in, her breathing slows, and she quickly drifts off to sleep.

Once Raven is sound asleep, Peter quietly slips out of the hotel room. He pulls on his jacket and steps into the hallway, the door closing softly behind him.

The streets of Nashville are cold and rain-soaked, the downpour relentless as it drums against the pavement. The December chill seeps through Peter's jacket, and he pulls it tighter around himself. The streetlamps cast long, distorted shadows on the wet ground, their light reflecting off the puddles that have begun to form in the gutters.

As he rounds a corner, he spots a small group of Antifa members moving with purpose, their faces partially obscured by masks and hoods, water streaming off them in rivulets. Peter falls into step behind them, keeping a safe distance, his curiosity piqued. He watches as they weave through the streets, their presence adding to the already charged atmosphere.

It's then that he notices someone familiar—a face he's seen before. Then it clicks. It's another CIA operative, an undercover agent he's spotted once or twice, embedded like he is, but on the opposite side of the ideological divide. Peter's heart skips a beat as he quickens his pace, following the man until they're both separated from the crowd.

Peter corners the operative in a dimly lit alley, the sound of the rain hitting the ground the only noise. The operative startles as Peter approaches, his hand instinctively reaching for the concealed weapon at his side. Then his eyes narrow in recognition.

"Peter?" the operative says, his voice tinged with surprise. "What the hell are you doing here?"

"Same as you, I guess," Peter replies. "What's going on?"

The operative relaxes slightly, though his eyes remain wary. "I've been embedded with the Anti-Capitalist Alliance and the Red Dawn Initiative. Everyone's talking about something big coming soon."

Peter nods, his mind racing as he processes the information. "My people on the right are saying the same thing. What's your handler saying?"

The operative's expression hardens with frustration. "Not much. They just keep telling me to monitor it. But if you wanna know the truth, I think someone's stopping me from getting any further."

Peter's gaze sharpens. "What do you mean?"

The operative leans in, his voice a whisper. "I mean, I've been undercover for the past year, and every time I start telling them about Leadership..."

"Leadership?"

"Yeah. You've heard of them, right?"

Peter nods.

"Well, every time I go upstairs with any information," the operative continues, "someone shuts it down. 'Just monitor them,' my handler tells me. 'Leave the rest to us.' I get a feeling someone in the CIA is feeding them intel."

"A double agent?"

"Yeah. Someone high up the chain."

"It just gets worse," Peter says quietly.

"Look," the operative says, "I need to go. It'll look bad if they see me talking to the enemy. Stay safe."

"You too," Peter says.

The operative nods. With a final glance around the rain-slicked alley, they part ways, each returning to their respective roles in the unfolding madness.

Two blocks away, Peter's pulse quickens as he dials Deacon, the phone pressed against his ear as the rain continues to pour around him. It rings several times before Deacon picks up, his voice gruff and tense.

"Peter? What's going on?"

"Deacon, we've got a problem," Peter begins, his voice low as he steps under the awning of a closed shop to shield himself from the relentless weather. "I just spoke to an operative working the other side. He thinks there's a double agent in the CIA—someone high up, feeding intel to Leadership."

There's a pause on the other end of the line. When Deacon finally responds, his tone is cautious. "That would explain a lot. But first, I need to tell you something. We had to abandon Petrov."

Peter's stomach drops. "What happened?"

"The security at that business park in Billings—it was tighter than we anticipated. As soon as we were made, things went south. We barely got out ourselves. There was no way we could get Petrov out with us."

Peter grits his teeth, frustration boiling just beneath the surface. "He was our only link to Leadership, Deacon. What now?"

"I know," Deacon sighs. "But we couldn't risk the entire operation for him. We'll regroup, figure out another angle."

Peter takes a deep breath. "This operative I talked to, he's embedded with the Anti-Capitalist Alliance and the Red Dawn Initiative. He said something big is coming, but every time he tries to pass information about Leadership up the chain, it gets shut down."

Deacon is silent for a moment, processing this. "If there's a mole high up, that means everything we've been doing could be compromised. We could be walking into traps, or worse—being used."

"Exactly," Peter says. "I'm worried the situation is spiraling out of our control. How much have you shared so far?"

"Not much. I've done my best to keep things as opaque as possible. I've not even told anyone except Kirsty that you're with the Brotherhood."

Peter feels slightly reassured. "Good. What's your next move?"

Deacon hesitates briefly before speaking. "Kirsty and I are heading to Colorado tomorrow. We found an old miner who's willing to take us into those mines. Maybe then we'll know what Grand Junction has to do with it all."

Peter glances up at the darkened sky, feeling the storm pressing down on him. "That's good. Keep me informed."

"Stay sharp, Peter," Deacon says. "If there's a double agent in the CIA, things are about to get a whole lot more dangerous. Watch your back."

"You too, Deacon," Peter replies before ending the call. He slips the phone back into his pocket, the cold rain seeping into his jacket as he turns back toward the hotel.

FORTY-THREE

THE NEXT DAY IS THE DAY OF THE RALLY. CROWDS OF protesters and counter-protesters flood the streets, their voices merging into a cacophony of defiance and anger.

The chant of "We will not be replaced" ricochets off the surrounding buildings, followed by opposition chants of "Every nation, every race, punch a Nazi in the face!" Then "Whose streets? Our streets!"

Peter and Raven are at the bar, tucked away from the chaos, sharing drinks with Ray Collins and the rest of the Brotherhood members. The bar is their refuge from the escalating tension outside. The smell of stale beer and cigarette smoke lingers in the air, mingling with the low murmur of conversation. Peter glances at the television above the bar, which shows live footage of the rally, but his mind is elsewhere, his thoughts as dark as the whiskey in his glass.

Just then the door to the bar swings open, and in walks none other than Marcus Kane. His presence is commanding, as always, but there's a subtle shift in the air. He exchanges brief, tight hugs with Peter and the others, then smirks, a glint of something unreadable in his eyes.

"I've got a surprise for you all," he says.

The words hang in the air, heavy with anticipation. Without further explanation, Marcus motions for Peter, Raven, and Ray Collins to follow him.

The four of them step out of the bar and into the thronging streets. The city is a battlefield. They weave their way through the dense crowd, dodging the skirmishes that are breaking out between Antifa and patriot groups. The air smells of smoke and sweat, and the sound of shouts and sirens creates a dissonant backdrop.

They push forward, slipping through narrow alleys and past makeshift barricades, until they arrive at a seedy-looking motel. The building's neon sign flickers ominously in the twilight. Marcus leads them to a room on the ground floor.

The door swings open, and they are greeted by a figure standing in the shadows. It takes a moment for Peter to recognize him, but when he does, his heart almost explodes—the fire engulfing his brain. It's David Smith, alive and well, though disguised in a way that makes him almost unrecognizable.

Raven, who had been walking beside Peter, suddenly breaks away. Without a word, she rushes to David, throwing her arms around him. The sight of them together, their embrace so familiar, makes Peter's stomach churn. He watches, fists curling at his sides, as Raven and David share a kiss. A rush of wrathful anger surges through him, the sight of Kara's killer so close, so casual, igniting a blaze deep within him.

Ray Collins steps forward, eyes wide with disbelief, and pulls David into a rough embrace. "I thought you were dead, brother," he mutters, his voice thick with emotion.

David Smith smirks as he pulls back from the hug. "Not yet," he replies before turning to face Peter. "You're Jack Reilly, right?"

Peter nods stiffly, every muscle in his body tensed.

"I've heard a lot about you," David says. He leaves Raven's side and approaches Peter, extending his hand. There's a firm grip as their hands meet, and Peter feels the weight of David's scrutiny, the unspoken challenge in his gaze.

David's voice lowers as he adds, "I hear you're one hell of a guy to have beside you in a fight."

Peter forces a calm reply, though his insides are roiling. "I just do my thing."

David's smirk deepens as he turns to the others, repeating in a mocking tone, "He just does his thing. Cold as ice."

Marcus finds a bottle of bourbon on the table and cracks it open. The amber liquid sloshes into chipped glasses. They take seats around a small, scratched-up table, Marcus handing a glass to each of them. David sits down and pulls Raven close to him, patting his lap as he says, "Raven, baby. Come sit with me."

Raven hesitates for a moment, her gaze flicking to Peter. There's something in her eyes—guilt, perhaps?—but she quickly masks it and moves to join David at the table.

"Wait," Ray Collins says. "Shouldn't we talk about things before we get too drunk? I mean, this changes everything. If Davey's here, then the whole him being dead thing was a ruse."

Raven chimes in. "But why? Why go through all that trouble?"

Marcus, leaning casually back in his chair with his arms crossed, speaks up, his tone matter-of-fact. "Isn't it obvious? To split us up. To make us paranoid, distrust each other. And it worked, didn't it?"

Ray nods, takes a sip of his whiskey, then speaks. "It certainly got us looking over our shoulders, wondering who's next to end up in a container. But now... now we know it's all bullshit. The Feds are playing us."

Marcus's gaze shifts to Peter, who is the only one not sitting. He stands at the back of the room, his face unreadable. "What about you, Reilly? What do you think?"

Peter takes a sip of his drink, then answers. "Whoever planted that news story wanted to drive a wedge between us. They knew we'd start pointing fingers, questioning each other. And now we're left wondering—who the hell is feeding them this intel?"

Marcus straightens up in his chair, his expression darkening as he looks each of them in the eye. "That's the real question, isn't it? We've got a snake in the grass. Someone's leaking our moves, setting us up to fail. And I'll be damned if we don't find out who it is."

FORTY-FOUR

A FULL MOON HANGS LOW IN THE SKY, CASTING A silver glow over the snow-covered forest of the Rocky Mountains. Deacon and Kirsty move cautiously between the tall pine trees, and in the distance, the howl of a coyote echoes in the frozen, black air.

They approach a small clearing where an old miner named Randy is waiting. Randy is a grizzled man, his face weathered by years of toil. A thick gray beard reaches down to his chest. He's dressed in a worn flannel shirt under a heavy coat, sturdy boots, and a battered cowboy hat. Despite his age, there's a sharpness in his neon-blue eyes that speaks of experience and a lifetime of surviving in harsh conditions.

The second he spots Deacon and Kirsty, Randy's keen eyes narrow, and he raises a hand to halt them. "Hold on," he says in a gravelly voice. "Before we go any farther, you two need to leave your cellphones behind. Down there, even deep in the mine, those things can still be detected."

Deacon replies, "Already done, Randy."

Randy nods approvingly. "Smart move." He adjusts his hat and adds, "Now I know these parts like the back of my wife's hands. Five generations of my family worked this place. From the day they opened the mine till the day it closed down. I worked it from the age of sixteen to the age of forty-five."

Deacon sizes up the old man. "So you can get us down there safely and without being spotted?"

Randy's grin widens, a glint of pride in his eyes. "Yup. I can."

With that, Randy turns and leads them deeper into the forest. After about ten minutes, he comes to a halt before a boarded-up opening in a rock face. The steel tracks that once carried coal carts are barely visible beneath the thick blanket of snow, but they are there, a relic of a time long past.

"This is it," Randy says. He pulls out a small crowbar from his pack, handing it to Deacon. "We pry these boards off, and we're in. Just be ready. The air down there can be a a little suffocating. The cold don't really reach that far down, and it's darker than a tomb."

Deacon nods, taking the crowbar and setting to work on the boards. The wood groans in protest as he pries it away. One by one, the boards come loose, revealing the dark, yawning mouth of the mine.

The three of them then step into the open pit, the weight of the mountain pressing down on them as they descend into the unknown. The walls of the tunnel loom around them like the throat of some ancient, slumbering beast. The wooden beams supporting the ceiling creak ominously with each step they take, as though protesting the intrusion of these outsiders into its forgotten depths.

As they descend farther, the scent of coal dust clings to their nostrils, mixing with the bitter tang of sweat and the underlying dampness that pervades the tunnel. The heat becomes almost unbearable, the close confines amplifying the stifling atmosphere. The narrow beams of their flashlights cut through the oppressive darkness, casting long, wavering shadows on the walls but offering little comfort against the overwhelming blackness that surrounds them.

Randy leads the way with the surety of someone who has

navigated these tunnels countless times before, but even he seems to move with more caution as they delve deeper into the heart of the mountain.

Finally, they reach a section that veers underneath Grand Junction. The atmosphere has grown even more oppressive, the air thick with the scent of earth and something else—something metallic and unnatural. Kirsty stops abruptly and pulls a Geiger counter from her backpack. The device immediately begins to tick, the sound growing faster and more insistent with each step they take.

"We're definitely getting close to something," she says. The sound of the ticking fills the tunnel, bouncing off the walls as if the very earth itself is warning them of the danger ahead.

Deacon nods. "Let's keep moving. We need to find out what exactly they're hiding down here."

But above ground, within the Grand Junction facility, a different kind of tension is building. In the control room, security guards are monitoring cameras, their eyes glued to the screens displaying the feeds from deep within the mine—the tunnels filled with hidden CCTV. The images show the three intruders—Deacon, Kirsty, and Randy—making their way farther into the tunnel, oblivious to the danger closing in around them.

One of the guards, a young man with a tense expression, leans forward, his eyes narrowing as he realizes the severity of the breach. His hand lifts a radio to his thin lips, his voice tight with urgency as he speaks into it. "Mr. Jacks, we've got a breach. Three individuals have made it into the tunnels. Sector Seven. What are your orders?"

A crackling response comes through the radio, the voice on the other end cold and authoritative. "Flood the tunnel. We can't risk them getting any farther. Not like the journalist last time."

The guard hesitates, his hand hovering over the switch that will release the water from the spent fuel pools. Trepidation grows around his heart as he glances at the monitor, seeing the three figures moving deeper into the mine, unaware of the imminent danger.

"Sir, they'll be killed," he says.

The voice on the other end of the radio is unrelenting, cutting through the guard's hesitation like a knife. "Exactly. Now that's an order, soldier. Flood the tunnel. Now!"

With a grimace, the guard closes his eyes for a brief moment, steeling himself, then pulls the switch.

A low rumble begins to build deep within the facility, reverberating through the tunnels like the growl of a waking beast. Water, cold and unstoppable, is released from one of the spent fuel ponds inside the facility, surging into the tunnel with terrifying speed. The force of it is immense, a relentless torrent that rushes through the confined space, swallowing everything in its path.

Deep underground, Deacon, Kirsty, and Randy feel the ground tremble beneath their feet. The rumbling grows louder, the air around them seeming to shift, bringing with it a sudden, chilling gust. Panic flickers in Randy's eyes as he turns to Deacon and Kirsty, the fear filling his voice as he shouts, "Run!"

They bolt, racing deeper and deeper. A deafening roar of rushing water fills the tunnel, the ground shaking violently as if the Earth itself is coming apart. Their breaths come in ragged gasps, their hearts pounding as they push themselves to their limits, the adrenaline coursing through their veins like fire.

But the water is faster. It crashes through the tunnel like a tidal wave, a wall of liquid fury that sweeps everything in its path. Unable to keep the pace, Randy is the first to be caught, the water slamming into the old miner with such force that he's swept away in an instant, his cries swallowed by the torrent. He disappears beneath the churning water, his figure vanishing in the blink of an eye.

Deacon and Kirsty push themselves harder, desperation giving them strength. Their lungs burn, their legs ache, but they keep running, driven by the primal instinct to survive. Just as the water is about to overtake them, Deacon spots a ventilation shaft to their right. Without a second thought, he grabs Kirsty and pulls her toward the narrow opening.

They scramble into the shaft, the roar of the water just inches behind them. The passage is tight, barely wide enough for them to squeeze through, the cold metal scraping against their skin as they claw their way upward, the water coming after them, rising up the vertical duct. Their breaths come in short, panicked bursts, but they don't stop, not until they've reached the top.

With a final, desperate push, they pull themselves up and out, emerging in another service tunnel. The moment they're free, they collapse on the ground, gasping for breath, their bodies trembling from the adrenaline. The sound of the water rushing below them is deafening, reminding them how close they came to being swept away.

They are safe—for now.

"We made it," Deacon gasps.

Kirsty nods, too exhausted to speak, her body trembling as she tries to steady her breathing. They sit in silence for a moment, until Deacon lifts himself up on shaking legs.

"Come on," he says, offering a hand to Kirsty. "We can't wait around for them to do something else."

Once he's helped her up, Kirsty pulls out the Geiger counter again. This time the device goes berserk, the ticking so rapid it's almost a continuous crackling hum. They exchange a worried glance.

Pressing on, the walls of the tunnel become more reinforced, the rough stone gradually giving way to concrete and steel. Finally, they pass through a large metal door and come to a massive manmade chamber, all of it held within the glare of the electric lights strung up all around. The size of the room is staggering, their footsteps echoing off the domed ceiling.

It is then that the pair come to a standstill. In the center of the chamber stands a series of metal cabins, their doors marked with radiation hazard symbols.

Kirsty approaches one of the cabins with a sign above the door that says *Hazardous Materials Suiting Area*, pushing open the door. Inside, they find hazmat suits, heavy and cumbersome but necessary for what lies ahead. They quickly don the suits, the rubbery material clinging to their sweat-soaked skin. The suits are uncomfortable, the weight of them oppressive, but they offer the only protection against the deadly radiation levels they are sure to face.

Leaving the cabin, they delve farther into the vast chamber, and it is in the center that they find what Kara Tate must have discovered when she snuck in here all those months ago. It is what is known as a hot cell—a containment chamber heavily shielded against nuclear radiation. The walls are lined with lead, and thick glass windows allow a view inside. Deacon steps forward, peering through one of the windows. His breath fogs up the screen of his hazmat suit as he gazes at the facility within—a facility for refining cesium from spent nuclear fuel.

Deacon and Kirsty exchange uneasy glances before entering the hot cell. Inside, the once powerful machines, designed for the delicate and dangerous task of cesium extraction, stand like ancient, dormant giants. The quiet is unnerving, amplifying the sense that something is terribly wrong. The only sound now is the steady, rhythmic hiss of their own breathing inside the hazmat suits.

Kirsty moves cautiously to a control panel set against the wall. Her eyes scan the array of buttons and levers, all of them in the 'off' position. Whatever process this facility was once engaged in, it has since ceased.

Deacon's voice is muffled by the suit. "Let's check the storage area. If there is cesium here, it should be stored nearby."

Kirsty nods, her heart pounding in her chest as they move toward a heavy, reinforced door on the far side of the chamber. The door is marked with another radiation hazard symbol, this one larger and more ominous than those they've seen before.

Deacon grabs the handle and, with some effort, pulls the door open.

Beyond lies a narrow corridor, the walls lined with thick, reinforced glass panels. The passage leads them to a storage room, the only door in sight. Deacon steps forward, pushing it open with a loud creak that echoes down the empty hallway. The room beyond is dark, the only light coming from their flashlights, which cut through the darkness in narrow beams.

As they step inside, the Geiger counter strapped to Kirsty's suit suddenly goes crazy. The rapid clicks of the counter fill the room, the needle jumping erratically from side to side.

"Mark..." Kirsty's voice trembles with unease.

Deacon raises his flashlight, sweeping it across the room. Metal shelves line the walls, their surfaces covered in a thin layer of dust. The shelves are empty, devoid of the heavy canisters that should have been there. His breath catches as the realization hits him.

"They've taken it," Deacon murmurs, the words barely audible over the Geiger counter's frantic clicking. "And you know what cesium is good for?"

"Dirty bombs," Kirsty says as she steps closer to one of the empty shelves. "Because it emits gamma radiation, which penetrates the body more easily than all other forms."

"But now it's been cleaned out," Deacon adds.

Kirsty nods grimly. "Then that raises the question: where is it?"

But before they can ponder this further, the sound of rocks falling catches their attention. The noise echoes through the chamber, sending a jolt of fear down their spines. They rush to the entrance of the hot cell and peer out into the tunnel at the edge of the vast room.

They listen intently. The cracking sound of falling shale is followed by a low, rumbling growl, slowly turning to the sound of voices. Deacon and Kirsty exchange a look.

"Someone's here," Kirsty whispers.

Deacon's hand moves to his backpack. Unzipping it, he pulls out a sidearm. Beside him, Kirsty does the same, her movements as quick and efficient as they can be in the cumbersome radiation hazmat suit that clings to her.

"Stay close," Deacon murmurs.

The entrance tunnel and the large metal door are at the top of a bank. Their eyes scan it. In the dim light, they spot figures moving—men in hazmat suits similar to their own, their faces hidden behind reflective visors that gleam under the lighting.

Deacon's heart skips a beat as he notices the glint of metal. These men are armed, their automatic rifles catching the light. The men begin positioning themselves with military precision, covering every angle of the chamber's entrance, their weapons trained on the hot cell below.

One of the men steps forward, raising a megaphone to his visor, right where his mouth is. The amplified voice that follows is cold and commanding, bouncing and echoing off the walls of the domed chamber.

"You are surrounded," the voice booms. "Come out with your hands up and surrender. Failure to do so will lead to your deaths."

Deacon and Kirsty exchange a quick glance, their eyes locking in silent understanding. There's no way they're surrendering. They both know what that would mean—capture, interrogation, and a fate worse than the one they face now.

"We'll have to make a run for it," Deacon whispers as the men change positions, fanning out. "Get ready to move."

Kirsty nods.

The man with the megaphone shouts again, his voice impatient. "This is your final warning! Surrender now, or we will open fire!"

"Run!" Deacon yells, grabbing Kirsty's arm and pulling her with him as they sprint from the door of the hot cell. Bullets ping off the metal machinery around them, sparks flying as they dive behind a stack of boxes. The metal containers provide minimal cover, but it's enough to give them a moment to catch their breath. Bullets continue to rain down around them, the force of the impacts causing the boxes to shudder.

"We can't stay here!" Kirsty gasps. "They'll pin us down! What do we do, Mark?

"Stay low, and stay close," he mutters back. "We'll use the crates and machinery for cover."

Suddenly, the impatient crack of gunfire erupts from above, the security team unleashing another storm of bullets. The chamber fills with the deafening roar.

"Move!" Deacon barks, popping up to return fire with his pistol. His shots ring out, targeting the men closest to the entrance. One of them stumbles back, clutching his shoulder, but the others keep firing, relentless.

Kirsty scrambles behind a nearby piece of machinery, her breath coming in sharp gasps. She steadies herself, then quickly pivots to the other side, her movements fluid despite the bulkiness of the hazmat suit. As she emerges from the far end, she opens fire, her shots precise and controlled, laying down suppressive fire to keep the security team pinned.

Deacon moves swiftly in her wake, Kirsty's covering fire keeping the security team at bay, buying them just enough time to reach the safety of another piece of cover—a gasoline-powered generator. They dive behind it together, gunfire reverberating through the chamber.

As he sits with his back against the cold metal, Deacon's eyes narrow on a plastic canister of gasoline tucked against the generator. An idea sparks in his mind. "I think I know how to give us cover," he says.

Kirsty nods, understanding without needing an explanation. As the men surrounding them home in on their position, Deacon yanks open the canister and suddenly bolts from cover, the bulky hazmat suit slowing him down but not enough to stop him. With bullets whipping past and pinging off the machinery around him, he pours a thick line of gasoline along the ground. He doesn't stop until he reaches a large telescopic forklift at the far end of the room, diving behind it.

Deacon fumbles with his lighter for a moment, the gloves of his suit making the task more difficult, but finally, he strikes a flame and drops it onto the trail of gasoline. The fire ignites instantly, roaring to life and racing along the fuel-soaked path. Ventilation shafts fill the room with fresh oxygen, making the air itself highly combustible. A wall of flames erupts between them and the security team, the intense heat radiating through the chamber.

"Go, Kirsty! Run!" Deacon shouts, watching as she dashes from cover, using the flames as a shield.

Deacon's eyes dart back to the half-full canister. He knows they need more to make it out alive. He yanks off his hazmat helmet, the cold air biting at his face as he rips a strip from his shirt, pours some gasoline on it, enough to soak the rag, then stuffs it into the canister's opening. His fingers move quickly, lighting the makeshift fuse. With a deep breath, he hurls the canister with all his strength into the midst of the advancing security team.

The canister lands upright, wobbling slightly before it steadies, the flame licking closer to the fuel inside. One of the men shouts in alarm, his voice cut off as the canister explodes with a deafening roar. A massive fireball engulfs the area, the intense heat and force knocking several of the men off their feet as the air catches fire.

The distraction is perfect. The chamber is filled with smoke and flames, the security men thrown into chaos. Deacon doesn't waste a second. "Let's go!" he yells, sprinting for the exit. Kirsty is right behind him, dodging through the smoke and flames that have engulfed the chamber.

But just as they near the heavy metal door, a sharp crack splits the air—a bullet tears through the smoke and slams into Kirsty's side. She gasps in pain, her steps faltering as the impact sends her crashing to the ground.

"Kirsty!" Deacon shouts, skidding to a stop. He rushes to her, grabbing her under the arms, his adrenaline surging as he drags her toward the exit. Bullets ping off the walls around them, the security men closing in fast. One catches Deacon's suit, cracking the visor but skimming off the surface.

Kirsty's face is pale, her breath coming in short, labored gasps, but she doesn't give up. She grits her teeth, forcing herself to move with Deacon's help.

They reach the thick metal door just as the security team emerges from the smoke, rifles aimed. With a final surge of strength, Deacon shoves Kirsty through the opening, then grabs the edge of the door, heaving it shut with all his might. The metal slams into place just as a barrage of bullets thuds against it from the other side.

Deacon twists the lock, securing it in place. The security men pound against the other side, their shouts muffled by the thick metal, but they're too late. The door holds, blocking their path.

"Kirsty!" Deacon turns to her. Blood seeps through her hazmat suit, staining the material dark red.

"I'm... I'm okay... I think," she gasps, wincing as she tries to sit up. "Just hit in the side... I'm pretty sure the bullet went straight through... I don't think it hit anything vital."

Deacon doesn't waste time with words. He quickly helps her out of the hazmat suit before undressing from his own. As soon as they're free, he wraps an arm around her, supporting her weight as they move as quickly as they can from the area. Kirsty holds her side just above the hip, blood oozing through her fingers.

The tunnel seems to stretch on forever, the darkness pressing in around them. But then, finally, after almost thirty minutes, a faint glimmer of light appears ahead—the tunnel's exit. With a final burst of energy, Deacon hauls Kirsty up the last stretch, and they burst out onto the surface, gasping for air.

The night is bitter cold, the snow falling in heavy lumps, the forest around them eerily silent compared to the chaos below.

Deacon wastes no time. He quickly helps Kirsty through the woods and into their pickup truck.

"Hold on," he mutters, sliding into the driver's seat. The engine roars to life, and Deacon floors the accelerator, the truck lurching forward as they tear through the snow-covered underbrush.

Their relief is short-lived. Headlights slice through the darkness behind them—the security team is in pursuit. Deacon grits his teeth, swerving through the forest, dodging trees and rocks as he tries to lose them.

The pickup bounces over the rough terrain, the wheels skidding on the snow-covered ground. Kirsty clutches her side, her hand slick with blood. "They're getting closer, Deacon!" she warns, her voice tight with fear.

"Not for long," Deacon growls, his eyes scanning the dark forest ahead. Just as the security vehicles close in, he spots a narrow path winding deeper into the woods, practically invisible to anyone not looking for it. He'd spotted it during the drive there, noticing on the satnav that it led to the highway. Without hesitation, Deacon veers off the main trail, the pickup squeezing through the tight space, branches scraping against the sides, snow showering down on them from the trees above.

The men in the security vehicles miss the maneuver, coming up over a ridge as it happens. Deacon watches in the rearview mirror as the headlights behind them pass the turn and fade away, swallowed by the dense woods and the falling snow. They've finally lost them.

Kirsty slumps back in her seat, her body trembling with pain and exhaustion as the pickup bounces up and down. "We made it," she whispers, more to herself than to Deacon.

Deacon doesn't respond, his focus still on the ragged road ahead. But a flicker of relief crosses his face as the reality of their escape sinks in. They've survived—barely.

FORTY-FIVE

THE BASEMENT OF THE NASHVILLE BAR IS CLOAKED IN shadow, the dim bulb overhead casting a sickly, flickering light on the faces of the ten or so people gathered—the last remnants of the Iron Brotherhood. Outside, the muffled roar of the city—a mix of protest chants, the blare of sirens, and the distant, thunderous rumble of scuffles.

Marcus Kane stands at the center of the loose circle, his figure dark and imposing. His presence commands attention, and one by one, the scattered conversations die down as everyone turns their focus to him.

"Brothers, sisters, the time has come," he begins. "We've waited, planned, and sacrificed for this moment. And now, the day is almost upon us. Leadership have given me our mission."

The group shifts, expectation rippling through the room. Marcus pauses, letting the tension build before he leans forward, his voice dropping to a conspiratorial whisper. "On the day of the State of the Union, while the nation's eyes are glued to their TV screens, we're going to deliver a message. Not just here, but across the world."

Murmurs run through the group. Nods of agreement, but

also flickers of unease. Marcus catches each glance, each uncertain shift, his gaze sharp as he continues.

"Our task," he goes on, "our mission, is the to be the most critical of them all. Historical is what I'd call it. You see, brothers and sisters, we've been chosen to hit the Capitol itself. To strike at the very heart of the federal beast."

There's a collective intake of breath as the gravity of his words sinks in.

Marcus's voice drops even lower, a growl that seems to reverberate through the room. "We'll be picking up a bomb. One that will ensure our message is heard loud and clear. This is what we've been waiting for. This is our moment."

"Hell yeah!" David Smith cries out as he stands beside Raven. Peter stands back from them, practically on his own.

Suddenly, the faint buzz of a phone interrupts the tense atmosphere. Marcus's expression hardens as he pulls out the encrypted device from his pocket. When he answers it, the room falls into an uneasy silence. As he listens to the voice on the other end, his eyes narrow, homing in on Peter, who shifts uncomfortably under the intense scrutiny.

The conversation ends abruptly, and Marcus lowers the phone, his hand tightening around it as if trying to crush the very information it delivered. His demeanor changes—darker, more ominous. The Brotherhood members sense the shift, their eyes flicking toward Marcus as he turns, slowly, deliberately, to face Peter. His gaze is cold, penetrating, and the subtle change in the air sends a shiver down Peter's spine.

"Now to the next agenda," Marcus says in a menacing tone. "How you doing, Reilly?"

Peter feels the full force of his dark eyes.

"Or should I say... Peter Black?" Marcus's voice, sharp and cutting, slices through the dank air of the basement like a knife. "That's right, brothers and sisters. I think we just found our rat."

Peter feels as if the ground has dropped out from beneath him. His heart skips a beat, the words striking him with the force of a physical blow. The room, once a place of unity and purpose, now feels suffocating, the walls pressing in on him. Panic surges through his veins, but before he can even begin to formulate a plan, the basement erupts into mayhem.

The Iron Brotherhood members—men who had fought by his side, shared drinks and war stories with him—turn on him with brutal efficiency. Peter fights back with everything he has, adrenaline coursing through his body, his fists flying in every direction. He lands a few solid hits, but the odds are stacked against him. The confined space of the basement limits his movements, and their numbers quickly overwhelm him.

He's forced to the cold, unforgiving floor, the rough concrete scraping against his skin as they pin him down. His vision blurs, the world around him narrowing to the immediate pain and the pounding in his head. Blood drips from his nose, mingling with the sweat that soaks his face, the metallic taste of it sharp on his tongue. In the background, he can hear Raven asking what he's done, who Peter Black is.

"A federal agent," Marcus hisses in reply to her questions.

Through the haze of pain and confusion, Peter watches David Smith step forward, his face devoid of emotion, his eyes as cold and merciless as the hunting knife he grips. He kneels beside Peter. The steel of the knife catches the dim light of the bulb hanging from the ceiling, and Peter glares up at David, refusing to show fear, even as his heart hammers in his chest.

"A goddamn Fed," David says in an undertone dripping with venom as he raises the knife high, the intent clear in his eyes.

Peter braces himself, every muscle in his body tensing for the inevitable. But just as the blade is about to descend, Marcus Kane's hand snaps out, gripping David's wrist with iron strength.

"Stop," Marcus commands. "Leadership wants him alive. They need to know what he knows."

For a moment, the room is frozen in time. David's eyes flick to Marcus, the knife still poised above Peter's chest. But finally, with a frustrated snarl, David lowers the blade, pulling back with clear reluctance.

"You're lucky," he spits, his voice dripping with disgust. "But this isn't over."

The Brotherhood members drag Peter to his feet. The rough grip on his arms pulls him forward, and he stumbles, barely able to keep up. As the basement spins around him, his gaze lands on Raven standing in the corner, her face pale, her eyes wide with shock. She's frozen, unable to move or speak, just watching in stunned silence as they pull him away. There's something in her expression that twists the knife of betrayal even deeper—utter disbelief, mingled with a pain that mirrors his own. For a brief moment, their eyes lock, and in that instant, Peter feels the full weight of her unspoken words, the sadness that cuts him to the core.

They drag him outside and bundle him into the back of a van, forcing zip-ties onto his wrists and legs. Sitting in the back, surrounded by leering faces, Peter forces himself to focus, to think past the searing indignation that blurs his thoughts.

Someone inside the CIA has betrayed him. It's that obvious. The realization hits him like a second blow, more painful than any of the punches and kicks he's just endured. Someone he trusted, someone who knew his mission, has leaked his identity—the mole he was told about. The bitterness of it gnaws at him, turning his stomach as the van's engine rumbles to life. One thought continuously goes through his head: *Who is the double agent?*

FORTY-SIX

The Colorado motel is a nondescript stretch of one-story buildings on the outskirts of town, the kind of place where people come to disappear for a night. The neon sign outside flickers intermittently, casting an eerie glow on the cracked asphalt of the parking lot.

Inside one of the rooms, Deacon and Kirsty wait in tense silence. Only a single lamp on the bedside table illuminates the shabby furniture and worn carpet. Deacon has just finished patching Kirsty up. The bullet went right through, missing anything vital, and her side is now wrapped in a makeshift bandage, the wound still fresh but no longer bleeding. She's propped up against the headboard, her face pale and lined with pain, but her eyes are sharp, focused.

Deacon sits on the edge of the bed, the adrenaline still pumping through his veins as he checks his handgun, only six bullets remaining.

The minutes tick by, each one feeling longer than the last, time stretching out, until finally, there's a gentle knock at the door. Deacon's head snaps up, his grip tightening on his gun, but he forces himself to relax. He knows it's her.

Standing, he moves to the door and peeks through the peephole. He sees the familiar face of CIA Director Sandy McLean, her blond hair tied back in a bun, her bony face bent into a tense expression.

She was the only person Deacon could think of calling, the fear of the mole forcing him to avoid anyone else.

He unlocks the door and opens it just enough to let her in before quickly shutting and locking it behind her.

Director McLean steps into the room, her eyes immediately going to Kirsty, assessing her condition.

"How is it?" the director asks her.

"Sore," Kirsty replies. "But I'll live."

McLean glances at Deacon. "You were right not to take her to a hospital. This needs to be handled quietly."

Deacon nods, coming away from the door and placing his handgun on the bedside table, the safety on.

McLean takes a position in the middle of the room. "You should have told me from the beginning what you were up to," she says, her tone scolding. "Especially the little fact of Peter Black having infiltrated a militia group. Christ, Deacon. Now, tell me. What did you find underneath Grand Junction that got you shot?"

Deacon glances at Kirsty, who is struggling to stay alert, then back at McLean. He takes a deep breath, knowing that what he's about to say could change everything.

"We found a hot cell," he says grimly. "They were using it to procure cesium from spent fuel rods. Grand Junction is full of them, so I'm guessing they're involved. Our old friend Thomas Jacks has some explaining to do."

Kirsty sits forward, wincing as she moves. "And you know what they use cesium for—dirty bombs."

"But here's the thing," Deacon continues. "When we inspected the storage in the hot cell, it was empty—all the cesium was gone. So whatever they're planning, it's already moved into the next phase. We need to inform the president and initiate a state of emergency. This is too big to keep under wraps."

McLean's face remains impassive, but there's a flicker of something in her blue eyes—something that Deacon can't quite place. She steps closer, her voice dropping to a near whisper as she asks, almost casually, "Does anyone else know about this?"

Deacon hesitates, sensing a subtle shift in her demeanor. There's something in the way she's looking at him now, a coldness that wasn't there before, but he dismisses it as nerves, assuming the weight of the situation is affecting them both. He shakes his head.

"No. Just us," he replies firmly.

"Good," McLean says coldly.

Without warning, she pulls a silenced pistol from inside her coat. The movement is smooth, practiced, almost too fast for Deacon to register. Before he can even react, she turns the gun on Kirsty and pulls the trigger. The muted pop of the gun is almost lost in the stillness of the room.

Kirsty's eyes widen in shock as the bullet strikes her in the chest. She gasps, blood blooming on her shirt as she slumps back against the pillows, her life snuffed out in an instant.

"No!" Deacon shouts, horror and disbelief crashing over him.

His instincts kick in, and he reaches for his own weapon, but McLean is faster. She spins on him, her finger squeezing the trigger. Deacon lunges forward, grabbing her arm just as the shots fire, sending the bullets into the ceiling. McLean snarls, kneeing him hard in the stomach. He loses his grip on her wrists, stumbling back. As she takes aim again, Deacon does the only thing he can. He dives toward the window. Another shot rings out, and pain flares in his buttocks, but he manages to throw himself through the glass.

He hits the frozen ground hard, pain shooting through his already battered body, but he grits his teeth and forces himself to move. Every breath is a struggle, his lungs burning as he staggers across the icy gravel to a line of parked cars.

McLean rushes to the window, but he's already behind the

cover of the vehicles, heading toward the trees that line the edge of the motel.

Cursing under her breath, she climbs out the window, avoiding the shards sticking up out of the frame and dropping down onto the lot. Her expression is cold and emotionless as she scans the darkness. The silenced pistol in her hand is still hot, its barrel faintly smoking in the cold night air as she moves with calculated precision, like a snake hunting a rat, her eyes slicing through the shadows in search of her prey.

Deacon, the pain in his rear spreading to his legs, pulls himself deeper into the trees. Spotting a ditch, he throws himself into it, rolling into the brush, the tall grass providing scant cover. His body trembles with pain and exhaustion, and his vision blurs as he fights to stay alert. The night is eerily quiet, the distant hum of highway traffic the only sound.

Then another sound. McLean's footsteps crunching on the compacted snow. He holds his breath as her shadow looms just feet from the ditch. She pauses, her gaze sweeping the area, the tension almost unbearable as Deacon wills himself to remain still, to blend into the darkness. The seconds stretch into an eternity, the cold air thick with the scent of earth and blood.

And then, miraculously, she turns away. The sound of doors opening and voices murmuring as people begin to emerge from their rooms, drawn by the noise of the breaking glass, seems to spook her. McLean curses under her breath once more before slipping away into the night, her figure fading into the shadows as quickly as she had appeared.

Deacon lies in the ditch, his body broken, his mind reeling from the betrayal. The pain is overwhelming, but what burns more than the bullet in his ass is the grief and rage that churns inside him, threatening to consume him whole. Kirsty is dead. The cesium is gone. And someone he trusted has just tried to end his life.

FORTY-SEVEN

UNTIL THEY CAN MOVE HIM TO LEADERSHIP, THEY'RE keeping Peter in a foreclosed house in another suburb of foreclosed, empty houses on the edge of Nashville.

The electricity is off, leaving the room they keep him in cold and damp. Peter sits slumped in a chair nailed to the floor, his hands bound tightly behind him with rough, coarse rope, and his legs duct-taped to the legs of the chair.

The oppressive silence is shattered by the creak of the door opening. Raven enters, her footsteps quick and light as she comes to Peter's side. Her face is a storm of emotions—anger, confusion, desperation—all fighting for control. The dim morning light seeping through the thin curtains catches the tears glistening in her eyes as she takes in the sight of Peter, beaten and vulnerable, a man she thought she knew.

"Jack... Peter... whatever your name is, we need to get you out of here. Now." Her voice is frantic as she says it.

Kneeling beside him, she fumbles with a knife to cut through the ropes and tape that bind him. As she saws through the bindings, Peter's eyes meet hers with a mixture of pain and sorrow.

"My real name... is Peter Black," he says, his voice rough, filled with regret as he looks at her.

Raven freezes, the knife slipping slightly in her trembling hands. She stares at him, the truth crashing down on her like a falling tower block. Her hands continue to shake as she processes what he's just said, the world around her seeming to tilt and spin. She had hoped, prayed that the others were wrong.

"So... it's true? You're CIA?" Raven's voice quivers.

Peter nods slowly, his heart aching as he sees the pain in her eyes, knowing that his next words will only deepen the wound.

"Yes. I'm sorry, Raven. I never wanted to lie to you... but I had to. It was my mission," he says in a voice heavy with regret.

Raven's breath catches in her throat. She pulls back, staring at him with a mixture of betrayal and hurt. The knife falls from her hand, clattering to the floor as she tries to make sense of the revelation.

"A mission? All this time... you were just using me? Using us? Was anything you said real?" Her voice is filled with anguish, the raw emotion cutting through the cold air.

Peter wishes he could erase the hurt he's caused, but all he can do now is tell her the truth.

"It was real, Raven. I swear to you," he pleads. "Everything I felt... everything I feel for you... it's real. But I had a job to do. I had to stop them. I have to stop what they're planning."

Raven's face crumples as she tries to process his words. She wants to believe him, wants to hold on to the connection they've shared, but the betrayal cuts too deep. She looks away, blinking back tears as she fights the storm of emotions threatening to overwhelm her.

"I never wanted to hurt you, Raven," Peter tells her. "But I couldn't let them win. Not after everything they've done, everything they're planning to do. Please, you have to believe me."

Raven looks at him, her eyes filled with a mix of anger, sorrow, and something else—something that might be the remnants of the trust they once shared. She hesitates, her hand trembling as she reaches for the knife again, cutting through the last of the ropes that bind him.

"You need to get out of here," she says quietly, her voice steady but devoid of the warmth it once held.

As Peter stands, he looks at her, trying to read the turmoil behind her eyes, but she avoids his gaze.

"Come on," she whispers, leading him out of the room. They move through a darkened hallway, the floorboards creaking under their weight, and begin passing the living room. Inside, three members of the Brotherhood are huddled around a makeshift fire, the only source of warmth in the otherwise frigid house. The men are deep in conversation, their voices raised in a heated argument over the smoke filling the room.

"Open the damn window, Joey. We're choking in here," one of them grumbles, coughing as he waves a hand in front of his face.

"And let the cold in? You out of your mind?" Joey snaps back.

Peter and Raven pause at the edge of the room, but the men are too engrossed in their bickering to notice the pair creeping past the doorway.

Finally, they make it to the back door. Raven reaches for the handle, opening it as quietly as possible, the cold morning air rushing in. Peter hesitates, turning to her with a pleading look.

"Come with me," he whispers urgently. "They'll turn on you when they find out you helped me. You know that."

Raven shakes her head. "I can't. My place is here. This is my family... my life. I can't just walk away."

"You don't have to stay," Peter insists. "We can figure this out together. Please, Raven... don't do this."

She looks at him, the internal battle evident in her eyes. For a moment, it seems as though she might relent, but then she takes a step back, pushing a set of car keys into his hand.

"The sedan parked on the street. Take it and go," she says, her tone final.

Peter looks down at the keys, feeling the weight of them in his palm, a physical manifestation of the choices laid before him. His heart sinks as he realizes there's nothing more he can say to change her mind. With a heavy heart, he nods, accepting her decision, though it tears him apart inside.

"Thank you," he murmurs.

Raven doesn't respond, her gaze fixed on the ground as if avoiding his eyes will make this easier. Peter steps out into the cold, the door closing softly behind him. He glances back one last time, seeing Raven standing in the doorway, her silhouette framed by the dim light inside. She watches him, her expression unreadable, a figure caught between worlds.

Peter climbs into the sedan, the engine coming to life as he turns the key. He looks back at Raven one last time, hoping for some sign, some flicker of emotion that might give him the strength to stay and fight for her. But she remains in the doorway, silent and still, her choice made.

With a resigned sigh, Peter shifts the car into gear and drives away, left with the bitter knowledge that he's lost some rare human connection.

FORTY-EIGHT

WHILE PETER ESCAPES, THE CORE MEMBERS OF THE Iron Brotherhood—Marcus Kane, Ray Collins, and David Smith —are busy a hundred miles away in Fayetteville. The lockup is a grim, isolated storage facility on the outskirts of the city, surrounded by rusting fences and overgrown weeds. The early morning is gray and dark.

Inside the lockup, the dim light of a single bulb reveals a large, unmarked white van parked in the center of the small, cluttered space. The vehicle is nondescript, just like a hundred others on the road, but its ordinary appearance hides something far more sinister.

The three men approach the van. With a heavy creak, David Smith pulls open the rear doors, revealing the bomb inside. It's covered with a heavy black tarp, and when David pulls it back, he reveals the dirty bomb, compact and rectangular. Its metal casing is dented, with haphazard wiring and a crude timer attached. Inside, cesium-137, encased in lead, waits to be dispersed by the plastic explosive packed tightly around it.

Ray Collins stares at the bomb, his mouth going dry as the reality of the situation sinks in. He swallows hard, trying to steady his nerves. "Wow. A nuclear bomb," he mutters.

"It's not a nuclear bomb, dumbass," Marcus Kane says. "You think we'd be able to get out of DC in time if it was a nuclear bomb?"

"Then what is it?"

"It's a dirty bomb. Packed with just enough explosives to bring the Capitol building down on top of all those assholes inside, and enough cesium to send a cloud of gamma radiation across the city—big enough to cover the Federal Triangle and the National Mall. Not only will it wipe out most of the swamp, it'll make the heart of the federal government uninhabitable for at least the next ten years."

David Smith's eyes widen as he thinks about it. "Once this goes off," he says, "there's no going back."

"There's no need to go back," Marcus replies, his voice taking on a dark, determined edge. "This is what's gonna set everyone free, Davey. We're not just making a statement—we're writing history."

FORTY-NINE

AFTER WAITING WHAT SEEMED LIKE A LIFETIME IN THE ditch, Deacon had managed to pull himself up and circle through the woods, praying all the time that Sandy McLean had fled the area. Stumbling along on pain-wracked legs, his butt completely numb, he had worked his way around to the front of the motel.

Ignoring the police cruisers parked in the lot, he had gotten into his pickup and driven away, the bullet still burning in his flesh.

Deacon is now lying on his front in a veterinarian office, the smell of antiseptic and animal musk hanging in the air. The vet, an old, gray-whiskered man with a perpetual frown, works on Deacon's wound with the steady hands of someone used to patching up more than just animals. Deacon winces as the needle pierces his skin, stitching up the nasty gash left by the removal of the slug.

His phone buzzes on the metal tray beside him, breaking the silence. Deacon glances at it, the screen illuminating the dim room. Picking it up, he answers the call, not speaking at first.

"Deacon?" comes Peter's voice.

The relief is instant. "Peter... we've got a serious problem.

More than we thought," Deacon says, his voice heavy with exhaustion.

"What happened?"

Deacon pauses, letting out a deep sigh before he continues. "We found a hot cell—deep underground, below Grand Junction. It was set up to extract cesium from spent fuel rods. The place was a goddamn fortress, but... the storage area was empty. Every bit of cesium had already been moved."

"Then they've already made the bomb," Peter says.

"What bomb?"

Peter takes a deep breath, the sound making it down the line. "The Iron Brotherhood are planning to hit the Capitol during the State of the Union. Leadership are giving them a bomb. It must be what's using the cesium from Grand Junction. The plan is to detonate it during the address, wiping out the President, the vice president, the Cabinet, Senators, Congress, the Supreme Court—everyone. It would decapitate the federal government in one strike and spread enough radiative material to make DC a no go for at least ten years."

Deacon feels his blood run cold. "Jesus, Peter... That's not just an attack. That's an assassination of America itself."

"Exactly," Peter replies, his tone grim. "They believe they're about to seize control—or at least plunge the country into a civil war where they come out on top. Little do they know, they're merely preparing the ground for a foreign invasion."

Deacon processes the information. "But you can stop them, right? I take it you're part of this plan?"

"No, I'm not," Peter replies, his words laced with frustration.

"What do you mean?"

"I mean, our mole outed me last night. The Brotherhood turned on me, and I'm only alive because one of them let me go."

The anger inside Deacon threatens to burn him up. He tenses as the vet pulls wire through his skin, the man tutting and telling him to be still.

"It's McLean," Deacon snarls down the phone. "She's the mole."

"Director McLean?"

"And that's not all. Kirsty... she's dead."

"What? No... How?"

Bitterness seeps into Deacon's voice. "McLean was the one who pulled the trigger. We were at a motel, waiting for her. She showed up, asked a few questions, and then... just like that, she shot Kirsty in cold blood. I barely got out alive."

Peter sounds dumbfounded. "McLean... the traitor. She must be the one who outed me. That has to be it. The Brotherhood knew everything. They knew who I really was—my name."

Deacon sighs. "I can take part of the blame for that. When I called her last night, before she showed up at the motel, I finally told her about you working undercover with the Brotherhood. She must have called her commie handler the second I hung up."

"You couldn't have known," Peter says.

"It also means that we're on our own. We can't go to the FBI, the police, and we certainly can't go to the CIA."

"It wouldn't be the first time I've been forced to work on my own, Deacon," Peter says. "But we have to move fast. They currently have everything. Kirsty's gone, the cesium's gone, and the Brotherhood is moving forward with their sick plan. We're running out of time."

"I know, Peter," Deacon replies, his voice heavy. "We need to head to DC, figure out our next move. If the Brotherhood is planning to hit the Capitol during the State of the Union, we have to be there to stop it."

"I'm heading there now," Peter says. "I'll let you know when I reach the city."

"Stay safe, Peter. We can't afford any more surprises. I'll see you in DC. Then we'll stop this thing once and for all."

Peter's final words are heavy with promise. "Count on it."

FIFTY

MARCUS KANE STANDS AT THE CENTER OF THE ROOM, his eyes scanning the scene with cold fury. The once-occupied chair now stands empty, the ropes that had bound Peter lying cut on the floor. The three Brotherhood members left to watch him —Joey, Hank, and Mitch—hover nearby, looking sheepish, their gazes darting between the empty chair and the floor.

"What the hell happened, boys?" Marcus's voice slices through the silence like a razor. The three men exchange nervous glances but remain silent, the shame of their incompetence hanging heavily in the air.

"Someone helped him escape," Marcus continues, stepping closer to the empty chair. His voice reverberates with anger, his eyes narrowing as he takes in the frayed ropes. He turns his gaze on the three men, his expression darkening. "You let him go."

Joey shifts uncomfortably, avoiding Marcus's gaze, while Hank and Mitch look down at their boots, their faces red with embarrassment. None of them dare to speak, the fear of Marcus's wrath keeping them silent.

"You idiots," Marcus snaps. "Do you have any idea what you've done? How could you let this happen?"

The men flinch at his words. Joey opens his mouth to speak,

but Marcus cuts him off with a sharp gesture. "Save it. I don't want to hear your excuses. Get out. Now."

The three men don't need to be told twice. They scramble out of the room, their heads hanging low, leaving Marcus standing alone with Ray Collins and David Smith.

Ray crouches down, picking up the frayed ropes, his face hardening as he realizes the truth. He looks up at Marcus, his voice grim. "It must have been Raven. She's the only one who could've gotten past them without raising suspicion."

David's face tightens in disbelief, his voice defensive as he steps forward. "No. Raven wouldn't do that. She's loyal—she's one of us."

Marcus turns slowly to face David, his eyes narrowing, a calculating look in his gaze. There's a pause, a moment of tension hanging in the air before he speaks. "Loyal? To us, or to him? You really don't know, do you?"

David looks confused. "What are you talking about?"

Ray, still holding the ropes, stands up and looks directly at David, his voice blunt, almost taunting. "Peter and Raven have been... involved for a while now. Pretty much since he showed up."

The words hit David like a ton of bricks. His face contorts with a mix of shock, anger, and betrayal. He takes a step back, his hands curling into fists at his sides, struggling to keep his composure. "No... she wouldn't. Not with him."

Marcus doesn't bother to soften the blow. He sees the fire in David's eyes, the storm brewing, and he knows it's exactly what he needs to hear. "She did, Davey. And now she's let him go. She betrayed all of us... for him."

David's breath comes in harsh, ragged bursts, his mind reeling from the revelation. His jaw clenches, fury overtaking reason. Before any of them can react further, Raven steps into the doorway. Her face is pale, her eyes red from crying, but there's a defiant strength in her stance. "I couldn't let him die," she says. "I'm sorry."

For a brief moment, the room is silent. Then, like a sudden storm breaking, David's rage explodes. He crosses the room in two quick strides and backhands her viciously across the face, the sound of the slap echoing in the small, cold space.

"You betrayed me. For him!" David snarls as Raven stumbles back, her head snapping to the side from the force of the blow. A cut opens on her lip, blood trickling down her chin. She doesn't cry out, doesn't defend herself. Instead, she looks at David with sad, tear-filled eyes, accepting the consequences of her actions with a quiet resignation.

But David's rage isn't sated. He grabs her roughly by the arms, dragging her farther into the room. Marcus and Ray exchange a quick glance before stepping forward to help restrain her, Ray using the piece of rope he's holding to bind her.

They then begin dragging her to the front door, Marcus's voice cold, devoid of any sympathy. "You've made your choice, Raven," he says. "Now you'll have to live with it."

"Please, you don't have to do this!" Raven's voice trembles with desperation as they haul her outside.

The night air is cold, biting against her skin as they push her toward the waiting van. Her feet barely touch the ground as they force her forward, the harsh grip of their hands unyielding. Ray Collins yanks the van's doors open with a sharp tug, revealing the ominous bomb inside, still covered by the heavy black tarp.

David's face is a mask of fury and pain as he forces her toward the device. She struggles, but the combined strength of the men is too much. They affix her to the bomb, her back pressed against the cold metal as they restrain her with straps and zip ties.

"Please, David... don't do this..." Raven's voice breaks, filled with despair as tears stream down her face.

David leans in close, his voice devoid of any emotion. "You're nothing to me now, Raven. You made your choice. This is where it ends."

FIFTY-ONE

Twelve hours later, in Washington, DC, the air buzzes with the anticipation surrounding the State of the Union. The city is on high alert, with security personnel visible on nearly every corner. Helicopters circle above, and the wail of sirens provides a constant backdrop to the bustling streets.

Deacon and Peter, heavily disguised, meet at a small, inconspicuous café tucked away from the main thoroughfares. The two men are almost unrecognizable, their wide-brimmed hats pulled low over their faces, oversized sunglasses obscuring their eyes and scarves wrapped tightly around their necks. The disguises are meticulously chosen to thwart any facial recognition software, a necessity given the precariousness of their situation.

The café is busy with patrons hurrying in and out, too preoccupied with their own concerns to notice the two men sitting in a shadowy corner, heads bent low in hushed conversation. The television above the counter drones on, playing the latest news headlines. A chilling report catches both their attention—a young woman found dead in a Colorado motel, shot to death. The screen flashes with the images of two men the police are seeking in connection with the crime. The grainy photos are unmistakable: it's them—Peter and Deacon. The captions don't name them, but if it wasn't for the disguises, they'd have every eye in that café on them right now.

Peter glances at the screen, his jaw tightening. "As if today wasn't already going to be hard enough," he mutters.

Deacon turns away from the screen, wincing slightly from the stitched-up wound on his buttock as he shifts in his seat. "So," he begins, "I reached out to the only person I think I can still trust—Aria Shah. She told me there's a team of CIA special forces guys in DC right now, hunting us down."

Peter's gaze sharpens. "Aria... can we really trust her?"

Deacon hesitates, then nods slightly. "I think so. She's risking everything just by talking to me. But she can't help us directly—it's too dangerous. She did, however, manage to send us this." Deacon reaches down, pulling a backpack from beside his chair, placing it on the table between them.

Peter's eyes flicker with curiosity and a hint of dread as he asks, "What's inside?"

Deacon unzips the pack, revealing a compact, sleek device. It looks menacing, a piece of high-tech equipment designed for serious work. Peter recognizes it instantly.

"An IPSI catcher," he says.

"That's right," Deacon says, zipping the bag back up. "It's a mobile stingray for tracking phone chatter—as well as their locations. But that's not all. It's also equipped to remotely hack into traffic cameras. We can use it to monitor communications in the area, get a lead on your old pals the Iron Brotherhood, and even tap into the city's camera feeds to track their movements in real-time."

"So we're not completely alone."

"No," Deacon says. "But Aria's warning is clear. This is it. We can't rely on anything else. She's sure McLean's got people watching her."

"Then we'll get it done with the stingray and the cameras," Peter says. "We need to start scouring the city for them straight away. They have to be somewhere, and I can guarantee you, they'll be in telephone communication. We should look for any cellphone that's encrypted. It won't let us listen in, but it'll still ping a location off the cell towers. And with the cameras, we might even catch a glimpse of them."

"That's my thinking," Deacon agrees.

They rise from their seats, the backpack with the IPSI catcher and the laptop to monitor it held tightly in Deacon's hand. Leaving the café, the two men blend into the crowd outside, just two more faces in the thronging city.

As they walk, Deacon speaks in a low voice, almost as an afterthought. "I called my old buddy in the FBI. Told him about the plot, hoping he might help."

Peter's eyes narrow, sensing the unease in Deacon's tone. "And?"

"He said he'd been told to inform his superiors if I got in touch. Told me that they've been briefed to expect something like this—some big warning about the State of the Union that would be a hoax. But because we go way back, he promised not to say anything this time. Still, he's certain they're listening."

Peter nods. "Then we'll just have to be quicker than them."

Deacon's lips tighten into a thin line, his eyes scanning the street ahead. "We don't have a choice."

FIFTY-TWO

The Brotherhood's van rolls into a dark, deserted parking garage on the outskirts of Washington, DC, the rumble of its engine echoing off the concrete walls.

The van parks in a shadowed corner where the strip lighting is out, and Marcus Kane, Ray Collins, and David Smith step out.

The men stand in the cold air, their breaths stretching out before them as they wait. It isn't long.

From the deeper recesses of the garage, two figures emerge—Jason Simons and Daniel Carter. As soon as they step into the light, smiles break out across their faces. The tension in the air melts away as they recognize David Smith standing alongside Marcus and Ray. Simons is the first to move, crossing the distance in a few long strides before enveloping David in a bear hug.

"Davey, you son of a bitch," Simons says, his voice thick with emotion. "We thought you were dead."

Carter isn't far behind, clapping David on the back before pulling him into a tight embrace. "Damn good to see you, man," he murmurs.

David grins, the weight of the past few hours momentarily lifting as he's reunited with his brothers. "I could say the same. It's good to be back."

Ray Collins watches the reunion with a faint smile. He turns to Simons and Carter, shaking his head. "I'm just glad you two aren't in some container at the Port of Baltimore."

Carter snorts, a smirk tugging at the corner of his mouth. "What a crock of shit that all was," he replies.

Simons glances over at the van, his eyes narrowing as he nods toward the back. "That where it's at?" he asks.

Marcus exchanges a brief look with Ray before jerking his head toward the van. "Take a look for yourselves," he says, his voice flat.

Simons steps forward, his heart pounding with curiosity and dread. He grips the handle of the van's rear doors, hesitating for just a moment before pulling them open. The doors swing wide, and the men's expressions shift from curiosity to shock.

There, strapped to the bomb, is Raven. Her eyes are wide with fear, her mouth gagged. The bomb's ominous presence fills the space, wires and circuits visible through the gaps in the tarp. The men stare in stunned silence.

Simons is the first to break it. "Why's she tied up like that?"

Marcus's expression hardens as he steps closer, his eyes fixed on Raven. "She betrayed us, Jason," he says coldly.

Carter's face pales. "Betrayed us? To who?"

"Jack Reilly," David Smith growls.

Simons furrows his brows. "Reilly?"

"Not Reilly," Marcus interjects in a bitter tone. "Peter Black, CIA operative."

"I knew it!" Carter snaps. "I never trusted that bastard."

Ray Collins steps forward, his face hardening as he explains. "We got ahold of him, had him tied up ready to be dropped off with Leadership. Then she betrayed us. Helped the son of a bitch escape."

Jason's eyes widen in shock while Carter's mouth tightens into a thin line. They hadn't expected this. Raven had always been one of them—trusted, loyal, or so they had thought.

"Now he's out there somewhere," Marcus adds. "In DC, and

he'll be trying to find us. He knows what we're planning, and he'll do everything in his power to stop us."

The men shift uneasily, the weight of Marcus's words sinking in. They've all seen Jack Reilly/Peter Black in action. They all know how deadly he can be.

FIFTY-THREE

DEACON'S FINGERS WORK QUICKLY ON THE KEYBOARD, hacking into the traffic camera network with practiced ease. The screen before him flickers, switching between various feeds as he scans the streets of Washington, DC, for any sign of a vehicle that could carry a large dirty bomb; namely a panel van. Peter keeps his eyes on the road, the tension growing inside the car as they drive through the city's labyrinth of side streets and back alleys, both men knowing that if they fail to find the Iron Brotherhood in time, they too will be hit by the wave of gamma radiation.

After five hours of searching, Deacon's face lights up. "I think I've got something," he says. "White van, sticking to the side streets. Not a typical delivery route."

Peter's eyes narrow as he glances across the car while navigating a tight turn onto a narrower street. "That could be them. Can you get a better look of who's inside?"

Deacon flips to another camera, one at the end of the street the van is driving down, heading straight toward it. He zooms in on the camera feed, the grainy footage sharpening until they get a clearer view. He adjusts the angle, and the van's windshield comes into focus. Inside, two figures are visible, their faces partially obscured by the dim lighting and the reflections on the glass. But even through the poor resolution, Peter recognizes them.

"It's them," he says, his grip tightening on the steering wheel. "Daniel Carter and Jason Simons. They're driving the van."

Deacon nods, his eyes glued to the screen. "They're heading west, but they're avoiding the main roads. They know what they're doing—trying to stay off the radar."

Peter accelerates slightly, heading toward the location of the van. "We can't lose them."

Deacon begins adjusting the settings on the IPSI catcher, enhancing the device's sensitivity to pick up any sudden changes in communication. "I've got their signals locked in. If they try to make a call or send a message, we'll know."

The chase tightens as Peter pushes their car to the limit, weaving through the streets of Washington, DC, with a laser focus. The city blurs around them.

"There it is," Deacon says sharply as he spots the van up ahead. It's moving rapidly through the traffic, but Peter is faster. He presses the gas pedal to the floor. The engine roars in response, and the car surges forward, closing the distance between them and their target.

As they pull alongside the van, Peter steadies the car with one hand and nods to Deacon, who already has his gun drawn. In a fluid motion, Deacon rolls down his window, leans out slightly, and takes aim at the van's tires. The sharp crack of gunfire splits the day as Deacon squeezes the trigger. The first shot misses, but the second hits its mark, puncturing the tire with a satisfying pop.

The van swerves violently as the tire blows out, but Peter is ready. He jerks the steering wheel hard, slamming into the side of the van with a bone-rattling impact. The van veers off course, careening toward the sidewalk. With one last push, Peter forces it off the road entirely, crashing into a row of parked cars before skidding to a halt.

Simons and Carter are out of the van in an instant, assault rifles in hand. They dive behind the vehicle, using it as cover as they unleash a hail of bullets in Peter and Deacon's direction. Peter and Deacon react just as quickly, ducking behind their car and returning fire. The sharp cracks echo through the streets, sending civilians scattering for cover like startled birds.

Peter's breath comes in short bursts as he peeks out from behind the car, aiming carefully before squeezing off a few shots. One of them finds its mark, and Simons slumps against the side of the van, a fatal wound in his chest. He slides to the ground, his rifle slipping from his grasp as life drains from his body.

Carter is hit by Deacon. Badly injured, he staggers back, clutching his side as blood pools beneath him. He leans heavily against the van, his face contorted with pain as his legs go weak and he sinks down to the ground.

"Drop it!" Peter shouts as he approaches. "It's over!"

Carter goes to lift his gun, but his arms are too weak, the blood filling his lungs, stealing his strength. Giving up on shooting Peter, he merely stares at him. The grimace on his face twists into a sick smile as he sits against the van, defiant even in his final moments. "You're too late..." he mutters, his voice thick with blood.

Peter exchanges a glance with Deacon before the latter cautiously approaches the back of the van, his gun still raised. Peter keeps his gun on Carter, scanning the area for any additional threats.

Deacon reaches the back of the van and yanks open the doors, his heart pounding in his chest. But as they swing open, his stomach drops. The back is empty. No bomb. No payload. Nothing but the cold, dark interior.

"It's empty!" Deacon shouts.

Frustration surges through Peter, his eyes locking on to Carter. "Where is it? Where's the bomb?" he demands.

Carter's smile doesn't falter, even as blood drips from the corner of his mouth. "I never liked you..." he whispers, the words laced with a venomous satisfaction. Then, with a final, shuddering breath, Carter's eyes glaze over, his body sagging lifelessly against the van.

Peter stares at the corpse, his mind racing. They're running out of time, and the bomb is still out there. He's about to turn to Deacon when a faint sound catches his attention. His eyes dart to the front of the van, where a cellphone buzzes on the dashboard. Without hesitation, Peter grabs it and answers the call.

"Carter, are you and Jason in position?" Marcus Kane's voice crackles through the line. "We're now heading to the Capitol. What's your status?"

Peter's blood runs cold as the realization hits him. Marcus and another team have the bomb—and they're now heading to the Capitol.

Peter cancels the call and exchanges a tense glance with Deacon. Without wasting another second, they dash back to their car. Peter hands the phone to Deacon before sliding into the driver's seat.

While Peter starts the engine, Deacon dives into the passenger side, the phone clutched tightly in his hand. With swift, practiced movements, Deacon grabs the IPSI Catcher, setting it up on the dashboard, quickly plugging the phone into the device.

"Come on, come on," he mutters, his fingers working rapidly to interface the phone with the IPSI Catcher. The device powers up, its screen flickering to life with a series of data streams and location pings. It begins searching, sending out signals to intercept and trace the origin of Marcus Kane's call.

Finally, the device pings with a location. "Got it," Deacon says as the first sirens reach their ears. "They've just entered Pennsylvania Avenue, about fifteen minutes from the Capitol. We need to move—now."

FIFTY-FOUR

THE STREETS OF WASHINGTON, DC, BLUR PAST AS Peter navigates the city with reckless abandon. As they speed down Pennsylvania Avenue, the Capitol Dome and the Statue of Freedom looming just blocks away, all that matters to them is the small dot on Deacon's IPSI catcher. The van is close to its destination, too close, and time is running out.

Peter's knuckles are white as he swerves around slower vehicles, ignoring red lights and the blare of car horns.

"It's right around this corner!" Deacon shouts. "We've got them!"

Peter's heart pounds in his chest as he slams his foot on the gas, sending the car hurtling toward the intersection. "Hold on!" he yells, his eyes narrowing as he takes the corner at breakneck speed.

But before he can react, another vehicle barrels into them from the side with a deafening crash. The impact is brutal, the sound of metal twisting and glass shattering filling the air as their car is thrown into a violent spin. Peter feels the world lurch sideways, everything turning upside down as the car rolls once, twice, before finally coming to a stop on its side.

Peter is momentarily stunned, the world around him spinning. He blinks rapidly, trying to shake off the dizziness as he registers the pain in his shoulder and the shards of glass embedded in his arm. Beside him, Deacon is groaning, a streak of blood running down his forehead from where he hit the dashboard.

"We've got to move," Peter grunts, his voice hoarse as he fumbles with his seatbelt. The car is a wreck, the windows shattered, the frame crumpled from the force of the impact, but they're still alive.

Deacon, dazed but conscious, nods and starts working on his own seatbelt. "Damn it," he mutters, his hand shaky as he finally releases the latch and drops down onto what used to be the car's side door.

Peter kicks at the windshield, his adrenaline surging as he forces it out of its frame. The shattered screen falls away in one piece, and he scrambles out of the wreck, pulling Deacon with him. They're bruised and battered but not broken. The mission isn't over yet.

As soon as they get to their feet, the air is torn apart by the sharp crack of gunfire. They dive for cover behind the twisted metal of their overturned vehicle, hearts pounding as bullets ricochet off the wreck.

"It's the SWAT team! They found us!" Peter yells over the cacophony, his voice strained as he peeks over the edge of the battered car.

Across the street, four black-clad figures move with deadly precision, taking up positions behind parked cars and concrete barriers. The CIA SWAT team, clad in tactical gear and armed with automatic rifles, is already closing in, their weapons trained on the two men.

"Move, now!" Deacon barks, already sending covering fire at them, forcing their attackers into cover. He's not looking to kill— just to incapacitate, to buy them time.

Peter squeezes the trigger of his own pistol, the recoil jolting up his arm as his shot finds its mark on one of the men's legs. The

SWAT agent crumples to the ground, clutching the leg with a pained grunt, his rifle skidding across the pavement.

Deacon follows suit, his shots precise and controlled. Another agent goes down, another leg shot, his weapon clattering to the ground as he retreats behind the safety of a nearby concrete barrier.

Peter risks a glance over the wreckage, spotting two more operatives advancing on their position. "We can't stay here!" he shouts, his voice hoarse as he reloads, the click of the magazine slotting into place drowned out by the returning gunfire. "They'll box us in!"

Deacon grits his teeth, nodding as he fires another shot, forcing an agent back behind a parked car. "We need to get to higher ground—get out of their sightlines!"

Peter scans the area, eyes locking on to a narrow alleyway just a few yards ahead. "There!" he yells, pointing it out.

Deacon follows his gaze, then nods. "Go! I'll cover you!"

Without hesitation, Peter pushes off from the wreckage, sprinting toward the alley, his heart hammering in his chest. Deacon lays down suppressive fire, his shots forcing the SWAT team to keep their heads down as Peter makes the dash.

Peter dives into the alley, pressing himself against the wall, breathing heavily. A moment later, Deacon is beside him, his own breaths heavy from the exertion as he reloads his weapon.

"They're gonna follow us," Deacon says. "We have to keep moving."

The maze of backstreets becomes their salvation as they weave through the labyrinth of alleys, the sound of sirens and shouts right behind them. The adrenaline drives them forward, every twist and turn in the alleys putting more distance between them and their pursuers.

But as they round a corner, their path is suddenly blocked. Police cruisers screech to a halt at the alley's entrance, sealing off their escape route. Deacon scans the area frantically. "Where now?"

Peter's eyes dart upward, spotting a fire escape bolted to the side of a nearby building. "Up there! Move!" he commands, already pulling out a wheeled trash can, climbing on top, and using it to leap onto the ladder.

They scramble up the fire escape, the metal rattling under their weight. Just as they reach the roof, the first police officers reach the fire escape, guns drawn. Shots ring out, bullets sparking off the metal railings as Peter pulls Deacon up onto the rooftop.

They dive behind a low wall, breathing heavily. But there is no respite. The brief moment of safety is shattered by the ominous whir of a helicopter's blades slicing through the air.

"We've got company!" Deacon shouts as the helicopter appears, rising up at the edge of the building.

Peter makes a snap decision. "Stay here. I'm getting us a ride," he says.

Without waiting for a response, he sprints across the rooftop toward the helicopter, so quick that the sniper onboard doesn't have time to get his shot away before Peter is there. Timing his leap perfectly, he launches himself from the edge of the roof, his hands latching on to the landing skids of the helicopter. The pilot, realizing what's happening, begins to jerk the controls. The chopper bucks and weaves, but Peter holds on, maneuvering himself across the underside of the craft, staying out of the sniper's line of sight.

While the sniper leans out of the door on one side, searching for the target, Peter climbs up the opposite side, his movements silent and precise as he opens the door and gets in. The sniper has his back to him, still focused on where Peter *was*, not where he *is*. He doesn't notice until it's too late. Peter grabs the sniper, yanking his rifle from his grip. The sniper struggles, but Peter quickly gets him into a tight hold.

"Hope you don't mind a short drop." Peter holds the sniper until they're over the rooftop where Deacon is waiting. Then he lets go, the sniper falling ten feet onto the roof with a bone-jarring thud. Deacon moves in swiftly, gun drawn, and secures the dazed sniper with the guy's own handcuffs.

Meanwhile, Peter climbs into the helicopter's cabin, taking the pilot by surprise. Drawing his gun, he presses it against the pilot's head, his voice cold and commanding. "Land on the roof. Now."

The pilot complies without protest. He eases the helicopter down onto the rooftop, the skids touching down just a few feet from where Deacon stands with the restrained sniper.

As soon as the helicopter is on the ground, Peter orders the pilot, "Get out. Walk away, and you get to live."

The pilot, pale and trembling, nods vigorously before scrambling out of the helicopter. He backs away, hands raised, before turning and sprinting toward the rooftop exit.

Deacon climbs into the helicopter as Peter takes the pilot's seat, quickly familiarizing himself with the controls.

"Let's end this," Peter says as the helicopter lifts off the rooftop, the city of Washington, DC sprawling beneath them, the Capitol appearing ominously in the distance.

FIFTY-FIVE

MARCUS KANE'S GRIP ON THE STEERING WHEEL IS tighter than tight as the van approaches the heavily guarded gatehouse that leads to the secured back entrance of the Capitol building. The area is fortified with barriers, and every guard is armed to the teeth, their eyes fixed on the white van as it inches forward.

As they near the gatehouse, the tension inside the vehicle coils tighter, like a boa constrictor. The guards, wearing body armor and gripping rifles, step forward, their expressions unreadable as they scrutinize the three men.

When the van finally comes to a halt, one of the guards motions for Marcus to lower the window. Marcus complies, his movements measured and deliberate, even as his heart pounds in his chest like a drum.

"IDs and paperwork," the guard demands.

Marcus hands over the forged documents and IDs with a steady hand, his face a picture of calm professionalism. This is the moment of truth. Leadership assured him that these documents were flawless, their fake identities already logged in the system.

The guard passes the IDs to a colleague, who methodically checks the photos against the faces in the van before using a hand-held PDA to scan the QR codes on each ID. Meanwhile, the first guard flips through the paperwork with a practiced eye.

Inside the van, the men sit as still as statues, their hands hovering near the guns taped under their seats. If anything goes wrong, they're prepared to fight their way beneath the building to deliver the bomb, no matter the cost.

"You're from C-SPAN," the guard comments as he reads through the documents.

"Yeah," Marcus replies. "We're here to deliver sound equipment."

"That's what it says," the guard mutters, scanning the papers. "Also says it doesn't need checking. In fact, it's adamant that the equipment isn't to be touched."

"It's sensitive equipment," Marcus explains smoothly. "Some of your guys checked it before we shipped out this morning."

The guard nods slightly, his brow furrowing as he glances around. "Well, you're in luck getting through quickly today. We've got some trouble happening at the moment—firefights in the city. Whole place is on high alert."

The tension inside the van tightens like a vise, the atmosphere nearly suffocating. The loss of contact with Carter and Simons, the abrupt cancellation of the call, and now the news of a firefight —it's all too much. The men know it has to be Peter. Their already frayed nerves are unraveling, inching closer to breaking point with every passing second.

The guard adds, "There's always some disgruntled fool wanting to start trouble. Just another day in DC, right?"

Marcus forces a chuckle, nodding in agreement. "Seems like it."

The guard with the IDs hands them back to Marcus without a word. The other guard finally nods, returning the paperwork. "You're cleared. Proceed to the underground area for deliveries," he says, his tone all business. "Just follow this road around."

Marcus breathes a silent sigh of relief, nodding curtly as he pulls the van forward, driving through the gatehouse.

"I think I need new underwear," Ray Collins mutters as they head toward the ramp leading into the underground storage area beneath the Capitol building.

The van rolls down the ramp, the dim strip lighting casting long shadows across the concrete walls, making the space feel even more oppressive.

"We're in," Ray murmurs.

Marcus guides the van deeper into the storage area. Rows of vehicles, boxes, and equipment are lined up in neat, organized sections. Each man keeps his eyes peeled, watching every shadow, every corner, for signs of anything out of the ordinary.

The van slows as Marcus expertly maneuvers it into position, pulling into a spot nestled between two rows of storage containers. This is it—moments away from the culmination of their deadly mission.

———

PETER'S KNUCKLES tighten on the helicopter's controls as he maneuvers the aircraft with precision, sweeping over the top of the Capitol building.

"They must be underneath," Deacon says. "In the underground storage area. That's where it'll cause the most damage."

"How long until the State of the Union speech starts?" Peter asks in a voice tight with urgency.

Deacon quickly checks his watch, his brow furrowing as he does the mental math. "Another eleven minutes. We need to move now."

Peter nods grimly. Every second counts, and he knows they're racing against time. The thought of what's at stake—thousands of lives, the heart of the nation—sharpens his focus to a razor's edge. He glances out the window at the sprawling Capitol Building below, its stately dome illuminated against the gray sky, the symbol of democracy now a target for complete devastation.

Deacon leans forward, his eyes scanning the Capitol grounds

as the helicopter hovers in place, the rotors slicing through the air with a steady, ominous hum. "The entrance is there," he says, pointing down at the back of the building. "We need to land right there."

Peter's eyes flick to the underground entrance. He quickly assesses the best spot to land—right in front of it.

"This is gonna be tight," he mutters, more to himself than to Deacon.

With a sharp intake of breath, Peter dips the nose of the helicopter and angles it toward the Capitol Building. The rotors whip through the air as he guides the aircraft down, the entrance coming into sharper focus with each passing second. He keeps the descent steady but quick, every movement calculated to shave precious seconds off their approach.

Peter's hands steady on the controls, he lowers the helicopter with expert precision, the skids making contact with the ground right in front of the entrance with a soft thud.

"Let's go!" Deacon barks, already unstrapping himself.

Peter shuts down the engine. The rotors slow to a halt as both men leap out of the helicopter, boots hitting the ground in unison. They're already moving, every step fueled by the adrenaline pumping through their veins, the weight of their mission driving them forward. The seconds tick away, each one bringing them closer to either success or absolute catastrophe.

———

INSIDE THE GRAND chamber of the United States House of Representatives, the atmosphere crackles. The room is filled with the nation's most powerful figures—members of Congress, the Cabinet, justices of the Supreme Court, Joint Chiefs of Staff, and other dignitaries, all seated in their designated areas.

The President stands at the podium, his hands resting on the edge as he surveys the room, minutes away from giving his address. While adjusting his tie, his sharp eyes scan the people before him. But something feels a little off. The usual sea of familiar faces is punctuated with empty seats, gaps that are too noticeable to ignore.

He leans slightly toward the vice president, his voice low but carrying a note of concern. "It looks like we have a low turnout this year. I expected to see more faces."

The vice president, always keenly attuned to the President's moods, glances around the chamber as well. He's noticed it too— the absence of certain key figures. "It's unusual, sir. I've noticed a few empty seats myself. And Sandy McLean's not here, either."

The speaker of the House, seated nearby, nods in agreement. "Director McLean sent word earlier. She's dealing with some fallout within the CIA—urgent, apparently."

The President's brow furrows as he absorbs this information. "I was hoping she'd be here. McLean's presence is a sign that we have the full support of our agencies."

The President takes a deep breath, steadying himself as he prepares to address the nation. But in the back of his mind, the unease lingers, a gnawing doubt that tonight's speech might be more than just another routine address—it might be the prelude to something far more dangerous.

FIFTY-SIX

Underground, beneath the Capitol, Marcus Kane, Ray Collins, and David Smith sit in a heavy, suffocating quiet. Their eyes watch as several people carry equipment into a service elevator.

When the elevator door clangs shut, Marcus says, "Okay. Let's go."

The men push open the van doors. The cold, sterile air of the underground storage area rushes in, mixing with the faint scent of concrete and machinery. Climbing out of the van, they move to the back.

"Open it," Marcus orders.

David nods and steps forward, gripping the cold metal handles of the van's rear doors. He hesitates for the briefest of moments, then, with a determined grunt, he pulls the doors open.

Inside the van, Raven is strapped tightly to the bomb, her eyes wide with fear and defiance.

Without a word, David climbs into the van. Behind him, Marcus Kane slips in as well, positioning himself on the opposite side of the bomb. While David comes before Raven, Marcus begins arming the device, setting the timer with a cold efficiency.

Ray Collins stands just outside the van, keeping a watchful eye on their surroundings, his hand resting on the grip of his gun.

"I really loved you, you know," David says, his voice seething with bitterness.

Raven glares at him, her eyes blazing with a fiery defiance that refuses to acknowledge the fear gnawing at her insides.

David leans in closer, his intent clear as he moves to steal one final kiss, a grotesque act of ownership. But as his lips meet hers Raven lashes out, her teeth sinking into his lip with a viciousness that surprises him. The sharp pain draws blood, and David recoils with a growl, the metallic taste mingling with his anger.

"You'll soon be in hell," David snarls.

"And you won't be far behind," she spits back, the taste of his blood in her mouth.

Before she can even flinch, his hand whips out, backhanding her across the face with a force that snaps her head to the side, the sting of the blow resonating through her entire being.

All the while, Marcus remains focused on the bomb. The timer clicks into place with an ominous beep, the display flashing nine minutes, the numbers ticking down with a finality that seals Raven's fate.

For a moment, David stands there, breathing heavily, his emotions warring inside him. Then he wipes the blood from his lip and composes himself, his gaze shifting to the bomb's timer. The numbers continue their relentless countdown.

"Goodbye, Raven," David says coldly. He steps back, watching as Marcus gives the final adjustments to the bomb. The deed is done.

Both men exit the van, shutting the doors behind them with a final, echoing thud that leaves Raven alone in the darkness.

"Let's go," Marcus says urgently. "We need to be at least a block away before this goes off. And once the wind catches the radiation, we'll need to be at least a couple of miles away. Otherwise, we'll be contaminated."

Ray Collins checks his watch. "We've got eight and a half minutes. So we need to move quickly."

Without wasting another moment, the trio begins moving swiftly toward the exit ramp. They have a car waiting for them not far from here, parked down an alley just off of Maryland Avenue. In all their runs, they were able to make it there within four minutes. That gives them another four to drive away from the area. The radius of the gamma radiation spread is estimated to reach no further than the Supreme Court.

The three of them race through the underground passage. As they climb the ramp toward the exit, relief begins to creep in, the thought of freedom just within their grasp. But that fleeting moment of hope is violently shattered when they spot the helicopter outside, followed by muzzle flash.

Ray Collins is hit multiple times in the chest and abdomen, the impact swift and brutal, his face contorting in shock and pain as he stumbles, barely registering what's happened before his body drops to the ground, lifeless.

Marcus Kane and David Smith dive for cover behind a nearby concrete barrier, narrowly avoiding the same fate. The air fills with the resonating echo of gunfire. The sudden violence draws the attention of security guards and Secret Service agents stationed nearby. Their weapons drawn, they converge on the scene, the confusion evident as they struggle to determine who is friend and who is foe in the midst of the melee.

From behind the barrier, Marcus Kane returns fire, his shots wild but filled with desperate fury. He knows he's cornered, the odds stacked against him, but he's not about to go down without a fight. David Smith follows suit, firing at Peter and Deacon as they advance from behind the helicopter.

Peter and Deacon move with practiced coordination, laying down suppressive fire to keep Marcus and David pinned down while they move from cover to cover along the edges of the ramp. They inch forward, using the alcoves and concrete columns of the underground space for protection.

The security personnel and Secret Service agents, caught in the maelstrom, split their focus. Some fire at Peter and Deacon, while others aim at Marcus Kane and David Smith, unsure of who poses the greatest threat. The confusion only adds to the frantic, dangerous atmosphere.

Amid the chaos, a Secret Service agent manages to get a clear shot at Marcus Kane. The bullet finds its mark, hitting him in the shoulder. He stumbles, the force of the shot nearly knocking him off his feet. Blood seeps through his jacket, but he grits his teeth, refusing to fall. With a defiant growl, he keeps firing, each shot more desperate than the last.

But the damage is done. Another shot, this one from a different angle, hits him square in the chest. The pain is overwhelming, his grip on his weapon faltering as the strength drains from his body. He gasps, dropping his gun as his legs buckle beneath him.

"You'll all... be with me... soon..." Marcus rasps, his voice barely more than a whisper, filled with the last vestiges of his defiance.

He collapses to the ground, the life draining from his eyes as blood pools around him. The end is quick and unforgiving.

Seeing Marcus fall, David Smith's resolve shatters. Panic floods his senses, the hopelessness of the situation crashing down on him. With survival instincts kicking in, he makes a desperate dash for the Capitol building, his figure disappearing into the shadows of a service entrance.

"Get to the van!" Peter shouts to Deacon, his voice cutting through the bedlam as he takes off after David Smith. Every instinct screams at him to stay with Deacon, to focus on the bomb, to save the Capitol. But the fire that has blazed inside him since he first stood over Kara Tate's lifeless body, since he learned who had pulled the trigger, now roars with an intensity that drowns out all reason. It consumes him, leaving room for only one thought: He has to catch David Smith. Nothing else matters.

"Peter, stop!" Deacon shouts, but it's no good.

Nevertheless, their sudden sprint creates the perfect distraction. As the Secret Service agents and security guards shift their attention toward the fleeing David and the pursuing Peter, Deacon finds his window of opportunity.

With the guards and agents preoccupied, Deacon keeps low as he dashes toward the van. Reaching it, his pulse quickens as he gets to the driver's side. He yanks the door open and jumps into the driver's seat.

Crouching low, he reaches beneath the steering column, prying open the panel to access the ignition wires. The sound of his own breathing fills his ears as he focuses, blocking out the distant shouts of the Secret Service as they search the area.

The wires spark as Deacon connects them, his eyes darting at the side-view mirrors as the engine finally roars to life.

———

THE SERVICE CORRIDOR David Smith ran into rises up into the Capitol building. The marble floors and towering columns now resonate with the rapid staccato of their footsteps. Staff and officials, all caught off guard, turn in shock as the two men barrel through.

David glances back, panic etched across his face as he raises his weapon and fires wildly behind him. The shots go wide, smashing into walls and sending chunks of plaster flying, but they're enough to send the crowd into a frenzy. People scream, diving for cover behind anything they can find—benches, statues, even the heavy doors of the Capitol offices. The once orderly, dignified atmosphere of the Capitol is replaced with a cacophony of shouts and frantic footsteps.

David rounds a corner, sweat pouring down his face. He fires again, the bullet whizzing past Peter's ear, close enough for him to feel the rush of air. Peter ducks instinctively, but he doesn't slow his pace. His focus is singular—he won't let David Smith escape.

As they charge down another corridor, David's desperation

grows. He's cornered, and he knows it. His eyes dart wildly, searching for an escape, any way out of this impossible situation. But before he can get much farther, a set of heavy doors at the end of the hall bursts open, and a group of Secret Service agents rush through, their service pistols drawn.

"Hold it right there!" one of the agents shouts as he trains his weapon on David.

David skids to a halt, his eyes wide with fear. He's trapped— Secret Service on one side, Peter closing in from the other. His mind races, adrenaline pumping through his veins as he realizes there's nowhere left to run.

But then he spots something out of the corner of his eye—a window to his right, followed by something that ignites the rage inside him. Beyond the glass, he catches a glimpse of the white van busting out of the Capitol grounds, barreling onto Constitution Avenue. The sight sends a surge of panic and adrenaline coursing through him. It's now or never.

In a flash of desperate inspiration, David dives toward the window, crashing through the glass with a thunderous shatter. Shards fly in every direction as he tumbles through the air, hitting the pavement a story below with a thud. For a brief moment, everything is still, the chaos of the Capitol fading into shocked silence.

Peter rushes to the broken window, peering down at David's crumpled form on the street. It looks like he's unconscious. A motorcycle cop, having heard the crash, runs over to assess the situation. The officer kneels beside David, cautiously reaching out to check his pulse. But just as the cop leans in, David's eyes snap open. Before the officer can react, David produces a knife from his jacket and plunges it into the side of the cop's neck.

The cop gasps in pain, his hand flying to the wound in his neck as he staggers back. David grits his teeth and pushes the officer aside, groaning as he forces himself to stand. He stumbles over to the cop's motorcycle, the keys still in the ignition.

With a roar, the motorcycle's engine comes to life, and David is off, the tires squealing against the pavement as he tears through the Capitol grounds.

Peter watches the scene unfold with growing horror. Kara's killer is getting away. Without hesitation, he does the only thing he can think of. As the Secret Service men shout for him to surrender, he leaps through the shattered window, following David's reckless path.

Peter's body slams into the ground, the impact jolting through his bones and knocking the wind out of him. Pain shoots through his legs and arms, but he pushes it into the corners. There's no time to stop, no time to think. He scrambles to his feet, his eyes locking on to another police motorcycle parked nearby.

Peter rushes to the bike, throwing himself onto the seat. With a determined snarl, he guns the throttle and tears off after David.

———

DEACON GRIPS the steering wheel mercilessly as he races down Constitution Avenue NW, his heart pounding in sync with the roaring engine. The cityscape rushes by in a blur of lights and shadows, the iconic buildings and monuments of Washington, DC, reduced to mere streaks of color as he pushes the van to its absolute limits.

The bomb in the back is a ticking time bomb—literally—and Deacon knows he's racing against the clock. Every second counts, and his only focus is reaching the Theodore Roosevelt Bridge and getting the van into the Potomac River before everything goes up in radiated flames. The depth of the river should, in theory, absorb most of the blast from the plastic explosives and contain the gamma radiation within the water. Sure, it'll contaminate the river for several miles, but at least there won't be a radioactive cloud covering the city.

But then, amidst the blur of his thoughts, he hears something that makes his blood run cold.

A faint, desperate cry comes from the back of the van.

At first, Deacon thinks it's just his imagination or the wind whipping through the van's interior. But the cries persist, growing louder and more frantic. He finally glances into the rearview mirror, and what he sees makes his heart skip a beat.

A woman is there, Raven, her face pale with terror, her body restrained tightly to the bomb. She's struggling against the zip ties, her eyes wide with fear.

"Help! Please, help me! Get me out of here!"

Deacon curses under his breath, the reality of the situation hitting him like a freight train. This was supposed to be a straightforward part of the mission—get the bomb to the river and sink it before it detonates. But now, with Raven trapped back there, everything has become infinitely more complicated.

He glances at the clock on the dashboard. Time is running out, and every instinct tells him to keep going, to focus on getting the van to the river. But he can't ignore Raven's terrified cries. He can't just leave her to die, strapped to a bomb with no hope of escape.

"Damn it," he mutters to himself. What the hell is he supposed to do now?

"Just hold on!" Deacon shouts back to her. "I'll get you away from that thing as soon as I can, but we need to get this van into the river first. Stay calm, okay?"

Raven nods weakly as she tries to control her panic. Deacon keeps his eyes on the road, weaving through traffic, his mind now split between navigating the streets and figuring out how he's going to save Raven.

———

WASHINGTON, DC is a blur of flashing lights and blaring sirens as Peter weaves through the crowded streets, the roar of his motorcycle bouncing off the buildings. His sole focus is on the figure ahead of him: David Smith, speeding just yards in front on a motorcycle.

Up ahead, the van turns onto Virginia Avenue NW, heading straight for the Theodore Roosevelt Bridge, its path parallel to the Potomac River. The bridge looms ominously in the distance, the dark waters of the river glinting in the gray day.

David Smith accelerates, his eyes locked on the van. With a sudden, calculated move, he veers closer, getting alongside it, then leaps from his bike. His body arches through the air before he latches on to the side of the van. He scrambles up, his hands gripping the vehicles' metal frame as he hauls himself onto the roof.

Peter watches the maneuver. There's no time to waste. He revs the engine, pushing the bike forward until it's nearly kissing the van's rear bumper. With a burst of speed, Peter jumps from the bike, his hands catching the rear of the van as he pulls himself up on top of it.

David Smith is already at the front, crouching low as he inches toward the cab. The wind tears at his clothes and hair, but his movements are steady, precise. His eyes are locked on the driver's side. In his hand, he clutches a knife, the blade glinting ominously in the dim light. He's preparing to strike, ready to lean over, smash the door window, and plunge the knife into Deacon.

But just as David raises the knife, Peter reaches him. In one swift, fluid motion, Peter swings his boot in a wide arc, aiming for David's hand.

The boot connects, striking the knife from David's grip. The blade skitters across the roof, spinning wildly before disappearing over the edge, clattering onto the asphalt below.

David twists around, his eyes flash with fury, his hands instantly shifting to grab Peter's leg, attempting to throw him off balance. Peter counters, shifting his weight and throwing a downward punch, his knuckles connecting with David's jaw in a satisfying crack.

David reels from the blow, but he recovers quickly, snarling as he lunges at Peter, both men grappling fiercely atop the speeding van. The wind howls around them, the city a dizzying blur as they struggle for dominance.

Deacon, inside the cab, glances at the mirror, catching sight of the battle raging above him. His grip tightens on the steering wheel as he swerves slightly, trying to keep the van steady despite everything going on around him.

On the roof, David Smith is no match for Peter. He struggles to maintain his balance on the swaying van as the two men stand apart. His eyes flicker with fear, but he tries to steady his nerves, preparing to fight.

Peter gives him no chance. With a fluid, predatory stride, he closes the distance between them, his movements precise and deadly, like a tiger coming in for the kill. David swings at him, but Peter effortlessly dodges the telegraphed punch, his body moving with the grace of Muay Thai as he shifts to the side and delivers a sharp elbow strike to David's ribs. The blow is quick and powerful, knocking the wind out of David and forcing him to stagger back.

Before David can recover, Peter is on him again. He grabs David's arm, twisting it into a painful lock, and with a swift motion, he sweeps David's legs out from under him. David crashes to the roof of the van, his body landing with a clattering thud.

"You knocked her teeth out," Peter growls, his voice low and deadly, each word dripping with cold, calculated rage. He yanks David up by the collar, pulling him close so their faces are just inches apart. David swings pathetically at him again, but Peter leans back just enough to avoid the blow, then counters with a brutal knee strike to David's abdomen, the force of the move driving the air from David's lungs.

As David doubles over in pain, Peter's fist comes crashing down, a hammer-fist strike that lands squarely on David's mouth, snapping his front teeth, almost choking him with the shards.

David tries to fight back, instinctively reaching up to shove Peter away, but Peter is relentless. He grabs David's hand, twisting it sharply, applying pressure to the tendons and bones until they snap with a sickening crack.

"You broke her fingers," Peter hisses, his voice a venomous whisper. With methodical precision, he begins to break David's fingers, one by one. The pain is unbearable, and David howls in agony, his body convulsing as he tries to pull away, but Peter's grip only tightens.

David Smith's subsequent attempts to fight back are pitifully weak, each of his movements easily countered with ruthless efficiency. Peter uses a mix of styles—Muay Thai, Pencak Silat, Krav Maga, and Aikido—each strike a masterful display of martial arts, breaking David down piece by piece. A sharp jab to the throat, a vicious elbow to the temple, a swift kick to the knee—all leaving David more bloodied and broken than before.

David's face becomes a grotesque mask of pain, barely recognizable under the relentless onslaught. His body is failing him, his strength drained by the overwhelming assault. Finally, with David barely clinging to consciousness, Peter grabs him by the scruff of his neck, lifting him effortlessly off the roof. Peter's eyes blaze with the furious fire burning within as he raises his fist, ready to deliver the final, killing blow.

"This is for Kara," he hisses, his voice trembling with righteous anger. But before he can strike, the van lurches violently, throwing both men off balance.

Deacon has taken the van off a ramp, sending it airborne for a moment before it begins its inevitable descent. The sudden momentum throws Peter and David into the air, both of them losing their grip on the van as they're flung toward the river below.

Time seems to slow as they plunge into the cold, dark waters of the Potomac River. The impact is jarring, forcing the air from Peter's lungs as he hits the surface hard. The frigid water engulfs him, pulling him down into its murky depths, disorienting him as he struggles to regain his bearings.

Nearby, David is thrashing in the water, his movements

frantic as he fights to stay afloat. But his body is battered, one arm broken, weakened by the brutal fight, and the river is relentless in its pull.

Peter breaks the surface, gasping for air, his chest heaving as he gulps down the precious oxygen. His eyes lock on to David, who is struggling to keep his head above water. Even the cold, unforgiving river can't quench Peter's thirst for vengeance.

Summoning every ounce of strength left in his body, Peter begins to swim toward David, the taste of revenge still fresh on his lips. The river may have interrupted his retribution, but it hasn't stopped it. Peter's resolve is unshakable—he will finish what he started.

———

INSIDE THE VAN, Deacon doesn't hesitate as it sinks deeper into the cold, dark waters of the Potomac River. Water floods into the vehicle, rising rapidly and adding weight to the sinking metal cage. Raven, still strapped to the bomb, watches the water climb with wide, fearful eyes.

Deacon pulls out a knife, and despite the urgency, his hands remain steady as he slices through the straps and zip ties binding Raven to the bomb. The water is already up to their waists, cold and unrelenting, but Deacon focuses only on freeing her.

With a final cut, Raven is released from her restraints. She gasps, her chest heaving with relief and fear, and locks eyes with Deacon.

"We need to move. Now," Deacon says.

He grabs Raven's hand, gripping it tightly as the water surges around them, rising quickly to their chests. Leading her into the front, Deacon uses the handle of his knife to smash the driver's side window. The glass shatters, the fragments quickly swept inwards by the rushing water.

Deacon then helps Raven squeeze through the narrow gap. He isn't far behind, the cold river water pulling at him as he forces his way out. The current outside the van is strong, but they kick with all their strength, propelling themselves upward, their lungs burning as they push toward the surface.

Finally, they break it, gasping for breath. They tread water for a brief moment, regaining their bearings, before they start swimming away from the van—and the bomb—with all their might. Deacon's heart pounds in his chest as he glances at his watch—less than a minute left.

"Keep going!" he shouts.

———

Pain contorts David Smith's face as he crawls onto the opposite riverbank. His mouth is a mangled mess of broken teeth, blood trickling down his chin as he drags himself up onto the muddy shore with busted, bent fingers. For a fleeting moment, he thinks he's escaped, that somehow, he's managed to survive Peter's relentless assault. But just as he starts to pull himself further up the bank, his broken hands clawing at the wet earth, he feels an iron grip clamp down on his legs. The suddenness of it shocks him, and his eyes widen in terror as he looks back over his shoulder.

Peter has emerged from the water, his face a mask of cold, unyielding fury. His eyes, dark and merciless, lock on to David's with a gaze that promises nothing but vengeance. Without a word, Peter yanks David back toward the water, his grip on his leg unrelenting, his strength fueled by a singular, burning resolve— the fire burning is now an inferno.

David struggles, thrashing and kicking, his hands digging into the mud as he tries to find purchase, but he's too weak, too broken. Every breath is a struggle, every movement a reminder of his impending doom. Peter's grip is unbreakable, dragging David closer to the water's edge.

As the cold water laps at David's legs, panic surges through him. His greatest fear, the one thing he's always dreaded, is now a horrifying reality. He fights with renewed desperation, but it's no use. Peter is stronger, his resolve like steel.

Peter's thoughts drift back to what Raven told him. David's fear of drowning. The memory sharpens his focus, fueling his determination. He forces David's head under the water, his hands pressing down with a relentless, almost methodical force. David's struggles are wild, his hands flailing as he tries to push himself up, but Peter holds him down, his mind fixed on one thing: justice for Kara.

Peter's grip doesn't waver as David thrashes beneath him. He watches the bubbles rise to the surface, his mind filled with thoughts of Kara—her smile, her laughter, the way she would light up a room. He can see her now, standing on the riverbank, her ghostly figure clear against the dark water, her eyes filled with a silent plea for justice.

Peter feels a surge of determination. For Kara, for everything that David had taken from him, from her, he presses down harder. David's struggles grow weaker, his movements slowing as the life begins to drain from him, the look of fear on his face reminding Peter of a frightened child. But Peter doesn't relent. He can't—not with Kara watching, urging him to finish it, to see it through to the bitter end. The resolve in her spectral gaze drives him forward, ensuring that justice is served, no matter the cost.

And so it is, the task done.

Peter finally lets go, releasing David's lifeless body to the current. It drifts away, carried by the river, the last remnants of a man who had caused so much pain now nothing more than a shadow in the water.

Looking up again, hoping to see Kara's face one last time, he sees that she's gone. Her presence, whether real or imagined, has served its purpose. The need for revenge that had driven him is gone, leaving only a hollow sense of finality in its place.

Peter stands on the riverbank, drenched and exhausted. Glancing up the river, his eyes scan the shoreline. In the dim light, he spots Deacon helping Raven up the muddy bank.

He's about to call to them when the bomb detonates. The explosion rips through the water with a deafening roar, and for a brief second, the river seems to rise, a towering wave surging upward, throwing spray and debris into the air. Peter is thrown off his feet by the force of the blast, his body hitting the ground hard. A searing flash of light momentarily blinds him, followed by a low, rumbling boom that shakes the very earth beneath him.

He scrambles to his feet, his heart pounding in his chest as he looks out over the river. The surface is now churning violently, bubbling and boiling. The Potomac, once a lifeline to the city, is now a poisoned artery, and the contamination will spread downstream, carried by the current into the heart of Washington, DC. But at least they have minimized the damage. At least they have saved America itself.

He glances down river, where Deacon and Raven are pulling themselves up, both of them dazed but alive, and he begins stumbling toward them. His legs are shaky, but there's no time to stop.

As he reaches them, they exchange a brief, wordless look. There's no time for explanations or reassurances; they all know what needs to be done. They have to get out of there, and fast.

Together, the three of them start running, their footsteps pounding against the wet earth. The sirens are closing in, the blue and red lights now visible in the distance. But they don't look back. They push forward, disappearing into the shadows, determined to stay ahead of the law and whatever consequences may come.

FIFTY-SEVEN

HOURS LATER, AS DUSK SETTLES OVER WASHINGTON, DC, the aftermath of the crisis unfolds near the Potomac River. Emergency vehicles flash their lights, and officials move swiftly through the scene. The atmosphere is tense, thick with the acrid smell of the river and a sense of urgency that hangs over everything.

A high-ranking official steps out of an armored SUV, his face set with determination. He strides toward the makeshift command center, where a FEMA coordinator, a Metropolitan Police captain, and an FBI agent are gathered around a map of the city.

"What's the status?" the official demands.

The FEMA coordinator looks up, clipboard in hand. "Hazmat teams are combing the river, and the EPA's already pulled water samples. The explosion was partially absorbed by the water, but we're picking up trace radiation. Cesium is in the water, and it's starting to spread downstream."

The police captain steps forward, his expression grim. "We've cordoned off the area, but the media's closing in fast. People are getting restless. We've recovered one body from the river—a male identified as David Smith—but we're still searching for others."

The FBI agent scans the map, his brow furrowed. "That makes five bodies total: the two at the Capitol and two more found shot on the road. Intel is patchy, and we're still piecing it all together. Right now, our priority is securing the Capitol and containing this situation before it spirals."

The high-ranking official frowns, looking between them. "And the bomb? Are we certain it's been neutralized?"

The FEMA coordinator hesitates before answering. "The blast was largely contained by the water, but the cesium spread is ongoing. The gamma radiation's being attenuated, but we won't know the full impact until the EPA finishes testing. This could contaminate the river for miles."

The official clenches his jaw, taking a deep breath. "Keep the public out of this. I want constant updates on the radiation levels, and make sure the media doesn't catch wind of how close we came to a catastrophe."

EPILOGUE

A DAY LATER, MICHAEL AND MAYU WORK QUICKLY, packing up whatever they'll need for what comes next. Their eyes cast sad looks over their Greenwich Village apartment, knowing that in all likelihood, they'll never see it again.

As Michael zips up his backpack, Mayu moves nervously toward the window. She pushes aside the blinds with two fingers, peering out onto the quiet street below. Her heart skips a beat when she sees a dark sedan pull up to the curb. The doors open, and several men in dark suits step out.

"Michael," Mayu whispers urgently, turning away from the window, her face pale. "We can't go out the front."

Michael looks up from his task, his eyes narrowing in concern as he sees the fear in Mayu's expression. He nods, grabbing his backpack and slinging it over his shoulder. "Okay, fire escape it is," he says.

They move quickly to the door that leads out to the fire escape, Michael yanking it open and stepping out onto the metal walkway. The cool evening air hits him, and he takes a deep breath to steady himself. But as Mayu follows him out, she freezes, her gaze fixed on the alley below.

"Michael, look," she says.

Michael glances down the alley, and his stomach twists in knots. More men are approaching the fire escape, their eyes scanning the building. It's clear they are being hunted, and there is no safe way down.

"Looks like it'll have to be the roof," Michael says. He grabs Mayu's hand and pulls her back into the apartment.

As they move swiftly through the narrow hallway, heading for the stairs that lead to the roof, Michael recalls his father's phone call. "They'll be coming for you," he'd said. "And if they catch you, they'll use you and Mayu to draw me out. You'll have to go on the run with me. I'm so sorry, Mikey."

The normal life that he had craved all those years on the run with Peter was now officially over.

As they ascend the stairs, Michael keeps a tight grip on Mayu's hand, his mind racing with thoughts of what might happen if they're cornered.

Finally, they burst through the door onto the rooftop. The night sky stretches out above them, stars twinkling faintly in the haze of the city lights. The noise of the street below seems distant, almost surreal, compared to the intense focus of the moment.

Mayu scans the rooftops, her breath coming in short bursts. "We need to keep moving," she says.

Michael nods, and they start across the rooftops, their footsteps quick and quiet. The buildings are close enough together that they can jump from one to the next, and they move with the practiced ease of people who have lived in the city long enough to know its ins and outs.

As they cross the final rooftop, Michael glances back, his heart pounding in his chest. The men are nowhere to be seen, but he knows they're still in pursuit. They can't afford to slow down—not until they are safely away.

They reach the edge of the building and climb down a rusted ladder that leads to a narrow backstreet. The city's noise envelops them once again, the hum of traffic and distant voices masking their movements.

Moving farther away from danger, Michael squeezes Mayu's hand, their fingers intertwined in a silent vow of determination. They're on the run now, and there's no turning back. They will meet up with Peter and Deacon, and together, they will face whatever happens next.

———

IN THE DIM, suffocating silence of a rundown motel room, the atmosphere is heavy with tension, lingering in the air like an unwelcome guest. The single, flickering bulb overhead casts jagged shadows across the room, highlighting the peeling wallpaper and the stains on the worn carpet.

Peter moves slowly, deliberately, as he packs his bag. Each movement seems weighted, his mind clearly elsewhere. He pauses, holding a sheet of lined paper in his hand, his eyes scanning the words he's written for what feels like the hundredth time. Emotions stir within him—a mixture of regret, sadness, and an inescapable sense of finality.

Across the room, Deacon packs the last of their gear. His face is a mask of focus, but even he can't entirely hide the tension etched in the lines around his eyes. He glances at Peter, seeing the conflict in his friend's expression, and knows what he's thinking.

"It's for the best, Peter," Deacon says, his voice low but firm, trying to keep them both on track.

Peter sighs, the sound heavy with resignation. "I know, but it doesn't make it any easier."

He carefully places the note on the bed, smoothing it out next to a small bundle of dollar bills.

The room, once filled with the detritus of their hurried stay, is now left in a tidy, almost deliberate state. Their departure is planned, calculated—no loose ends, no trace of their presence beyond what they intend to leave behind.

With one last look at the room, Peter turns and joins Deacon at the door. They exchange a silent nod, a shared understanding of the road that lies ahead—one filled with uncertainty, danger, and the weight of being hunted by the very country they swore to protect. The very country they have saved.

They exit the motel, stepping into the cool morning air. The pickup truck waits in the parking lot. Peter takes the wheel while Deacon settles into the passenger seat, his gaze fixed straight ahead.

As the truck pulls out onto the empty highway, the motel quickly disappears into the distance, swallowed by the morning mist. The drive is silent as the two men face forward, leaving behind everything they've known. The road stretches out before them, a long, uncertain path that offers no comfort, only the grim reality of their new existence as fugitives.

———

RAVEN'S HEELS click softly against the asphalt as she walks across the nearly empty motel lot, the morning sun casting long shadows in front of her. In one hand, she carries a paper bag filled with breakfast—warm, comforting smells of coffee, eggs, and bacon wafting through the air.

As Raven reaches the door to their room, she feels a small pang of something—a strange mixture of hope and apprehension, as if she is on the cusp of something both fragile and significant. She juggles the bag in one hand as she turns the knob, her thoughts focused on the relief of seeing Peter and Deacon again, on sitting down together for a meal, a small act of normalcy, even if only for a moment.

But as she steps inside, her heart sinks.

The room is empty. The silence is heavy, almost oppressive, and the absence of Peter and Deacon is immediately palpable. Confusion furrows her brow, and she takes a few tentative steps inside, her eyes scanning the space as if they might appear from some hidden corner.

"Peter? Deacon?" she calls out, her voice soft, almost hesitant.

There is no answer. Just the quiet hum of the old motel refrigerator and the distant sounds of traffic outside. The breakfast bag slips from her fingers, landing with a muted thud on the floor. Her gaze sweeps over the room, her mind racing to make sense of what she's seeing—or rather, what she isn't seeing.

And then she spots it—the note.

It's lying on the bed, perfectly placed, waiting for her. Her breath catches in her throat as she reaches for it, her fingers trembling. The weight of the paper is disproportionate to its size, heavy with the words she is about to read. She unfolds it slowly, her heart pounding in her chest, and begins to read.

RAVEN,

I'm sorry for leaving you like this, but it's the only way. I hope one day you can understand why I had to do this. You've been the only light in one of the darkest times of my life, and I'll always be grateful for that. But right now, the only way to keep you safe is to let you go.

The media and authorities haven't mentioned your name—and Deacon's FBI buddy says there's nothing on you. That means you're in the clear. As long as you stay away from me, you'll be safe. I know this is a lot to ask, but please don't try to find me. There's nothing ahead for me except a fight I can't walk away from, but you can still have a life. You deserve that much.

Take the money and get away from all of this. Go see your sister in California, start fresh. You've always wanted that, and now's your chance. I wish I could be there with you, but this is how it has to be.

Please, Raven, don't look back. Just go and live the life you deserve. I'm sorry it can't be with me.

Take care of yourself.

Peter

. . .

Tears well in Raven's eyes, blurring the words on the page as she finishes reading. She stands there, the note clutched tightly in her hand, her mind a whirl of emotions—sadness, frustration, anger, and a deep, aching loss. The room seems to close in around her, the emptiness echoing the void Peter has left behind.

Don't miss DAWNLIGHT. The riveting sequel in the Peter Black Thriller series.

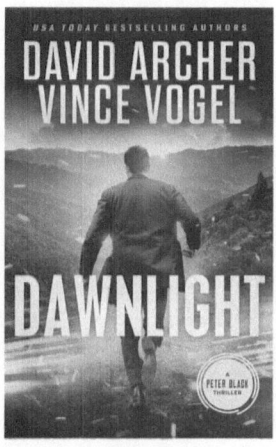

Scan the QR code below to purchase DAWNLIGHT.

Or go to: righthouse.com/dawnlight

NOTE: flip to the very end to read an exclusive sneak peak...

DON'T MISS ANYTHING!

If you want to stay up to date on all new releases in this series, with these authors, or with any of our new deals, you can do so by joining our newsletters below.

In addition, you will immediately gain access to our entire *Right House VIP Library*, which includes many riveting Mystery and Thriller novels for your enjoyment.

righthouse.com/email

(Easy to unsubscribe. No spam. Ever.)

ALSO BY DAVID ARCHER

Up to date books can be found at:
www.righthouse.com/david-archer

ROGUE THRILLERS
Gates of Hell (Book 1)
Hell's Fury (Book 2)
Ice Burn (Book 3)

BEN CARTER LEGAL THRILLERS
Dead Man's Jury (Book 1)
Trail by Murder (Book 2)

JACOB HUNTER THRILLERS
The Kyiv File (Book 1)
The Bogota File (Book 2)
The Havana File (Book 3)

PETER BLACK THRILLERS
Burden of the Assassin (Book 1)
The Man Without A Face (Book 2)
Unpunished Deeds (Book 3)
Hunter Killer (Book 4)
Silent Shadows (Book 5)
The Last Run (Book 6)
Dark Corners (Book 7)
Ghost Operative (Book 8)
A Fire Burning (Book 9)
Dawnlight (Book 10)

ALEX MASON THRILLERS

Odin (Book 1)
Ice Cold Spy (Book 2)
Mason's Law (Book 3)
Assets and Liabilities (Book 4)
Russian Roulette (Book 5)
Executive Order (Book 6)
Dead Man Talking (Book 7)
All The King's Men (Book 8)
Flashpoint (Book 9)
Brotherhood of the Goat (Book 10)
Dead Hot (Book 11)
Blood on Megiddo (Book 12)
Son of Hell (Book 13)
Merchant of Death (Book 14)

NOAH WOLF THRILLERS
Code Name Camelot (Book 1)
Lone Wolf (Book 2)
In Sheep's Clothing (Book 3)
Hit for Hire (Book 4)
The Wolf's Bite (Book 5)
Black Sheep (Book 6)
Balance of Power (Book 7)
Time to Hunt (Book 8)
Red Square (Book 9)
Highest Order (Book 10)
Edge of Anarchy (Book 11)
Unknown Evil (Book 12)
Black Harvest (Book 13)
World Order (Book 14)
Caged Animal (Book 15)
Deep Allegiance (Book 16)
Pack Leader (Book 17)
High Treason (Book 18)
A Wolf Among Men (Book 19)

Rogue Intelligence (Book 20)
Alpha (Book 21)
Rogue Wolf (Book 22)
Shadows of Allegiance (Book 23)
In the Grip of Darkness (Book 24)
Wolves in the Dark (Book 25)

SAM PRICHARD MYSTERIES
The Grave Man (Book 1)
Death Sung Softly (Book 2)
Love and War (Book 3)
Framed (Book 4)
The Kill List (Book 5)
Drifter: Part One (Book 6)
Drifter: Part Two (Book 7)
Drifter: Part Three (Book 8)
The Last Song (Book 9)
Ghost (Book 10)
Hidden Agenda (Book 11)

SAM AND INDIE MYSTERIES
Aces and Eights (Book 1)
Fact or Fiction (Book 2)
Close to Home (Book 3)
Brave New World (Book 4)
Innocent Conspiracy (Book 5)
Unfinished Business (Book 6)
Live Bait (Book 7)
Alter Ego (Book 8)
More Than It Seems (Book 9)
Moving On (Book 10)
Worst Nightmare (Book 11)
Chasing Ghosts (Book 12)
Serial Superstition (Book 13)

CHANCE REDDICK THRILLERS
Innocent Injustice (Book 1)
Angel of Justice (Book 2)
High Stakes Hunting (Book 3)
Personal Asset (Book 4)

CASSIE MCGRAW MYSTERIES
What Lies Beneath (Book 1)
Can't Fight Fate (Book 2)
One Last Game (Book 3)
Never Really Gone (Book 4)

ALSO BY VINCE VOGEL

Never Came Home (Book 11)

ALEX DORRING THRILLER

Agent 192 (Book 1)

The Hitman's Death (Book 2)

The Wrong Man (Book 3)

Who Dares Wins (Book 4)

The Highwaymen (Book 5)

The Ring (Book 6)

ABOUT US

Right House is an independent publisher created by authors for readers. We specialize in Action, Thriller, Mystery, and Crime novels.

If you enjoyed this novel, then there is a good chance you will like what else we have to offer! Please stay up to date by using any of the links below.

Join our mailing lists to stay up to date -->
righthouse.com/email
Visit our website --> righthouse.com
Contact us --> contact@righthouse.com

 facebook.com/righthousebooks
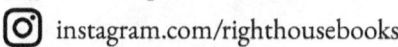 x.com/righthousebooks
instagram.com/righthousebooks

EXCLUSIVE SNEAK PEAK OF...

DAWNLIGHT

PROLOGUE

1985

THE LATE AFTERNOON SUN CAST A WARM, GOLDEN glow over the quiet suburban street. Seventeen-year-old Sandy McLean walked side by side with her best friend Gloria, her schoolbag slung casually over a shoulder. The trees shaded their path as the teens strolled and chatted, their voices blending softly with the quiet of the neighborhood.

"Jeez, Sandy," Gloria said, shaking her head in mock despair. "You've got it all. Good grades and looks. I'm so jealous I could murder you right here on this sidewalk."

Sandy laughed, her strawberry blond hair catching the sunlight as she turned. "Oh, please. It's just one test."

"One test? You aced every test this semester. Don't pretend it's nothing."

Sandy shrugged, trying to downplay the compliment, though a small, proud smile tugged at the corners of her mouth. "You've been doing fine too."

"Fine doesn't get me into Harvard. You'll be running the world before we've even finished college."

They reached the driveway to Sandy's house. It was a modest

but well-kept home with a neatly trimmed lawn and a porch swing swaying gently in the breeze. The curtains in one of the windows fluttered, drawing Sandy's attention. Her stomach tightened.

"I'll see you at Cory Chapman's party tonight," Sandy said quickly, hoping to divert her friend's gaze.

But there was no need to worry. As usual, Gloria was too preoccupied to notice. Her gaze lingered down the street toward Chad Ullman's house—Ullman being the school's hottest senior and football captain.

"Seven o'clock, right?" she said, finally glancing back at Sandy with a distracted smile.

"Yeah, Brad's picking me up. We'll meet you there."

Her friend grinned. "Brad. Lucky you." She gave Sandy a playful nudge before heading off down the sidewalk.

Sandy waited until her friend was out of sight before turning toward the house. Her eyes lingered on the window. The curtains had gone still, but she knew someone had been watching.

She opened the door, the familiar creak of the hinges echoing through the entryway. The smell of lavender and lemon polish greeted her, as it always did. Her mother was standing in the hallway, arms folded, her expression unreadable.

"Do you have to be so obvious?" Sandy asked, dropping her school bag near the stairs.

Her mother tilted her head slightly, a faint frown crossing her face. "What do you mean?"

"The curtains," Sandy said, motioning toward the window. "She could've seen you."

Her mother didn't respond to the accusation. Instead, her lips curved into a soft smile. "How was your day?"

Sandy hesitated, debating whether to push the issue. But she let it drop. "It was fine. I scored high on the history test."

Her mother's smile widened. "Of course you did. My brilliant girl." She reached out and smoothed a stray strand of Sandy's hair. "Next stop, Harvard."

Sandy managed a small smile in return. Her mother's pride was as heavy as it was gratifying. It wasn't enough to be good; she had to be the best.

"What time's dinner?" Sandy asked.

"Five."

"Good," Sandy said, moving toward the stairs. "It'll give me plenty of time before Brad picks me up for the party."

Her mother's voice followed her up. "Don't stay out too late."

"Don't worry. I won't," Sandy replied, but she didn't look back.

As she climbed the stairs, she couldn't shake the feeling that her mother's watchful eyes were still on her.

A little while later, the dining room was bathed in the soft glow of candles, their flickering light reflecting off polished wood and fine china. Sandy sat at the table with her parents, the clink of cutlery and the murmur of conversation filling the room. Her father was slicing into his steak with precise, measured movements, while her mother absentmindedly swirled her wine.

Her father, always the one to break the silence, glanced up. "So what's on the agenda tonight, Sandy? It's Friday, and you're not babysitting for the Hendersons."

Sandy rolled her eyes, already bracing for the conversation. "Why even ask, Dad? You always know exactly what I'm doing."

Her father smirked, a hint of pride behind the expression. "Fair enough. You're going to the Chapman party tonight. His parents are in France for the week, which means their nice home is about to play host to a horde of teenagers hopped up on hormones. I give their new carpets a day before they're ruined."

Sandy groaned. "So what's the verdict? Am I banned?"

"Oh, no," he said, pointing his fork at her. "You're going. Not going would be a social faux pas, akin to your mother and me skipping the yacht club's annual jamboree. But let's be clear— what I don't want is you anywhere near the narcotics that will surely be attending the Chapman house as well."

"Daddy!" Sandy exclaimed, leaning back in her chair. "You don't actually think—"

"Marijuana? Yes, Sandy, I do," he interrupted, his tone casual but his gaze sharp. "Cory Chapman picked up six ounces of it last night in a Home Depot parking lot. He's planning to play the entrepreneur by selling it at his own party."

Sandy froze mid-bite. "You've been spying on him?"

Her father raised a hand as if to calm her. "I keep an eye on things. You know that. It's my job to know."

"It's creepy," Sandy said, turning to her mother. "Mom?"

Her mother sighed, her fingers grazing the stem of her wineglass. "Your father's right, Sandy. You're too important for us not to worry."

Sandy shook her head. "I'm not going to smoke anything! You don't have to—"

Her mother interrupted, her voice soft but firm. "Your father smelled it."

Sandy snapped her gaze back to him. "What?"

"On your jacket. Earlier this week," he said, his tone calm but pointed.

"That's impossible!" Sandy protested, but he held up a hand to stop her.

"No excuses," he said, leaning forward, his hand resting warmly on hers. His voice softened, but the weight of his words pressed down on her. "Go to the party. Have fun. But don't jeopardize everything we've worked for by getting caught doing something stupid. As much as I can smooth things over, it'll leave a mark. An arrest. A story. Something we can't erase, even with all the friends I've made in high places."

Sandy opened her mouth to argue, but her father continued, his expression unyielding. "If you want Harvard—if you want the life we've planned for you—you need to be perfect. No blemishes. No mistakes."

Her mother finally spoke, her voice softer now. "He's right, Sandy. You're too close to risk it all now."

Sandy looked between them, her appetite gone. "Fine," she muttered, pushing her plate away.

Her father smiled faintly, as though he'd won. "That's my girl. Now go enjoy yourself. Just remember—there's no margin for error."

Sandy nodded, but the weight of their expectations felt heavier than ever.

Later that evening, Sandy sat at her vanity, applying a touch of blush to her cheeks. The soft glow of her bedroom lamp reflected in the mirror as she secured a pair of silver earrings, their delicate sparkle catching the light. Outside, the muffled rumble of a car horn broke the quiet. She leaned toward the window and pulled back the curtain. Brad sat in his red Corvette convertible, the engine idling, a grin plastered across his face as he revved the motor for effect.

She smiled faintly, then grabbed her bag from the bed. As she descended the stairs, her mother appeared at the base, hands folded neatly in front of her.

"Your father would like to see you before you leave," she said, her voice calm but with an edge of seriousness that Sandy knew better than to challenge.

"Now?" Sandy asked, glancing toward the door.

Her mother nodded. "He's downstairs."

Sandy hesitated but then turned toward the door leading to the basement. The wooden stairs creaked under her weight as she descended into the dimly lit space. The faint hum of machinery and the low whir of tape reels filled the air. She found her father seated at a desk in a cramped room, surrounded by banks of sound equipment and rows of filing cabinets stacked two deep against the walls. A pair of headphones sat snugly over his ears, and he scribbled notes into a notebook as he listened to a conversation crackling over the line.

She stepped inside, her heels clicking softly on the concrete floor. "Dad?"

He glanced up, his face lighting briefly with a smile before he removed the headphones and set them down with care. "Sandy. Come in," he said, gesturing for her to sit in the chair opposite him.

Sandy sat, her gaze drifting over the equipment. The room smelled faintly of old paper and machine oil. She caught the faint murmur of voices coming through the headphones. It sounded like a telephone call—two people speaking—but the words were indistinct, just a tinny echo of a faraway conversation.

"Mom said you wanted to see me."

Her father leaned back in his chair, folding his hands in his lap. "I did. Before you leave, I wanted to remind you of something important."

She raised an eyebrow, already bracing for another lecture. "More warnings about not smoking pot?"

He shook his head. "No. This is bigger than that." He leaned forward, his voice lowering slightly. "As you are well aware, there are fifty other candidates being prepared for what you're being set for. Fifty."

Sandy frowned, unsure where he was going with this. "And?"

"And most of them are male," he said bluntly. "Which means they statistically have an eighty percent higher chance of making it into the CIA than you do. That's just the reality of the numbers and the times."

Her frown deepened. "Great pep talk, Dad."

"Let me finish," he said, his tone firm but patient. "They may have the odds in their favor, but none of them—none of them—have your drive. Your grades. Your ingenuity. Your guile. Do you know how rare that combination is?"

She didn't respond, her eyes fixed on the desk, where his notebook sat open, filled with his tight, meticulous handwriting.

"Many of them," he continued, "will ruin their chances before they've even started. They'll get caught up in distractions —stupid decisions, lapses in judgment. You, on the other hand, have a real chance to fulfill something extraordinary."

He leaned closer, his voice dropping to a conspiratorial whisper. "To achieve something none of them ever will. To be the first female head of the CIA—and to be the golden worm that eats this rotten apple from the inside. A divine blow for international communism."

Sandy blinked, caught off guard by the sudden fervor in his tone. "The head of the CIA? It'll be hard enough to get in."

"Why not? To control the American intelligence apparatus," he went, his eyes glinting with a strange intensity, "would place us in an unassailable position. Then, my girl, we will have truly led the world into socialist revolution."

She stared at him, her heart thudding in her chest. "You're serious."

"Deadly serious." He reached across the desk and placed a hand on hers. "But none of it happens if you lose focus. If you let them catch you making mistakes. Do you understand?"

Sandy swallowed hard and nodded. "I understand."

"Good." He leaned back, his expression softening into something closer to paternal pride. "Go to your party. Have fun. But remember, you are destined for something far greater than your peers can imagine."

She stood, her legs feeling shaky beneath her. "I'll keep that in mind."

He smiled faintly. "That's my girl."

As she climbed back up the stairs, the sound of the tape reels and his scribbling followed her, a constant reminder of the weight now pressing on her shoulders. When she stepped outside into the cool night air and slid into Brad's convertible, she couldn't shake the feeling that her life was to be just as her father said: destined to help reshape the world.

CHAPTER 1

Thirty years later, Sandy McLean sits at her desk, staring at the skyline of Washington, D.C., the world on the brink of the monumental change her father had always dreamed of. The Capitol dome glows softly in the distance, a faint silhouette against the rising dawn. And here she sits, one of its eventual destroyers. Her office is silent, save for the hum of the air conditioning. She should feel victorious at the pinnacle of power, but her thoughts drift, unbidden, to the past.

The carefree days of youth. That's what people call them, don't they? For Sandy, they were never carefree. There was always something to care about, something that demanded her attention: the mission. The one she was quite literally born for. It had always been there, quietly shaping her life, an invisible thread binding her to a cause she hadn't chosen but could never escape.

The mission predated her. It had been set in motion eight years before her birth—the day two idealistic beatniks with socialist leanings decided to turn on their own country. Her parents. Intellectuals, radicals, dreamers. And traitors. They hadn't just flirted with subversion; they'd jumped headfirst into it. They'd pledged themselves to the KGB, and in doing so, they'd pledged her, too. Their *gifted* daughter.

Sandy's brilliance was evident from the moment she could speak in full sentences before her second birthday and read advanced texts by the time she was four. Her parents nurtured her intelligence with a cold determination, shaping her into a prodigy of both academics and ideology. By the time she reached adolescence, Sandy spoke three languages fluently, excelled in mathematics and logic, and had memorized entire treatises on Marxist theory. This last one, of course, she kept strictly between her and her parents.

Since the day her parents first realized what they had, Sandy's path to becoming the CIA's first female director had been meticulously planned. She had been groomed to infiltrate the system, rising through the ranks with a sharp mind, a commanding presence, and an uncanny ability to manipulate both allies and adversaries. While the world hailed her as a trailblazer, few knew she was also its greatest threat—a communist agent at the heart of America's intelligence apparatus.

Sandy leans back in her chair, her fingers steepled as her gaze shifts to the framed photographs lining her shelves. Diplomatic receptions, handshakes with presidents, and carefully curated images of a life that isn't entirely hers.

Her thoughts turn to Kim Philby. The name still echoes in certain circles—a symbol of cunning and betrayal. A British intelligence officer turned Soviet spy, Philby lived a life that parallels hers in unnerving ways. Like her, he was born to privilege, raised to see the world in shades of ideology rather than allegiance. Like her, he operated in the shadows, always one step away from discovery.

And, like her, he'd believed in the mission.

But Philby's story didn't end well. Sandy knows it too well—the ignoble retreat, the exile to Moscow, where he spent his final days drinking himself to death in a dingy apartment, far from the country he'd once called home. A man who'd given everything for a cause, only to be discarded when his usefulness ran out.

She shudders. The thought of ending up like Philby—out in

the cold, a relic of a bygone era—gnaws at her. Yet her story isn't his. It can't be. Philby never got this close to seeing his ideals triumph. He never stood on the precipice of victory.

Sandy straightens in her chair, forcing herself to focus. Her mission isn't over. Not yet. And if she succeeds, if she truly brings the American intelligence apparatus under control, it will all have been worth it.

The phone on her desk buzzes, breaking her reverie. She picks it up, her voice crisp and steady. "Yes?"

"They're here," her assistant says.

Sandy places the receiver back in its cradle, her expression hardening. The past is just that—the past. What matters now is the future, and the future is still hers to shape.

Sandy rises, smoothing the lapels of her blazer, and strides down the corridor toward the briefing room. Her heels click against the polished floor, each step deliberate, echoing her authority.

When she enters, the room falls silent. Four operatives sit around an oval table, their postures rigid, their eyes sharp. The tension in the air is palpable. These are some of the best operatives the agency has ever fielded, yet even they can feel the weight of what's coming.

"Good morning," Sandy begins, her voice smooth, authoritative. She takes her place at the head of the table, her hands resting lightly on its edge. "You four have been chosen for a reason. Before we proceed, I want you to understand why you're here."

She lets the silence stretch, her gaze sweeping across the room, meeting each agent's eyes in turn. A slight shift in their seats betrays the anticipation they're trying to suppress.

Sandy turns to the large screen behind her and presses a button on the remote. The display flickers to life, shifting to four profiles, each corresponding to the operatives before her.

"Senior Operations Officer Callum Drake," she begins, her eyes locking on the tall man sitting to her left. He's in his forties with short-cropped brown hair and a steely gaze that doesn't waver. "Twenty-two years in the Agency, eight of those spent infiltrating domestic terrorist cells. Ph.D. in human psychology with a focus on behavioral deviations. You tracked and dismantled the North Cascadia Front. Fluent in Russian and Arabic. Firearm proficiency scores in the top one percent of the agency. Nine confirmed kills—classified, of course."

Drake inclines his head slightly, his expression unreadable, though there's a flicker of pride in his eyes.

"Collection Management Officer Olivia Wren," McLean continues, shifting her focus to the woman two seats away. Wren is in her early thirties, her sharp eyes taking in every detail of the room. Her lean, athletic build speaks of agility and discipline. "Stanford graduate, dual degrees in criminology and psychology. You led the operation that uncovered the sleeper network known as 'Operation Midnight Rose.' Five confirmed kills during active duty. Your profiling skills are unmatched in the agency."

Wren's lips twitch in a faint smile, professional but self-assured.

"Operations Officer Samuel Ortiz," Sandy says, turning to the heavyset man with broad shoulders and an intensity in his dark eyes. "Former Marine. Three tours before joining the agency. Expert in close-quarters combat and counter-terrorism tactics. Covert operations in South America and Eastern Europe. You dismantled 'The Black Circle,' a splinter cell recruiting sleeper agents in high-profile sectors. Twelve confirmed kills."

Ortiz's jaw tightens, his eyes flicking briefly to the screen before he nods, his expression carved from stone.

Finally, McLean's gaze lands on the last agent, a man leaning back in his chair with calculated ease. A small scar runs down the left side of his face, giving him an air of quiet danger. "Operations Officer Marcus Langston. An enigma, even among your peers. Former MI6, transferred under our cooperative program. Specializes in subterfuge and deep-cover missions. Cambridge graduate, focus on geopolitical psychology. No confirmed kills on record—

which, as we all know, means you're particularly skilled at leaving no trace."

Langston's lips curl into a faint grin, the glint of amusement in his eyes not quite masking the sharp edge beneath.

McLean steps back from the table, folding her hands behind her back. "Each of you has been chosen not just for your tactical and academic expertise, but because you understand what it means to live between two worlds. Sleeper agents. Terrorist cells. You know how they think, how they blend in, and, most importantly, how to find them and eliminate them."

She presses another button on the remote. The screen changes, displaying an image of a man's face: Peter Black. His features are shadowed, his expression intense. The grainy footage seems almost alive, his gray eyes staring directly ahead.

The agents sit up straighter, their attention fixed.

"This," McLean says, her voice dropping a notch, "is your target. Peter Black."

The silence in the room sharpens. Each operative's eyes remain locked on the screen, absorbing the image, the implications. McLean's words cut through the stillness like a blade.

"The reason I've created this team," Sandy says, her voice sharp and deliberate, "is to hunt this man." She gestures to the screen, where Peter Black's face stares back at the room. "His name is Peter Black, and he is one of the CIA's deadliest assassins. Or at least, he was—until he set off a dirty bomb beneath the Potomac River in Washington, D.C. weeks ago."

A murmur ripples across the table. Agent Marcus Langston leans forward, his expression alight with a mix of disbelief and excitement. "It's Azrael, isn't it? We're going after Azrael."

Sandy's gaze locks on to his, cool and unwavering. "Yes."

The room seems to hold its collective breath as the screen flickers, transitioning to grainy footage. A South American cocaine factory fills the display, dimly lit and teeming with guards. They watch as a shape—a phantom—moves through the shadows, eliminating the men one by one with surgical precision. Each strike is swift, silent, and final.

"This is Peter at work," Sandy says, her tone flat. Onscreen, Peter disappears into the darkness, leaving only lifeless bodies in his wake. "As you can see, he has a propensity for sneaking up on people and killing them. Don't let it happen to you."

She clicks the remote again, and a new image appears—a man's sharp, serious face fills the screen. "This," Sandy continues, "is Mark Deacon. You may have encountered him during your time at the Agency."

Drake gives a small nod, while Wren and Ortiz exchange glances, acknowledging the name without speaking.

"Deacon," Sandy says, "planned and orchestrated the D.C. attack. We have evidence linking him to the operational blueprint."

The screen shifts again, this time displaying a bright, confident face. Kirsty Lange. The room's atmosphere darkens as Sandy speaks.

"As you know, one of our own was found murdered in a Colorado motel two days before the D.C. hit. We strongly believe Mark Deacon was the one who pulled the trigger."

The mood in the room tightens, especially for Operations Officer Olivia Wren. Her jaw clenches, and her dark eyes narrow with controlled anger.

"Did any of you know Kirsty?" Sandy asks, her gaze sweeping the table.

Wren speaks up, her voice tight with emotion. "I did. We trained together. Shared an apartment for five years. She was like a..." She starts to say "sister" but stops herself. Instead, she finishes softly, "We were close."

Sandy nods, her expression neutral but her words precise. "Then you understand what's at stake. This mission isn't just about preventing future attacks. It's about justice—for her and for everyone who's suffered at the hands of Peter Black, Mark Deacon, and the people with them."

The screen shifts again, revealing two new faces. Sandy points to the first, a younger man with sharp features and cold eyes.

"Michael Black," she says. "Trained by Peter since he was thirteen while they were on the run. He is not just a bystander. He has confirmed kills to his name."

The agents exchange glances, absorbing the information.

"And Mayu Tanaka," Sandy continues, her voice hardening. A striking woman appears on the screen, her delicate features belying the lethal nature described next. "The daughter of Koji Tanaka, one of the world's foremost creators of chemical weapons. Her father may be in prison now, but he left her with skills that make her just as dangerous. Martial arts, weapons training, survival expertise—don't underestimate her."

Drake shifts in his chair, the hint of a smirk crossing his lips. "Quite the team they've put together."

Sandy's gaze snaps to him, sharp as a blade. "And that's why you're here. Together, they have the skills to evade us: unmatched combat abilities, psychological resilience, and survival instincts honed over years of living off the grid. But make no mistake," she adds, her eyes sweeping the room, "you four are the best we have. Each of you brings the expertise needed to hunt them down. I expect nothing less than success."

Wren nods, her expression resolute. "Are we coordinating with the FBI and US Marshals?"

Sandy's face darkens, her tone cutting. "Yes, but understand this: I want you to lead the charge. This stays in-house. We can't afford leaks, and we won't let outsiders compromise the mission. You are the spearhead. I expect results."

The agents straighten in their seats, a shared determination settling across their faces. They are ready. They understand what is at stake.

Sandy stands, looking over them one last time. "This mission begins now. Go."

CHAPTER 2

ABOUT 600 MILES NORTHWEST OF SANDY MCLEAN'S office in D.C., a passenger ferry slices through the cold waters of Lake Michigan, its engines rumbling faintly beneath the deck. The midday sun gleams off the lake's surface, but the mood aboard is far from serene. Peter Black takes a seat near the stern, the few scattered tourists keeping to themselves. His hood is pulled low over his face, a ball cap shadowing his sharp, reconstructed features.

Across the aisle, a man with salt-and-pepper stubble and a newly healed nose scar slides into the adjacent seat. Mark Deacon. They don't exchange greetings—just a brief glance before settling into the kind of quiet camaraderie shared only by those who've faced death together.

Around them, a muted news broadcast plays on a wall-mounted screen. The anchor's voice is clipped and grim.

"The dollar hits another historic low today, sparking fresh concerns about the country's economic stability. Some military personnel report missed paychecks as Congress fails to reach a budget agreement for the fifth consecutive week."

Deacon leans back, eyes flicking toward the screen. "What a mess," he mutters.

Peter says nothing, watching as the broadcast shifts to footage from Kyiv. Tanks roll through broken streets. Soldiers huddle in rubble-strewn corners, their faces hard with exhaustion.

"In Ukraine," the reporter continues, "Russian forces are days away from taking Kyiv. Experts fear Western Europe could be next on Moscow's list."

Deacon exhales sharply, a low whistle escaping his lips. "We're days from seeing Europe invaded. China's kicking our asses in space, and unemployment's breaking records. This country's circling the drain."

Peter finally speaks, his tone dry. "At least the ferries still run on time."

Deacon chuckles, glancing at Peter's face. His eyes narrow as he studies the subtle changes—the sharper cheekbones, the slightly fuller lips. "The doc did good work. Doesn't even look like you anymore."

Peter smirks. "That's the idea. You?"

Deacon taps his new nose with a finger. "Got this in Mexico. Cheap and quick. Hurt like hell, though."

The news shifts again, this time to footage of a Chinese rocket launch. A sleek, futuristic spacecraft ascends into the stratosphere, leaving a trail of fire behind it.

"China aims to establish a Mars base by 2030," the anchor says. "With this timeline five years ahead of NASA's current projections."

Deacon shakes his head. "We can't even pay the Army, but sure, let's race to Mars." He pauses, his tone darkening. "Had a visitor the other day. Came for me."

Peter straightens slightly. "An assassin?"

Deacon nods. "Didn't stick around long. Let's just say he won't be reporting back to whoever sent him."

Peter's jaw tightens. "Any more since then?"

"Not yet. You?"

"Two weeks back," Peter says, his voice low. "Quick work. Haven't seen another since."

Three months ago, Peter Black and Mark Deacon uncovered a decades-long conspiracy by Cold War-era foreign powers to destabilize the West through extremist militias, economic sabotage, and political chaos. Infiltrating the extremist group known as the Iron Brotherhood, Peter discovered a plot to detonate a cesium-based dirty bomb in Washington, D.C. His cover was blown when CIA Director Sandy McLean, revealed as a double agent, betrayed him. Despite overwhelming odds, Peter and Deacon pursued the bomb, battling militia forces and evading SWAT teams, ultimately driving the bomb-laden van into the Potomac River to minimize the fallout. However, McLean manipulated the narrative, branding them as traitors. Now fugitives, Peter and Deacon are hunted by foreign agents and their own government, carrying the weight of a truth no one wants exposed.

"Could be McLean's shadow force," Deacon says.

Peter's eyes narrow. "Shadow force?"

Deacon leans in, lowering his voice. "She's put together a team of her best operatives to track us down. I heard it from a source—she's built herself a squad of killers."

"What source? Where'd you get this?"

Deacon's grin is faint but sly.

Peter groans. "Not this John Doe guy again."

Deacon nods.

"Mark, come on. I told you, it's a ruse. It's McLean behind those emails."

"They've been good to us," Deacon insists. "John Doe warned us about Pittsburgh, didn't they? Got us out of that mess."

"They were establishing trust. Just like we were trained to do in the CIA."

Deacon smirks. "They also warned me about the guy coming for me. Sent the message right as he was climbing through my window."

"That's because they're watching you, Mark." Peter's gaze sweeps the passengers milling about the ferry, then the choppy surface of the lake. "Hell, they could be watching both of us right now."

"No one's watching us," Deacon says with forced certainty.

Peter's eyes harden. "It's probably the communists. You know that, right?"

Deacon shakes his head. "No. I don't think so. I think John Doe's a group inside the intelligence community. They're trying to bring down the International and want us to take out McLean."

Peter doesn't answer immediately. His eyes drift back to the lake. "What else have they told you?"

Deacon glances around, making sure no one's too close. "They sent me a dossier on McLean. Did you know she's never been married? No serious relationships, either. Lone wolf all the way."

"Figures," Peter says.

Deacon leans closer, his voice lowering further. "And get this: According to the dossier, McLean's parents were recruited by the KGB in the 1960s. Her father was a diplomat and her mother a journalist. They became deep-cover agents. Operated in the States for decades."

Peter's expression tightens. "McLean, too?"

"Not officially. But she was groomed. Honor student. Straight As. Went to Harvard on a scholarship. Right after graduation, she was recruited into the CIA. Climbed the ranks so fast, nobody thought to question it. She's been there the whole time, right under our noses."

Peter's jaw clenches, his voice low and sharp. "And now she's running the agency."

Deacon exhales, his frustration evident. "If I'd seen it earlier... if I'd known what she was, I might've saved Kirsty." His voice falters for a moment, then hardens. "McLean's shadow force isn't just after us—they're part of a system she's been building for decades. And we all missed it."

Peter stares out at the choppy water, his expression unreadable. "Where are the parents now?"

"They died in a car accident when McLean was in her early thirties. But here's the kicker—John Doe gave me a name. Bill Hammond."

Peter's brows furrow. "Who's that?"

Deacon smirks. "He worked with Ken McLean—that's Sandy McLean's father—at the embassy in the 1970s. Turns out he's also Sandy McLean's godfather."

Peter leans back, absorbing this. "What's he up to now?"

"Investor in green energy. Rich as hell. Bought up islands around the US for green energy projects. Wind farms, tidal plants, geothermal facilities—you name it."

Peter's lips curl into a faint smile. "Sounds like a saint."

Deacon's grin is colder. "Or he's got secrets worth digging into."

Peter nods slowly. "You think he's the key?"

"He's a start. But it's a four-man job," Deacon says, his tone final. "We'll need the others."

Peter doesn't hesitate. "Then I'll send out the message. Bring them in."

Deacon shifts in his seat, lowering his voice even further. "While we're on it—have Michael and Mayu made any progress with that encrypted device we pulled off the Iron Brotherhood?"

Peter's brow furrows. "Michael hasn't said anything. But that's not to say he and Mayu haven't been looking. There's got to be someone out there who can crack it."

Deacon sighs, his frustration evident. "We better hope. Because if we can access the intel in that device, we might be able to expose the sleeper agents planted all over America—all over the Western Hemisphere. Until we break into it, though, Bill Hammond is all we've got."

The ferry horn blares as it approaches the dock. The two men rise, their movements casual but deliberate. Around them, the tourists are still glued to the screens, watching the collapse of a nation in real time. Peter and Deacon step off the ferry and go their separate ways, blending into the crowd, two shadows disappearing into the chaos.

Scan the QR code below to purchase DAWNLIGHT.
Or go to: righthouse.com/dawnlight